PENGUIN BO

# Undercover PRINCESS

Connie Glynn has always loved writing and wrote her first story when she was six, with her mum at a typewriter acting as her scribe. She had a love for performing stories from a young age and attended Guildhall drama classes as a teenager. This passion for stories has never left her, and Connie recently finished her degree in film theory.

It was at university that Connie started her hugely successful YouTube channel *Noodlerella* (named after her favourite food and favourite Disney princess). Here Connie vlogs about her passions, which include comics, cartoons, impressions, video games, cosplay and all things cute. Connie recently passed 700,000 subscribers and has over 56 million views. The year 2016 saw Connie make her first appearance in a cinematic film release as she made a cameo as the voice of Moxie Dewdrop in Dreamworks' *Trolls*.

**Follow Connie on YouTube, Twitter, Instagram and Tumblr**
**@Noodlerella**
**#RosewoodChronicles**

# The ROSEWOOD CHRONICLES

# Undercover PRINCESS

## CONNIE GLYNN

PENGUIN BOOKS

PENGUIN BOOKS

UK | USA | Canada | Ireland | Australia
India | New Zealand | South Africa

Penguin Books is part of the Penguin Random House group of companies
whose addresses can be found at global.penguinrandomhouse.com.

www.penguin.co.uk
www.puffin.co.uk
www.ladybird.co.uk

First published 2017
This edition published 2018

001

Set in 11.7/14.4 pt Goudy Old Style
Typeset by Jouve (UK), Milton Keynes

Printed in Great Britain by Clays Ltd, St Ives plc

A CIP catalogue record for this book is available from the British Library

ISBN: 978-0-141-37989-0

All correspondence to:
Penguin Books
Penguin Random House Children's
80 Strand, London WC2R ORL

MIX
Paper from
responsible sources
FSC® C018179
www.fsc.org

Penguin Random House is committed to a
sustainable future for our business, our readers
and our planet. This book is made from Forest
Stewardship Council® certified paper.

*For my wonderful family and all the gorgeous witches
who've charmed my life.*

*Special thanks to Richard and Mark, who have supported me
ferociously in every step I've taken, Holly and Ruth for pushing
me and helping me achieve my vision, and Evan for the much-
appreciated maths help. And one last thank you to my beautiful
and kind audience – thank you, thank you, thank you.*

# PART ONE
## *Welcome to Rosewood Hall*

# Prologue

There are places in our world in which wondrous and whimsical things seem more capable of happening than anywhere else. You can recognize them because they are thick with an atmosphere that seems out of time and place with the rest of reality. Sometimes they exist naturally, such as hidden waterfalls or secret meadows filled with flourishing wild flowers. Sometimes they are man-made, like empty playgrounds at twilight or dusty antique shops rich with history. But occasionally, although it is rare, these spaces exist in a certain type of person. You may have met such a person yourself. They may not at first glance seem particularly charismatic or especially intellectual, but, as you spend more time with them, it seems they possess the power to change and achieve anything . . .

Princess Eleanor Prudence Wolfson, sole heir of King Alexander Wolfson and next in line for the throne of Maradova, did not live in one of these spaces, nor was she one of these people, but she was in desperate need of both.

'I am going to this school!' Eleanor slammed the brochure on the table with a loud *thwack*, causing the cups of breakfast tea to wobble on top of their saucers.

Alexander Wolfson didn't even look up from his newspaper to reply.

'No,' he said blankly.

'I am next in line for the Maravish throne. I think the teeny-tiny decision of which school I attend is something I am capable of managing myself.'

Alexander looked up at his wife, Queen Matilde, who was sitting across the table from him.

She shrugged. 'She does have a point, Alex,' she said amiably, delicately dropping a lump of sugar into her teacup and stirring it slowly while stifling a smile.

This was not the parental solidarity King Alexander had been hoping for.

'See?' said Eleanor. 'Even Mum agrees with me.'

Alexander remained firmly fixated on his newspaper, feigning an image of complete composure. He took a sip of tea.

'Edwina –' he gestured to their maid – 'would you kindly take the empty plates to the kitchen, please?'

'Of course, Your Majesty.' Edwina expertly stacked the crumb-covered trays and exited the dining hall with a skilled smoothness, her feet barely making a sound on the oak flooring. The large double doors closed behind her, creaking softly as she eased them shut.

Once Alexander was sure she was a reasonable distance down the hall, and safely away from any domestic outbursts, he looked back down at his newspaper and said, 'My answer is no.'

Eleanor let out an exasperated screech and stamped her foot. 'You could at least *look* at the brochure!' she snapped, snatching the newspaper from her father's fingertips.

Alexander was forced to look up at his daughter.

Eleanor had always been a challenging child. She was anything but a typical princess; she would take fiery political arguments and sneaking out to loud, rowdy concerts over mild polite conversation any day, and more than anything she *despised* elaborate formal functions – or at least she assumed she did, having refused to ever attend one. But she was smart, she was confident and she was passionate – and for Alexander that was all far more important than any of the traditional values expected of her. Although occasionally he did wish she'd watch her language around her grandparents.

As much as he wanted Eleanor to be happy and live a life free of the commitments of royalty, the fact remained that she would be queen one day and would eventually need to accept that responsibility. He was determined to find a way to make his daughter realize she could enjoy her royal obligations; something he'd had to learn himself when he was younger.

'You are going to Aston Court, as have all the rulers of Maradova for the last hundred years, and you're going to like it whether you like it or not.'

Matilde chuckled softly across the table as she sipped her tea.

'No.' Eleanor echoed her father's stern tone. 'I'm going to Rosewood Hall in England.'

Eleanor's voice didn't waver. She was determined. She would be kicking and screaming long before she was caught entering the gates of Aston Court.

Alexander sighed deeply.

For Eleanor, attending Aston Court wasn't about simply 'not getting her way' as it would be for most teenagers. It would be the end of her freedom as an undeclared royal altogether. She would officially have to come out to the public as the heir to the Maravish throne; she would no longer be able to sneak out or refuse to attend royal functions, and she'd have to stop dyeing her hair and start dressing more appropriately. Her responsibilities would begin and she could never lead any semblance of a normal life again.

Alexander picked up his newspaper and folded it neatly. He prepared himself for the ensuing heated shouting match, a regular occurrence since Eleanor had hit her teenage years.

'Please, Dad.'

This caught Alexander completely off-guard, so rarely did his daughter plead; she was far too stubborn. He looked up, expecting to see her usual indomitable pout, but instead was confronted with a look of real desperation. He found himself struggling to remember why he was so determined to say no, before quickly reminding himself that Aston Court was the only school that could guarantee her safety once she was officially announced to the public as their princess. There she would be under expert surveillance; she'd be safe and she'd be perfectly prepared for her future. It was Aston Court or nothing. Yet for all his certainty he found himself gingerly reaching out his hand as Eleanor placed the Rosewood brochure in his palm.

She wrapped her hands around his and squeezed lightly. 'All you have to do is read it, that's all I ask.'

Across the table Queen Matilde took another discreet sip of her tea before delicately placing the cup on her saucer. 'You know, it may be the tea talking, but I've always been fond of England, haven't you, Alexander?' She looked up at her husband, her carefree expression dropping momentarily as her eyes locked with his. The Maravish king held his wife's gaze for what felt like the longest few seconds of his life. She had that effect on him.

He let out a long sigh before finally giving up.

'Fine, I will read the brochure, but that's it.'

Eleanor let out a squeal of delight and relief. 'Yes! Thank you, thank you, thank you! I know you'll be happy with it, Dad, I promise.' And with that she stuffed a croissant in her mouth and ran out before he had time to fully register what had just happened.

The door slammed behind her, leaving Alexander and Matilde to sit in the wake of its echo. He looked up at his wife again as the sound slowly faded to silence. She smiled sweetly back at him.

'She can't go,' he said. 'It's too dangerous to have the sole heir to the Maravish throne traipsing around some British boarding school when she should be learning everything she needs to rule one day.'

Matilde turned serious again, delicately repositioning her cutlery in front of her so that each fork, knife and spoon was perfectly in line.

As she looked up, Alexander was acutely aware of the fire twinkling behind her eyes.

'You know as well as I do that Rosewood is no ordinary school, and, secondly –' she stopped for a moment, forcing him to look her directly in the eye – 'as you've stated before, she has not yet been formally announced. No one knows she's the princess, so this may very well be the best way for her to live her last few years as a carefree teenager before

7

taking on her royal duties and I *know* you wish you'd had that chance.'

Alexander was momentarily taken aback. Was his wife really suggesting what he thought she was?

'You want her to go to this school undercover?' he asked.

Matilde instantly smiled again, dropping her intensity like it was as simple as putting on and taking off a hat.

'Right now all you have to do is read the brochure.' She lifted her teacup to her mouth, then paused and added, 'Besides, if things turn sour we can always send in Jamie.'

Alexander stared at his wife in bewilderment and adoration. He chuckled softly to himself. Something told him that reading the Rosewood brochure was not going to be the end of the matter.

# 1

There is a small blue bakery in St Ives with bushy clumps of wisteria growing on the pebbledashed walls. Through the front windows there lies a visible thick coat of dust over the sheet-covered surfaces that glitters in the air when the sun shines. A faded candy-striped canopy covers the doors with a sign above reading MS PUMPKIN'S PASTRIES, although no baking has taken place for many years. Above the bakery you will find a previously humble home, now crammed with gaudy items and kitsch displays, a futile attempt by the new owner to enhance the homely setting. Yet one room remains untouched by the new inhabitant, a soft haven filled with the house's happy memories.

Lottie Pumpkin lives in the attic of 12 Bethesda Hill, St Ives, with her stepmother, Beady. There she has made herself a sanctuary, hidden away in the cosy loft overlooking the sea. It is a room of creaky floorboards, walls lined with photos from her childhood and books bursting with fairy tales. But today she will be leaving her bedroom and her house, and Cornwall. Today she will be moving away to live at Rosewood Hall.

*

'Lottie!' Beady's piercing tone rang in Lottie's ears, making her freeze as she lowered the last item of clothing into a suitcase.

'Yes?' Lottie replied, her eyes involuntarily squeezing shut. She heard movement and Lottie's stepmother appeared in the doorway. A creamy green mask covered her face, and her red hair was hidden away in a neat towel bun. Beady was an incredibly beautiful woman who took her appearance very seriously. She was also far too young to be burdened with the responsibility of taking care of Lottie and it was extremely generous of her to sacrifice her life for someone else's kid, which she regularly reminded Lottie about.

'I completely forgot you were leaving today!' She said this as if it were extremely amusing.

Lottie gave her a pleasing smile that she'd performed a million times. 'That's OK, I'm –'

Before she could finish, Beady let out a loud cackle.

'I mean, how could I forget? You never shut up about the place –' she laughed again – 'although if they're letting you in it can't be *that* prestigious.' Lottie flinched a little and Beady paused in her laughter. 'I'm only kidding, Lottie. Don't take things so seriously.'

Lottie held her smile tightly and attempted a laugh, but Beady's eyes had moved to the two pink suitcases on the floor.

'Those are big. I hope you're not expecting a lift. That's a lot to ask of someone.' Beady gave her an injured look, as if she were being very patient.

'No, it's fine,' Lottie replied, trying to be as pleasant as she could. She absolutely did not want to upset Beady: she knew how difficult it had been for her having to look after Lottie when her mother passed away. All she wanted was to make life easy for her. 'Ollie and his mum are giving me a lift.'

Beady's eyebrows shot up in a disapproving way.

'That's very generous of them. I hope you make sure his mum knows how grateful you are she has to do that for you.'

'Of course.' Lottie nodded and that appeared to satisfy Beady.

'Good, well . . .' Beady paused, looking around the room as if taking it in for the first time. She chewed the side of her mouth, turning her gaze to give Lottie a once-over, then she took in a long breath as if preparing herself for what she was about to say. 'You worked hard . . . I hope it doesn't disappoint you.'

Lottie gulped. She knew Beady was happy she'd got into Rosewood; it meant she could have the house to herself at last. Getting into Rosewood not only fulfilled a promise Lottie had made to her mum but it was the greatest gift she could give her stepmother.

'Thank you,' Lottie replied.

Beady waved her hand as if dismissing the conversation.

'Anyway, I need to go and wash off this face mask. Have a safe trip.'

As soon as she was gone, Lottie quickly got back to packing, but it wasn't long before she was interrupted again.

'What on earth are you wearing?' Ollie's sarcastic tone drifted into Lottie's bedroom. He stood leaning against the door frame, his arms crossed as he watched Lottie pack up the last items in her room.

'Ollie!' Lottie's hand rushed to her chest in shock at the sudden appearance of her best friend. 'How did you get up here? And how many times do I have to tell you to knock?' Lottie was huffing slightly from trying to squish down her suitcases. Ollie was fourteen, the same age as Lottie, yet even though he was taller than her he'd retained his baby face, which reminded her of soft-serve ice cream on the beach and other happy memories.

'I had to sneak past the wicked witch. Did you know her skin's turned green finally?' Ollie said with a devilish smile.

Lottie giggled, but she couldn't ignore his comment. She looked down at her outfit, brushing down her dress self-consciously. 'And what exactly is wrong with my outfit?' she said indignantly.

Ollie laughed, grinning at her with his signature cheeky smile. Clumps of dog hair dotted his jeans, a permanent feature that he never seemed to care about.

'Isn't it a little too fancy for the first day of school?'

'*Too fancy?!*' Lottie couldn't believe he'd suggest something so ridiculous. 'Nothing is *too fancy* for Rosewood Hall. I need to fit in. I can't have my clothes making me an outcast on the first day.'

Lottie began picking at a non-existent spot on the collar of her dress. 'Most of the students probably have their clothes tailor-made out of gold or something.'

Ollie casually strolled into the room, taking a seat on Lottie's bed. He pursed his lips as he glanced around the bedroom. Usually so alive with Lottie's special brand of handmade quirkiness, it was now stripped bare, everything she owned crammed into two pink suitcases.

'Well,' Ollie began, reaching into his pocket, 'if you can take a moment off from worrying about what other people think of you . . .' He pulled out a crumpled envelope and a worn-out Polaroid that Lottie recognized from his bedroom wall. 'These are for you.'

Lottie reached out for them, but Ollie whipped his hand back.

'You can't open the letter until you're on the train.'

Lottie nodded with an exasperated smile and he slowly placed both gifts in her hand. It was a photograph she'd seen thousands of times: the two of them at the beach, their noses covered in ice cream and beaming grins on both their greedy faces. Even though the colours had begun to fade to sepia, you could still see the tiara on Lottie's head and the horns on Ollie's. As children, the two had demanded to wear these fancy-dress items every day and everywhere. Ollie had declared he was the fairy Puck from Shakespeare's *A Midsummer Night's Dream* after they'd watched an open-air performance at the beach one evening. He'd been completely infatuated with all the mischief the character got away with and assumed he too could get away with being naughty so long as he was wearing his horns. Lottie's tiara, on the other hand, had a less happy-go-lucky origin. Her thumb lingered over the accessory in the photo, a little pang striking her heart as she remembered the day she'd received it.

'I'll give you some time to say goodbye,' he said, before effortlessly picking up both her suitcases and carrying them down the stairs to the car. When he was gone she thoughtfully placed Ollie's gifts with the rest of her most important belongings, which she'd laid out on the now-bare bed so as not to forget them. She put each item into her handbag: first the weathered Polaroid and letter from Ollie, followed by her favourite sketchbook, her most loyal stuffed companion, Mr Truffles, a framed photo of her mother, Marguerite, in her graduation gown, and, finally – looking very out of place among the other objects – a crescent-moon tiara, her most valued possession. It had taken Lottie all of sixty minutes to pack her entire life into two pink suitcases, one denim backpack and a small over-shoulder handbag with a sturdy white strap. She looked over the now-empty room.

*I did it, Mum,* she thought. *I got into Rosewood just like I promised.*

# 2

To Lottie (the Honorary Princess of St Ives),

Feels like I barely saw you this past year you were studying so much, and now you're off to live on the other side of the country. It won't be the same without you, but I'm sure you'll have enough adventures for the both of us.

I wanted to get you a fairy-tale book as a goodbye present as I know how much you love them, but I fear you own them all already so I figured I'd give you this Polaroid to remind you of my existence every day.

Can't wait to hear about all the crazy things you get up to at Rosewood. I'm so proud of you for getting in, but I'll miss you a lot *pauses to shed a tear* AND HOW DARE YOU LEAVE ME ALONE IN THIS TOURIST TRAP!!! TRAITOR!! (See how I turn my difficult emotions into anger as a defence mechanism??)

Your friend, Ollie

PS Bring me back a gold crown or something – I assume you get one upon arrival ;)

Lottie smiled as she reread the note from her best friend and allowed herself a moment to feel a little sentimental about leaving her humble life in Cornwall. She gazed out of the train window at the lush countryside thundering past and thought back to the day last year when she had submitted her application to Rosewood Hall. Five years ago she'd promised her mother that she would find a way to go there. There had been a storm the night before and the world outside was soggy and wet. Her mother lay wrapped in four different blankets, her body skinny and weak from the sickness that had consumed her, but an unyielding strength persisted in her eyes. She'd looked at Lottie and smiled her familiar warm smile.

'You can do anything you put your mind to, little princess.'

The submission process had been arduous and intimidating. Rosewood rarely accepted applicants on a bursary unless they showed outstanding potential; it was a school that prided itself on excellence. Rosewood was not the type of school one just *decided* to go to; you couldn't simply pick up a brochure and say you wanted to attend. And, as Lottie lived alone with her stepmother in her late mother's bakery, there was no way she could pull together the funds to pay the school fees. But Lottie had persisted. She'd worked tirelessly, forgone social activities and hobbies, waking up early to do the chores before locking herself away in her room to study relentlessly. All the while she dreamed of the day she would walk through the gates of Rosewood and take her place among the children of the elite. Ready, of course, to make a positive impact on the world.

'*We are now approaching Rosewood Central. Please ensure you take all your belongings with you as you leave the train.*'

16

As she grabbed her two suitcases, Lottie wondered momentarily if she would be the only Rosewood student travelling to the boarding school on public transport. She assumed most of the students would have private cars, but on the school map she and Ollie had spent hours unravelling they'd seen what could only be a landing pad – did students really travel by helicopter? Should she have made the effort to also travel by helicopter? She knew it was a silly thought, but it succeeded in reminding her how different she was from the other students.

Suddenly feeling very anxious, she felt around in her bag for her crescent-moon tiara. Her mother had been a fantastic storyteller and had read to Lottie every night before bed. *The Glass Slipper* was Lottie's favourite tale and she had asked her mum to read her every version of the story they could find, fascinated by how different they all were. Her mother had explained how fairy tales, like most things in the world, had evolved and adapted, but what Lottie was most drawn to was the prevailing sense of putting goodness out into the world. No matter which version of the story she read, the kindness of the princess remained, and more than anything that was what Lottie wanted to emulate. And so, for her seventh birthday, Lottie's mother had given her a silver tiara heirloom with a crescent moon on top. It had been handed down through generations of Pumpkins, sharing the legacy of Rosewood Hall.

Lottie watched as the scenery outside the train window blurred into the memory of her seventh birthday party.

'This was gifted to one of our ancestors, who had the privilege of attending Rosewood hundreds of years ago. He passed it down, and eventually my grandfather bestowed it to me. One day, if you have children of your own, you can pass it on to them.'

Lottie barely took in her mother's words, unable to pull her eyes away from the object in the box.

She delicately placed the tiara upon her crown. But, alas, her tiny seven-year-old head had been simply . . . too tiny. The tiara had fallen almost immediately, landing on the hard wood of her living-room floor and looking very out of place among the sea of birthday-cake-stuffed children. Being the sensitive girl that she was, Lottie had proceeded to cry. It was not necessarily the fact the tiara didn't fit that had the young Lottie feeling so overwhelmed, but that the tiara – this pristine object of magnificence, so incongruous in her humble home – made everything surrounding it seem so painfully ordinary. It appeared to glow with a glittering grandeur, yet its light only succeeded in illuminating quite how plain the world around it was.

'Lottie's crying *again*,' grumbled one of the party attendees.

'Shut up, Kate,' Ollie said. 'Don't be mean just because you didn't win Pass-the-Parcel.'

'THE SONG STOPPED ON ME!'

This sharp exchange had only served to make Lottie more upset – now her party guests were unhappy too. Just as Lottie had been ready to escalate into true floods of tears at the end-of-the-world scenario, her mother appeared at her side to save the day.

'OK, settle down, everyone. Kate, there's a special treat for you, if you let Thomas keep his Pass-the-Parcel prize,

18

and, Lottie darling, you can clip the tiara on with these.'
Marguerite reached into her apron pocket and presented her
with two crocodile hair clips.

'Now, everyone – this tiara is actually very special.' She
picked it up and Lottie noticed how natural it looked in her
hand. 'You see, this tiara has magic powers.'

All the children calmed down instantly, eagerly awaiting
one of Marguerite's enchanting stories.

'Whoever wears this tiara can achieve anything they put
their mind to, and touching it grants the wearer all the good
qualities of a princess.'

As she spoke, Marguerite Pumpkin carefully clipped the
tiara on to Lottie's head, delicately sweeping her hair back to
cover the clips.

'Now, what are three good qualities princesses have that
we can think of?' She looked at the children, but they went
shy, as children often do when put on the spot. 'How about
brave? Do you think princesses are brave?' They nodded their
heads. 'Now what else?'

'Oh, oh, they're pretty!' Ollie blurted.

Marguerite chuckled softly, impressed by his innocent
sincerity.

'Well, yes, they are often pretty, but that prettiness comes
from within because they are . . .' She put out her hand,
inviting someone to fill in the blank.

'They're kind!' said Kate, smiling at Lottie.

'Yes, good, Kate, what else?'

Lottie, feeling encouraged by Kate's smile, decided to add
her own thoughts. 'They never give up on their dreams.'

'Excellent, Lottie. What's a word we could use to describe that?'

'DELUSIONAL!' Ollie shouted. Everyone laughed, except Lottie, who simply rolled her eyes.

'Er . . . helpful?' offered Charlie. There was a moment of silence as the children continued to hum and haw, all trying to think of an appropriate word. Until it came to Lottie like a lightning bolt. It was so clear; this word suddenly seemed the most powerful and important word in the world and it would change Lottie's attitude forever.

'*Unstoppable.*'

Lottie knew as soon as she'd spoken it that this was the power she wanted the tiara to grant her: the power to never, ever give up, to be an unstoppable force of good whether the world liked it or not.

To think it was now seven years since she'd received it seemed so odd. Her life had become vastly different after her mother passed away only two years later, and sometimes she still struggled to believe it wasn't all just a terrible, sad dream. She shook her head, forcing the bad feelings away, and put the Polaroid back in her purse before her fingers located the tiara in her bag. She took a moment to squeeze it, lightly caressing the little gems along the front. She would have preferred to put the tiara on, but touching it would have to do while she was on the train.

She then recited to herself her personal mantra. 'I will be kind, I will be brave, I will be unstoppable.'

She could do this. She would fit in. She would succeed at Rosewood, just like she'd promised her mother.

'This station is Rosewood Central. Alight here for Rosewood Hall.'

Lottie picked up her suitcases with a flood of determination. She was ready to start the next magical chapter of her life and she would prove she belonged in this world.

## 3

Lottie took one of the shuttle cars from the station. It dropped her off at the school entrance, a grand double set of cast-iron gates, ornately embellished with the letters R and H, set in the massive wall that enclosed the front grounds of Rosewood Hall. The open gates led to a large canopied structure, under which all the incoming students were gathering. The roof was supported by stone pillars that were adorned with carved intricate thorns and roses. The wind through the pillars made an odd siren call, the noise sending a strangely pleasant shudder down her spine.

She gazed around and felt a pang of nerves as she took in the other students and their incredible array of luxury cars. Lottie recognized a few of the vehicles from spending so much time with Ollie; she was sure he would be drooling if he could see them. None of the other students seemed to be carrying their own luggage and most of them were enthusiastically chatting or intently tapping away at their phones before they would have to hand them over for the start of term.

Rosewood was open to students from the age of eleven, so many of these children would know each other already, making Lottie feel even more like an outsider. Lottie went to thank her driver but an unexpectedly strong breeze blew through the pillars, drowning out the sounds of the student chatter. That's when she saw her.

A mysterious figure on the periphery.

Behind the car that had brought her here was a girl – tall and lean with cropped, jet-black hair and clad in a beaten-up black leather jacket, a guitar case casually slung over her shoulder. She was not like the other students; something about the girl screamed of passion – she was like a dark brooding storm cloud. She was pulling suitcases out of the back of a private car with ease; the chauffeur tried to help but was met with dismissive hand gestures, so he stood to the side looking distressed. Lottie couldn't see the girl's face properly as it was covered by a large pair of sunglasses. She felt a sudden instinctive need to get a closer look at the girl. It felt as if there were an energy between them – something was drawing her towards her. But before she could come to terms with this strange sensation of familiarity, her view was cut off by a pile of books with legs.

'Excuse me, sorry, coming through!'

Lottie hurriedly pulled her pink suitcases out of the way. She'd never seen such a small person carry so much stuff. It looked as if she should topple over at any moment and yet somehow she managed to appear balanced and composed. Clearly this girl was much stronger than her size suggested. Even though her face was hidden behind piles of books and cases, Lottie could see masses of tight dark ringlets. How on earth she knew where she was going was a mystery. She stepped around Lottie just as a group of Year Sevens raced past, as if she'd timed it perfectly.

'*Greetings!*'

Lottie jumped as a girl's face popped out from the side of the books and cases with a beaming grin, revealing two large brown eyes magnified by a thick pair of round spectacles. Lottie's brain immediately conjured up the image of an owl.

The tiny owl girl glanced down at Lottie's cases. 'You must be a Rosewood fledgling – how exciting!' She looked up at Lottie, considering her curiously before her grin burst back on to her face and she laughed. 'I appreciate your commitment to the colour pink,' she said, nodding at Lottie's outfit, cases and accessories.

Lottie felt her cheeks going hot, a reflex she'd been cursed with since she was little.

'Thank you, I . . .'

'That's quite a prominent idiopathic craniofacial erythema you suffer from.'

The owl girl leaned forward to scrutinize Lottie's face, causing her to involuntarily lean back and blink. She considered herself to have a pretty good vocabulary, but this was beyond her.

'Blushing, that is. It's quite charming really; although it can be an early symptom of erythematotelangiectatic rosacea . . .'

As the owl girl continued on like this, Lottie followed her along the path towards the school entrance, nodding dumbly.

Already Lottie felt like she had entered another world as she looked around. The pathway was framed by three stone arches. As they walked through them, Lottie could make out an intricately engraved copper portrait mounted at the top of each arch. She recognized the figures as the patrons of the three legacies to Rosewood: Florence Ivy in the middle, Balthazar Conch to the left, and the last one on the right was occupied by the twins Shray and Sana Stratus. They glared down at the students, the weight of their expectant gaze causing Lottie to gulp involuntarily.

*Be brave!* she repeated to herself.

'I personally think it's cute, but if you were also prone to erythrophobia that could be a problem.'

The owl girl giggled to herself and turned to Lottie, smiling. It took her a moment to realize the other girl had finished talking and that she needed to respond.

'Erythrophobia?' she asked. Should she know this word? Had she just exposed herself as stupid?

The owl girl stared at her before unexpectedly bursting into laughter again. The sound of her giggling was so adorable that Lottie felt as if she were being licked by a puppy.

'Sorry, I was definitely rambling. Here . . .' The girl did a strange shimmy, transferring her luggage to one hand.

Lottie was sure everything would topple this time, but to her amazement it stayed upright, like some kind of bizarre circus performance. The owl girl reached into her pocket with her newly freed hand and pulled out a small piece of paper. 'I'm Binah.'

Lottie took the offering and quickly realized it was a business card. A BUSINESS CARD? They were fourteen; what could any fourteen-year-old possibly need a business card for?

### Binah Fae
Volunteer library assistant
For study advice and tutoring
please send all requests by mail to:
*Binah Fae, Stratus 304B, Rosewood Hall, Oxfordshire*

Lottie was momentarily overcome with dread; did she need a business card too? Was that the done thing for children of the 'elite'?

She struggled to speak for a moment before replying.

'Hi, Binah. I'm Charlotte . . . but please call me Lottie.' She prayed that her first name alone would be sufficient and, to her relief, Binah smiled with total sincerity. All thoughts of the enigmatic leather-clad girl melted away as Lottie took in her warm expression.

'It's a pleasure to meet you, Lottie.'

The two girls stepped out through the final archway and Lottie followed suit as Binah left her luggage with a woman in a golf buggy, giving her name and year and watching her luggage disappear up the huge hill towards the main school buildings. Lottie slowly turned a full circle, taking in the boundary, which enclosed the school grounds. Behind her was the massive wall; to her right and left, disappearing round the back of the distant buildings, were the ancient rosewood trees that gave the school its name. The path was lined with roses of all different colours and species. They didn't simply flourish; they appeared to glow with a hidden magic.

The uphill path took them to a stone archway that gave entry to a courtyard in front of the reception hall. The entrance to the reception was a vast pair of oak doors, framed by a stone arch that was carved with a thorny pattern. The delicate thorns escalated upward to reveal the name of each Rosewood house – Ivy, Conch and Stratus, their order reflecting what they symbolized in the school motto: 'Righteous, resolute, resourceful.' Above this was a huge gold engraving that read ROSEWOOD HALL: ACADEMY OF REMARKABLE ACHIEVEMENT.

She stopped a moment, her stepmother's words echoing in her head.

'I hope it doesn't disappoint you.'

Lottie only faltered for a second, but it caught Binah's attention.

'Are you OK?' Binah asked, cocking her head to the side inquisitively.

'I'm just . . .' Lottie trailed off, not wanting to admit how nervous she was to see the school for the first time. 'Tired from travelling so far.'

If she'd only known in that moment the domino effect those words would have.

'You're from another country?' Binah asked, her enthusiasm bubbling back.

'Yes.' Wait, what? Did she say county or country?

'That's wonderful. We have so many international students; you'll fit in no problem!'

'Wait, I think –' Lottie tried to interject, to explain she was just from Cornwall, but Binah continued on in excitement.

'No, no, don't worry at all.' Binah beamed up at her with a brilliant smile that showed all her pearly teeth and left Lottie feeling a little dazzled. 'You're a Rosewood novice and I take it upon myself to know everything so I can help everyone.'

Lottie blinked a few times, amazed at how much Binah's words reminded her of her own desire to put good into the world. She quickly remembered herself and opened her mouth to correct the misunderstanding, but Binah's eyes had moved behind her, squinting at whatever she was seeing.

'And, speaking of things you should know, here come three of them right now.'

Lottie followed Binah's gaze as three impeccably well-dressed students walked towards them.

One of the girls had an iced coffee in one hand and a phone in the other that she was furiously talking into. She was clad in an oversized fur coat and Lottie could see designer logos peeking from her ensemble. This girl could have easily been a brunette Barbie doll come to life. The other students were a boy and girl who seemed to move in unison; they were so identical in build and appearance that they must have been twins. They were like shiny little doves, dressed almost entirely in white.

'*Binah!*' called the girl twin in a high-pitched squeal, leaping forward to give her a big squeeze.

Binah hugged her in return, then they all seemed to notice Lottie at the same time.

'Anastacia, Lola, Micky – meet Lottie. She's international.'

Lottie groaned internally, praying no one asked to see her passport. The Barbie girl said a curt goodbye into her phone then turned to Lottie.

'Pleasure,' said Barbie flatly, holding out her hand, a slight French accent dripping through the word. Lottie shook her hand slowly, noticing how cold it was. 'I love your dress,' she added.

Lottie blushed, realizing that this girl probably had no idea how reassuring and kind that little compliment had been for her.

'Oh, thank y–'

But before Lottie could finish, the Barbie girl interjected, saying, 'OK, enough chit-chat. I'm sick of standing around and I want to make sure my luggage isn't being mistreated.'

The twins giggled to themselves.

Binah leaned over to Lottie and whispered in her ear. 'That one's Anastacia, daughter of the French ambassador. She's very entertaining.'

Lottie nodded, watching as Anastacia and the others sauntered through the archway. Yet Lottie found she couldn't follow. She was overcome by the thick fragrance that seemed to flood the air around them. The mixture of lavender and roses gave the air a deep, dreamy feel, like being plunged into another world. She looked up at the building looming over her. Lottie felt as though the school was calling to her, pulling her in with an atmosphere of its own. She was meant to be here; she knew it deep in her bones. The tiara that lay hidden away in her bag burned at her side. She'd really done it. She'd made it to Rosewood. She realized then that it wasn't that she was scared the school would disappoint *her*; she was scared that she would disappoint the *school*.

'*Allez!* Some of us would like to get to Rosewood before they die of old age, thank you.'

Anastacia's voice pierced Lottie's ear, pulling her out of her daze and forcing her legs back into action. 'What are you doing?' she asked.

'I have absolutely no idea,' Lottie replied as she took her first steps into Rosewood Hall.

# 4

The heavy doors of the magnificent oak-walled reception were wide open to welcome the students, new and old, who were pouring in, all of them buzzing with enthusiasm like well-dressed bees in a hive. The way the light hit the archway behind Lottie in strange dappled sections gave the impression that the courtyard was a painting, as if crossing the threshold had plummeted her into another world.

'The welcome speech and fireworks aren't until later tonight,' Binah explained, 'so you'll want to get settled in to your dorm and relax, maybe try on your uniform. We can meet up before all that.'

The five of them were standing in line for registration and Binah had pulled out a large beautifully bound document that Lottie recognized from her own Rosewood Hall welcome pack, but where Lottie's was purple, Binah's was yellow.

'Which house were you assigned after your aptitude test?'

Micky, Lola and even Anastacia perked up at this question, each turning round to hear Lottie's response.

Along with the application, Lottie had had to take an aptitude test filled with 'what if' and multiple-choice questions to evaluate which house would be the best fit for her.

'I'm in Florence Ivy.'

The other students shared a look and Lottie wondered if she'd said something stupid.

Binah laughed and patted Lottie's shoulder, which would have felt condescending coming from anyone else, but her sincere smile made it impossible to take it as an insult. 'Sorry, sorry! We never call them by their full names. It's just Ivy, Conch and Stratus.'

Lottie couldn't stop herself blushing yet again.

'I see you're in Stratus –' Lottie said, pointing to Binah's yellow notebooks.

'*C'est n'importe quoi,*' Anastacia interrupted, her expression inscrutable behind her sunglasses.

Lottie had a limited understanding of French, but she could still grasp that Anastacia had said something along the lines of *nonsense*.

'Binah was one of the only students ever to be offered all three houses – and for some reason she chose Stratus over Conch,' explained Anastacia.

'Hey!' exclaimed Lola, looking genuinely hurt.

'Nothing personal, Lola. It's just Conch is clearly the superior house and red is a superior colour.'

Lola and Micky rolled their eyes in unison, obviously used to this kind of statement from Anastacia.

Binah shrugged at Lottie, trying to act as if it were no big deal to be invited to all three of the Rosewood houses, but her bashful smile suggested she knew exactly how impressive it was.

At the front of the line an Ivy prefect, whose purple badge said FREDDIE BUTTERFIELD, took her phone for the term and handed her another welcome pack. Lottie had known this was coming – phones were strictly prohibited during term time – yet it felt as if she were handing over a part of herself. Since her mother had passed away she'd spent so long studying as hard as she could that she hadn't had time for friends, so Ollie was the only one she ever really messaged. She couldn't even email him because internet usage was strictly monitored. The idea of him not being easily contactable made her a little nervous, but she quickly gulped it back down.

'Welcome to Rosewood, Miss . . . Pumpkin.' Lottie felt a twinge of embarrassment at the boy's hesitation over her last name but quickly quashed it. 'This bag contains some gifts from the school to you; it also contains the keys to your room and your fob for entry to the Ivy dorm. All other necessary equipment will be found in your room. You will get your phone back at the end of term. Thank you. Have a lovely day.' His tone suggested that he may have been enthusiastic earlier in the day but was now struggling to keep chipper, having had to follow the same script with many other Rosewood students.

They stepped out of the reception hall and parted ways with Anastacia, who went off towards a bridge in the direction of Conch House, accompanied by a frizzy-haired blonde girl who appeared to have been waiting for her. Lottie watched curiously as Anastacia wrapped the blonde girl in a tight embrace. She almost wondered if she was imagining the scene; it seemed so out of character for the girl she'd just met to display so much emotion.

Binah took her on a scenic route through the school. They passed the main quarters of Stratus Side, the Stratus House dormitory, which, as the name suggested, was in the topmost tower of the school. Very fittingly, Stratus House was represented by the merlin falcon, a symbol for resourcefulness, which was carved on a plaque above the tower's entrance. They left the twins there, who gave Lottie a synchronized wave before ascending the tower.

As soon as they were into the main school grounds, Binah began an impromptu lesson on the buildings they passed. Her lips moved faster than Lottie could keep up with and she spoke with such an intense vocabulary that it bordered on being another language altogether.

'The intricate fenestration on the assembly hall's walls is an intentional pastiche of eighteenth-century gothic styles . . .'

Lottie nodded. Were all Rosewood students this articulate?

Anastacia had said that Binah was the only student to ever be invited to all three houses and Lottie felt a sudden intense determination.

*I want to be this smart.*

She was going to use her time at Rosewood to work as hard as possible and make her mother proud.

Once they were out of the main school cluster, which was not a short walk at all and Lottie was very happy she didn't have to carry her luggage, the path became cobbled, which meant they were getting close to the Ivy dorms. A quarter of the way down the hill, nestled among dense rhododendron trees that backed on to Rose Wood, was a grand-looking stone building. Through its cast-iron gate was Ivy Wood, her new dormitory. It was beautiful and looked like a hotel, such was its size – and indeed it was almost like one. Lottie had read that, along with many en-suite bedrooms, Ivy Wood had its own reception area, kitchen, dining hall, library and study rooms. Ivy clung to the grey stone walls in tangled heaps, climbing up the sides of the buildings. The path to the front door was lined with thick bushels of wisteria covering trellised alcoves . . . and there it was: her home for the next four years.

'What kind of architecture is popular in your country?'

Lottie was jolted out of her daydreaming by the unexpected question. She looked at Binah and her voice caught in her throat; it would be completely humiliating to admit to the misunderstanding, but she had to do it. Now was her chance.

'I . . .'

But that's as far as she could get.

'Oh, look, isn't he wonderful?' Binah clapped her hands together in excitement.

Lottie looked up and found her gaze drawn to the pond at the centre of the Ivy garden. There was a bronze statue of a stag, its horns outstretched like a crown above its head, eyes piercing her own with an odd familiarity.

Binah sighed wistfully as she led Lottie towards it.

'He's called Ryley – he's the guardian of Rosewood, and your house symbol.'

Lottie found she was struggling to pull her eyes away. She once again found herself forgetting to set Binah straight on the mix-up, almost as if the deer were intentionally distracting her.

'Come on.' Binah gently reached out and stroked Lottie's palm with her thumb, as she escorted her away from Ryley to the entrance of the dorm. 'Let's get you checked in and to your dorm; you must be tired from your travels.'

Lottie groaned internally. Being at Rosewood was already completely exhausting and she hadn't even started classes yet.

Binah marched her up to the door for the Ivy dorm and left her with a clear set of instructions for meeting later.

'I'll pick you up by the Ivy Wood gate at seven p.m. and take you to the Miracle Marquee to meet the others. If you need any help after I go, your house mother is Professor Devine . . .' Binah paused for a moment, bringing her finger to her lips in thought. 'Although she won't be around now as she's giving the orientation speech, but I'm sure one of the prefects will be happy to assist you.'

Lottie had religiously memorized the names of all her teachers and heads of faculty, but out of all of them she was most excited to meet deputy headmistress and Ivy house mother Professor Adina Devine.

Ollie had made numerous 'jokes' about how that sounded like a witch's name. Lottie had reminded him that she was sensitive to jokes at the expense of people's names and pointed out that '*It sounds more like the name of a fairy godmother, thank you very much.*'

'You're lucky; Professor Devine is an amazing woman,' said Binah, a wide smile spread across her face. 'Just be sure not to get on her bad side. She can shout loud enough to shatter glass.'

Lottie gulped at this thought; she did not deal well with being shouted at.

Binah swiftly hugged her and Lottie found herself wrapping her arms around her and squeezing tightly, realizing that she didn't want her to go. Binah had helped her so much already. Lottie worried she'd be completely lost without her.

'Thank you so much, Binah.' She gave her another little squeeze before pulling away.

Binah smiled at her again, her teeth glittering in a wide, comforting grin.

'You'll fit in just fine here, Lottie. I think you're exactly what this school needs.' And off she went, skipping away towards the Stratus dormitory.

Lottie felt odd not having Binah at her side any more. Everything seemed much bigger than it had a few minutes ago and she felt that same anxious loneliness creeping back.

*Be brave.*

Upon entering the dorm, she was greeted by an ornately decorated reception room with a large oak-framed painting of a tiny but stern black-haired woman in purple with a deer by her side. It was, of course, Florence Ivy. She scowled out at the world from inside the frame, demanding to be taken seriously and inspiring resolve in all who gazed upon her.

*I won't let you down, Miss Ivy.*

A chubby red-haired prefect with a badge that said ELIZA LOOPER was sitting at a desk at the entrance. She smiled at Lottie and checked her in. There was a distinct smell of gingerbread around her, and her heavily freckled face was like a little constellation map. Unlike Freddie from earlier, she seemed genuinely enthusiastic to be helping.

'Lovely to meet you, Lottie!' She handed Lottie a small booklet with TERM TIMETABLE printed in gorgeous calligraphy on the front.

'This is your finalized timetable. You'll find out who you'll be in a company with, that is who you'll be sharing most classes with –'

Lottie nodded. She'd already researched how the Rosewood Hall classes were structured. Each year was split into companies of about twenty students all from the same house. Most classes were attended in these companies and she was praying she had a nice group.

'If you want to send and receive any letters, your personal PO box address is in your welcome pack and you can send and retrieve larger packages from the mail room next to the Stratus building.'

Again Lottie nodded; she'd been through the mail system about a million times with Ollie, reassuring him that they'd find a way to keep in touch.

'You're in Room 221. Your room-mate arrived about thirty minutes ago. She's new too, so if either of you have any more questions let me know,' she said, beaming.

*Room-mate!* The word was like an alarm bell in Lottie's head. How could she have forgotten she was going to be meeting her *room-mate*. The girl she'd be spending at least the next two years of her life sharing a room with. She headed up two flights of stairs and reached Room 221 at the end of the corridor. The door loomed in front of her, large and white with glittering gold numbers. She took a deep breath, mentally preparing herself.

The first thing Lottie noted as she opened the door was how huge the room was; it made her little attic room in Cornwall seem like a closet. It even had a balcony, one of the perks of being on the second floor. There were two white metal-framed double beds on opposite sides of the room; between them was a large purple Persian rug, perfectly centred on the lacquered wooden floorboards. As expected, her new tartan Ivy uniform, also purple, was lying on the empty bed waiting for her. The bare bed and walls actually excited her; there was so much decorating potential.

However, something seemed slightly off as she took in the side of the room that had already been occupied. It was almost completely bare apart from a framed poster for the film *Rebel Without a Cause* on the wall. Her room-mate hadn't even bothered to put her bedding on yet. Instead she was lying sprawled on her mattress with a book covering her face.

Was she . . . asleep?

Lottie was still jittery with the excitement of the day, and yet here was this girl, napping. She felt an odd sense of impatience. She knew she should let her sleep but she couldn't help herself. Lottie grabbed the door handle and slammed the door shut.

The girl sat up abruptly, the book falling off her face to reveal a mop of short black hair and dark piercing eyes that felt like they looked directly into her soul.

Lottie couldn't believe it. It was her, the girl from the drop-off.

## 5

'It's you,' Lottie breathed.

If she'd thought this mysterious girl was thrilling at first sight, up close she was like a whirlwind. She practically oozed teenage rebellion. Chaos and anarchy in human form. They could not have been more different. For everything Lottie was, this girl was the antithesis. Yet there was something eerily familiar about her that Lottie couldn't quite place.

She held herself with an enviable confidence and ease that made Lottie feel shy and awkward in comparison. Lottie suspected her cropped hair was dyed; it seemed too dark to be naturally black. Her make-up was bold and she wore a T-shirt for a band Lottie had never heard of and suddenly worried she should have.

'Excuse me?'

'Hi, sorry . . . Hi!' Lottie stumbled over her words, desperately trying to remedy any awkwardness from her moment of stunned silence. 'Have we . . . have we met before?'

Something flashed across the girl's face, her eyes squinting before turning into an almost cocky smirk. 'That's highly unlikely,' the girl replied, raising an eyebrow like some kind of eighties teen heart-throb.

Lottie immediately started blushing but she couldn't quite figure out why.

The girl extended her hand for Lottie to shake. Even their hands were completely different. Her tattered wristbands and chipped black polish on cracked nails made Lottie feel embarrassed about her own little gold bow ring and meticulously painted pink nails.

'I'm Ellie, Ellie Wolf.'

Lottie grabbed her hand and there was a tiny static shock between them that almost made her jump. She shuddered at the sensation but didn't find it unpleasant.

'Lottie . . . Lottie Pumpkin,' she replied.

'Pumpkin?'

Lottie mentally prepared herself for an onslaught of jokes at the expense of her odd last name that she'd have to pretend to find funny, but she was pleasantly surprised when Ellie smiled.

'Cute.'

The light from the balcony window beamed in, illuminating her delicate collarbones and reflecting off a silver diamond-shaped locket around her neck, which had a wolf crest in the centre.

Lottie blushed again and instinctively looked down. 'Thank you.'

An awkward silence crept its way into the room that Lottie felt she had to remedy.

'Do you know what company you're in?' she asked excitedly, and immediately told herself to calm down before she seemed overly keen.

'I'm in Epsilon, I think,' Ellie replied indifferently, pouring one of her bags out on to her bed.

'ME TOO!'

*What did I just say about being too keen?* Lottie mentally chastised herself, but Ellie turned and gave her a little side smile as if she found her enthusiasm endearing.

Lottie felt suddenly very uncool, but Ellie didn't even seem to notice as she began rummaging through the objects on her bed.

It didn't take Lottie long to have her side of the room exactly how she wanted it. She'd always been good with decoration, keeping scrapbooks and sketchbooks her whole life. Back in Cornwall, in the oaky attic of the bakery, her bedroom walls were covered in art pieces, Polaroid pictures strung up with clothes pegs, an assortment of fairy lights and colourful bunting in pretty pastels. It was her cosy retreat, a little haven where she could hide away.

She smiled to herself, dusting off her hands and admiring her handiwork. It was perfect. The rosy bedsheets, the flowerpots filled with pink roses, the candles on the shelves in colourful crystal holders. Everything blended just as she'd planned with the white and purple furniture of the Ivy dorm that she'd seen in the online brochure. She had also allowed herself to bring her most beautiful hardback fairy-tale books, along with a collection of paperbacks, all her stationery and Mr Truffles, her stuffed pig, who looked very comfortable amid her lacy cushions. She'd done it. She'd officially moved in, and she'd made the place hers . . .

Lottie turned round to find a war zone had broken out behind her. She gasped at the chaos on the other side of the room. If she hadn't known any better, she'd have thought a bomb had gone off. Piles of CDs and DVDs were spewed across the floor. *Who even owns CDs any more?* Dark clothes lay in crumpled heaps next to mountains of dog-eared books and papers. It was the messiest room she'd ever seen and it hadn't even been lived in for a day. The only thing Ellie had bothered to place carefully was a framed photo of herself with her tongue out, an arm round a very irritated-looking boy in a black suit.

After all Lottie's careful planning for her perfect dorm room it hadn't even occurred to her that her room-mate might be . . . a slob.

In the midst of the chaos was Ellie, sitting cross-legged on her bare bed with her big black boots, hunched over an unfinished sudoku with one earphone in, scruffy strands of hair obscuring her eyes.

'Interesting choice of decor!' Lottie tried to say this light-heartedly, but an involuntary twinge of nervousness squeaked out.

Ellie looked up slowly, pulling her earphone out and letting it dangle over the bed.

'What . . .? Whoa.' She pushed her hair back out of her eyes, letting out a long whistle of astonishment as she took in the room. 'You just did all this?' The words came out less impressed than bewildered.

'Having a nice room is important to me,' Lottie said quietly, the implication behind the words – she hoped – coming out very clear.

'Ha!' Ellie swung her legs over the bed. 'Oh! I'm guessing my eclectic style is not so much to your liking?' Her voice was dripping with sarcasm, her earlier charm replaced with a cockiness Lottie wasn't sure she liked.

'Well . . .' Lottie began, not one hundred per cent sure of the best way to approach the situation when what she really wanted to say was exactly what she'd say to Ollie in the same circumstances: *Clean your room, you animal.* 'I'd be more than happy to help you sort it out, if you'd like?'

Ellie stood up and crossed her arms in front of Lottie, who had her hands firmly placed on her hips.

'And I suppose you want me to clean it all up then,' Ellie said indignantly.

'It's not like the fairies are going to do it,' Lottie said, surprising herself with her own sarcastic tone, something that was very unlike her.

Ellie exhaled through her nose in an ironic laugh.

'Well, maybe I like it like this?' She was enjoying winding Lottie up. She sauntered over to Lottie's perfectly made bed and grabbed Mr Truffles.

'Hey!' Lottie exclaimed. 'Be careful with him!'

'It's fine, it's fine,' Ellie replied, tossing him over her shoulder. 'I'm just going to use him to even out the sides a bit . . . seeing as you clearly don't like my *aesthetic*.' She said the word slowly, drawing out the syllables and making little quote marks with her fingers.

Lottie was terrified of any confrontation so watched as Ellie placed him on top of a messy heap of stuff by her bed.

'Ta-da!' She grinned. 'Now you have your perfect room.'

Lottie stared at her, mouth wide open. *She was being teased.* She felt tears sting the back of her eyes. She'd grown used to slights and jabs from living with Beady but had never imagined she'd have to deal with it at Rosewood. She took a deep breath and performed her mental ritual that had got her through so much before. Closing her eyes, she imagined wearing her mother's tiara.

*I will be kind, I will be brave, I will be unstoppable.*

She was determined not to crumble.

'Ellie, that's not funny.' She tried to sound as firm as possible but she wasn't used to taking a tone of authority. 'Give him back,' she said, holding her hand out.

Ellie turned back to her and cocked an eyebrow. 'Just come get him,' Ellie replied, sliding to the floor. 'Better yet, why don't you come and join me in my trash pile?' She beckoned for Lottie to sit next to her. 'Or do you not want to ruin your pretty little dress?'

Lottie found herself particularly upset by that statement. She'd been so happy after Anastacia had complimented the dress that she'd saved up so much money for, but now that joy had been dashed by Ellie's mocking words.

Ellie lay back in her pile of mess and began flapping her arms, making a junk angel on the floor, becoming at one with her piles of possessions.

'Ellie, stop you're going to –'

But it was too late; Ellie's arm had caught the pile of stuff with Mr Truffles on top. That, in turn, knocked over her can of Coke that was on the floor, spilling the whole thing and turning her mess into a puddle of sticky jumbled objects.

'Oops!' Ellie sat up and stared at the dark bubbling liquid as it spread across the wood towards Lottie, making no attempt to stop it. To Lottie's horror, a small splash had landed on Mr Truffle's foot and she quickly swept him up.

'*Oops?* What do you mean, "*oops*"?' Lottie found herself overcome with frustration. She'd never met anyone who made her feel this way before. It was as if her whole body was on fire and she realized for the first time since her mother had died that she was letting herself get angry. It felt like all the negative feelings she'd bottled up her whole life were ready to explode.

Ellie just shrugged in response.

'Urgh, fine!' Lottie stormed into the bathroom, gritting her teeth to stop from shouting, and grabbed a towel. 'If you won't clean this up then I will.'

She began soaking up the black liquid, decidedly ignoring Ellie's aloofness.

'Relax – jeez!' Ellie grabbed one of her books off the floor and sat cross-legged on her bed again, casually flicking a strand of loose black hair out of her eyes. 'I'm sure you have a maid or something who can come and clean this up.' She chuckled to herself and Lottie felt her stomach drop.

*That is it!*

It was clear Ellie had some chip on her shoulder and Lottie would not have anyone make any prejudgements about her. Watching Ellie lounging on the bed, Lottie felt a storm building inside her.

'Look, I don't know what kind of assumptions you've made about me but I worked really hard to get into this school. I can't afford the school fees and I had to really prove myself, so the *least* you can do is keep your side of the room clean on the first day.' She slammed the towel down on Ellie's bed. 'Oh, and you're right, I don't want to ruin this dress, because unlike some people I don't have the luxury of not caring about things.'

Ellie immediately stopped laughing.

There was an awkward long pause. Lottie couldn't remember the last time she'd been so honest. She glanced at Ellie, suddenly terrified of the repercussions, but to her shock she saw what seemed to be genuine regret.

'I . . . didn't realize . . .' Ellie looked away, pushing her hands through her hair in what was probably the closest she got to showing embarrassment.

Lottie unclenched her hands, which had unconsciously turned into nervous fists at her side. Then she noticed the clock on the wall that was ticking away. It was five to seven, just five minutes before she was meant to be meeting Binah.

Ellie's look of shame clicked with Lottie in a way she didn't quite understand and she felt like something important had just happened between them. *Be kind*, she reminded herself. She sucked in all her frustration and let it out in one long sigh.

'Are you coming to the fireworks?'

Ellie blinked in surprise, obviously not expecting the sudden change in tone.

'I'm going with some people I met earlier . . . I'm sure they wouldn't mind if you tagged along.'

She looked thoughtfully at Lottie for a moment before turning away, her hair quickly falling back in front of her eyes.

'I'm gonna pass. I'm really tired from all the travelling and . . .' Ellie began fiddling with the locket around her neck. 'I should probably tidy this up a bit anyway.' She faced Lottie as she said the last words and gave her an apologetic smile.

For some reason Lottie couldn't quite figure out, the idea of leaving this girl now made her chest feel heavy; even after their awkward introduction. It had been years since anyone had upset her and she was still subconsciously waiting for her new acquaintance to punish her for her outburst. But she didn't. Instead she looked at Lottie in a way that made her feel as if she understood her and it made her instinctively pull her hand to her chest.

'Thank you.' Lottie surprised herself with the words, not entirely sure what she was thanking her for.

Ellie smiled – and Lottie felt like an unspoken truce had been agreed.

'No problem.'

# 6

Binah collected Lottie at the Ivy Wood gate as planned and they walked together across a bridge to the Miracle Marquee. Thoughts of her spat with Ellie melted away and Lottie focused on how she was going to clear up the misunderstanding about her coming from another country and explain that she'd just been too shy to correct Binah earlier.

Luckily the school in the evening made a welcome distraction from her nerves. To her surprise, it was even more breathtaking at night, with soft flickering candles guiding you along the pathways. When they reached the marquee Lottie immediately understood its nickname. Wooden beams were obscured by hundreds of roses making the rooftop look as though it were floating. Inside, hanging out by the seating area, were Anastacia, who even in the dark was still wearing sunglasses, Lola and Micky, who were both eating lollipops, and a dark-skinned boy who Lottie didn't recognize.

As she walked towards them, she could hear the boy saying, 'I still think they should extend curfew to ten p.m. for the Year Ten students. Someone should complain.'

Anastacia scoffed. 'Oh, please be our guest, Raphael, and let us know how it works out for you the fiftieth time around.'

The conversation was dropped as they spotted Binah and Lottie approaching.

'Yay, Lottie!' Lola ran over to her and gave her a big squeeze as if they had been best friends forever. There was a sweet smell like baby powder as she hugged her.

'Lottie, this is Raphael. Raphael, meet Lottie.'

Raphael made a spectacle of bowing. 'A pleasure to meet you, Miss . . .?'

'Pumpkin,' said Binah.

Raphael chuckled softly. 'Binah, it's too early in the year for your strange jokes,' he said, straightening up. There was a very subtle American accent as he spoke that Lottie couldn't quite place.

'No . . . that's really my last name.' Lottie could feel the blush creeping up her cheeks and prayed they didn't ask any more about it.

'OK, people,' Anastacia suddenly barked. 'Professor Devine's speech starts in twenty minutes and Saskia's saved us a good place for the fireworks. Let's move!'

Everyone immediately picked up their bags to walk to the viewing point. Lottie couldn't help but wonder if Anastacia had said that to get the attention away from her, but was Anastacia that considerate?

As they walked towards the field where the speeches were being held, Micky pocketed his lollipop stick, only to start eating another lollipop immediately.

He noticed Lottie staring, and asked 'Want one?' He pulled a bunch from his trouser pocket and held them out to her.

Lottie politely took one and put it in her bag for later.

'They're Tompkins branded.' Lottie jumped as Binah whispered in her ear. 'The lollipops . . . and Lola and Micky, they're Tompkins.' It took Lottie a moment to register what Binah was saying to her. The twins were actual Tompkins? Tompkins was the most luxurious and delicious sweet company in the world. No wonder Micky had such a sweet tooth. And suddenly Lottie realized what they reminded her of, with their striking white hair and soft blush with dark lips. They were like human candy canes.

As Lottie processed this new information, they stopped walking and found themselves among a crowd of students, facing the frizzy-haired girl she'd seen Anastacia embracing earlier. Her mass of hair and lean body made her appear taller than everyone else and she held herself in such a way that it made her simultaneously unthreatening yet commanding. She wore a red sash with the bear symbol of Conch House – which indicated her position as head of year.

She scrutinized Lottie for a moment before smiling.

'So this is the new Ivy student you mentioned, Anastacia.'

*This must be Saskia*, Lottie thought to herself. She wondered what else Anastacia had said about her. She gave a polite smile in response and the girl returned it with a look of inquisitiveness. She held out a bag of books, asking, 'Do you mind holding this for a moment?'

'Er, sure, no problem.' Lottie took the bag and watched as Saskia rummaged around in her pocket before pulling out a business card and handed it to Lottie in exchange for the bag.

Lottie groaned internally. *I really need to get some cards.*

'I'm Saskia,' Saskia said, offering a tanned hand. 'Year Eleven head of Conch House.' She relayed the information as if it were no big deal, but Lottie knew it meant she had a lot of power in the school.

'I'm Lottie,' she replied, suddenly feeling very shy.

'That's a nice name.' Saskia gave Anastacia a sideways glance. 'I hope Ani is being nice to you; we're childhood friends so –'

Before she could finish, Anastacia barged between the two of them, planting herself next to Saskia. Saskia gave Lottie a little knowing smile and giggled.

As they took their places, Lottie noticed adults in dark suits scattered around the perimeter, looking very serious. They made her inexplicably nervous. They seemed to radiate danger. What on earth were they doing in a school?

'Who are all those people dotted around in the black uniforms?' Lottie asked curiously.

'You don't know?' Raphael sounded so shocked you'd think Lottie had just told him she didn't know how to count to three, but Binah quickly chimed in.

'They're bodyguards. There are a lot of children of very important people here, as you know –'

'I heard some of the bodyguards are Partizans,' interrupted Raphael.

Lottie noted that Anastacia looked up over her sunglasses for a split second but quickly glanced back down.

Lottie, of course, had absolutely no idea what he was talking about.

'What's a Partizan?'

At this seemingly innocent question, they all looked at her, their heads snapping round in unison. Micky's jaw literally dropped, causing his lollipop to fall out of his mouth, which would have been comical but right now just made Lottie feel extremely anxious. Saskia raised an eyebrow, a unfathomable look on her face. Lottie rattled her brain, trying to think of a way to get out of this but nothing was coming to her.

'Where did you say you were from again?' Anastacia said coolly.

*Crap!*

Lottie opened her mouth but couldn't seem to form any words. She could feel her palms going clammy. *This is it – now's the time to come clean and tell them about the misunderstanding. Do it! Quickly!*

'. . . I'm not –'

'Students of Rosewood, welcome!' A melodic voice rang out across the field, immediately capturing everyone's attention. Lottie turned to see an Indonesian lady, possibly in her forties, wearing a white suit with a purple rose brooch on her chest. She stood at the centre of the outdoor stage, arms outstretched, like she was beckoning to the world. Professor Adina Devine was every bit as mesmerizing in person as she had been in Lottie's mind. She exuded a powerful aura. As she smiled out at the gathered Rosewood students and faculty, there was such genuine warmth behind her eyes that Lottie felt the look was personally intended for her. Professor Devine's pristine white suit, lit by the stage lights, appeared to glow in the dark, and the long overlapping shadows behind her intersected like giant iridescent wings. Lottie looked over at the others and found they were all as deeply captivated by the deputy headmistress as she was. To Professor Devine's left was a larger woman with long flowing hair, who was covered in jewels and wearing a yellow rose, and to her right was a tall bald ebony-skinned woman with fiery eyes, who was wearing a red rose: the Stratus and Conch house mothers, respectively. And behind them, barely noticeable in the shadows, was a stout-looking man, who resembled a baked bean thanks to his short stature and red face. Lottie instantly recognized him as Professor Croak, headmaster of Rosewood and a fantastically underwhelming individual when placed next to these three forces of nature.

Professor Devine went on, now that she had her audience's attention. 'Before we continue with the festivities I must inform you that the outdoor swimming pool by Conch House is undergoing refurbishment and is strictly out of bounds until after Christmas. I expect you all to respect these orders or there will be serious punishment.' She paused to give the crowd a stern look, hinting at how terrifying she could be. Satisfied, she went back to her speech.

'Righteous, Resolute and Resourceful! These are the three pillars of Rosewood Hall and each house is the keeper of one of these pillars and each pillar supports the other. At Rosewood Hall we believe that each student, teacher, house and company must rely on one another to achieve greatness. Each house needs the other to truly reach its potential and it is through the unity of all these pillars of aspiration that we will prosper.'

*Kind, brave, unstoppable. Righteous, resolute, resourceful.* Lottie couldn't help feeling her own mantra fitted well, and felt the fire of her determination to succeed at this school burn inside her.

'To those of you returning to us from your summer holiday, we are delighted to have you back and I encourage and anticipate that you shall all strive to achieve even greater feats than last year. To those of you who are new to us, I give you an extra-special welcome and ask that you take this moment to look around at your fellow students.' Lottie complied, turning to Lola and Micky, who grinned back at her and made a peace sign. 'Among your peers is an endless fountain of potential. One of you is likely to be the next ruler of a country, an Olympic gold medallist, a Nobel Peace Prize winner.' Raphael gave a little bow to Binah at the mention of this and she mimed an act of humble acceptance in response that made Lottie and the others have to stifle their laughter. 'Do not fail the potential you have within you. This school aches to see you reach your most exceptional self: use your time here wisely; use your time here to become remarkable and above all never give up on yourself, or each other.'

*Unstoppable.*

'Thank you, everyone, and enjoy this year at Rosewood.'

Lottie stood for a moment in wonder as Professor Devine left the stage and walked off in a glowing pool of pristine white. Headmaster Croak nodded to the professor and slowly approached the podium with a happy little smile on his face, adding hastily, 'Enjoy the fireworks!' before following the women off the stage.

Everyone looked up as the first firework went off in a magnificent burst of yellow. It was quickly followed by a succession of multicoloured spurts, fizzling in the sky. Lottie slowly let out a breath she hadn't realized she'd been holding.

'They're like trained assassins,' Binah's voice whispered softly in Lottie's ear, once again making her jump in surprise. 'Partizans, that is. They're trained from a young age in many fields from languages to martial arts and are assigned to a single member of an important family or group. And they will stop at *nothing* to protect them.'

Lottie had almost forgotten about the whole Partizan thing; she'd been so engrossed in Professor Devine's speech. The idea of secret trained bodyguards seemed a little over the top, and yet . . . she turned again to look at the fireworks. In the distance she could see the reception building that she'd come through that morning, with its grand arched doorway that separated Rosewood from the rest of the world. Everything glowed with the lights of the fireworks, dazzling flashes highlighting the architecture. It truly was like she'd entered a magical realm. Were lethal undercover guards necessary here?

'There's not so much need for them in our modern society,' Binah continued, 'but some people still hire them as a status symbol.'

Binah leaned back and glanced at one of the suited guards. She smiled wistfully. 'I find the idea of them quite romantic, don't you?'

Lottie followed Binah's gaze. *Romantic?* It wasn't exactly how she'd describe a potential personal killer, but she had to admit it was pretty exciting.

*I wonder if I'll ever meet one . . .*

\*

After the fireworks, when Lottie got back to her dorm room, she almost tripped over a small white gift bag that had been left by her door. She picked it up curiously, wondering if maybe it was for Ellie but the tag on the handle read: *For the Pumpkin princess.*

Lottie prepared herself for some kind of mean jab at her last name but instead found something far more bizarre. She carefully pulled out a tattered book called *The Company of Wolves*. She scrutinized it for a moment in confusion then flicked through the pages. There, on the inside of the cover, in gold calligraphy was written:

*I know your secret.*

# 7

Lottie woke up with a heavy feeling in her chest. She hadn't slept very well, trying to figure out what the 'gift' had meant and who it was from. She'd wanted to ask Ellie if she'd seen anything but her room-mate had been asleep when she got back. Another more worrying thought had occurred to Lottie, that maybe Ellie had left it – had she even bothered to attend the speech and fireworks? – but pushed that notion out of her mind . . .

She had this horrible sick feeling in her stomach that the gift might refer to the 'from another country' misunderstanding. They probably all thought she was some awful liar. She decided that first thing that morning she was going to march straight to Stratus Side and tell Binah and the rest of them before her first class.

As they headed into the Ivy Wood dining hall together, Lottie just grabbed a piece of toast and mumbled an excuse to Ellie, saying she had 'some business to attend to'. Ellie, aloof as always, simply nodded and offered to sign in Lottie if she wanted to skip their first class.

'What? Oh, gosh, no. I would never dream of doing something like that. I couldn't skip my first class!' Lottie was shocked at how easily Ellie suggested it.

Ellie smirked at her response but didn't press her.

'Well, I'm gonna make the most of this famous Rosewood breakfast. Come back and join me if you finish your "business" early, but if not I'll see you in class.' Ellie grinned at her, chucking a blueberry into her mouth and winking.

Lottie gazed at Ellie's pile of food with envy. She would have given anything to stay for the magnificent breakfast buffet, laid out with every possible breakfast food you could imagine. Wooden tables lined the high-ceilinged hall, while huge windows looked out over the garden with a clear view of the pond and the statue of Ryley the deer. Lottie took one last lingering look before shoving her toast in her mouth and legging it out of Ivy Wood and up the hill towards Stratus Side.

To Lottie's disappointment, when she reached Stratus Side she found she didn't have access. She was about to give up and head back to breakfast when a large blonde woman came bustling down the corridor with an armful of art supplies.

'Oopsy!' The woman missed a step and proceeded to drop all her stuff over the floor, revealing her face. Lottie instantly recognized her from last night's welcome party as Ms Kuma, the Stratus house mother. Immediately Lottie bent down to pick up the fallen items. Ms Kuma was a wonderfully poetic woman; as well as being the Stratus house mother, she was also head of the English department and would be teaching Lottie her favourite subject. She dressed in deep colours, unafraid of bold patterns and adorned herself in spellbinding jewels. Something about her seemed supernatural, like she might be capable of making the impossible happen.

'Oh, thank you . . .?' She paused to allow Lottie to give her name.

'Lottie,' she replied, grabbing the last item from the floor.

'Thank you, Lottie. That's very kind of you. I need to get this back to the art-supply cupboard before our staff meeting, but goodness knows how I'll get there in time.'

'I can do it – just pass everything to me,' offered Lottie with no hesitation.

'Oh, that would be marvellous,' Ms Kuma said, and clapped her hands together, a melodic trill in her voice. 'It's the little wooden door if you follow the corridor to the end and go down the right set of stairs.'

Lottie smiled up at her new teacher, careful to keep her balance. 'No problem!'

It was tricky to get down the stairs with her arms full and she almost walked right past the art-supply cupboard door, which was tiny with a strange wooden knob that looked like a face. It looked like it belonged in Wonderland, not a school building.

She eased the door open to find that it wasn't quite a cupboard as such but a small cluttered room with shelves crammed with art supplies, and chests of drawers lining the back wall. She was carefully putting everything away when a huge pot of glitter fell off one of the shelves.

'Oh no!' Lottie groaned but then fell silent as she watched, mesmerized, as the cloud of glitter wafted through the air, settling behind one of the sets of drawers. Intrigued, Lottie heaved the drawers back with all her strength and gasped at what she found behind it. There was a hatch in the wall, hidden by the drawers. There was a small metal handle that sparkled, calling for her to open it. Curiosity got the better of her; she opened the hatch and began crawling through the tiny space. Inside was mostly wooden board and heaps of discarded fabrics. There was plenty of space for her to crawl but it was far too dark not to be a little bit creepy. In the distance she could hear the sound of rushing water and wondered how far out this tunnel went. She could see weak rays of light filtering into the tunnel, possibly from side openings, and began hurriedly crawling towards them while trying to keep as quiet as possible.

After a few minutes, she heard a familiar giggle from an opening ahead of her. It was *Lola*. Lottie crept forward and discreetly peeked round the corner.

'She *looks* like she could be a princess, I guess . . . You know, with all that pink.'

Lottie almost yelped as she came face-to-face with Lola and Anastacia. But they didn't seem to see her; in fact Lola continued fixing her hair, as she spoke, and Lottie realized in shock, *I'm behind a mirror*!

'I *thought* Pumpkin was kind of an odd name.' Lola snorted. 'Do you think she transforms at the stroke of midnight?' She began inanely giggling at her own joke.

Lottie almost choked. They were talking about *her* . . . and they seemed to think she was a princess? Lottie willed her breath to be as quiet as possible as she listened on.

'It's true, she's the undercover princess – it's the only logical explanation,' Anastacia replied.

This took Lottie completely by surprise. Had she misheard or was Anastacia, the most serious person she'd ever met, genuinely suggesting that Lottie was an undercover princess? Was this a joke? Or did that mean there was really a princess somewhere in the school?

*The gift!*

Was this what that creepy message in the book had been about? An unpleasant shiver ran up Lottie's spine for whoever the real princess was.

'Are you serious? How are you so sure?' said Lola.

Lottie leaned forward, listening intently to catch every word.

'Well –' Anastacia paused and moved closer to Lola – 'you didn't hear it from me, but I heard a rumour from someone else that the unannounced princess of Maradova chose Rosewood over Aston Court and look . . .' She pulled a magazine out of her bag and flicked to a page, which Lottie couldn't see. 'That's the queen of Maradova. Doesn't she look familiar?'

'Holy chocolate biscuit!'

Lottie jumped and had to cover her mouth to stop from accidentally squeaking with laughter at this strange outcry from Lola.

'Shh, quiet,' Anastacia snapped. 'We cannot tell anyone. If this is true, then she obviously wants to keep her identity secret. Why else would she come up with a fake name like Lottie Pumpkin?'

Lottie felt a little wounded at this jab at her name. She'd spent a lifetime defending her unusual name and now it appeared to have got her caught in some strange princess theory.

'Besides,' Anastacia added, 'if she is the princess of Maradova, I definitely want to be on her good side.'

Lottie almost burst out laughing at this. The scenario had become too surreal. She wondered momentarily if she'd ever even made it to Rosewood Hall at all. Maybe she'd fallen asleep on the train and this was all some elaborate dream. The idea that *anyone* could ever think someone as plain as her could be a princess made her feel like a terrible phoney. How could they not see how completely ridiculous that was?

'The rumour is that she wants to lead a normal life,' said Anastacia.

Lottie thought back to the previous night and their reaction to her not knowing what a Partizan was.

*They must think I was pretending!*

'But surely people know what the princess looks like?' argued Lola. 'Surely you've seen her at one of the international events?'

Lottie leaned in further, curious about this too.

'She never attends any; she refuses – part of the whole *I want to be a normal girl* thing.'

Lottie felt her mind boggle at the idea of anyone wanting to be normal, especially a princess. What kind of person was this princess of Maradova?

'Micky and I definitely won't say anything, and Binah is always discreet and . . . Raphael will do whatever you say –'

'Good,' said Anastacia, quickly cutting her off. 'Then it's just between the five of us, OK?'

'OK,' replied Lola.

'*No way,*' Lottie breathed from behind the mirror.

She had to fix this rumour before it got out of control.

## 8

Even though it was on the other side of Rosewood, Lottie made it to her first class fifteen minutes early. She looked down at her new uniform regretfully. With all the running around she had been doing, her purple Ivy pinafore had become significantly crinkled already, with a touch of glitter from her tumble in the supply cupboard.

Ellie arrived just before the bell went and took a seat at the desk next to her. She had opted for a tight pair of the purple tartan trousers and a set of braces with a shirt underneath showcasing the Ivy emblem of a stag on the pocket. All she needed was a buzz cut and she'd look like a classic sixties skinhead.

Lottie sailed through her first two classes effortlessly. English was one of her best subjects, and having helped Ms Kuma that morning she'd cemented herself as a favourite student. It wasn't until her lesson before lunch that she felt the weight of how intense the Rosewood classes could be. Maths had never been Lottie's strong point – she'd had to work extra hard on the maths part of her Rosewood application – and although she tried her best to concentrate she soon became distracted thinking about how she could quell the rumour when she saw Anastacia and the others at lunch. How should she bring it up? Should she tell them she heard their conversation and that they had got it wrong?

'Oh, hey, guys. I was spying on you earlier in the girls' loos after I followed a magical cloud of glitter to a secret passage and I thought you should know I'm not actually an undercover princess, but thanks for the compliment. Love ya.'

Yeah . . . somehow she didn't see that going down well. To take her mind off it, she began doodling tiaras and gowns in her notebook, wondering what the princess of Maradova was really like.

'Miss Pumpkin, would you please remove your head from whatever cloud it is in and complete the equation?'

Lottie blinked at the sound of her name and looked up to find the whole class staring at her. She instinctively turned to Ellie, who had revealed herself to be a maths prodigy. She'd raced through the textbook work and would probably be moved on to an advanced class pretty soon. It made Lottie feel completely inadequate sitting next to her. She gave Ellie a pleading look but was met with a side smile.

Mr Trigwell was clearly not the type of teacher to let daydreaming slide, and she could not have planned a worse first interaction. He was tall and thin in an almost inhuman way, as if his limbs were a little too long for his body. His nose was slightly hooked and his build paired with his attire reminded her of the Slender Man urban legend she'd read about online. She struggled with maths on a good day, but, with her distracted mind and her instinctive fear of Mr Slender-Man–Trigwell, her inability to think logically with numbers was amplified to an embarrassing level. She finished the class with 'extra homework for Lottie Pumpkin' as her 'distracted mind is craving something to fill up the empty space'. She was mortified: she refused to fall behind in any subject and she had to prove herself, but she didn't know how she would get ahead in maths without a supportive teacher.

'I can tutor you if you want?' Ellie said as they packed up their bags.

'Really?' Lottie felt a huge sense of relief fill her chest. 'That would be amazing! If there's anything you need help with so I can thank you, let me know.'

Ellie gave her a little side smile. 'I can think of a few things . . .' she said slyly. 'Hey, are you doing anything after classes?' she asked unexpectedly. Lottie was about to answer when she continued. 'Actually it doesn't matter – just don't come back before five thirty. I have a surprise.' Before Lottie could respond, Ellie swung her backpack over her shoulder and headed out of the door, calling back, 'Remember – not before five thirty!'

Lottie blinked for a moment, wondering what on earth her room-mate had planned.

Lottie had assumed she'd eat her first lunch at Rosewood in the main cafeteria that overlooked the pond by the flower house with her new friends, using the time to properly get to know each other. Instead she found herself at a table on the patio, alone, eating artichoke soup and some kind of strange pickled vegetable that she didn't recognize. She'd considered looking for everyone she'd met the night before, but she still had no idea how to handle the ridiculous rumour, and an even more sinister thought had occurred to her: *What if one of them left that creepy gift?* She wished her mum was still around to ask for advice – but she was on her own. She didn't want to burden Ellie with her problem and Ollie would be of no help. She stirred her soup absent-mindedly. As she stared out over the pond, a delicate red dragonfly landed on one of the lily pads, resting its wings, only to be swallowed whole by a large frog. Lottie winced as she watched the helpless creature being devoured.

'*Lottie!*' She jumped at the sound of a boy calling her name from behind her. 'We've been looking *everywhere* for you.' Before she had time to process the situation she found her previously empty table completely filled by Lola and Micky, Anastacia and Raphael.

'I was just . . . eating lunch,' Lottie said stupidly, wanting to kick herself for saying something so obvious. She couldn't exactly say she was avoiding them because she knew they thought she was a princess.

They all proceeded to place their plates on the table and Lola leaned over, placing a slice of strawberry cake in front of Lottie.

'We got this for you. It took us *forever* to find you,' she said dramatically.

Lunch had only started fifteen minutes ago and Lottie smiled at the exaggeration.

'You can't hide from us, though!' Raphael laughed as he said this, but Lottie froze at his words. Lola squirmed in her seat and Anastacia gave Raphael a quick scowl. 'I mean, as in, in the school . . . you can't hide,' he said, stumbling.

'Right,' Lottie said, trying not to sound nervous. 'What else could you have meant?'

A noise like a mouse squeaking escaped from Lola's mouth and Anastacia turned her scowl on her.

Lottie found it unexpectedly fun to mess with them.

'Thank you so much for the cake,' she said, scooping a bit of whipped cream on to her finger. 'Strawberries are my favourite. How did you know?' She licked the cream, trying to act as casual as possible.

'Oh, we know everything about you,' Raphael said with a wink.

*He is really not good at keeping secrets, is he?*

He let out a little yelp as Anastacia obviously kicked him under the table.

Lola squeaked again and Anastacia gave her another look.

This was becoming very exhausting for her and Lottie realized what she had to do. She had to get one of them to crack and tell her that they knew so she could put them straight.

'All this food is so exciting,' she began, putting as much wistfulness in her voice as possible. 'I've never eaten anything so fancy in my life.' That was actually not a lie.

Lola's eyes widened and once again she began squirming restlessly.

Anastacia tried to remain calm but her lip twitched. 'Is that so?' she said through gritted teeth.

'Yes, and I love the uniform; it's so much nicer than anything I've ever worn before.' This wasn't quite true, but Lottie couldn't help hamming it up.

Lola's face turned red and it looked like she was biting her tongue.

*It's working!*

Lottie only needed one more thing to push Lola over the edge. She let out a long sigh as she rested her chin on her hand. 'I wish my life was always like this,' she said, not having to fake any of the dreaminess in her voice. She turned her eyes to Lola just as she exploded.

'I CAN'T TAKE IT ANY MORE!'

*Bingo.* Lottie had to stifle her smile.

'We-know-that-you're-the-undercover-princess-of-Maradova-and-we-know-you're-pretending-to-be-someone-else-and-we-promise-we-haven't-told-anyone-and-it's-only-us-and-Binah-and-Saskia-who know-and-we-won't-tell-a-soul-we-PROMISE!'

'*Lola!*' Anastacia shouted out, but it was clearly too late.

A tense silence filled the air. It was obviously taking a lot of effort on Raphael's part not to start laughing and Lottie felt a similar sensation. Completely unaware of the tension, Micky leaned over and helped himself to the strawberry on Lottie's plate, which would have annoyed most people but she just found it added to the comedy of the situation.

'Interesting . . .' Lottie said slowly, remaining calm when what she really wanted to do was burst out laughing and tell them all how completely silly this idea was, 'but I think you have the wrong person.' Anastacia turned her scowl to Lottie and it sent a cold feeling through her bones. 'I'm flattered really, but I'm not sure why you all think this.'

'Because –' Lola began indignantly, a pout forming on her lips.

'It's *obvious*!' Anastacia interrupted, looking annoyed. 'You can't hide it from us! You look exactly like your mother . . .

and your name is, quite frankly, ridiculous –' *Ouch!* – 'and you already let it slip that you're from another country, but as soon as we pressed you about it you froze up.'

*It's time to come clean*, Lottie thought. She couldn't have them thinking this, even if it meant they wouldn't want to be friends with her any more.

'About that . . .' she began. 'I'm not actually from another country; that was a misunderstanding.' She smiled at them, hoping it might help. 'I'm from Cornwall and my name . . . really *is* Lottie Pumpkin.' They were all silent again, Anastacia's eyes squinting as they scrutinized her until finally Raphael cracked. A snort escaped his throat and he burst into laughter; Anastacia gave him another sour look, but he ignored it.

'Lottie, or whatever you want us to call you –' he paused to catch his breath between chuckles – 'you are absolutely the worst liar I've ever met.'

*Huh?*

He quickly continued. 'If you want to keep your identity as a princess secret, you are seriously going to need our help.'

*Oh, come on!* Lottie's mind was about ready to explode.

'But . . . I'm not lying. I really am Lottie Pumpkin.'

This only caused Raphael to burst out into more laughter, and this time Lola and Micky started to giggle too.

'Stop, oh my God, I can't breathe!'

Lottie internally groaned. She'd tried to come clean, and she'd been as honest as possible but it seemed that no matter what she said they wouldn't believe her. She groaned again, out loud this time, and buried her head under her arms on the table.

'We promise we won't tell anyone,' Lola reiterated. 'Your secret's safe with us.'

Lottie kept her head planted on the table. 'Thanks.'

This was not how she'd planned her first day of school.

## 9

Lottie stood outside her dormitory door for what felt like a million years.

Her last two classes of the day had been options, so weren't with Ellie and the rest of their company, Epsilon. It appeared there would actually be a lot of classes they wouldn't have together as Lottie had chosen mostly art subjects while Ellie had picked advanced science and maths. Lottie had gone to the library until half past five as instructed and she had absolutely no idea what Ellie had planned. At least she felt better about the 'princess' misunderstanding. As far as she was concerned, she'd tried to explain it and they hadn't believed her, so as long as they kept it between themselves then it wasn't her problem any more. Right now, what she wanted to do more than anything was fix her less-than-fabulous first impression with Ellie.

So here she was, standing nervously outside Room 221 again, trying to think of a nice gesture while also worrying that some kind of terrible prank lay on the other side. She'd also made the decision to introduce Ellie to Binah and the others at some point, though she wasn't exactly sure how that would go down. Lottie suddenly conjured the image of

Anastacia and Ellie painting each other's nails at a sleepover and the whole scene was so completely unnatural that she found herself giggling involuntarily. Somehow she struggled to imagine they'd get along too well.

Lottie took a deep breath and slowly eased the door open. To her total shock, she found the room almost completely spotless . . . well, as spotless as it could be with all Lottie's books and Ellie's CDs. She must have come back and finished decorating her side of the room and, to Lottie's surprise, it looked kind of amazing. Their two sides were the complete antitheses of each other, split in the middle by the Persian rug. Ellie's collection of books, DVDs, CDs and video games was stacked on the bookshelves, but she'd done an excellent job of shoving them all in as best she could. Posters for an array of cult films were hanging on her side of the room and her shelves were crammed with band merchandise. Everything had a pleasantly motley vibe about it that fitted Ellie's stormy aura perfectly.

'Ellie?' Lottie called cautiously, as she walked through her new and improved room. There was no response, but she could hear angry music drifting from the bathroom.

'ELLIE!' she called louder.

'In here! Erm . . . Can you come and give me a hand with something?' Ellie's voice echoed out from their less-than-little bathroom.

'The room looks ama– OH MY GOD!' Lottie abruptly covered her eyes. Ellie was standing in just a bra and a pair of briefs, leaning over the roll-top bath with thick glops of black hair dye dripping down her neck. Lottie noticed that she was still wearing her wolf locket.

'I'm so sorry. I shouldn't have barged in.' Lottie could feel her face going bright red with embarrassment.

Ellie's relaxed laughter floated through the room. 'It's fine, Lottie,' she chuckled. 'We're both girls. I don't care.' She heard splashes of water as Ellie turned on the handheld shower head. 'Now get in here. I need help washing this dye out.'

And so Lottie found herself leaning over their pristine white bathtub, gently washing thick black dye out of the hair of a half-naked girl she'd known for barely more than a day. She'd never, ever dyed someone's hair before and she found the whole process of massaging the shampoo in, pouring the water over each section of hair and making sure the temperature was comfortable to be a very intimate experience.

'You're good at this,' said Ellie cheerily as Lottie began applying the last part of the shampoo. 'You sure you've never done it before?'

'Never. I didn't really have any girl friends back home.'

There was a short pause before Ellie added in a sad tone that implied she completely understood, 'Me neither.'

They continued in silence, watching the water trickle down the drain in a dark oily display. To Lottie's relief, Ellie had switched the music to The Velvet Underground, a less heavy alternative for her benefit.

'I'm really sorry about the mess in the room before,' said Ellie suddenly, her voice very quiet but equally clear. 'And your pig.'

'Mr Truffles,' Lottie added quickly.

'Right, Mr Truffles,' Ellie said, smiling slightly.

Lottie didn't know what to say, and Ellie gently pushed the shower head away to turn and face her. The dark dye was still dripping down her scalp, leaving lines of black across her white chest. She slicked her hair back out of her face. Like this, raw with no make-up on, hair pushed back, almost completely naked and revealing her sinewy, flat-chested body, Ellie could easily have been mistaken for a boy. Yet there was nothing masculine about her; her frame was somehow soft and delicate, almost genderless.

'Most people here have their lives handed to them on a plate,' she said, looking suddenly very serious. 'They don't realize how lucky they are to get to come here . . . If I'd known you were here on a bursary, I . . .' Her voice trailed off and she pushed back a loose strand of hair. 'You're not like them.'

Lottie hadn't really thought of it like that. She very much lived her life believing if you were an exceptional person then you got to do exceptional things. All the time she'd been working hard to get into Rosewood, she hadn't spent much time thinking about how easy it had been for the other students. Yet even though the words were intended as a compliment – 'you're not like them' – they still made her feel like a failure.

'You're different, because you had to work to get here. You can really appreciate it and actually do something good with your time here.' Ellie grinned at her. 'I'm really glad they put us in a room together.'

Lottie felt totally lost. She'd spent the last year of her life desperately trying to prove she was as worthy as the other Rosewood students to attend the school; she'd wanted nothing more than to be just like them, yet here was this storm of a girl suggesting the other students should have to match up to *her*. She didn't want to think like that; she couldn't get complacent and she couldn't let Ellie isolate herself from everyone in the school because she felt this way.

'Me too,' said Lottie, and both girls smiled at each other, each perhaps thinking they would change the other's mind.

'Oh, and if anyone makes you feel like you don't belong here, I will gladly beat them up for you,' Ellie added, flexing her arm muscles like a bodybuilder, accentuating the definition of her collarbone and revealing how delicate her frame actually was.

Lottie giggled. 'Thank you, but please don't beat anyone up.' Ellie faked an indignant pout. 'I'm perfectly capable of beating up my own enemies,' she said, mimicking Ellie's arm flex.

'Fine. I'll leave all the posh, rich kids alone.' Ellie sighed sarcastically, as if this was a huge ask for her, and leaned back over the tub. They went back to their routine of rinsing and scrubbing. Lottie watched in wonder as the water turned from black to clear as it washed down the drain, leaving no trace of the thick dark dye. As potions for friendship went, Ellie's hair dye was certainly a potent one.

The atmosphere felt completely different that night when they went to dinner. They decided to grab some food from the Ivy kitchen instead of eating in the main hall so they could spend the night alone and start on their homework. The kitchen was stocked with finger foods and snacks every morning, as well as the ingredients to make light meals like sandwiches and pasta, although Lottie doubted many of the students were familiar with preparing food for themselves.

When they finally went to bed there was no more tension between them. Lottie realized she felt completely relaxed around Ellie like she'd found a little home with her. With Ellie she didn't feel the need to prove herself, she didn't need to watch her words, she could just . . . be herself. She drifted off happily, completely unprepared for what she would wake up to.

'Lottie! Wake up!'

Lottie jolted awake to find Ellie leaning over her, grinning wildly, the whites of her eyes glowing acid in the dark, looking manic.

'I've done something really bad.' She was huffing slightly as if she'd just been running. 'Quick, get up!'

Lottie sat up quickly, her mind coming up with numerous worst-case scenarios: she's started a fire, she's murdered the headmaster, she's messed up the room again.

'What's going on? What time is it?' Lottie whispered, sleep lingering in her voice. She could hear furious thuds echoing down the lit hallway, getting closer to their door. 'Ellie, what on earth have you done?'

Ellie abruptly shoved something under Lottie's pillow and bolted over to her bed just as their door flew open.

Lottie covered her eyes from the harsh light streaming in from the corridor.

'Miss Wolf!' A voice came booming in from the doorway.

Lottie winced and to her shock saw deputy headmistress and Ivy house mother Professor Devine.

She was standing in a flowing white nightgown, the light spilling in around her as if she were glowing, her hair in jagged little tufts like she'd just rolled out of bed. 'Would you please explain what you were doing in the Ivy House kitchen at three in the morning?'

Lottie had to bite her tongue to stop herself from screaming a line of expletives at Ellie. *Yes, Ellie, what WERE you doing, you big idiot?* she thought.

Ellie feigned a sleepy yawn as if she'd just been woken up. *Oh please! There's no way the professor will fall for that.*

'What . . . what's going on?'

Lottie was surprised by how convincingly Ellie's sleepy tone came out. Clearly this wasn't the first time she'd done something like this.

'Ha!' Professor Devine's cynical laugh came out more like a statement. 'Do you take me for a fool, Miss Wolf?' Although her tone was sharp, Lottie spotted a glint of humour in her eyes.

Ellie stared her down for a moment. She had met her match.

'Come, both of you.'

*Both of us!* That seemed very unfair.

'Oh, and, Ellie, you can bring those chocolate bars you stuffed under Lottie's pillow.'

Ellie turned to Lottie with a look of total bewilderment. They were both baffled how the professor could possibly have known this information.

They followed their house mother in reluctant silence down the corridor, Lottie in her pink Disney princess nightgown, and Ellie in her Star Wars two-piece, both looking very odd against the dimly lit baroque-style corridor. Lottie could only imagine the terrible punishment they were going to get. This all seemed completely unjust. She had been asleep; she was an innocent victim in all this.

As if hearing her mental frustration, Ellie leaned towards Lottie and whispered. 'I was just trying to get us a midnight feast or something, you know, to cement our friendship or whatever . . .'

Lottie turned to Ellie and gave her the best *You've got to be kidding me* look she could muster, but it must have been pretty weak because they both snorted, having to use all their willpower not to burst out laughing at how ridiculous the situation was.

They came to an area of the Ivy dorm Lottie hadn't been to yet. The corridor was wider and it was even more ornate and luxurious than the regular dormitory. At the end, above the door to the house mother's rooms, there was a huge gold-framed painting of an effeminate-looking man with little square glasses smiling out at the world. Lottie recognized him as the founder of Rosewood, William Tufty.

Professor Devine opened the door and gestured for the girls to go in. Lottie was expecting an imposing office, with dark grand furniture, a perfect scene for a mortifying reprimanding, but to her surprise they entered the quaintest little room she'd ever seen. The floor was a peachy marble, with a large plush rug in the centre, on top of which was an intricately decorated cream coffee table, its glass topped with a sophisticated rose pattern. Two pink-trimmed love seats with gorgeous woodwork and golden lining sat on either side. Soft light from velvet lampshades gave the whole room a dreamy glow that seemed to mimic Professor Devine's own natural luminescence. Lottie felt completely out of place in her nightgown and half expected the room to come alive and refuse her and Ellie entry for being too scruffy.

'Take a seat, girls.'

Ellie and Lottie sat next to each other, Lottie with her hands nervously in her lap, Ellie leaning back, getting instantly more comfortable than she should have been in the situation.

Professor Devine brought out a tray with a beautiful floral tea set and biscuits. This was not the punishment Lottie had been expecting. The deputy headmistress set them down upon the coffee table and sat on the love seat opposite them.

'Miss Wolf, this is your first warning,' she said sternly. 'Do not let me catch you getting up to mischief again.'

Lottie noted the odd choice of words. If she didn't know any better, she would have thought the professor was encouraging Ellie to be more cunning next time. They shared a look that Lottie couldn't quite understand. It was a tense stand-off, until finally Ellie sighed in defeat.

'How did you know I was there? I was so quiet.'

Lottie held her breath for a moment, thinking Ellie had been tricked into confessing but the professor simply laughed.

'I want you to know, Ellie, that I have eyes and ears all over this school.' She tapped her nose twice. 'Nothing gets past me.' Ellie raised a disbelieving eyebrow in response. 'Now, if you're going to wake me up, the least you can do is offer me some polite company for a while. That is your punishment.' Her tone was humorous and light, a sharp smile spreading across her lips as she poured a cup of tea for each of them.

'To be fair, Professor, Lottie didn't actually do anything. She wasn't even awake,' Ellie said honestly. 'I wanted to surprise her with a big feast in the room for breakfast or something –'

Professor Devine held a finger up to silence her and turned to Lottie. 'Miss Pumpkin, is it?'

Lottie nodded nervously. This whole event was just too strange; she was half convinced she was dreaming the whole thing.

'Pumpkin, what a charming name.' The professor said the word melodically, seeming to truly delight in it. 'I suppose you are a fan of Cinderella?' she added, gesturing to Lottie's nightgown.

'Oh yes,' Lottie replied enthusiastically. 'I love all the interpretations of old fairy tales.'

Ellie smirked and Lottie instinctively stuck her tongue out at her.

The professor laughed good-humouredly and took a sip of tea. 'I have met many girls like you, Miss Wolf. It seems I have quite the mischief-maker on my hands.'

Ellie shrugged as if this were no big deal.

'Now I know you did nothing wrong, Miss Pumpkin,' she said, turning back to Lottie with a warm smile on her face, 'but the fates have placed Miss Wolf in a room with you, so you must look out for her. The same goes for you, Ellie. This is a vital lesson for you both.' Her face turned very serious all of a sudden. 'I cannot express how important it is that you young girls do everything you can to support each other in a world that is so ready to belittle you and bring you down. We can achieve amazing things when we uplift one another.'

Lottie and Ellie turned to face each other; it truly was amazing that two girls that were so vastly different would end up sharing a room.

'Now off to bed, both of you. What on earth were you thinking, getting me to serve you tea so late at night. Dreadful, completely unprofessional!' The professor winked at them before sending them off and heading back down the corridor in a floating vision of silky white fabric.

Lottie realized that neither she nor Ellie had even touched their tea.

*What an odd night*, thought Lottie.

'She's fun,' said Ellie, grinning.

Lottie and Ellie clambered back into their beds, snuggling under the duvets. A warm feeling started to spread through Lottie as she looked around at their odd-couple decoration. Her place with Ellie had become their little sanctuary. She smiled to herself, feeling suddenly very at home. Maybe she'd be happy at Rosewood after all.

As the girls fell back asleep, something was stirring around Rosewood Hall, something that had all the students giddy and excited. A rumour like an unstoppable weed was spreading its way through the roses of the grounds and it was going to have a life-changing effect.

## 10

The next day was one of the most perplexing days of Lottie's life. Somehow everyone in Rosewood seemed to have discovered Lottie's royal secret, and they weren't very subtle about it. As she walked through the Ivy dining hall that morning, she could hear hushed voices gossiping at her expense and, worst of all, Lottie realized she was kind of enjoying it.

'*Look, that's her!*'

'*She certainly looks the part.*'

'*I thought* Pumpkin *was kind of a weird name.*'

Lottie purposefully ignored that last comment as she took her seat next to Ellie. *This Maravish princess must be a big deal*, she said to herself.

She'd already had little gifts left outside their door that morning, from bath bombs to perfume, all accompanied by business cards. *How are they so good at networking and manipulating already?* she thought. Luckily she was able to hide them without Ellie noticing, one of the few perks of her terrible habit of 'sleeping in'. The idea of Ellie finding out about this ridiculous mess made her cringe. If Ellie was going to discover the misunderstanding, she wanted to tell her herself.

'Good morning.' A tall dark-haired boy with round spectacles stood at the front of the hall on a speaker's podium, a short purple-trimmed cloak with a stag emblem round his shoulders.

'I'm George Ogawa, Year Thirteen head of Ivy House. I trust you are all settling in well,' he continued, smiling at everyone with a charismatic expression that he'd probably practised many times in the mirror. It fell a little short as the dining hall continued to buzz with hushed whispers. 'While those of you who are new here get settled into your classes over the next few weeks, I have been asked to remind you that you will soon be given the opportunity to join a club or team, an honour that should be thoroughly respected.' He paused a moment to clear his throat and Ellie made a gagging motion. Lottie huffed at her, knowing how prestigious some of the extracurricular classes at Rosewood were. 'So it will be in your best interests to consider carefully in which position you feel you will best represent Rosewood. Thank you and enjoy your breakfast.'

George exited the stage and the hall immediately began chatting enthusiastically again. Lottie was acutely aware of the word 'princess' being thrown about and was tempted to shove her face into a loaf of bread to hide.

'Here –' Ellie pushed a little apple tart on a rosy dish across the table – 'I had one of these yesterday. They're really good.'

'Oh, I can't. I'm allergic to apples,' replied Lottie, sliding it back.

'You're . . . ?' Ellie's voice trailed off and she looked around the hall, which had been so lively and loud the morning before, to find only hushed whispers and pointing fingers.

'Umm . . . why is everyone staring at you?' she asked, grabbing a *pain au chocolat* from the middle of the table and gnawing off a big chunk.

Lottie was amazed at how completely indifferent Ellie was to all the gossiping. She almost wondered if Ellie was teasing her again and actually knew about the whole thing.

'You seriously don't know?' The words came out a little harsher than Lottie intended, but Ellie didn't seem to notice, instead taking another big bite of her pastry.

'We've only been here two days,' she said, gulping down her food and immediately stuffing the rest in her mouth. 'What could *you* possibly have done that's got everyone so worked up?' The words came out muffled through the food, but the 'two days' was loud and clear. How on earth *had* she managed to cause such chaos in two days? Lottie felt like she should get a prize.

'Basically . . .' Lottie began. What difference would it make if she told her now? Better she tell her herself now, she'd probably just find it hilarious. 'There's this ridiculous rumour –'

Lottie was abruptly cut off when Lola and Anastacia appeared at her side. Anastacia looked immaculate already. Her red Conch tartan dress was somehow more starched and pristine than anyone else's, and her hair was a perfect silky pool of chestnut brown cascading to her waist, a contrast to Lottie's sleepy bedhead. Looking at her made Lottie want to run upstairs and put a paper bag over her own head in shame.

The only odd thing was that Anastacia was wearing sunglasses again. *What does she have to hide?*

'WE ARE SO SORRY!' Lola proceeded to get down on her knees and began making a big show of grovelling.

Anastacia removed her sunglasses and rolled her eyes. *Did she seriously just take off her sunglasses for the sole purpose of rolling her eyes?*

'We promise we didn't tell ANYONE; we have no idea how this happened!' Lola remained firmly on her knees, looking up at Lottie like a little puppy. Everyone was staring now. She reached into her bag and pulled out a box. 'These chocolates are for you. I'm so sorry, Lottie. I'm so, so sorry.' Her bottom lip was quivering slightly and she looked like she might be about to cry.

Lottie stared at the box. TOMPKINS CONFECTIONERY CHOCOLATE CARAMELS COLLECTION. Lottie mentally kicked herself for being excited by the chocolates. How could she have let this get so out of hand?

'Oh, get up, Lola, for God's sake – you're being ridiculous.' Anastacia's French accent came out particularly strong as she pulled Lola off the floor.

'We didn't tell anyone,' she said sternly. 'I promise. None of us did. We really have no idea how this happened.' Anastacia was deadly serious, so serious that she'd kept her sunglasses off and Lottie noticed her eyes were bloodshot, as if she hadn't slept well.

All of a sudden they both became aware of Ellie, who was sitting chewing her food like it was popcorn and watching them as if they were performing a play.

'Who's this?' Anastacia said, pointing at Ellie without actually looking at her.

'That's Ellie.'

'I'm Ellie.'

Their two voices came out in unison.

Anastacia seemed dissatisfied with this answer. 'OK, but WHO is she?'

Lottie decided to ignore how rude that sounded, as if everyone needed permission to be in Anastacia's presence.

'She's my room-mate.'

'I'm her room-mate.'

Again they spoke in unison. Lottie had to resist the temptation to shout 'jinx', thinking this might not be the appropriate time.

'Can someone please explain what's going on here?' Ellie interjected. 'You guys are kind of ruining breakfast, which, in my family, is actually punishable by death.'

Lottie kicked Ellie under the table but had to stop herself from laughing.

'She doesn't know? Everyone in the school knows *except* your room-mate?' Anastacia looked like she was about ready to explode.

'Hey! I know plenty of things,' Ellie replied, as she forked some of the apple tart into her mouth. 'Like . . . you know she's allergic to apples?'

'SHE'S WHAT?!' Lola screeched in disbelief. 'Oh my God, it's perfect. A princess who's allergic to apples. It's like you're a Disney character!' Lola's burst of giggles was cut short by Ellie choking on her tart.

She quickly downed her orange juice trying to catch her breath. '*What?*'

Lottie had a sudden distinct feeling of déjà vu.

'OK, this is getting tedious.' Anastacia rolled her eyes again and turned to Ellie. 'Your room-mate Lottie Pumpkin is actually the undercover Maravish princess.'

Ellie's eyes shot open so wide they looked like they might pop out of their sockets.

'Lottie?' She turned to her questioningly, and there was suddenly an intense and slightly terrifying energy radiating from Ellie that completely contrasted with her jokey mood a few minutes ago.

The severity of this change made Lottie gasp and she found her words getting muddled in her throat. 'I . . . couldn't stop it spreading.'

Lottie wished she could kick herself in the face, she sounded like such an idiot.

'I thought you said you were attending on a bursary?' There was a coldness now in the way Ellie was speaking.

'Yes . . . I didn't . . . this is . . .' Lottie tried to reply, but she was still stumbling over her words.

Ellie abruptly stood up, pushing her plates away. 'I have to go,' she said coolly, and just like that she stormed out of the dining hall.

Lottie's heart was thudding. That had got . . . unexpectedly extreme.

Anastacia turned back to Lottie and shrugged.

Lola grinned and waved after Ellie as she left. 'She seems nice!' she said.

Lottie tried to get through the rest of the day, praying that Ellie would show up to class. Lottie had looked everywhere: the library, the field – she'd even checked the little hidden spot she'd found by Stratus Side. Ellie had vanished. She went back to the

Ivy dorm at lunch to look for her, but Ellie clearly did not want to be found. Lottie hoped she'd show up at their room later but she was also nervous about seeing her again. Ellie had made it very clear to Lottie what she thought of all the Rosewood students whose lives had been handed to them on a plate and as far as she was concerned now, Lottie was one of them. Not just one of them, but a big stupid liar as well. The worst part was this wasn't a lie; she really was attending on a bursary and she really *had* worked her butt off to get in – but she didn't know how she'd even begin to explain the misunderstanding. Yet still, for all that, Ellie's reaction seemed too intense. Why had she reacted like that? It didn't make any sense. She knew they had their differences but this was just . . . odd.

Lottie had one more look around campus after her last class but she knew deep down that she needed to head back to the dorm. She bumped into the prefect Eliza on her way through the gate and asked her if she'd seen Ellie at all.

'Oh, I think she came in about an hour ago. She said she wasn't feeling well.'

Lottie said a quick thank-you, then hurried upstairs. She was just about to open the door to their room when she suddenly felt a wave of anxiety. *What if Ellie is really mad about this? Maybe she knows the Maravish princess?* All these possibilities started popping into Lottie's head and she found herself not wanting to open the door. She reached into her bag and felt her tiara, finding comfort in always having it by her side. *You can do this*, she thought. *Face your fears.* Lottie gently pushed the door open and found . . .

Nothing. There was no one; the room was dimly lit and she couldn't see Ellie anywhere. She was just about to turn and leave to hunt for Ellie somewhere else when a voice came from behind her.

'You're a liar.'

Lottie jumped as she turned to find Ellie waiting by their door. She looked furious. Her hair hung in front of her face, causing a dark shadow to mask her eyes, and her fists were clenched so hard Lottie feared she may draw blood from her palms.

Lottie quivered. 'Excuse me?'

'I said –' Ellie shut the door firmly behind her before repeating more aggressively: 'you're a liar.'

Lottie was acutely aware that there was no way out of the room without going directly through Ellie.

'W-what are you talking about?' Lottie could feel herself begin to tremble but willed herself to stay composed.

'You're not the princess of Maradova,' snapped Ellie.

Cold droplets of sweat began to build on Lottie's skin, her stomach knotted inside her and her tongue felt like lead in her mouth. How could she get her to believe this was all a big misunderstanding?

'Ellie, let me explain . . .' Lottie's words came out shaky and oddly pitched.

Ellie's face twisted into a humourless smirk. 'I *know* that you lied because . . .' She paused to move to her bed and started to rummage through her bag, violently chucking various objects and pieces of paper to the side.

Lottie momentarily considered bolting for the door and running all the way back to Cornwall, but before she could finish that thought Ellie had located the item she was looking for and shoved the new-found object in Lottie's face. It was the diamond-shaped locket with the wolf crest expertly engraved on the surface. Ellie popped it open to reveal a small family photo: a king and a queen with a young girl at their side.

Lottie's face went deathly pale as she realized who the little girl in the photo was. Lottie turned her gaze back to Ellie, but she already knew how her sentence was going to end.

'Because . . .' she repeated, '*I'm* the princess of Maradova.'

# 11

The tension in the room was so thick Lottie was sure she would suffocate under it. The awkward silence as the two stared each other down was only broken by the soft ticking of the clock above the door. Ellie's eyes were ablaze. She was truly furious and Lottie could feel the intense anger radiating towards her – that same storm she'd felt when she first saw Ellie at the school entrance. She willed herself to say something, anything to break the oppressive silence before it consumed them both.

'I tried to tell them it wasn't true.'

Ellie laughed humourlessly. 'You are so selfish – it's unbelievable.'

Lottie flinched as if she'd been slapped. That stung. She prided herself on being kind, on being welcoming, helpful. Selfishness was the exact opposite of her nature. She hung her head in shame. 'I'm so –'

'I bet it didn't even cross your mind once what this means for the real princess, did it?'

She couldn't argue with that; it hadn't. Not once had it occurred to her that the Maravish princess might actually be at Rosewood. She'd thought it all sounded like a fairy tale. She suddenly felt exceptionally stupid, not just because of her lack of thought but the idea that she could ever pass as an actual princess. A feeling she had never experienced had settled firmly in the bottom of her stomach, hard and cold, and wound its way up through her chest and caught in her throat. She was truly horrified. By not clearing up the misunderstanding as soon as it happened she'd been partly responsible for the rumour spreading. She prayed that this wouldn't affect Ellie's attempt at a normal life.

Ellie stared at her, but Lottie couldn't think of any way to make it better.

'I'm sorry. I tried to tell people it wasn't true, but it got out of hand.' Somehow the words felt empty and useless.

Ellie grunted in furious exasperation. She grabbed the photo of her and the mystery boy from her bedside table and sank into her bed, shoulders hunched over in a protective little shell. Her raggedy hair covered her face as she stared intently at the picture. Lottie wondered if the boy in the photo was her boyfriend.

Ellie sighed deeply, placing the picture frame back on the table. 'I'm not going to tell anyone it's not you,' she said firmly.

Lottie was incredibly confused. If Ellie was saying this to make her feel better, then she had to stop her – she couldn't face that much guilt.

'You can if you want to. I know I should have tried harder to correct everyone.' Lottie sat opposite her on her own bed with a new feeling of resolution. 'You can shame me as much as you want; I completely deserve it.'

'No, you don't understand,' replied Ellie. 'I'm not even mad at you. I'm mad at the situation but . . .' She looked down at the photo again. 'This might actually be a blessing.'

Lottie blinked a few times, trying to understand how this could be a good thing for either of them.

'Maybe –' Ellie paused and took a deep breath – 'maybe it'll be OK if we keep pretending it's you.'

'*What?*' There was no way she'd heard that right.

Ellie responded with her usual little side smile.

Lottie quickly composed herself. 'I mean, if that's really what you want?' The idea that she would actually get to pretend to be a princess sounded like a story she'd made up as a kid.

This caused Ellie to burst into fits of laughter. Lottie was starting to get the feeling she might be better suited for the title Princess of Mood Swings.

Ellie wiped the tears forming at the sides of her eyes as she snorted. 'It's just so funny. I would do *anything* to be in your position, Lottie. All I've ever wanted is to not be a princess . . . And then I end up getting roomed with a girl who's obsessed with them.' She let out a long breath. 'You know before I came to Rosewood I'd only met twenty people in my life? Twenty!'

Lottie's jaw literally dropped at this statement.

'Wow!' she said in amazement. 'How is that possible?'

Ellie chewed her lip and began fiddling with her locket. 'I'm the sole heir to the throne of Maradova, but I never wanted to be announced or play the part of the perfect princess so . . . the only option was to hide me away in the palace until one day I'd be ready to take on my role.'

Lottie listened with fascination, her heart aching for the lonely little girl Ellie.

'Don't get me wrong. I'd sneak out sometimes, but that started some rumours and my parents had to put me on lockdown. So here I am, fifteen years old, and only the most trusted members of the royal Maravish household even know what I look like.' Ellie didn't look up as she finished speaking.

Lottie had thought her life had been challenging, but at least she'd been free to make her own choices.

'I'm not obsessed . . . with princesses, that is.' Lottie said the words before she had even processed them. 'I know it probably seems really childish but –' Lottie paused but she owed Ellie the truth considering she'd just shared so much with her – 'it's my mum. See . . . I got this tiara from my mum before she passed away . . . and she taught me this silly phrase that I say to remind myself to be like a princess when I'm anxious or frightened.' She was sure Ellie was going to laugh at her, but she couldn't stop herself. 'I say "*I will be kind, I will be brave, I will be unstoppable*". And then everything seems clearer and I'm OK again . . .' Lottie looked away, scared to see the reaction on Ellie's face at her childish mantra.

'It's not silly,' Ellie said sternly, surprising her. 'You're not silly, Lottie – you're very smart.'

Lottie looked up to see Ellie looking at her with complete and utter candour. She felt the sting of tears prick at the corner of her eyes. She hadn't realized how much she needed the validation until she got it.

'Thank you,' she said softly.

Ellie gave her a little reassuring smile before lying back down again. She absent-mindedly began tracing circles in the air until she abruptly stopped and turned to Lottie again.

'Eleanor Prudence Wolfson,' she said quietly. 'That's my real name. Not a lot of people know it.'

Lottie looked at her properly then, as if they were meeting for the first time.

'It's lovely to meet you, Princess Wolfson.'

Ellie grinned at her, clearly finding it funny to hear Lottie using her title, but her face slowly turned pensive again and Lottie waited calmly for her to unravel her thoughts.

'What I don't understand –' Ellie paused, rubbing her forehead in consideration – 'I don't understand how anyone figured out I was coming to Rosewood. We didn't even tell the headmaster who I really am.'

Lottie didn't know what to say. She just assumed everyone knew everything here; they were all so inherently gossipy.

'Anastacia said she heard a rumour, but I don't know how the rest of the school knew or where the rumour started. She promised she didn't tell anyone.'

'Do you trust her?'

Lottie took a moment to ask herself if she really did and found there was hesitation in her gut. 'I would like to trust her, but I don't know who else could have told everyone.' She hated playing the blame game but she couldn't think of any other logical explanation.

Ellie bit her lip before turning over to look up at the ceiling. 'It's probably nothing to worry about.'

Something told Lottie that she definitely didn't believe that.

## 12

It was a testament to how occupied Lottie was with studying and fixing her less-than-perfect maths grades that she didn't remember the ominous book message until a week later. She was sitting with Binah and Ellie in the small oak-lined Stratus library that was open to Stratus students and registered guests. It was shortly before the 9:30 p.m. curfew and Lottie was writing her first letter to Ollie. Most students were still thrilled by the idea of Lottie being the secret Maravish princess so the cosy Stratus library was a pleasant retreat from all the whispering.

*Dear Ollie (the resident troublemaker of St Ives),*

*My personal PO Box is very easy to use so I'll be expecting lots of letters from you and your mum, please. The address is: Ivy 221A, Rosewood Hall, Oxfordshire.*

*You will truly laugh at me when you find out about the pickle I've got myself into. I promise I'll tell you all about it when I come home for Christmas. Give your dog a cuddle for me and make sure your mum knows I'm doing really well here.*

*Miss you so much,*
*Lottie*

*PS You can help yourself to the stash of chocolate hidden under the floorboard in my room but only if you check up on what Beady's doing to the house.*

'Big puffy rats make Dora always scared.' Lottie looked up from her letter to see Binah leaning over Ellie's shoulder, the two of them staring intently down at the numbers on the paper. 'That's how I always remembered it,' explained Binah.

Ellie laughed in response to Binah's odd statement. 'I suppose,' Ellie said, rubbing her chin as she filled in another number on the paper. 'I just always remembered the calculation order as BPRMDAS. I never bothered with cheats.'

'It's not a *cheat*!' Binah protested. 'It's mathematical mnemonics.'

Ellie gave Binah a teasing smile that led to giggles from both of them. They had quickly bonded over a love of puzzles, particularly numerical ones. Although Lottie couldn't understand what they were talking about half the time, she loved watching them get enthusiastic about numbers.

Binah's face turned pouty and she reached into her bag. 'Ellie, you're banned from teasing me until you crack my code.' She laid a piece of paper down on the table that was filled with complex equations. Lottie watched in fascination as Ellie's cockiness melted.

$$x_1 = .92 * x_{12}$$
$$x_2 = (x_1 + 4)/3$$

$$x3=(x1+1)/2$$
$$x4=x3$$
$$x5=(3/4)x3$$
$$x6=(x8-x9)^2$$
$$x7=(x1+x10)-x3*x4/x5$$
$$x8=x9-1$$
$$x9=(x4+x5)$$
$$x10=ROOT(x5)+ROOT(x12)+2i^2$$
$$x11=x1-x2+x3-x4+x5-x6-x7+x8-x9+2*x10$$
$$x12=((x4-x3)-5)^2$$

Lottie had never seen anything so confusing in her life. She could not even begin to imagine how to solve something so complicated.

'I made this puzzle especially for you, Ellie, and I have a little something for you both to go with it.' Binah reached into her bag again and placed two blue leather-bound boxes on the table, a cool, iridescent sheen twinkling on their surface. Ellie immediately went to open hers.

'Uh-uh-uh!' Binah tutted, pulling the box out of her reach. 'Neither of you is allowed to open these boxes until Ellie figures out this puzzle.'

At this, Ellie pouted with indignation.

'Well, you *could*,' Binah added, 'but it would be a futile endeavour because they won't make sense until you've unlocked the message.'

Lottie was relieved to see that Ellie seemed equally perplexed by this statement.

'Message?' asked Lottie in bewilderment.

Binah gave her a knowing smile.

'Yes, the coded message in the maths problem.'

Ellie and Lottie looked at each other again.

'How am I supposed to decode the message?' asked Ellie, frowning.

'You'll find a way,' Binah replied with a little giggle, delighted at their baffled expressions. 'Oh, and one more thing. I know how much you love fairy tales, Lottie, so . . .'

She pulled a beautiful red hardback book out of her bag. A large wolf's head was engraved on the cover. Across the top in big gold letters it read LITTLE RED RIDING HOOD.

Lottie gasped, the memory of the 'gift' from her first day flooding back: *The Company of Wolves.*

Binah looked confused at Lottie's expression. 'Is something the matter?'

'No, no, not at all! It's gorgeous – thank you so much.'

Lottie was suddenly desperate to get back to their room and show Ellie the creepy message. She took the book and gave Binah her best reassuring smile. 'I just realized how close to curfew it is. We'd better get back before we get in trouble.'

This wasn't exactly a lie. Lottie really was terrified of breaking any rules, especially after their little run-in with Professor Devine. She couldn't imagine her being so lenient a second time.

Binah nodded, but Ellie's expression remained sceptical so Lottie gave her a quick look to signal she'd explain when they got back to their room. They said their goodbyes and as soon as Binah was out of sight Ellie turned to Lottie with an eyebrow raised.

'What's so urgent?' she asked, struggling to keep the excitement out of her tone.

Lottie took a deep breath before she spoke. 'Ellie . . .' she began, nervous of how she'd react. 'There's something I need to show you.'

'You got this on the *first night*? And you didn't think to say anything! That was a whole week ago!' Ellie's voice came out a tight-lipped screech as she read the gold text inside the cover of the book.

Lottie looked away sheepishly. 'Well . . . I was kind of worried you might have put it there yourself.' Ellie choked out a laugh and Lottie quickly corrected herself. 'Just at first . . . because you seemed so grumpy . . . and . . . it was before I knew you were, you know . . . a princess.'

The laughter stopped as Ellie stuck out her bottom lip in thoughtful agreement.

'Whoever did it was obviously trying to intimidate you . . . me . . . I mean, the princess, into reacting. It was an experiment. We need to find out who did this,' she said abruptly, closing the book with a loud thud. 'Whoever they are; they're probably also responsible for telling the whole school.'

Lottie nodded; she'd been thinking the same thing. Together they sat on the floor and started thinking of potential suspects who could have left the book until they had fifteen names. All three Ivy heads of year and the six Ivy prefects from Years Eleven to Thirteen, as they all had access to the dorms without looking suspicious. Then all the people Lottie had met on her first day, who thought she'd said she was from another country: Raphael, Saskia, Lola, Micky, Binah and Anastacia.

'Well, it definitely can't be Lola or Micky because they didn't know until Anastacia told them,' Lottie said defensively, 'and Saskia didn't even meet me until before the fireworks, and there's no way the Year Eleven head of Conch House could go by unnoticed.'

Ellie nodded but was not really paying attention as she started flicking through *The Company of Wolves* again.

'Ellie?'

'It's a library book,' she said flatly.

'It's . . . what?'

Ellie handed the book back to her and Lottie opened the back cover to see the little tear-away marks where a library-ticket holder had previously been.

'Ellie!' she exclaimed in excitement. 'You're a genius! All we need to do is find out which students accessed the main library on the first day.' She grabbed Ellie and hugged her.

Ellie returned it by softly patting her back, clearly not used to such sudden displays of affection.

Lottie quickly pulled away feeling embarrassed, a hot pink blush creeping on to her cheeks. 'Right, anyway, we can do that first thing tomorrow.'

'Tomorrow?' Ellie's face shifted into a mischievous smile. 'There's no way I'm waiting that long.'

'But it's past curfew,' Lottie replied in confusion.

Ellie's face turned into a full-on grin, baring her teeth like a wild animal. 'That's why they invented sneaking out.'

# 13

Lottie could not believe she was doing this. She'd always prided herself on being a paragon of good behaviour. She'd never had a single black mark on a school report or anything close to a pink slip and yet here she was, dressed in a black shirt and jeans that she'd had to borrow from Ellie, climbing down the side of their balcony to break into the library. Lottie had protested, but Ellie declared she would be going whether Lottie came or not.

'And look at the vines on the wall,' Ellie had said, 'they're practically begging us to sneak out.'

So once again Lottie found herself doing something completely out of character, overcome by a peculiar thrill that felt both foreign and familiar all at once.

The lights outside the dorm room were dimmed after curfew, but the bright full moon lit up the grounds, leaving them feeling exposed on the path. They knew that the on-campus bodyguards would be watching the gate, so they would have to figure out another way round.

'We could walk back through the woods, under the bridge and back round to the front entrance?' Ellie whispered. Lottie shook her head. There would definitely be surveillance at the front entrance too and, if they were going to do this, she was *not* letting them get caught. Professor Devine would definitely not forgive such a transgression.

'No, we'll go through the woods.' She conjured up the map of the school in her head and the secret tunnel she'd found on the first day through the glitter cloud. She wondered if the tunnel might lead down towards the bridge. 'I might know a secret way into the school.'

Ellie looked at her with genuine shock, then gave her the little side smile that had Lottie feeling like a proud puppy.

'You sure do love to surprise me,' she said with a hushed laugh.

Lottie blushed at the compliment and quickly moved forward, signalling for Ellie to follow her while she explained about the tunnel she'd found. They ducked into the shrubbery and crawled to a clear spot before legging it into the woods. Lottie had not prepared for how intensely dense the woods would be at night and thoughts of werewolves and ghosts began invading her mind. The Rose Wood was mostly untouched with little in the way of a path for guidance, so they had to stay close enough to the school not to get lost but far enough away to avoid getting caught. Ellie strode over the moss and exposed roots of the oak trees fearlessly, as if this was nothing more than a stroll in the park. Something barked in the distance, making Lottie jump and grab Ellie's arm for protection.

'It's just a deer,' Ellie snickered, trying to contain her laughter.

Lottie did not find it so funny and had to muster up all her courage to let go.

It took a good ten minutes of walking until the soil turned soft as they reached the river and the bridge. The sound of the water gushing meant they were free to talk more, but it was far too dark to see where they were going without a torch and Lottie feared they might put a foot wrong and wind up in the water. They slid their hands along the riverbank, clinging to the dirt as they looked for any give that might be an opening. There was nothing there but sludge. She'd led them to a muddy ditch in the dark where they would most likely get caught and be in so much trouble that Ellie's undercover princess plan would be ruined.

Lottie's mind did a little hiccup. *Under!* she thought excitedly.

'Ellie, it's not on the side of the ditch – it might be beneath us,' she hissed.

Ellie needed no persuading, walking directly to the river's edge and crawling around like a feral creature looking for an opening. Lottie froze, shocked by how much faith Ellie had in her tunnel theory. Before Lottie could protest, Ellie disappeared under the water.

'Ellie!' Lottie tried to keep quiet but couldn't stop her voice coming out in a screech. Before she knew what she was doing she ran into the river to find Ellie, wading desperately into the cold to find her. Something grabbed her leg and her heart stopped. She opened her mouth to scream when Ellie popped up in front of her, quickly covering her mouth to stifle her scream.

'It's me!' Ellie was completely soaked, her hair dripping with river water. Lottie's heart was racing as she looked at her, her breath hot against Ellie's palm. Ellie grinned, her teeth glowing in the moonlight like a wolf baring its fangs. She slowly led Lottie through the water and signalled downward, still smiling. Lottie looked where Ellie was pointing. There it was, reflecting the starry light, a tiny metal latch glistening just above the water's surface. They looked at each other for a moment before leaning in together and pulling on the latch. It was much easier to open than Lottie had expected, but they had to be quick as the river water splashed into the opening.

'Wow!' Ellie exclaimed. 'Good job, little princess.'

Lottie felt her whole body glow but didn't have any time to dwell on the praise as Ellie immediately climbed into the tunnel.

'Ellie!' Lottie called. They had no idea how deep it was and it was impossible to see what was down there.

'Come down – I'll catch you,' called the hushed voice from below her. Lottie stood shivering over the hatch, her heart still racing. She looked back at the woods once more, wondering how on earth she'd got here and realizing there was no going back. ·

*Down the rabbit hole I go.*

She lowered herself down into the tunnel, not caring that she was getting completely soaked. Two arms wrapped round her waist and helped her down. It wasn't as low as she'd expected and she could easily reach up and shut the latch with Ellie holding her. Lottie could barely see in the tunnel, the only light coming through a sliver of space at the top of the hatch in the riverbank. Ellie's hand grabbed hers; Lottie felt her body go hot and suddenly felt inexplicably nervous. Ellie leaned closer, her breath brushing against Lottie's cheek.

'OK!' she whispered. 'To the library office.'

They took careful, deliberate steps through the tunnel, relieved to find it winding upwards and, at last, they reached the art-supplies cupboard. Thankfully Lottie had forgotten to move the chest of drawers against the hatch and they were able to escape into the school. Quietly they crept through the school hallways, every tap on the stone floor seeming far too loud. Lottie had half expected to find teachers still hanging around as it was only midnight, but there was no one in sight. There was something unmistakably creepy about the abandoned corridors at night, and she couldn't stop herself imagining that the eyes in the huge paintings were watching her.

They had to go the long way round the hall to avoid the entrance of the Stratus quarters where there would be guards. Once safely out of the main building, they zipped through the courtyard and over a hedge to the back of the library building. It was locked. They couldn't enter with their student cards without it being a dead giveaway that they had sneaked out. Rosewood Hall kept a log of every student who entered and at what time.

Another thought occurred to Lottie. Did she even want to know who had taken the book out? Everyone was getting along; she was starting to feel like Rosewood was her home. Although people were still gossiping and whispering, she didn't feel like she was in any danger. So maybe whoever left the *gift* really hadn't meant any harm by it.

Before she could articulate these thoughts to Ellie, she watched in amazement as the princess jemmied open the glass panel of the door, reaching in to turn the handle from the inside. Ellie clearly had experience with not just sneaking out but breaking in as well. Next thing she knew Lottie would probably find out she had a personal trained assassin at her beck and call.

'I can't believe you persuaded me to do this,' Lottie said in disbelief as they walked in. Ellie just grinned at her. The office was located on the second level of the library, a pristine crystal-decorated dome that overlooked the whole building. It was managed by a waif of a man named Clark. He kept the office so well organized that it was easy to find what they were looking for: a meticulous record of exactly who had checked out a book and when.

'Got it!' Ellie said, her tongue sticking out in concentration as she meticulously rifled through the folder.

Lottie felt her heart rate escalate again. She didn't want to know.

'You need to see this,' Ellie said, failing to hide the satisfaction in her tone.

There were only a few names for the first day of school, and only three that they recognized. Written clearly on the paper in their own handwriting:

Binah Fae
Raphael Wilcox
Anastacia Alcroft

# 14

It took Lottie a whole night of begging to persuade Ellie not to confront anyone on the library sign-in list. They couldn't assume anything: it was not sufficient evidence and she didn't want to risk upsetting anyone over a hunch.

'It'd be better to retain this information and add it to anything new we discover,' Lottie had pleaded. Ellie had agreed, but it was clear that she'd decided Anastacia was her enemy – and it was about to reach breaking point.

The next day was oppressively hot. The weather had remained sunny and dry, making the air feel sticky, and there was a thick, stuffy tension as if the sky could explode at any moment. Although the majority of classes at Rosewood Hall were attended in companies, there were a few exceptions, and one of those was sports, which the whole year took together. This should have been great, a chance for everyone to get to know each other, but, as she soon discovered, Ivy House and Conch House did *not* play well together – especially when they had Ellie and Anastacia on opposing teams.

'Anastacia. Ellie,' called Dame Bolter. 'Would the two of you please come forward as captains and pick your teams? Thank you.'

Ellie and Anastacia glared at each other with such intensity that Lottie imagined sparks between them. They broke off their heated look and took their places at the edge of the field, ready to build their lacrosse teams. For Anastacia, sports lessons were very much about Conch House pride, but for Ellie it was personal. She was not only intensely competitive but had found a worthy opponent in Anastacia.

'Anastacia, you get first pick!' Dame Bolter shouted across the field. It was no coincidence that Conch always seemed to get first pick; Dame Bolter was the Conch house mother, and she was not like any sports teacher Lottie had ever had before. She was fiercely intimidating in a way that commanded respect. She was also the stable keeper and moved with just as much poise and elegance as if she were performing dressage. She was easily the most feared teacher in the school and Lottie couldn't imagine anyone in Dame Bolter's classes approaching anything even close to mis-behaviour.

'Raphael,' Anastacia said matter-of-factly.

*And here we go*, thought Lottie. Anastacia would pick all Conch students and Ellie would pick all Ivy, and they'd both have a scattering of Stratus, who were quite frankly above all this competitive nonsense. Lottie almost envied them, sometimes wishing she could throw all her purple Ivy stuff away and join the nice soft yellow world of Stratus, never having to worry about this silly rivalry.

Raphael sauntered over to stand by Anastacia, giving Ellie a little wink as he walked past, which earned him an eye-roll.

'Binah,' called Ellie. Lottie was not surprised by this choice. Ellie had been adamant that there was no way that Binah, one of the first friends she'd ever managed to make, could possibly have been the culprit. It also helped that Binah was an outstanding athlete.

Lottie reminded herself that Binah was the only student ever to be offered a place in all three houses so it made sense she was good at everything. Lottie was second to be called by Ellie, which was entirely undeserved as she was truly terrible at sports, and lacrosse in particular left her completely bewildered.

'OK. This week we are going to *win*!' Ellie encouraged. Once she'd picked her team, she had them all huddled in a group to listen to her pep talk. 'I believe in you, and, Lottie –' she looked over at her, her face turning surprisingly serious – 'that means you too.' Lottie groaned internally. She usually just stayed out of the way in team sports, tending to do more harm than good if she tried to help in any way. She'd never been at a school where they took physical exercise so seriously.

'Now, those Conch boys and girls might seem bigger and more intimidating and I know that four of them are on the school lacrosse team, but I believe with enough naive underdog spirit we can win this.' As motivational speeches went, Ellie wasn't exactly the best at them, her sense of irony tending to get in the way. 'Now let's do this.'

'With the heart and stomach of a king,' added Binah under her breath a little mockingly. At least it was a reference Lottie actually understood for once.

Dame Bolter blew the whistle and the first game began. Lottie stayed firmly out of the way as the lacrosse sticks violently smashed into each other.

*How can anyone enjoy such a ferocious game?*

Anastacia barely broke a sweat, expertly catching the ball in her stick and forcing it from the Ivy team. Raphael seemed to find extra joy in teasing Ellie, using every opportunity he could to intercept her. Watching his dubious tactics, it was becoming easier to imagine he may not be trustworthy.

Lottie sighed as she watched them, feeling completely ridiculous as she wandered up and down the field avoiding the action at all costs.

As they approached the end of the class, most people were panting and sweaty, except for Anastacia who appeared completely unaffected. Binah and Ellie had scored a majority of the goals but the score was an even 4–4, and with only five minutes left of game time it didn't seem likely that either team would be victorious.

Lottie was about to get back into position for the next whistle when Ellie grabbed her arm from behind.

'Lottie, listen to me a second.' Ellie had a very rare look of sincerity on her face. 'I know you think you're no help, but I really think if you try, you'll be amazed at what you can do.' She squeezed her arm a little. 'Be unstoppable.' Before Lottie could respond, Ellie winked at her and ran back to her position.

The whistle blew and the game resumed. Binah managed to stick-check the ball off a Stratus boy on the other team and passed it to Ellie who caught it effortlessly. She was instantly surrounded by the opposing team. She looked around for someone to pass it to but there was no one open. No one except . . . Lottie. She turned to her and got into position to pass the ball.

*No, no, no! Don't do it, Ellie!*

She could sense Ellie pulling her little side smile and then, sure enough, she pelted the ball in Lottie's direction.

It came flying towards her, whizzing as it split the air like a furious hornet intent on stinging her.

*It's going to hit me on the head*, she thought with reluctant acceptance.

It felt as if the world began to move in slow motion. The ball was getting closer and closer, and there was no way she could stop it. She held her stick up in a last-ditch attempt to stop it whacking her and . . .

She caught it. Lottie stood in complete bewilderment for a moment staring at the ball that was very much in her stick. She'd really done it; she had really truly caught the ball.

'I DID IT!' she cried, doing an excited little jump.

'Look out!' came a boy's voice from down the field.

She looked up to see Anastacia bearing down on her, eyes cool and calculating, not even remotely flushed in the heat as she raised her stick ready to knock Lottie down and take the ball. Lottie gravely accepted her fate, her moment of pride bursting as she realized there was, of course, no way she could get to the net.

'*BRIKTAH!*' screamed Ellie as she smacked Anastacia's stick hard with her own, making a loud *thwack* that could be heard across the field.

Lottie had no idea what that meant but the intention behind it was clear.

Ellie's eyes blazed as she stared Anastacia down, blocking her way to Lottie. Anastacia moved her weight over to her left side and did a graceful little pivot, sliding her stick away ready to come back round, but Ellie was too quick. She spun back and caught Anastacia's stick again mid-swing – the whole interaction like a strange furious dance.

'Lottie, *run!*' Ellie cried.

Lottie quickly pulled herself out of her daze and mustered all her strength and determination, tearing off as fast as she could possibly go towards the net. Ellie had faith in her, Ellie believed she could do this and she didn't want to let her down. On the periphery she could see Raphael and a Stratus girl homing in on her from both sides.

*Just keep running, just keep running!*

There was no way she would make it all the way to the net, they were running too fast, she would have to risk throwing it from further away, but the huge Conch boy in the goal would surely catch it if she didn't get close enough. Her heart was racing but the net was just about close enough now to risk it. Raphael was only inches away from her, *a little further* and . . . In a sudden moment of determination she mimicked the move she'd seen Anastacia pull earlier, veering left then pivoting back round to his other side. It was nowhere near as graceful as when Anastacia had done it but it worked and Lottie found herself on the other side of Raphael with a perfect view of the net.

'GO, LOTTIE!' she could hear Ellie scream across the field.

She summoned all her willpower and let out a furious war cry as she catapulted the ball as hard as she could at the net. It zipped out of the stick, burning through the air as it raced towards the goal like a comet. Everyone went silent, watching the ball in awe as it whizzed by. There was nothing the Conch boy at the net could do; it was moving too quickly and too powerfully.

*It was unstoppable.*

It hit the goal with such force it tore a hole through the netting and flew out of the back until finally it rolled to a stop.

Lottie took off her helmet and turned back to look at her team, her hair falling in sweaty clumps around her shoulders. 'I DID IT!' she called, lifting her helmet up in the air in celebration and giving Ellie a big grin.

Both teams and Dame Bolter stared at her in shock for a moment before finally Ellie pumped her stick in the air and let out a victory cry, the sound tearing through the air like a wolf's howl. The rest of the team followed suit and began cheering along. Even some members of the other team were clapping in admiration.

Ellie pulled off her helmet, dropped her stick and came tearing down the field. She grabbed Lottie round the waist and spun her around, still howling.

Lottie giggled uncontrollably as she turned, feeling completely elated. Ellie slowly put her down and said softly in her ear, 'I knew you could do it, little princess.' Lottie found herself blushing and looked down at the floor, the heat nothing to do with the sun.

A whistle rang through the air, causing everyone to stop and turn to Dame Bolter.

'Congratulations, young lady – your team wins the game.' Everyone started cheering again, except Anastacia, who was noticeably gritting her teeth, the least composed display she'd probably ever shown in her life.

Dame Bolter raised her hand to silence them.

'Miss Wolf, Miss Pumpkin, Miss Alcroft, please see me after class,' she said sternly.

Lottie gulped. She wasn't sure exactly what they'd done but it couldn't be good.

Ellie, Anastacia and Lottie stood in a line opposite Dame Bolter's desk. Her office was a beautiful eclectic mix of gorgeous traditional African ornaments as well as trophies and medals of all shapes and sizes. Her desk was large, made of dark mahogany and intricately patterned with a winding array of vines. In this setting, her looming presence was amplified to a gargantuan level.

'I would prefer it in the future if you did not turn my sports classes into a sword fight, Miss Alcroft, Miss Wolf.'

Ellie opened her mouth to protest, but Lottie quickly pinched her before she could, earning a scowl in her direction.

'But –' Dame Bolter turned from her desk and began admiring one of the trophies on the shelf, polishing a speck of non-existent dirt – 'you both communicated excellent stamina, agility and poise. Now I know you will be allowed to pick your extracurricular classes soon –'

'I'm sorry, Dame Bolter, but I have absolutely no desire to join the lacrosse team,' Ellie said bluntly, cutting her off.

'Oh no, I don't want you two to join the lacrosse team.' Dame Bolter smiled slightly, proffering a paper she'd lifted from her desk. 'I want you to become sword fighters. I want you to join the fencing team.'

Lottie was sure she caught Anastacia's fingers twitch, but other than that she displayed no sign of her excitement.

'We very rarely offer places in the fencing team. Being a part of the Rosewood lancers is a tremendous honour, so consider the proposal seriously, girls. The try-outs are in the first week of December; you may practise with the current after-school classes but I advise you to make a hasty decision.' She nodded at each of them. 'Thank you, girls, you are dismissed.'

Ellie shot Lottie a look of concern as they left her alone with Dame Bolter. Anastacia looked at Lottie, her eyes appearing to pass right through her before she too turned and left.

They stood for a moment in silence until the door was completely shut. Lottie wouldn't have been surprised if Ellie was outside with her ear pressed up against it, ready to come and fight if she felt Lottie was being treated unfairly.

'Miss Pumpkin . . . may I call you Charlotte?'

This didn't surprise Lottie. A lot of adults she met had trouble with her last name, finding it a little too silly.

'Yes, of course, Dame Bolter,' she said, pretending not to mind.

'Charlotte, I am a firm believer in the ethos of this school. It's why I love working here so much.' She gestured for Lottie to sit in the seat opposite her and she happily complied. 'I understand you are here under the Florence Ivy bursary programme.'

It was not a question, but Lottie felt the need to nod.

'I take it upon myself each year to properly introduce myself to any bursary winners. Charlotte, are you aware you are the first exceptional-circumstances bursary winner in twelve years?'

'No, ma'am.' Lottie could feel her hands trembling in her lap. She'd known it was a tremendous feat to get into Rosewood on a bursary, but she hadn't realized how special her circumstances were.

'At the start of this class, I must admit, I thought maybe we'd made a mistake.'

Lottie sat firmly, refusing to let the hurt show on her face yet she couldn't deny that she had made little attempt before now to participate during sports classes.

'But today you surprised me. You pushed yourself and did something exceptional. You became exceptional.'

Lottie's hands stopped trembling. 'I . . . thank you,' Lottie replied carefully.

'We will be monitoring your progress in the school carefully, Lottie. Do not disappoint us. We expect great things from you.' She smiled at her then and it was such a wonderful sight that Lottie felt momentarily dazzled.

Lottie found herself leaving Dame Bolter's office feeling quite overwhelmed. She thought about her mother, about the tiara sitting on her bedside table, about Ellie and how she'd encouraged her so much already. She did not want to disappoint anyone. She was going to work her hardest to prove to everyone that she was worth having faith in. All she had to do was keep pushing herself and not get distracted by any silly princess rumours or gossip.

As long as she stayed focused and didn't let anything distract her, she could definitely make them proud.

*I will be unstoppable!*

# 15

As the unseasonably hot September drew to a close, the girls awoke one Friday morning to a particularly splendid thunderstorm. The lightning illuminated their room through the chiffon curtains. Ellie threw off her covers and ran to the glass doors, throwing them open and running out on to the balcony into the embrace of the torrential downpour.

Her Star Wars pyjamas were quickly soaked through, hanging thick and sticky on her body, but she continued to dance around with her arms wide open, beckoning to the sky. She clamped her hands on the terrace wall and let out a howl in perfect unison with a burst of cracking thunder. Lottie stared, mesmerized by her affinity with the storm, and for a moment she was sure the thunder called out to Ellie in a deep growl through the dawn sky: *Let down your hair.*

The electricity in the air had the whole Ivy dorm giddy at breakfast that morning and for the first time in weeks the buzz seemed not to be aimed at Lottie. Ellie and Lottie took their usual seats in the dining hall next to the window overlooking the small pond with the statue of Ryley. Having a space in the hall that was basically reserved for them was definitely a nice perk of having people think she was a princess.

The rain was still pelting down outside, clattering loudly as it hit the glass. The whole outside world was a watery blur through the giant two-storey windows.

'This weather is insane!' exclaimed Ellie, stabbing a fork into a huge chunk of honey-roast ham and lifting the whole thing up in one. Lottie internally grimaced. She was already getting used to the extravagant Rosewood dining but, as a proud vegetarian from the age of five, the sight of meat made her queasy. Eating animals just didn't seem very princessy. How could she expect little woodland critters to assist her in her daily tasks if she was going to turn round and eat them?

'I'm more concerned about you catching a cold from running around in it,' Lottie said seriously.

Ellie beamed at Lottie with a toothy grin. 'I can't help it. Storms make people act strange.' She gestured to the room. 'Look.'

Lottie followed her gaze around the hall. Ellie had picked up on a strange buzz that seemed to be spilling out of all the students. There was more giggling, whispering and giddy mumbling than usual. Something was definitely causing a stir.

'It's probably due to the extreme changes in air pressure.'

Lottie and Ellie both jumped and turned to find Binah at the side of their table, dripping wet with an excited grin on her face. *How did she even get in here?*

'Good morning, Ellie. Good morning, Lottie.'

'Binah, oh my goodness, sit down – you must be freezing.' Lottie quickly pulled off her purple Ivy blazer and wrapped it over Binah's shoulders. Her huge round glasses were almost completely steamed up and it was a mystery how she could

119

even see anything. What was it with these girls and running around in thunderstorms?

'Looks like the air pressure may have got to you as well, Binah,' Ellie teased, that familiar little side smile working its way on to her face.

Binah tutted in response, waving her hand as if batting the comment away. 'Oh please. It takes more than a cumulonimbus cloud formation to affect my cognitive abilities . . . but you on the other hand . . .' She rested her chin on her hands, a wry smile crawling on to her lips. 'How are you getting on with that puzzle?'

Ellie looked away in irritation and Binah laughed. She gently patted Ellie's hand. 'Try to figure it out from the answers, not the equations.'

Ellie was about to question Binah on this when she cut them off, a glimmer in her eye.

'I need you both to do me a favour.'

Ellie and Lottie exchanged a look. Binah was usually doing favours for people, not asking for them.

'There's a new student joining our year and your company.'

Lottie looked out over the hall and realized this must be what had everyone so excited.

'No one knows anything about them and, as you know, I like to know everything so I can help everyone.' Lottie smiled at this, remembering how helpful Binah had been on her first day.

'So what do you want us to do?'

'I want you to find out everything you can about them, of course.'

Ellie hesitated for a moment, her eyebrows narrowing.

'Do you do this to every student?' she asked, a slight edge in her voice.

'Only the mysterious ones. Why do you ask?'

Lottie held her breath. *Could Binah have looked into Ellie?*

To her relief Ellie held her cool. 'Just curious,' she said, beaming.

'So what's her name?' Lottie asked, quickly changing the subject.

'Her? It's not a girl; it's a boy.' Binah's eyes shot up to the clock at the front of the hall. 'Oh my! I'd better be off or I'll be late to class.' She picked up her soaking-wet backpack and threw it over her shoulder, her massive ringlets flicking water across the room as she spun round. 'See you later.' She delicately skipped away before they had a chance to respond, indifferent to the trail of chaos she'd left in her wake.

Lottie breathed out slowly. 'A new boy . . .' *That's what everyone is getting so excited about?* She had to wonder if there was something special about him to have everyone so giddy and before she knew it her mind began asking a million questions. Why was he arriving over two weeks into term? What was he like? Did he bring the storm with him? She wondered if he was some sort of Prince Charming. The last time everyone had been this excited was when they had decided she was a princess.

'Lottie?'

Lottie was pulled out of her daydreaming to find Ellie standing up, looking very distressed. 'I've been saying your name for ages; what's wrong with you?'

Lottie couldn't help feeling embarrassed. She wasn't sure if it was due to accidentally ignoring Ellie or at the absurd thought that Ellie might be able to guess what she'd been fantasizing about.

'Sorry I was just . . .' *Being a cliché*, she thought to herself.

Ellie didn't even wait for her to finish, furiously grabbing her stuff and turning to leave.

'Let's go. I don't want to be in here any more. Everyone's acting like idiots about a stupid new boy.' She grabbed another pastry and shoved it in her mouth. 'What's so special about a boy anyway?' Ellie was being uncharacteristically moody and the tension in her voice had Lottie feeling a little nervous.

'I'm sure . . .'

Lottie found her voice trailing off. She had no idea why this information was stressing Ellie out so she didn't know what to say to make her feel better. She followed her as she stormed out of the dining hall.

'I'm sure this new boy is just a boring kid who will have absolutely no impact on our lives whatsoever,' Lottie said firmly.

She was not surprised when Ellie ignored these words of encouragement. Whatever was bothering her was clearly out of Lottie's hands.

# 16

Lottie found herself alone in the English classroom twenty minutes before the class was due to start, nervously sharpening her pencils and wondering if Ellie would get in trouble for skipping a lesson. Their discussion after breakfast hadn't gone how Lottie had hoped. As soon as they had arrived back at their room, Ellie had proceeded to face-plant on to her bed with no intention of getting ready for class.

'Aren't you coming?'

'I'll see you there,' came the pillow-muffled response.

'Will I, though? Skipping classes can become a very bad habit, Ellie.'

'Well, we'll see if I'll see you there.'

'What does that even mean?'

'You'll see.'

Lottie groaned and slammed her head down on the desk. She was starting to feel responsible for Ellie. If these really were her last few years of freedom before her royal duties began, then she wanted her to get as much out of them as possible.

'Excuse me.'

Lottie jolted at the unfamiliar voice and shot upright. She proceeded to hit the owner of the voice hard on the chin with the back of her head, not realizing that the mystery person had been leaning over her.

She let out a little yelp at what felt undeniably like static electricity.

'You scared me!' she cried, rubbing her head. She could feel tears springing to her eyes at the shock and had to will herself to calm down.

The boy behind her seemed completely unaffected by the collision. The only sign he showed of any pain was on the slow stroking of his chin as he sat down at a desk one space over from her.

Lottie found her shock turn to a feeling she couldn't quite place. *This* was the new boy. He was dressed in the soft plum blazer of Ivy House. Although it fitted him perfectly, he seemed too dark, too wild for such a tame uniform. An uncomfortable feeling began to creep through her and she felt the unbearable desire to both look away and stare at him forever all at once. But there was something more. As Lottie gazed at him, she felt like she knew him. He looked . . . familiar.

'Usually it's common practice to apologize when you hit someone,' he said smoothly.

'I . . . excuse me?' Lottie blinked. 'You can't be serious?'

'You hit me.'

'You sneaked up on me,' she retorted, outraged by his callous rudeness. '*You* should be apologizing to *me*.'

'Well, good luck with that,' he said curtly.

She rolled her eyes, all thoughts of Prince Charming vanishing with every irritating breath he took. It took all her willpower to be the bigger person and not say something she'd regret. Maybe it was the impulsive influence of Ellie, or maybe there was just something about this boy, but as it turned out 'all her willpower' was not strong enough.

'You're going to regret being so rude to me, you know,' she said sweetly, pretending to be looking at something in her book. Lottie was surprised with the words that came out of her mouth. This was so unlike her. *Be kind* was such a huge part of her mantra and yet she couldn't stop herself.

His ears pricked up as he looked over at her.

*Ha ha*, thought Lottie. *Got you!*

A little half smile crept on to his face as a lock of shaggy dark hair flopped in front of his intense brown eyes and Lottie had a severe sense of déjà vu.

'And why is that then?' he purred.

*Right into my trap*. Lottie had to stop herself from squealing, the thought of embarrassing this pompous brat was too good to be true.

'You're forgiven, of course, as you're new. Let it never be said that the Maravish family aren't forgiving,' she said, feigning a haughty tone.

'Maravish?' he said quizzically.

'Why, yes –' she closed the book and looked up at him with as much majestic posture as she could manage – 'I'm the Maravish princess . . . but you can call me Lottie.'

There was a pause in which the new boy simply stared at her blankly for a moment, his eyes showing no emotion and making Lottie a little nervous.

'Amazing,' he said with no emotion.

This had not been the response Lottie was expecting.

'Do you seriously not know who that is?' Lottie neglected to remind herself that *she* hadn't known who that was until a month ago.

'Oh I do.' He smiled, the gesture not quite reaching his eyes. He looked her up and down before smirking with obvious cynicism. 'I just didn't expect her to be . . . you.'

Lottie found herself genuinely hurt by the insult, though she had to admit she wasn't acting particularly like a princess right now. She mentally recited her mantra to calm herself down.

*I will be kind, I will be brave, I will be unstoppable.*

No stupid boy would make her doubt herself. She realized she was sitting there opening and closing her mouth like a fish as she tried to come up with a clever reply, but before she could respond the door swung open and in walked Ms Kuma followed by the rest of the class.

'Ah fantastic, you're already here, and making friends it would seem. Thank you, Lottie.' She beamed over at her, her long embroidered cloak swaying with her lyrical movements as she took to the front of the class.

At least Lottie could count on English to be a pleasant distraction from her strange morning. She'd always loved English and she adored Ms Kuma. It was no secret that her love of English stemmed from her childhood obsession with fairy tales. She was so fascinated by words and how they could be used as signifiers to express abstract thoughts and feelings; it all seemed so beautiful and romantic to her.

'Jamie, please do stand up and introduce yourself,' Ms Kuma said grandly.

Some of the girls in the class blushed and giggled as he stood up.

'Good morning. My name is Jamie Volk and I'm not sure how long I will be at this school. My parents travel a lot so I doubt there's much point in me getting too comfortable here.' With that, he sat back down. An awkward silence wriggled its way over the previously charmed students as the rest of the company tried and failed to figure out if he was joking.

As he finished his curt introduction, Lottie was distracted by the sight of Ellie. She was peering in through the circular glass window in the door, her mop of wet black hair suggesting she'd neglected to bring an umbrella with her. Lottie waved subtly at her, but Ellie's gaze seemed fixed on Jamie. She looked . . . uncharacteristically terrified. Jamie glanced over at the door just as Ellie turned round and bolted away. Out of the corner of her eye Lottie was sure she could see Jamie's fists clench.

*This is getting weird*, she thought. Her whole body went rigid as a troubling thought came to her. *He could be a bad guy; maybe that's the weird feeling I felt earlier?* And she'd just told him she was the princess. She tried to steady her breathing.

'It says here that English is your best subject?' continued Ms Kuma, seemingly unaware of any awkwardness. She gave a short humorous snort. 'Looks like you have some competition, Lottie.'

Jamie's eyes were still fixed on the door.

*Who are you, Jamie Volk? And what do you want with my princess?*

As if he'd heard his name spoken, he turned back and gave Lottie a vacant smile. To anyone else in the room it would have seemed like a harmless nod to their supposed joint love of English, but there was something more in his eyes that made Lottie shiver.

After what felt like the most tense and uncomfortable hour of Lottie's life, Ms Kuma finally dismissed the class for first break, pleasantly reminding everyone as they left their desks to bring in their *A Midsummer Night's Dream* homework for next week.

The second they were dismissed Lottie made a beeline for the door and bolted for the stairs as soon as she was out of the classroom.

Behind her she heard a boy's voice. 'Wait.'

She knew it was Jamie, but she wanted to get as far away from him as possible and find Ellie. Luckily Jamie was new so he wouldn't know the shortcuts back to the dorm. Something odd was going on and she wouldn't feel comfortable until she got some answers from Ellie.

She continued sprinting down the hill to Ivy Wood, determined to get as far away from Jamie Volk as possible. The air was heavy with the smell of wet soil, and the flora was lush from the storm, brushing her uniform with thick strokes of rainwater as she ran past them. Panting heavily she squeezed down a side trail, hidden by some ornamental bushes that Raphael and some of the other 'rebellious' kids had commandeered as a secret place to smoke cigarettes.

The hidden trail led directly to the pond outside the Ivy dining hall, if you crawled under the bush at the end. She would have to sacrifice her uniform to the mud but that felt like the least of her troubles. She turned on to the last bit of pathway expecting to come face-to-face with the bush but instead found herself confronted by . . . Jamie Volk.

They stood staring at each other.

Jamie was composed, serious and dry, his face partially masked by the shadows of the overgrown trees. He was the complete opposite of Lottie, who stood panting, her uniform and hair wet, and she was sure she had little twigs stuck in her blonde curls. The dappled light on her face through the leaves seemed only to accentuate her puffy red cheeks. Her mind was racing.

How did he know she'd come this way? How did he get here before her? What on earth did he want from her?

It hit her that she was in a secret area that no one knew about, trapped with a strange boy who thought she was the Maravish princess, and she felt hot red panic begin to prickle her skin. She had to run. She tried to turn round, but he grabbed her arm.

'I said "wait",' he commanded, pulling her back.

'Let go of me!' she screamed. She swiped at him with her free hand, but he caught it effortlessly.

'Lottie –'

'I will call the police,' she continued, trying to pull away from him, but she seemed to only be mildly annoying him.

*How is he so strong?*

'Lottie, please, just listen for a –'

'LET GO OF ME!' She gave one final tug with all her energy and stamped down on his foot. He tried to pull his leg back but a strange static sensation shook him and the two tumbled quite ungracefully into the mud.

'Eek!' Lottie fell flat on her back, immediately thinking of her poor ruined uniform and hair. She had to remind herself that these were the least of her concerns right now and that she needed to deal with the boy on top of her. She was ready to scream when a pendant round his neck fell against her chest; there was a familiar crest on it with an engraved wolf symbol.

The Wolfson family crest, the same one Ellie wore.

He glanced up and they were forced to look each other in the eyes. Their breath came out in steamy wisps as they slowly panted. Out of the shadows now she could see his cold, vacant mask had dropped momentarily and Lottie found herself suddenly mesmerized by the soft warm glow of his hazel eyes. There was something there, something vulnerable, something that made her feel both comforted and nervous. A clap of thunder filled the pregnant air around them and jolted Lottie out of her trance.

'You . . .' Lottie's eyes lit up with sudden, intense understanding. She looked into Jamie's eyes and felt all the pieces slot together. All at once she realized how she knew him, why he was so strangely familiar. She had seen him every day since she'd arrived at Rosewood.

He was the boy from Ellie's photo.

## 17

Jamie and Lottie stood awkwardly outside her bedroom door. Their uniforms were both filthy but he wore it naturally, as if it made perfect sense for him to be covered in mud. Lottie felt like she was about to burst with worry. She was absolutely dreading Ellie's reaction to her bringing Jamie to their room, plus it was her fault he was there in the first place. After their little tumble in the hidden trail, they had talked and Jamie's true purpose for transferring to Rosewood Hall had come to light.

He had been sent by Ellie's family to figure out what exactly was going on, and why their newspapers were reporting that the Maravish princess was at a school in England. He had known the whole time that Lottie wasn't the Maravish princess, which explained his attitude towards her and it left Lottie absolutely mortified.

'I'm the Maravish princess . . . but you can call me Lottie.' If she could go back in time, that would be the moment she'd choose to kick herself in the face. Upon realizing he'd known she was lying, she had stood blushing furiously and wondered if she could bury her head in the ground and maybe never,

ever come out again. She would live there forever and never have the chance to embarrass herself again.

'I'm not sorry for embarrassing you; I think you quite deserved it,' Jamie had said sternly.

She couldn't disagree with him.

The west side of the dormitory was the girls' side, and boys were not supposed to be there. Jamie was quite clearly a boy and if anyone, particularly Professor Devine, caught them, they'd both be in tremendous trouble. Which led to her current predicament. She wanted nothing more than to be safe in the confines of her room where she could chuck Jamie out over the balcony should a teacher come by to check on them; he might break his leg or something but it was a small price to pay for her perfect school record. She could explain that she'd fallen in the mud and had to run back to change and everything would be fine. But she couldn't bring herself to open the door. She was just too mortified by this whole series of events. Their decision not to fix this princess mix-up may very well result in Ellie being flown back to Maradova, and Lottie felt like it was all her fault.

*How many times will I find myself standing nervously outside 221?* she wondered regretfully.

'And I suppose opening doors for yourself is against the rules of a princess, Miss Pumpkin?' The sarcasm came from Jamie, who was making a point of tapping his foot impatiently.

All thoughts of worry quickly changed to irritation again. There was something particularly annoying about how well spoken he was. It added about fifty per cent more exasperation to the whole experience.

'You know what –' Lottie turned to him, clenching her fists in frustration – 'I am getting a bit sick of your sarcastic tone.'

Jamie did not miss a beat: 'And I'm getting a bit sick of waiting for you to open this door.'

'Well, I was just about to.' Lottie puffed up her cheeks in a particularly childish display of stubbornness, causing Jamie to roll his eyes.

They heard the latch on the dormitory door click and the door began to creak open. They both turned their heads in unison to see Ellie, jaw wide open, looking very confused at the sight of the two of them covered in mud.

'Lottie?' Ellie suddenly blinked as if coming back down to earth and her expression changed from shock to aggravation. 'WHAT THE . . .?' she started yelling, but Lottie and Jamie both had the same reaction, to push Ellie back inside and cover her mouth to stop her shouting.

'*Shh!*' hushed Jamie as he pulled the door shut behind them. 'Do you want us to get caught? You need to think about your school record.'

Lottie snorted in annoyance.

He rolled his eyes again. She had a feeling she'd be seeing him do that a lot.

Lottie felt a hand grab her arm and pull her backwards. Ellie positioned herself in the middle of Lottie and Jamie, creating a block between them. There was a look on her face, the same fire she'd possessed when taking down Anastacia the other day on the field. Lottie moved to step out from behind her, but Ellie put her arm out protectively, pushing Lottie back. She looked up at her and Ellie gave her that trademark little side smile and affectionately pulled a twig out of a lock of her blonde hair. 'I see you've met my childhood friend, Jamie Volk.'

She turned to Jamie and for a split second Lottie was sure Ellie gave him a heated look, like some kind of angry warning, but she couldn't figure out why. The atmosphere in the room had turned uncomfortably harsh. The whole exchange was very confusing. Jamie had said he'd known Ellie her whole life: surely she should be happy to see him?

'Jamie.' She said the name curtly.

They stood staring at each other for a moment, really taking the other in for the first time since being reunited, the Wolfson crest lockets around their necks perfectly lining up.

'You haven't sent a single letter; your parents have been worried sick,' Jamie said flatly. Ellie looked away and Lottie could see she was biting her lip anxiously. 'Not to mention you've been skipping classes and breaking curfew and –'

'It doesn't even matter!' Ellie suddenly protested. 'Lottie has perfect attendance and, as far as anyone knows, *she's* the Maravish princess so I can do whatever I want!' She tried to say the words with a sense of humour but it didn't have the desired effect.

'That is not how it works, Ellie,' he said coldly, his tone the complete antithesis of Ellie's lackadaisical attitude.

'But what if it did?' There was the tiniest trace of desperation in Ellie's voice that made Lottie wince.

'You know we can't . . .'

'But she's basically a P–'

'*Briktah!*' Jamie barked.

*Uh-oh*, thought Lottie. That was definitely not a good word.

Ellie stamped her foot down hard, making Lottie jump. She barked something in another language, which Lottie guessed must be an old Maravish dialect, and started gesturing wildly with her hands. Lottie had never seen her like this and it was almost frightening. Her tone was completely different to a few moments ago and Lottie was reminded just how intense Ellie's mood swings could be.

It was a strange sight, watching this mud-covered boy argue with a furious storm of a girl against the pretty rose-decorated background of Lottie's side of the room. There was something almost hilarious about it but, although she couldn't understand the language, the words 'Lottie' and 'Portman' kept popping up and it was clear they were discussing something critical. Lottie wondered if she should maybe leave them alone, but when she made a move to the side Ellie instinctively pushed her back without looking at her.

Finally, whatever they'd been arguing about, they seemed to reach an impasse. It was impossible to tell who'd won as they both still seemed frustrated. Jamie ran his hands through his hair in exasperation and sat on Lottie's bed. He picked up her stuffed pig Mr Truffles and to Lottie's amazement he began absent-mindedly rubbing its head before gesturing with his other hand as if giving Ellie permission to do something.

Ellie turned suddenly to Lottie, and the look on her face was so out of character – she appeared to be almost apprehensive – that Lottie felt very uncomfortable.

'Do you know what a Partizan is, Lottie?' Ellie asked uneasily.

Lottie instantly perked up at the use of a word she actually knew.

'Why, yes,' she said proudly. 'Binah told me on the first day actually. They're like fancy bodyguards . . .' The serious look on their faces had Lottie second-guessing herself. 'I believe,' she added more hesitantly.

'No, no . . . I mean, yes . . . you're right. They are.' Ellie looked over at Jamie and something odd flashed across her face, something akin to regret. It was quickly replaced by her usual mask of confidence.

'Anyone willing to go through the arduous process and strict criteria can train to be a Partizan nowadays, but a true Partizan is raised from birth for their role. Primed from childhood to be a lethal protector, loyal only to their master, they are very effective and very dangerous but, most importantly, they're discreet.' Ellie looked up at Lottie again, a glint in her eyes.

Lottie found she was holding her breath. Binah had said Partizans seemed romantic, and she realized now what she'd meant. They were like something out of a story. Deadly, devoted assassins, trained from birth to protect their lord or lady.

*I wonder how often they fall in love with each other?* she thought to herself.

'Wow,' she said aloud, then a thought struck her and she asked curiously, 'Do you have one?'

Jamie and Ellie turned to each other then, and a look passed between them. They seemed to share some kind of telepathic conversation that Jamie responded to by giving a swift nod.

Ellie turned back to Lottie and started rubbing the back of her head sheepishly as if she were embarrassed to continue.

'Jamie . . . Jamie's my Partizan.' She bared her teeth in a little grin as if this information was no big deal. 'The agreement was they'd send him here if anything went wrong and, well . . .'

A million questions began shooting around Lottie's head and she didn't know where to begin. *Who else had a Partizan in this school? Were Jamie's parents also Partizans? Had Jamie ever had to kill anyone?* She quickly crushed that last thought as she found it sent an unpleasant shiver down her spine.

'Lottie?' Ellie asked with concern.

Lottie sat down hard on Ellie's bed, feeling a little dizzy.

'Sorry, this is just a lot to take in,' she replied, still in a daze. She looked over at Jamie apprehensively. If he looked odd against Lottie's pretty pink half of the room before, he now looked like a fish in the desert. No wonder he had been so cold and intense when they had first met.

This boy had been raised from birth to protect Princess Eleanor Wolfson of Maradova, and Lottie had unwittingly almost exposed her and put her in danger. To Jamie, Lottie must represent everything he'd spent his life guarding Ellie from.

So why did he make her feel so nervous?

'Do you have your passport with you?' This came from Jamie who was avoiding eye contact on the other side of the room, seemingly concentrating hard on something opposite him.

'I . . . yes, I do. It's in my bedside table.' The words came out a little edgier than she expected and she knew there was no way she could hide her uneasy feelings from him.

'Good,' he replied. 'You'll be needing it.'

He stood up finally and Lottie flinched. He was completely different to her now she knew he was a lethal killing machine.

'What does that mean?' she asked as calmly as possible.

'It means, Lottie –' he walked over to the side of her bed and opened the drawer to pull out her passport and his fingers traced along the rosy pink cover, a smirk on his lips – 'you're coming to Maradova.'

It was the last thing Lottie had expected to hear.

# 18

Lottie had hoped that attending Rosewood would change her life dramatically, but she had never in her wildest dreams imagined that just a few weeks after she started she would be flying in a private jet with the riot-girl princess of Maradova and her deadly killing-machine-in-a-teen-boy sidekick. And she definitely wasn't dreaming, she'd checked.

'You don't need to be scared of Jamie.' Ellie was distracting herself by trying to solve the puzzle Binah had given her but was clearly having no luck. 'He's harmless, honestly.'

Somehow Lottie didn't believe that. No matter what Ellie said, she couldn't bring herself to trust him. She didn't like not being able to tell what he was thinking. He was sitting on the other side of the plane, apparently engrossed in a book but she was sure he was discreetly surveying the area.

'Are you *sure*? How do you know he's not gone rogue and secretly informed someone at the school that you were coming to Rosewood?' It was a thought Lottie had been mulling over during the flight. She was sure he was hiding something and it was driving her mad. She quickly cut herself off as she saw Jamie looking over at them. Lowering her voice, she added half seriously, 'Does he have superhuman hearing as well?'

Ellie blinked at her for a moment, then burst out laughing. 'Lottie, you are hilarious.'

Ellie and Jamie would not tell Lottie why she had to come to Maradova. Ellie's irritatingly enigmatic response was: 'If my plan works, then you'll find out why you needed to be there . . . and if it doesn't . . . well, let's not think about that.' So that's exactly what Lottie was doing. Trying not to think about it.

The flight took five hours and landed at around 7 p.m. British time. Lottie had only ever flown twice in her life and she had never been ushered straight through border control by an entourage of smartly dressed bodyguards in sunglasses. This was evidently a royalty perk. As soon as they were outside, Lottie was overcome by how very cold it was. There was ice on the ground and the air seemed frozen. They moved in relative silence once the entourage showed up. Ellie nervously chewed her bottom lip and distractedly rubbed the locket around her neck. Jamie remained completely composed and unreadable as always.

They all piled into a fancy black car as Jamie politely held the door open for them. As Lottie was about to follow Ellie into the vehicle, Jamie grabbed her arm and stopped her.

He looked at her with a fiery intensity. 'You need to be on your absolute best behaviour when we get to the palace, do you understand?' His voice came out as a low growl and made Lottie's whole body tremble, but she simply nodded in response. 'And, no –' he leaned down and whispered in her ear – 'I don't have superhuman hearing.'

They drove in total silence and when they entered the palace grounds Lottie realized that the estate was so large she couldn't see the top of the building out of the tinted car window. They had to go through two elaborate gilded gates before they even reached the driveway of the palace, although 'driveway' was a pathetically insufficient word to describe it.

Finally they pulled up by the door to the palace: magnificent in white oak with a gold, life-size snarling wolf's head in the middle, a knocker hanging from its bared jaws. The crunching gravel underneath the wheels seemed to echo like a low growl as they came to a halt.

One of the mysterious bodyguards opened the car door, but Ellie scooted over and let herself out of the other side. Jamie tensed for a moment and gritted his teeth, but Ellie simply smirked at him before sauntering over to the front door. As they approached the looming figure of the wolf head, the door opened inwards and they were greeted by two women in pristine aprons and black working dresses, hair neatly arranged. Lottie didn't get a chance to look directly at the wolf.

It was late and the palace was seeped in a milky-blue glow. Even the thick walls of the grounds couldn't keep the chill out of the hallways and Lottie stared nervously at the paintings of previous rulers that stared down at her, the eyes following them through the corridors in what seemed like a never-ending walk.

They were informed by a muscular woman, who introduced herself as Edwina, that the trial would take place the next morning, and that they should rest for the night. Lottie had no idea what she meant by that, but the word 'trial' made her shudder.

Lottie was given her own room in the left wing of the palace with a view of the vast gardens.

Ellie quickly joined Lottie, but Jamie kept himself scarce once they were safely in the palace walls.

'I didn't know places like this really existed.' Lottie couldn't conceal the wonder in her voice as she tiptoed around the guest room, absorbing every amazing detail of the lavish space. 'I can't believe how beautiful everything is.'

The vanity table had a collection of designer perfumes in gorgeous bottles that Lottie lined up to admire. Lottie had assumed that Rosewood Hall would be the height of her luxury experience, but if Rosewood was magnificent then Maradova was otherworldly. It was a very welcome distraction from the trial, whatever that would be, the next day.

'I always found it too excessive,' Ellie replied. As if on cue, the door swung open and in came a red-headed maid with a tray piled high with far too much food for two people.

'Please enjoy your dinner, Princess,' said the maid, curtseying respectfully.

'Thank you, Hanna, but please don't call me that.'

'Of course, Princess.' Ellie gave the maid a devilish smile and they both laughed before she exited the room, leaving them on their own. They sat on the bed to eat, but Lottie found herself too anxious to enjoy the food.

'It feels weird hearing you called princess,' she said at last.

Ellie had been very quiet since they'd arrived at the palace, clearly lost in thought.

'It feels weird to me too,' she said honestly.

Lottie watched Ellie as she distractedly piled bread and cheese into her mouth, her gaze distant and worried. She didn't like seeing Ellie like this; the palace obviously had a negative effect on her. Lottie wanted nothing more than to wrap her up and save her from her princess duties. *But how?*

Lottie was awoken in her soft bed the next morning by the same maid who'd brought them food the night before. She entered Lottie's room with a tray of tea and traditional Maravish pastries that reminded her of baklava and tasted heavenly. Without Lottie's knowledge, her clothes had been cleaned and pressed for her and laid out conveniently on the dresser. The same maid then offered to run her a bubble bath, which she enthusiastically accepted. She sat in the circular tub in her en suite for an extra-long time, wanting to prolong the luxurious experience as long as possible before coming back to reality and the looming trial. She sank her head under the warm water, squeezed her eyes shut and pretended for a moment that she really was a princess and this really was her home.

At 10 a.m. she was collected by an unassuming maid who took her into a plush living space in which Jamie and Ellie were waiting.

Jamie immediately began prepping her, and the enchantment she'd felt quickly crumbled as she came hurtling back to reality.

'When we are allowed entry into the throne room you will stand unless told otherwise. You will avoid eye contact unless told otherwise. And, above anything else, you will be silent unless told otherwise.'

Lottie nodded at these instructions, feeling more out of place than she'd ever felt in her life and desperately trying to be as accommodating as possible.

Jamie was pacing slowly back and forth in front of a large gold-framed mirror on the wall as if addressing an army regiment. Ellie was slumped on a gold-embroidered sofa, her boots carelessly kicking the fabric.

'Jamie, you need to relax. You always act like the world is ending and it's always fine.'

Jamie let out an exasperated breath from his nose and turned to face Ellie. 'Ellie, this isn't about things being fine. This is the single most significant action you've ever made regarding your future.' Jamie's tone was sombre, yet Ellie reacted by grinning.

'I know, this is the best plan I've ever had!' There was excitement in Ellie's voice that annoyed Lottie. She suddenly had the horrible feeling she was a chess piece in someone else's game.

'Umm,' Lottie began, and Jamie swiftly turned his head towards her, making her jump, but she found the courage to continue. 'If this is all so significant, can you please tell me what the trial is exactly?'

There was a short pause where they both looked at her as if remembering she were in the room.

'No!' was their simultaneous response.

'Well, can you at least tell me what to expect?'

Jamie raised an eyebrow, a strand of his slightly messy hair falling in front of his eyes.

'Expect the absolute worst,' he said flatly.

Lottie gulped.

'Ha!' Ellie stood up and patted Lottie on the head. Lottie usually quite liked the gesture but in this scenario she felt patronized. 'You're going to meet my parents, and they're going to love you.'

Jamie quite literally growled at this. 'You . . .' he started, but quickly took a deep breath to calm himself. 'You need to take this seriously, Ellie. This is not like before.'

Her face distorted into a furious mask of indignation. 'It's. Going. To. Be. Fine.'

'Ellie, you don't understand. They're really serious.' His tone was almost pleading and it made Lottie flinch. She wondered how many times Jamie found himself in situations like this, trying – and failing – to help Ellie.

'No, Jamie, *you* don't understand. Mum and Dad make *everything* seem like a huge deal but it's always fine in the end, and this time isn't going to be any different.'

'Ellie, this *is* different, I promise. They've –' he faltered for a moment, then looked back into Ellie's eyes – 'they've brought your grandmother.'

Lottie almost snickered at this as it seemed like such an anti-climax, but the horrified look on Ellie's face made her think better of it. Her eyes began darting around very quickly as if she were thinking really fast.

'Lottie, listen to me. I need you to –'

Before Ellie could finish the door swung open.

The red-haired maid curtsied. 'They will see you in the main hall now, Princess.'

'Hanna, *please*, I told you not to call me that,' Ellie said, jokingly rolling her eyes. She smiled at the girl and the maid giggled discreetly in response, still not looking up. Lottie could hardly believe that Ellie could behave so normally considering the tension in the room just seconds before Hanna had entered.

'Thank you, Hanna.' Jamie smiled charmingly at her, showing no sign of stress.

'Ellie, I need to *what*?' Lottie whispered, so Hanna wouldn't hear. 'You can't start saying something, then walk out. Tell me what you need me to do!'

Ellie turned back to her with a big smile on her face that seemed painfully forced. 'There's no time left.'

## 19

The large oak doors creaked open. Light flooded out of the throne room, bathing them in a bright white stream that caused Lottie to catch her breath and cover her eyes. As soon as she'd adjusted to the strange lighting, she had to stop herself from gasping at the storybook scene in front of her.

The room seemed to glow from within. Intricate patterns were etched into the white walls and above them. Peering down was a scene of strange mythical monsters and beasts, surrounding a crystal chandelier that reflected the light in little delicate dots like snow.

In the middle of the room sat Ellie's father, the king of Maradova. There was a distinct family resemblance in their dark eyes, but his hair was light and immaculately cut around his sharp features. The back of the throne on which he sat towered over his already tall frame in a way that made it seem part of him. He gazed at the three teenagers in turn and gave a single terse nod to Jamie, which he returned straight-faced.

A thin old woman sat to the right of him, mounds and mounds of long silver hair lavishly layered on top of her head. It did not take much deductive skill to figure out she was Ellie's grandmother. Her chair had a dark blue cushion with little gold tassels propped up to support her and in her right hand she held a magnificent cane topped with a solid gold wolf head. The way her hand gripped the cane suggested nothing of frailty but rather control, demanding respect and submission. Her eyes locked with Lottie's and for a split second Lottie felt a chill run through her. *The Evil Witch*, Lottie thought involuntarily; there was something undeniably terrifying about her.

On the king's left, standing with his hands clasped behind his back, was a tall man with what appeared to be a glass eye. He smiled at each of them, his eyes lingering on Lottie for a little longer than she felt comfortable with.

'Her Highness Princess Eleanor Prudence Wolfson . . .' started the glass-eyed man.

*What am I doing here?* Lottie thought to herself. *I don't belong here.*

'You have requested an official audience with the king to enact Act Six. Official enquiries into the suitability and benefit of this request have begun. The counterargument is . . .' He cleared his throat before continuing. 'The counterargument,' he repeated, 'is that the princess has, to quote the queen mother, "continually disappointed on all previous arrangements without exception".'

Lottie thought back to Ellie telling her how she'd sneaked out before – and how naturally she could deceive.

Ellie's grandmother banged her cane on the marble floor once and let out a little laugh that sounded more like a cackle.

'Disappointed?' There was a sharpness in her voice that made Lottie flinch. 'I think that is not quite the term I used. That would suggest we had any hope for you in the first place, dear Eleanor.'

Neither Jamie nor Ellie reacted.

The king rubbed his forehead and sighed in frustration. 'Duly noted, Mother.' It became instantly apparent to Lottie that the king wanted to be there about as much as Lottie did. 'Very well. Begin the enquiry.'

The glass-eyed man cleared his throat again. 'Miss Charlotte Edith Pumpkin . . .' he began.

'*Pumpkin?*' spat the old woman. 'What a peculiar name.' Her voice was taut as she said the word 'peculiar', as if she were really saying '*what a completely ridiculous name*'.

Lottie looked down at the glowing floor, trying her hardest to hide her embarrassment and also her growing sense of fear. The king cleared his throat before gesturing to the man to continue.

'Miss Charlotte Pumpkin, born Charlotte Edith Curran –' Lottie took in a sharp breath at having this information read aloud and turned to see Ellie chewing her bottom lip nervously. Jamie's face remained blank – 'Year Ten at Rosewood Hall, rooming with Eleanor, of no notable nobility, lived in St Ives, Cornwall, with her stepmother, Beady Curran, until September when she moved to permanent boarding at Rosewood. Mother passed away five years ago from leukaemia, father works as a . . .'

The list seemed endless and, although she was fully clothed, she'd never felt more naked in her life. Why was this happening? Why was this necessary? She felt sick. She felt dizzy. These were all parts of herself she wanted to hide from, and now strangers were picking at her life as if she were a specimen in a biology class. She suddenly felt very angry with Ellie. She wished she'd been warned. She wished she knew why any of this was required. She wished she knew anything at all.

'Enough!'

'OK, we get it.'

Ellie and Jamie had simultaneously come to her rescue.

*Maybe Jamie wasn't so bad . . .*

The king looked surprisingly sympathetic.

'Skip to the end,' he said bluntly. The glass-eyed man cleared his throat once again and Lottie slowly unclenched her fists, which had balled up at her sides.

'In the top two per cent of most of her classes, excluding sports and maths, currently the second-highest achiever in English literature and history.'

Jamie's blank mask slipped as he looked at Lottie, as if checking people were aware she was the same girl they were talking about, but there was a humour in his smirk that threw her back to their first meeting.

'One of only twenty-two students in the history of Rosewood to be offered the exceptional-circumstances bursary and it seems she was personally chosen by Professor Devine to join Ivy House.'

Lottie felt her heart hammering wildly and was sure they must be able to see it under her shirt. They knew information about her that even she didn't know. She was a hard worker, everyone knew that; she prided herself on it, and she wanted to be great and do great things, but to have her past shoved in her face followed by having her achievements read out among royalty – achievements she hadn't even known about – somehow it made her feel . . . humiliated.

Was Jamie questioning the legitimacy of these accomplishments? Why would it be funny that a girl so ordinary could push herself so hard?

'Quite the diligent little worker it would seem,' the king said with a dry smile.

Lottie was about to burst into tears right then and there on the marble floor.

*Be brave, be brave, be brave*, she repeated to herself.

'Ellie, you shame us.' The king's tone was cold. 'If even this girl, under her circumstances, can push herself to achieve such feats, then you, a future queen, have no reason to deny yourself similar accomplishments.' His eyes drifted over Jamie and a look like regret flashed on his face but was gone too quickly for Lottie to register completely. 'You forget how fortunate you are.' Ellie looked as if she were about to speak but the king held up his hand. 'You were allowed to attend Rosewood under the agreement that you would keep your identity secret with no exceptions. An agreement that you would acclimatize to school rules without the pressure of your royal obligations. You have failed on both these counts.'

The king's face seemed almost pained as he said these words. It was clear to her that he truly must have hoped Rosewood would be the right choice for Ellie. Ellie's grandmother continued to sit stony-faced at his side.

Ellie's expression was still hard, determined not to let anything show, but Lottie could see the strain in her eyes: the misty look of someone desperately trying not to cry.

*This is my fault*, thought Lottie.

All at once her anxiety for her own fate dissipated as she realized what was really at stake here. Ellie opened her mouth to protest, but before she could get any words out something rang in the back of Lottie's mind. The voice of Professor Devine.

*The fates have placed Miss Wolf in a room with you, so you must look out for her.*

Was this it? Was this her calling to Rosewood? Had her drive to become exceptional been entirely designed to bring her and Ellie together? That thought was comforting and suddenly she didn't feel so afraid.

'She's going to join the fencing team,' Lottie stated matter-of-factly.

The whole hall turned to stare at her like a pack of wolves. Jamie looked completely horrified and mouthed the word '*Don't*', but Lottie swallowed hard and continued.

'That is, with all due respect, you're wrong about her not acclimatizing to school life. She's been invited personally by Dame Bolter herself, an Olympic gold medallist, to join the fencing team. She also helps others excel: she helps me with my maths homework, she's improved my grades in sports, she studies for fun with the smartest girl in school, and she even gives Anastacia Alcroft a run for her money in lacrosse. She belongs at Rosewood and I will do anything to keep her there.'

Lottie paused and blinked, completely thrown by her own words.

'*Anything*, Miss Pumpkin?' The words came from a twinkling little voice behind her.

Lottie turned to see a petite blonde woman with porcelain skin and eyes so icy-blue they almost froze her on the spot. She was smiling ever so slightly, but her eyes shone with a clear sense of cunning. Although she was small in size, this woman gave off an edge that suggested she was most certainly not to be taken lightly.

Lottie hesitated for only a moment. 'Yes,' she said emphatically.

'Quite.' The woman's smile widened and she took a small step from the edge of the room towards Lottie. 'Would you even sign your life over to the Maravish royal family?'

*Wait, what?* And that was the moment everything went completely mad.

## 20

'Absolutely not!' cried Ellie's grandmother, her face screwed up in a furious mask of indignation. 'This is out of the question!'

The blonde woman seemed entirely unaffected by this outburst and simply waved her hand, as if dismissing the statement.

Grandmother Wolfson did not appreciate this gesture and turned to the king. 'Alexander, control your wife.' The words came out more as a bark than a request.

*That's Ellie's mother?* Lottie turned back to stare at the wispy, ethereal blonde woman and saw almost no physical resemblance between the two, and yet . . . the confident way she held herself, and her piercing eyes, the bold way she had dismissed the most terrifying woman Lottie had ever met. Maybe it wasn't so shocking after all.

The king turned to his mother then and, to Lottie's complete and utter surprise, he looked offended.

'Mother, may I remind you, this audience is requested for the sole purpose of an Act Six request? Or have you not been paying attention?'

Lottie almost laughed at this, even though she still had no idea what Act 6 was.

'Oh lord,' Ellie groaned under her breath, rubbing the bridge of her nose as if this were a regular occurrence. Jamie remained impassive, although his eyes seemed to be larger than usual.

The king turned then to Ellie's mother and his face softened; her presence seemed to have dissipated some of the tension in the room.

*So this is where she gets those mood swings from!* Lottie thought to herself. These people made Ellie look normal in comparison.

'Umm, excuse me –' Lottie began, but was cut off as Ellie's mother gently ran a lock of her curly blonde hair through her fingers, making Lottie jump in surprise.

'Alexander, she could be one of ours – it's uncanny.' She leaned into Lottie very closely, but it didn't feel like she was really looking at *her*. It made her feel as though she were a racehorse being inspected for purchase.

'Did you enjoy your night in the palace? We would love to have you again.'

It took Lottie a moment to realize the queen was talking to her.

'Yes, I –'

'You cannot seriously be considering the idea that this –' the king's mother cut her off and gestured furiously to Lottie without looking at her directly – 'common girl could possibly take the role of a Portman?'

*Portman!* Lottie remembered the term from Ellie and Jamie's earlier argument. *Whatever could she mean?*

'Your daughter is merely looking for yet another excuse to avoid her responsibilities and this time she's dragged an ordinary girl along with her.'

'Ordinary?' Ellie's mother laughed. 'In this instance I think we can all agree that her inconsequential background is most beneficial.'

She began circling Lottie slowly as if she were her prey. 'I, for one, think she's perfect. Too perfect, a blessing even?'

'See, I told you; she's totally right.' Ellie had regained the power of speech.

Jamie was clenching his jaw.

'I must agree,' the king said. 'It is a strangely fortunate situation we find ourselves in with this Miss Pumpkin.'

Lottie found she was struggling to understand. 'Excuse me, I –'

She was cut off by the glass-eyed man.

'She certainly meets the criteria, but the questions is, Your Majesty –' he bent down so he was closer to the king's ear, the words coming out with a hiss – 'will the princess truly uphold her end of the bargain? As has been said before, she tends to disappoint.' He gave Ellie a sharp look as he finished speaking, a nasty grin creeping on to his lips. Ellie was noticeably gritting her teeth.

'That is, indeed, the question,' the king agreed.

'Could I please . . .' Lottie tried to raise her hand this time.

The old woman cackled. 'Bah! If that's the only question, then the answer is a blindingly obvious no. I suggest you pull her from the school, and send her to St Agnes's Correctional Facility for Young Ladies where they will whip her into a woman worthy of the Maravish crown.'

'If someone could just . . .'

'I think it's a splendid idea, and shows that our Eleanor is making active decisions in her role as princess, which we

156

should be eagerly encouraging.' Ellie's mother beamed at her husband and he nodded in response.

'If you can call the choice to be passive an *active decision*.' The glass-eyed man chuckled softly.

The king and his mother openly laughed at this and Lottie found herself suddenly very angry.

'WOULD SOMEBODY EXPLAIN TO ME WHAT IS GOING ON?'

The hall went quiet again, the wolf pack turning to stare at her as if they had forgotten she was even there.

'Please,' she added quickly.

The silence that filled the room was almost deafening. Jamie broke his mask for just a moment and looked at Lottie in astonishment before quickly regaining composure.

'Lottie . . .' Ellie's face softened. She clenched her fists and turned back to the king with a hard look on her face. 'Dad!' she said resolutely. 'I don't care what the decision is. I'll accept whatever course of action you choose, but you need to make it now. I can't keep my friend in the dark any more.' She extended her hand to Lottie's and gave it a little squeeze. Lottie felt a pleasant sense of static between them.

Jamie let out a relieved sigh, the tension he had felt building during the discussion dissipating.

The king eyed his daughter with fresh consideration, struck with the loyalty and severity in her stare. His dark eyes squinted as he contemplated a side of her he'd never seen before. His gaze moved to the young girls' hands that were still clasped in solidarity.

'Very well.' He turned to his wife, and she beamed at him with a knowing smile. 'Based on the absurdly convenient

157

suitability of the proposed Portman and what I, as the king, have deemed a clear sign of positive influence –' he paused for dramatic effect – 'I sanction this request for Princess Eleanor Prudence Wolfson to enact Act Six with Charlotte Edith Pumpkin. Let it be written.'

Grandmother Wolfson let out a furious cry, but the king held up his hand and she reluctantly simmered down.

'I fear this is a grave mistake,' she said darkly.

The king ignored this statement. 'And, to put us all at ease, Jamie will continue his placement at Rosewood Hall. The school will be informed of the special arrangement.'

Jamie tensed and the glass-eyed man seemed to be stifling a snigger.

'You are all excused.'

Ellie let out an excited little squeal and grabbed Lottie's arm, leading her through the ornate doors with so much giddy energy she was almost skipping. Lottie followed, only dimly aware of her body moving, and still not entirely sure what had just been decided. Behind them, Jamie gave the king a look that went unnoticed by the two girls, but he quickly recovered his stone-faced mask and went back to his position of unwavering loyalty.

'Did you see that?' the king whispered to his wife when the door was firmly shut.

'Yes!' she replied excitedly. 'Eleanor's made a friend!'

# 21

'Portman: one who is hired to officially act in the place of a member of royalty in order to protect their true identity. All public appearances and official duties are to be carried out with the utmost respect and *blah*, *blah*, *blah*, *blah*, so on and so forth . . .'

Lottie blinked in bewilderment as Ellie read aloud the passage from a dusty old book they'd been given by the glass-eyed man, who Ellie had informed her was the king's advisor, Simien Smirnov.

'So this is *my* job now?' Lottie said, pointing to herself, her eyes bulging.

'Well, if you want it to be. You were basically doing it already,' she said good-humouredly. 'Now you'd just . . . be getting paid to do it.'

'OK, but . . . wait, paid?'

'Yes, you'll get a monthly payment, as well as travel, food and clothing expenses.'

Lottie almost choked; did they realize this was a dream come true? This hardly seemed like a job at all, getting all the benefits of being a princess *and* being paid for it.

'And this way, in the future when you inevitably have to tell everyone that you're, in fact, *not* the princess of Maradova, you'll be able to say with complete truthfulness that it's because you were an official Portman. Sorted!' She gave Lottie a thumbs-up, which she responded to by blinking again.

The three teenagers had convened in Ellie's bedroom, which, although large, was surprisingly bare. Lacking Ellie's motley charm, it could be anyone's room. It was evidently not a place Ellie considered home. Ellie and Lottie sat on the vast four-poster bed while Jamie stood by the door with one foot propped up against the wood frame, resting his head back in silent thought. He'd informed her that as soon as they started back at school he would begin training her to be a perfect Portman. Something she was a little apprehensive about.

'How long have you been planning this?' Lottie asked, afraid to hear the truth.

Ellie looked sheepish. 'Pretty much as soon I confronted you in our first week.'

Lottie baulked at this. 'You didn't ask me. You didn't . . .' She had to pause to stop herself from getting flustered; she was just so overwhelmed. 'You should have told me what I was here for. You can trust me.'

'You don't understand, Lottie. I couldn't! It would be breaking too many rules,' Ellie pleaded.

'But you always break the rules!'

'Lottie, stop!' This came from Jamie, but his words weren't angry or cold; they were calm. 'She really couldn't tell you, Lottie. Portmans are a royal secret; barely anyone knows they exist and half the people who do know think they're just a fairy tale, and we need to keep it that way to protect those who need them, do you understand?'

Lottie nodded. It did make sense, but it felt like they didn't have faith in her.

'I understand that, but *you* have to understand that I have Ellie's best interests at heart as much as you do.' She turned to her friend, a fiery feeling in her belly. 'If you trust me enough to be your Portman, then you should trust me enough to tell me about them.'

Ellie chewed her lip for a moment, while Jamie straightened up and walked over to Lottie.

'You're right,' he said.

'I am?' she asked in confusion. Had she just imagined that? Had Jamie just *agreed* with her?

'Yes. We should have told you. But Ellie truly had no choice in the matter,' he said matter-of-factly.

'I'm really sorry, Lottie.' Ellie pushed her hair out of her eyes as she spoke and Lottie knew she meant it.

'I forgive you, Ellie, and I really am happy to do this for you; it feels right. But we have to promise no more secrets going forward.' She held her little finger out like she used to as a kid, and Ellie laughed as she wrapped her own finger round it.

'I promise.'

As Lottie sat on the aeroplane the next morning, preparing for take-off, Jamie came and took the seat beside her. He was so quiet that she didn't even realize he was there until he said her name.

She turned abruptly and nearly banged her head into his, but this time he dodged it easily. His face was inscrutable as

161

usual. She was starting to trust him more, but he still made her nervous.

'I really do agree with you,' he said. 'It was wrong of them not to tell you. In fact, you should not have been brought here at all. You should not have been told about Portmans, and you absolutely should not have been asked to take on the role of one.'

Lottie was lost for words. She should've known Jamie felt this way, that he didn't think her capable or worthy to take on the role of an official Portman. She'd spent the majority of her life having people doubt her capabilities, yet hearing his words still hurt her deeply.

'I . . .' Her voice cracked and she took a breath to calm herself. She wanted them to believe in her, to see that she was capable of this role, even if she wasn't sure if she believed it herself yet. 'I'm going to impress you, Jamie.'

He looked at her with a slightly sad expression that she couldn't quite understand, sighed, and took a little beaten-up book out of his jacket pocket. It was leather-bound with a silver floral pattern that reflected the light. He placed it on her lap and she flinched as his hand grazed her knee.

'I'm sure you will,' he said, his smirk returning. Then he stood up and left for his own seat without another word.

Lottie looked down at the book and carefully opened the first page to a beautiful cursive script:

*I, Oscar Oddwood, Portman to the late Henric Wolfson, have collected the tales and advice of Portmans from around the world so that our collective wisdom may be passed down and augmented. May this book assist any of those that take on the ambiguous role of the Faithful Fake.*

Lottie gently flipped through it and saw an abundance of illustrated pages and different handwritings and languages. She felt as if there were magic radiating from the book, as if the item were sacred. She gently tucked the book away in her bag, feeling too tired to appreciate it properly now. She leaned her head against the window to watch the take-off.

The fluffy clouds parted below the plane, creating a peephole into the icy landscape of Maradova beneath them. She looked over at Ellie who was asleep, her face covered by a book entitled *Well-behaved Women Seldom Make History*. Jamie had his copy of *A Midsummer Night's Dream* out and was earnestly taking notes. They seemed entirely unaffected by the attentive staff and luxury of a private jet. There was something effortless and exciting about the two of them: they were so sure of belonging, so confidently radiating their purpose into the world.

Lottie felt as though she was being allowed an insight into a realm in which she didn't truly belong. Rosewood Hall, royal Portmans, the Wolfsons – they were all so magnificent, and after her alluring night in the palace she felt a deep desire to be part of it all. The clouds quickly re-formed under the plane and Lottie lost her view of the land below, suddenly feeling very far from the ground and determined to find her place in the world.

# PART TWO
## How to be a Princess

## 22

Lottie tossed and turned in her bed, but no matter what position she tried, she could not fall asleep. The covers were too hot and the air was too cold and no amount of counting sheep helped. This was the tenth sleepless night since her return from Maradova, and Lottie was starting to think she'd never dream again.

She looked over to see Ellie's resting face across the room and reluctantly sat up to start getting ready for the day. No matter what, she absolutely could not let Jamie or Ellie know she was having trouble sleeping or they'd think she wasn't cut out for her role as Portman. The strawberry-shaped alarm clock on her bedside table went off, signalling that it was time for her Saturday-morning class with Jamie, something she was calling her *princess lessons*. Ellie stretched in her bed and made a huge yawning sound, lethargically sitting up and swinging her legs over the side of the mattress.

'Ellie, you really don't have to come. You can go back to sleep if you want,' Lottie said softly, worrying that speaking too loud might disturb the early-morning air.

Ellie yawned once more, her eyes not fully focusing. 'Nope!' She rubbed her cheeks in an attempt to force herself awake.

'If you have to get up early for these princess lessons, then I will suffer with you. It's only fair.'

Lottie couldn't help feeling happy at Ellie's words.

They met Jamie in one of the Ivy study rooms overlooking the Rose Wood. The sun had not risen yet and it was difficult for Lottie to keep her eyes open in the warm room filled with dusty books. Jamie was pacing back and forth, asking her to translate ancient Maravish words while Ellie plugged away at homework. Since returning from Maradova, Lottie's days had become a strict timetable of school, homework, tutoring and princess lessons. She was used to working overtime from when she'd studied to get into Rosewood, but with the addition of insomnia she was starting to feel rundown.

'Sets?'

'Prince.'

'Sessa?'

'Princess.'

'Good.'

Jamie ticked something off in his little notebook that he kept for their lessons. His face remained unreadable and she had no idea if he was happy with her progress.

'Honestly, I don't see the point in her learning the ancient Maravish dialect. It hasn't been used in nearly a hundred years.'

Jamie scowled at Ellie, who'd been doing nothing but making digs at his lesson plan since they'd started.

'That's a good point, Ellie. Lottie, recite the history of the Maravish language.'

Lottie groaned internally. It seemed like every time Ellie made a comment, she had to recite something. She squeezed her eyes shut for a second, willing away some of her tiredness.

'Maravish: of Latin origin; a dialect grown from mixing English and Russian. After the treaty of Serego, when Maradova gained independence from the British Empire, the people of Maradova kept English as their main language. The ancient Maravish dialect is now only used to –'

'OK. Good.' Jamie cut her off. 'See how quickly Lottie's picked this all up, Ellie? You should be taking notes.'

Lottie resented that the only real feedback she got from Jamie was in the form of a verbal jab at Ellie.

Ellie stuck her tongue out at him before turning back to her textbook.

Two Ivy girls on their way to tennis practice walked past the door and giggled to themselves as they saw Jamie before blushing and scampering off. Jamie was fitting in at Rosewood in his own way. The king had decided it was acceptable to make Jamie's role as a bodyguard public knowledge – although everyone thought he was Lottie's bodyguard, not Ellie's. This had unsurprisingly resulted in establishing him as a heart-throb among the girls of Rosewood. Lottie wanted to gag at how pre-dictable it was, forgetting that she herself had been swooning over the concept of a Partizan just last month. She wasn't sure exactly what the school faculty had been told about her being a princess, but it didn't seem to have changed much.

Lottie took the opportunity to yawn while neither of them were looking, wondering how long she'd be able to keep them in the dark about her sleepless nights. She was pulled out of her thoughts when Jamie put a piece of paper down on her desk.

'I want you to name each of these members of the Maravish royal family.' Lottie peered at the faces on the paper. She recognized Ellie's parents and the previous rulers, Ellie's grandmother and King Henric, but there was something not quite right about it. Someone was missing.

'In Oscar's diary he said the last king, Henric, had two sons. Doesn't that mean King Alexander should have a brother, Ellie's uncle?'

Both Ellie and Jamie stared at her as if she'd just cursed, their faces serious as they exchanged a look.

'Claude,' Ellie said slowly, looking away. 'He was meant to be king, but . . . he refused his royal duties . . .'

'He was banished from the kingdom,' Jamie said bluntly. 'The Maravish royal family are meticulous when it comes to rules. It's important you understand that.'

Lottie felt as if a piece of a puzzle had just slotted into place. This is what Ellie faced if she didn't want to rule. Banishment. Total denial of her existence. A shiver ran up her spine.

'How scary . . .' Lottie whispered under her breath.

'Quite, and speaking of scary things . . .' Jamie smiled as he retrieved a letter from his backpack.

He placed it in her hand and she marvelled in wonder and confusion at the maroon wax seal that had already been broken. It was a strange symbol she'd never seen before: four triangles arranged in a square, overlapping to create two diamonds in the middle that made her think of wolf teeth.

'What is this?' she asked.

'This is our invitation to the Maravish Summer Ball,' Ellie replied, 'or rather, the Flower Festival.' She said the name with an exaggerated eye-roll. Lottie, on the other hand, had been lost at the word 'ball'. 'It's completely ridiculous. They do it every year, but it's always thick with snow, and there's nothing summery about it.'

But Lottie wasn't paying attention.

A royal ball! She was going to a real royal ball. She'd get to wear a gown, and there would probably be princes and princesses there! A REAL ROYAL BALL!

'Lottie!'

She blinked, crashing out of her daze to find Ellie waving her hand in front of her eyes, and Jamie's top lip twitching in annoyance.

'Royal ball, you say? Sounds great – where do I sign up?' She beamed at Ellie with her best *please let me go to the royal ball* look.

Ellie laughed, pushing her thick black hair out of her eyes. 'You're in luck, Miss Pumpkin, the Flower Festival will be our . . . I mean, *your* debut as princess.'

'*Really?*' Lottie stood up, pushing her seat back and smacking her hands on the table in excitement. Suddenly all the fatigue had evaporated from her body. This was like a fairy tale come true . . . until she saw Jamie's face. She coughed discreetly and slowly lowered herself back into her chair, blushing furiously. 'I mean . . . that sounds perfectly enchanting.'

Ellie snorted at Lottie's attempt at eloquence. Although Lottie knew that Jamie was trustworthy, she still felt odd around him and had a deep desire to prove herself.

Jamie sighed in a way that suggested he resented whatever he had to tell her next. 'It's not that simple. Ellie will be attending formally as your guest, which makes her presence at events easy to explain, but all first-time principal attendees must partake in one full day at Lady Priscilla's Etiquette Assembly, which, fortunately for you, is being hosted at Rosewood this year.'

Lottie blinked in confusion, having absolutely no idea what any of this meant.

'That means you have to attend an etiquette class, Lottie!' Ellie said, stifling her laughter.

'An . . . etiquette class?' Were they making fun of her? Was this all some elaborate joke?

'This is not a joke, Lottie.'

Lottie shivered, feeling like Jamie had just read her mind. 'You will need to attend this class in two weeks and you need to make the absolute best impression you can. There will be other young royalty and children of important families and you need to fit in.' He held her gaze, making sure she absorbed every word he said. She nodded.

'And if you can trip any of the snobby princes over during the waltz you get extra points from me.'

Jamie grumbled at Ellie's joke, making Lottie laugh.

Then he looked up at the clock and began packing up their stuff meticulously. 'Here –' he held out a piece of paper filled with instructions – 'this is everything we'll need to go over before the etiquette class. I'm meeting Raphael for a run. I'll see you both later.'

Ellie made a retching motion with her finger. Jamie and Raphael had both been placed in the same language classes and had quickly bonded over their multilingual backgrounds and love of long-distance running. It seemed like an odd pairing considering how humourless Jamie seemed. She wondered if, like Ellie, this was the first friend outside the Maravish family that Jamie had ever made.

Jamie paused by the door and turned back to them. 'If you need anything, let me know –' he gave Ellie a sharp look – 'and that does not mean coffee runs for fencing practice.' Ellie grinned up at him, feigning innocence. 'And, Lottie, try to get some better sleep tonight.'

Lottie held her breath as he exited the room. She thought she'd hid her tiredness well. As soon as he was out of sight, Lottie slowly exhaled. She needed to prove to Jamie she was cut out for this. She couldn't let any cracks show.

Thoughtfully watching Lottie, Ellie reached over across the table to grab her hand, gently stroking her palm with her thumb.

'I promise you'll be fine, little princess. You're a natural and this etiquette class will be easy-peasy.'

Lottie blushed, realizing that Ellie had mistaken her worry to be about the etiquette class, and looked down at the instructions in her hand.

'Fine isn't good enough,' she whispered to herself.

## 23

With the weather turning cold, the students of Rosewood Hall were gifted with a pleasant October evening. Pretty little cut-outs of bats and black cats lined the halls and all the dormitories were filled with carved pumpkins, giving the air an over-ripe smell.

Lottie stood in the queue for the main library cafe with Ellie and Binah, who were chatting about imaginary numbers, something Ellie had been teaching Lottie about in their tutoring sessions. Jamie had been given permission to use the school's phone to call the Maravish kingdom, to keep them updated on their well-being, and he'd be meeting them later. She looked out of the window at how dark it already was, even though school had ended less than an hour ago, and wondered if she'd be able to sleep that night.

'I'll have a slice of pumpkin bread and a white chocolate mocha –' Lottie checked to make sure Ellie wasn't paying attention – 'with an extra espresso shot, please.' She'd discovered a temporary remedy for her symptoms of sleeplessness: coffee and concealer, lots of both.

The library had quickly become Lottie's favourite place in Rosewood. She'd been apprehensive to return at first, after their little break-in adventure, but the unrivalled collection of books soon lured her back and, despite its magnitude, it somehow felt cosy. Being surrounded by so much inspiring literature filled her with a happy, warm feeling.

As they went to take a seat in the study area, a few heads turned to Lottie. She'd become very good at pretending she didn't notice, but no matter how much time passed people couldn't get over the secret-Maravish-princess thing. Lottie couldn't blame them, though; she couldn't quite get over it either.

'Let's sit there!' Binah suddenly exclaimed, marching towards a table by the window.

Ellie and Lottie froze. Seated at the round table were Lola, Micky, Saskia and Anastacia. Lottie was happy to sit with them, but she knew Ellie still felt weird about Anastacia, especially now she was her fencing competition.

Before Lottie could say anything, Ellie's eyes narrowed and she took a bold step forward to join them at the table.

'Hey, guys! Is it OK if we sit here?' Lottie quickly asked as Ellie sat down next to Binah.

Lola beamed. 'Of course!' She immediately got out a bag of Tompkins Fizzy Toffees and proceeded to hold the packet out to them. 'Help yourself!' she said enthusiastically.

Lottie watched as both Ellie and Saskia leaned forward together, their hands catching as they went into the bag. She held her breath, not sure how Ellie would respond.

'Sorry, I – Have we met?' Ellie asked, a little smile creeping on to her face that gave Lottie an unpleasant feeling in her stomach.

'Not formally!' Saskia pulled a toffee out and handed it to Ellie. 'I'm Saskia.'

'Ellie.'

'I know,' Saskia said coyly. Their eyes lingered on each other for a moment as Ellie placed the toffee in her mouth.

'She's the head of Conch House for the year above us,' Lottie said quickly, feeling the need to distract them. They both turned to Lottie and an odd sense of embarrassment overtook her.

'I like being in charge!' Saskia grinned at Ellie, and the two laughed.

Lottie slowly sat down in the spare seat next to Anastacia, who was focused on her textbook. She looked over as Ellie laughed again at something that Saskia had said and was overcome with an odd feeling of being left out.

'I can see why you have so much trouble sleeping when you have such a raucous room-mate.' Anastacia's voice came out low and icy beside her.

'Excuse me?' Lottie asked in confusion. *How does she know?*

'Ellie, she's wild.'

Before Lottie could process what she'd said, Anastacia turned to her, a serious look in her eyes as she considered Lottie's tired face. 'I have something for you.'

Lottie blinked in confusion as Anastacia reached into her bag, pulling out a packet of pills and placing them purposefully on the table.

'What are they?' Lottie asked as Ellie leaned forward, grabbing the pink packet and reading the cover aloud.

'*Princess and the Pea Sleeping Remedy. For any princess who struggles to sleep at night . . .*'

Lottie gulped.

How did Anastacia know she wasn't sleeping? And why did she have to give me those in front of Ellie? Lottie wanted to bang her head against the table; the last thing she needed right now was for Ellie and Jamie to be worrying about this.

'Lottie, are you not sleeping?'

She jumped at the sound of Jamie's voice and turned to see him looming over her. *When on earth did he get here?* It was clear she couldn't evade his question, though.

Lottie became acutely aware that everyone in the library cafe was now staring at them. Jamie seemed to have that effect. She smiled at him as best she could and his eyes widened a bit.

'Your eyes . . .' he added, a hint of concern creeping into his voice.

'I thought you weren't going to get here until later?' It was a rubbish attempt at sidestepping, but she absolutely could not have him thinking this was because she was stressed about her job as a Portman. Jamie was already convinced she wasn't cut out for it and she didn't want to prove him right.

'Lottie, why didn't you tell me?'

There was hurt in Ellie's voice, and Lottie suddenly found herself feeling very angry at Anastacia for getting her into this mess. She looked over at her, but everyone had their heads back in their books, pretending not to listen.

'It's fine. I'll explain later during maths tutoring when everyone's calmed down,' Lottie said, giving both Jamie and Ellie as firm a look as she could manage.

Ellie's face dropped and she looked a little sheepish. 'Lottie, I thought I'd told you . . . I'm really sorry, but I don't know how much time I'll have to tutor you any more because of fencing practice.' Lottie felt her heart sink. She loved Ellie's tutoring, and for the first time in her life she actually felt like she was getting good at maths.

'That's fine.' The words came out automatically. She couldn't ruin fencing for Ellie by making her feel guilty, especially when she was still getting up on Saturdays to keep her company during her princess lessons. 'Everything's fine. I can manage.' However, she wasn't one hundred per cent sure who that last statement was aimed at.

'You need to keep your maths grades up, Lottie,' Jamie said unhelpfully.

'I can tutor you.'

They turned to Saskia, who was leaning back on her chair casually. 'If you want me to. I'm top of my year.'

'Really?' Lottie couldn't hide the surprise in her voice; it was such a convenient solution. 'That would be amazing. Thank you.'

'No!' All eyes spun to Anastacia who'd slammed her hand on the table. 'We always hang out after school.' Her voice came out uncharacteristically unhinged and Lottie almost thought she was joking.

Saskia didn't seem affected by the outburst and simply smirked. 'But aren't you gonna be in fencing practice too? The trials are only a few weeks away.'

'Yes, but . . .'

'Then it's settled. I'll tutor Lottie.'

The library intercom crackled overhead. '*Would the students at table eight please keep the noise down.*'

Lottie looked at everyone, sensing that there were a million more things they all wanted to say, but they silently turned back to their books.

*What on earth just happened?*

## 24

Lottie was practising basic etiquette with Jamie after school in the small gymnasium by Conch House, learning the fundamentals that the other students would most likely already know. They practised everything from dinnerware placement to the correct way to eat an oyster, but the one thing he remained reserved about was the waltz, which he asked Ellie to teach her instead.

*I didn't think he found me THAT annoying*, Lottie had thought to herself.

There were only three days to go and Lottie had been working extra hard to hide her tiredness. The pills Anastacia had given her helped a little but nowhere near enough to fix whatever was stopping her sleeping. She stifled a yawn as they went over the appropriate greetings for different levels of nobility, causing Jamie to glare at her. He was still angry at her for not telling them about her sleep problems. He looked as if he were about to comment on it when Ellie let out a low groan that sounded like a growl.

'THIS PUZZLE IS DRIVING ME MAD!' she shouted, throwing her workbook across the room. Lottie watched in amazement as Jamie effortlessly jumped up and caught it mid-air. Ellie had taken to spending the 'boring' parts of the lessons, as she called them, working on Binah's puzzle, which she was still having no luck with. Lottie had long given up on ever being allowed to open their gifts.

Jamie flipped through its pages indifferently before closing it with a loud smack.

'We'd appreciate if you could do your strange anagrams in silence,' he said coldly, placing the book down on the bench that Ellie had commandeered.

She sat up like a jolt of lightning had gone through her body.

'Anagram?' she breathed, raising an eyebrow.

'Yes!' he replied, turning back to Lottie to adjust her arm to the correct position for her curtsy. 'You haven't converted the numbers into letters yet, but it clearly spells out the founder of the school, William –'

'WILLIAM TUFTY!' the two girls shouted in unison.

Lottie broke her position as Ellie came running over. It all made sense now. Ellie had been so concerned with figuring out what the puzzle meant numerically that she hadn't bothered to look for words in it.

'Jamie, we're finishing early,' Ellie called behind her as she pulled Lottie by the arm.

Jamie reached out to grab Lottie's hand but hesitated. 'Fine, you're dismissed.'

The two girls sat in the Ivy common room on a purple love-seat underneath a large painting of Florence Ivy. Three other Ivy students were sitting by the TV, giggling as they stared at Jamie who stood by the window overlooking the pond and dining hall, doing an amazing job of appearing uninterested in everything. He'd demanded to inspect the gifts before they were allowed to open them, something he'd declared was common practice but which had Ellie groaning impatiently. They'd bumped into a Stratus girl on their way back and asked her to tell Binah that they'd solved her puzzle if she saw her.

'I can't believe we've had these for weeks and not been able to open them,' Lottie said as they held the lids of their boxes. They counted to three before pulling the lids and Lottie squeezed her eyes shut, terrified of an impending anti-climax. And that's exactly what she got.

Inside her box was a tiny fox brooch no bigger than her little fingernail. She looked over at Ellie who was equally puzzled, holding a small enamel mouse.

'I don't get it,' Ellie said bluntly, looking up at Jamie as if he could give her another hint.

Lottie chewed the inside of her lip in thought.

'Well, it must have some significance.' She grabbed Ellie's gift and held them both up in front of her. 'A mouse and a fox, a mouse and a fox.' She repeated the words to herself in the hope it might unlock something. She saw Jamie's lip twitch out of the corner of her eye. 'Am I doing something wrong?' she asked apprehensively.

'It just reminds me of something,' Jamie replied, turning to stare out of the window again. His face showed an emotion Lottie hadn't seen before and she found she didn't want to look away. She forced herself to turn her attention back to their gifts.

Lottie felt her mind go cloudy, her eyes glossing over as a ghost from her childhood whispered in her ear. Somewhere in the back of her mind, she could hear her mother's voice reciting a verse from her distant past.

> *They found each other in the woods.*
> *Together they did build a house.*

A story her mother used to tell her, before she knew how brutal the world could be.

> *One was smart and the other was soft . . .*

A rhyme about two very different creatures, coming together to help each other: 'The Vixen and the Delicate Mouse'.

'William Tufty wrote nursery rhymes!' Lottie exclaimed. The words jumped out of her before she'd fully processed the thought. She looked over at Jamie, who was looking at her in surprise. 'And you know it too – you remember the story!' For a moment she entirely forgot her nerves with Jamie. 'The Vixen and –'

'– the Delicate Mouse,' Jamie finished, and she felt her heart skip a beat unexpectedly. 'I'd almost forgotten the name.'

Lottie grinned at Ellie, returning her brooch. 'I never would have guessed that the founder of Rosewood had written my favourite nursery rhyme as a kid. It was my mum's favourite rhyme too.' She looked down affectionately at her gift, stroking the metal with her thumb. *Thank you, Binah.*

Ellie reached out and gently rubbed her hand, a soft look in her eyes. 'So you think that's it? Binah wanted to tell us about his poems?'

Lottie felt a discomfort in her stomach, the kind that tells you when something isn't quite right. She racked her brain for more of the story and gradually fragments came back to her – of paintings and oak trees – but the memories were not enough to form a full picture.

'I think we need to find the whole rhyme . . .' she said, her eyes still lingering on the brooches. She turned to Jamie expectantly and he nodded. She wondered if he was excited about the poem too.

It did not take long to locate the William Tufty section in the library. He had an entire area dedicated to not only his work and any work he featured in but also a section of books and poems he'd loved.

They found the rhyme in an anthology of children's stories, and Lottie sat down opposite the others as they waited for her to read it aloud. She cleared her throat, feeling nervous under Jamie's gaze.

> 'They found each other in the woods.
> Together they did build a house.
> One was smart and the other was soft,
> The Vixen and the Delicate Mouse.
> They were champions of hide-and-seek.
> Every day they'd play a game.
> The Vixen was so clever that
> She hid inside the painting frames.
> The oak trees grew and soon they held
> A home for others to learn their tricks:
> Wisdom, valour and righteousness.
> They built their houses with stones and bricks.

*And now within the master's office,*
*Where he looks down on his house,*
*His gaze on them with a gaze on him*
*Of the Vixen and the Delicate Mouse.'*

She looked up at Ellie when she was done, light bulbs going off in her head.

'I think it's in the paintings.' Ellie's eyes narrowed, and Lottie continued: 'There're paintings of him all over the school . . . I think one of them might have the next clue in it.'

Ellie stood, pulling Lottie up too and swinging her bag over her shoulders, ready to leave. Jamie didn't say a word.

'Well, what are you waiting for?' said Ellie. 'Let's go and check them out.'

Jamie seemed to remember himself and his face once again regained its moody composure and he stood up between them.

'You can save your painting appreciation for another day,' he said drily. 'It's nearly curfew and I'm sure you both have homework to finish and, Lottie –' he looked at her sharply and all the anxious feelings she associated with him came flooding back – 'you need to get back to thinking about this etiquette class, which is in less than three days.'

Lottie gulped. Jamie was right. Before she could get excited about any mysteries, she needed to survive this class.

# 25

The main hall of Rosewood had been commandeered for the sake of the five-hour etiquette class run by a woman named Lady Priscilla. It was a rite of passage for the children of important families to attend one of these classes before their first public appearance at a significant function.

Although Lottie had walked through the main hall many times in her months at Rosewood and had become familiar with the grand space, it had never felt as cold and forbidding as it did then. Every step seemed to echo louder than usual; every breath seemed to be more visible in the air. There were children of her age from all over the world. They looked immaculate and natural in their attire, ranging from saris to embroidered jackets with tassels. Lottie had had to borrow a dress from Lola, who'd been more than delighted to dress up Lottie, and they'd found an appropriate, semi-sensible mid-length white dress that she hoped met the dress code.

Jamie stood by her side. They had arrived early and watched the others slowly trickle in. Everyone had either a bodyguard or an assistant with them. Lottie wondered if any of the bodyguards were Partizans, but they all seemed much older than their wards.

Jamie was running through the names of each attendee as they entered, which Lottie tried her best to remember: Veevee Indriani, royalty from Rajasthan living in the USA and set to be an Olympic figure skater; Lachlan Kidman-Dolman, son of Angus Dolman the painter and Ingrid Kidman the opera singer; Edmund Ashwick –

Lottie's attention was suddenly cut off by the entrants who followed Edmund Ashwick. To her complete amazement, Anastacia, Raphael and Saskia walked through the door!

'Wh-what are you guys doing here?' Lottie spluttered. She hadn't spoken to Anastacia since the library incident the previous week yet she felt a little better about having people she knew in this class. Anastacia was wearing a demure, floor-length black-and-silver dress, stylishly complemented by Raphael's black-and-silver tuxedo. She was several inches taller than Lottie and her sharp heels accentuated the height difference. Behind her, Saskia was dressed sensibly in a dark shift dress, her golden mane tied up neatly.

'I assumed you knew,' replied Anastacia smoothly. 'This will be my first year attending your family's summer ball.' Lottie blinked a few times and Jamie tensed at her side. Was this something she should have known? But before Lottie could reply, Anastacia continued. 'And Raphael is here because he –' she coughed – 'he suddenly decided he simply must get this class out of the way upon hearing I was attending.'

Raphael choked out a laugh. 'Well, no one else is going to volunteer to practise the waltz with the wicked bitch of the west dorm.' He smirked at her but she ignored him. 'I'm totally doing you a favour by being here.'

Raphael winked at Jamie, and Lottie was pleased to see he didn't respond. She and Anastacia might not be the best of friends, but she didn't like the idea of her being spoken to like that.

'I'm . . .' Lottie faltered for a moment then decided to just say it. 'I'm really glad you're here.' And she was: she hadn't realized until they walked in how nervous she'd actually been, and even though Anastacia was generally a little cold, at least she was consistent. She looked as if she were about to respond when suddenly Saskia interrupted.

'Lottie, I'm really looking forward to our first tutoring session.' Her voice was level and calming, instantly making Lottie feel more relaxed. Saskia curtsied, then looked up and gave Lottie a clear smile that made her feel odd in her fake princess role. 'I promise I'll get you a good grade; I'm a pro.'

Lottie smiled back as best she could, wondering what Ellie would make of this whole situation.

'Saskia is attending as my plus-one. Just like Miss Wolf is yours,' Anastacia added, checking her nails for any non-existent scuffs.

At the mention of 'Wolf', Lottie's mind flashed back to that first day and the mysterious book left at her door. A strange feeling fluttered in her stomach, as if there were something she ought to know but it was somehow out of her mind's reach.

'Thank you, Saskia,' Lottie said, ignoring Anastacia and amazing herself with how calm she sounded. She couldn't explain why but she was suddenly very uneasy.

Jamie coughed loudly, pulling her out of her thoughts. 'OK – time's up. Remember the protocol.'

188

In the distance Lottie could hear loud clicks of heels on marble coming down the corridor to the hall.

'Good luck,' Lottie said quickly to her friends.

Raphael grinned, but Anastacia simply nodded before they all stood in a line.

The door burst open dramatically making Lottie jump. *Red.* That was the first thing Lottie thought when she saw her. Lady Priscilla wore a tight red skirt suit with elaborate ruffles and a white vest. She looked older than Lottie expected and there was a tightness in her face that suggested she spent a lot of time scowling. Lady Priscilla entered the room with slow yet easy grace, gently tapping a cane in the palm of her hand, taking in the room methodically. A thin smile appeared on her face but it did not reach her eyes.

'There is little that pleases me more than when a child learns their place.' Her voice was prickly like pins and needles in Lottie's ears, making her shiver. 'Most of you are broken, tainted by a lack of discipline, and I delight in the opportunity to fix you. By the end of my class you will no longer be an embarrassment to high society. I will shape you until you fit in with the world into which you were all so undeservingly born.'

Lottie felt queasy. Suddenly Jamie's rigorous preparation for the class made perfect sense. This woman was terrifying. She moved down the line purposefully, her rigid posture giving the impression of a cobra poised to attack. Her hair was coiled atop her head in a tight red bundle with a small jade ornament in the centre like she had a little snake eye on the back of her head.

'You are all here because you were born into an important family, and it is my job to make sure that importance isn't wasted on you.'

189

She stopped at Anastacia. 'Miss Alcroft . . .' She tilted her head slightly, eyes slanted. 'Good posture, modest choice of attire . . . Good.'

She continued to move along the line, her heels making sharp clicking sounds. Lottie held her breath and chanced a quick glance at Jamie who stood with the other assistants and bodyguards against the left wall. His face was blank but his jaw was clenched. He did not return her glance.

'Master Singh.' A thin smile spread across her lips that made Lottie shudder. 'I had your brother in my class three years ago,' she spat the words out like they were poison. 'I sincerely hope you are more graceful than him.'

The heels clicked closer and closer to Lottie.

*Please don't stop at me! Please don't stop at me!*

The bright red leather shoes stopped directly in front of Lottie.

'And this –' the woman loomed over Lottie, gesturing coldly at her with her cane – 'must be the notorious Maravish princess.' She lifted her nose up as if she were smelling something foul. 'I must say, I for one was expecting someone a little more stimulating. From what I've heard of you I fear even my expertise will be lost on a calamity such as yourself.' She slapped her cane into her hand, making a piercing thwack sound that echoed through the hall.

Lottie felt the dread sink into her stomach. After all her careful planning and preparation, it never occurred to her that she would have to remedy the reputation Ellie had already built for herself. She felt tears pricking the corners of her eyes and had to bite her cheek to stop herself from crying.

'I . . .'

'YOU WILL ONLY SPEAK WHEN SPOKEN TO!' Lady Priscilla's voice boomed, making Lottie nearly jump out of her skin in shock. The silence that followed was deafening. Lottie had never felt so humiliated in her life. She firmly believed there was no excuse *ever* to shout at someone like that, no matter what the circumstance. No one has the right to belittle anyone like that.

Lottie bit her cheek even harder, desperately willing herself not to say anything more. She thought of Anastacia, Saskia, Raphael and Jamie, who would all be watching her. She nodded slowly, looking straight ahead, thinking only of what it would mean for Ellie if she messed this up.

Lady Priscilla twitched her nose like a little rat and sniffed. 'Good.' She slapped her cane in her hand again. This time Lottie didn't even flinch. 'Now let us begin our first lesson.'

# 26

'WRONG!'

Lady Priscilla smacked her cane on the table next to Lottie. She had done this three times already but it never failed to make Lottie jump.

They were sitting at the large oak table that had been laid out with a full formal place setting for every student. There was a wide gap between Lottie and the two students on either side of her, as if they didn't want to catch the wrath of Lady Priscilla. They were practising the order of cutlery and the correct way to hold each item, but apparently Lottie was doing everything wrong.

The worst part was that she wasn't doing it wrong. Lottie *knew* she was doing it right – she'd studied this over and over, but each time Lady Priscilla somehow managed to find one tiny detail that she was messing up, from moving slightly too fast to having her feet crossed improperly. Lottie quickly realized there was nothing she could do except drown her ego, nod along, and say, 'Yes, ma'am.'

Anastacia and Raphael were adamantly avoiding eye contact with her, while Jamie remained completely unreadable with the rest of the left-wall ensemble. Lottie felt like a total outcast. It was all her worst nightmares come true: not only was she failing but she wasn't even blending in. Lady Priscilla was determined to make an example of her and there was nothing she could do about it.

*Ellie, what did you do to get this reputation? You've only ever met twenty people!*

Lottie fought on. She didn't think anything could get worse than the humiliating posture training, for which she was made to walk the hall twice in front of everyone while Lady Priscilla pointed out all her errors.

But she was wrong. It did get worse.

Lady Priscilla had them all stand in a line once more. Lottie was painfully aware of the large gap between her and the other students to her left and right.

'It's time for the most important lesson.' Lady Priscilla tapped her fingernails along the side of her cane, her thin little smile creeping on to her lips. 'You are going to practise the waltz.'

Lottie's stomach sank. She'd been so excited about waltz practice but now all she felt was pure terror.

'Everyone pair up. Chop-chop!'

*Oh my God! Pair up?*

No one was going to want to pair with her after she'd been singled out by Lady Priscilla so many times. The only thing that could make this worse was if she looked down and realized she was in her underwear. Lottie stood frozen in place as she watched all the other students find a dance partner.

'Oh dear.' The voice came harsh and cold behind her, not a hint of regret. 'It seems no one wants to dance with the sad little princess.' Lady Priscilla tapped her cane sharply. 'And if you can't do the waltz, then I'll have no choice but to fail you.' Lottie imagined a cruel smile on Lady Priscilla's lips as she said this.

Lottie gulped. If she failed the class, she'd fail Ellie too – she had to do something. She looked over at Jamie but knew as well as he did that assistants and bodyguards could not partake in the class. What could she do? She would not let this woman stop her going to the ball.

'I suppose you think dancing, along with all your other royal obligations, is completely asinine?' said Lady Priscilla, stepping round and aiming her steely glare on Lottie.

*Maybe Ellie's right. Maybe these people are as awful as she says!*

'No, please, I don't think –'

But Lady Priscilla cut her off. 'No one wants to dance with you because you are a *shrew*.'

Lottie mustered all her strength and discipline to stop herself from flinching – she would *not* give Lady Priscilla the satisfaction of seeing her react.

'Everyone knows about the untameable princess of Maradova, and if you think for a second I will be fooled by your quiet act today, you are as senseless as I expected.'

Lottie felt her fists clench at her sides. This woman didn't know anything about Ellie; she didn't know that she had taken time out of her day to help Lottie with her maths homework, that she went to the gym every evening because she was so determined to get into the fencing team, that she cared deeply about her friends and was trying her absolute best. Lottie suddenly empathized deeply with Ellie. She'd spent all this time baffled that Ellie wanted to escape being a princess, but, standing there being victimized by this snake of a woman, Lottie found herself suppressing an overwhelming temptation to rip her dress and trash the room. Ellie didn't fit into the cookie-cutter image of a girl, let alone a princess. She was unapologetic and ferocious and this aristocratic world resented her for it. Lottie felt her fists tighten even more. Ellie didn't deserve this, Ellie wouldn't take this, Ellie was better than this.

'How dare –' Lottie was ready to tear this nasty woman down when she was cut off.

'May I interject, Lady Priscilla?' The smooth voice came from behind. A surreal calm washed over her and she felt her anger slowly evaporating. She dared not turn round to put a face to the voice for fear of further irking Lady Priscilla. 'I would be much obliged to have the honour of dancing with the princess myself.' A gloved hand gently rested on Lottie's back, causing her to inhale sharply. 'I believe all she needs is a positive influence.'

Lady Priscilla's entire demeanour shifted instantly. Her shoulders relaxed and her face turned from sour to saccharine, as if this mysterious boy had melted all the ice within her.

'Why, Prince Ashwick, I could not allow you to take on that burden.'

Lottie felt a pang of irritation at 'burden' but was distracted by the word 'prince'.

The boy purred a soft laugh. 'Any shrew can be tamed with the right suitor, ma'am.'

Lady Priscilla lifted her head slowly, scrutinizing the two of them. Lottie shoved the insulting Shakespeare reference to the back of her mind, telling herself that whoever this boy was he must know that the only way to persuade Lady Priscilla was to agree with her.

'Very well, Edmund.' She gave her cane another thwack for good measure. 'Let's see if some of your outstanding discipline can be absorbed.' Lady Priscilla turned round abruptly and walked towards the record player. 'Everyone assume a starting position.'

At last, Lottie turned to face her partner and gasped out loud. *An angel!* He was beautiful. Prince Ashwick stood elegant and graceful before her, dressed in a princely white outfit with gilded shoulder pads. His blond hair reflected the light and seemed to be made of gold. He turned to her and bowed low, but with complete sincerity. As he straightened up, Lottie was greeted with a soft smile and warm hazel eyes that contrasted with his sharp bone structure.

'May I have the honour of dancing with you, Princess?'

Lottie was speechless. *Prince Charming is real and he rescued me.*

'Y-yes,' she said, breathlessly. The world seemed to melt around her as he took her hand into his own. His other hand rested delicately on her back, pulling her towards him. He smiled at her, a friendly glint in his eyes.

'Now, it is usually customary to bow or curtsy to your partner before the dance begins,' said Lady Priscilla sternly, 'but until I deem your dancing worthy enough, no one shall be bowing to anyone.'

The music began to swell into the room, an elegant ensemble of strings and piano that harmonized in a way that sounded magical.

'We shall begin with the simple box step. Hear the rhythm: one, two, three; one, two, three; one, two, three . . .'

The prince eased into the dance effortlessly, and Lottie found she could match his steps faultlessly, as if they were a mirror image of the other. He led her gracefully across the floor. Both in white, they were snowflakes in the cold room, gliding smoothly around the hall as if they were floating. She felt weightless in his arms, the rest of the world melting around her in a hazy cloud. She forgot Jamie; she forgot Anastacia and Raphael, her insomnia, the pressures of her role as Portman – it all dissolved with the music.

'You know you're far better at dancing than half the girls here.'

Lottie blushed involuntarily, feeling silly for finding the compliment so pleasing. She didn't know how to respond. He was just so . . . charming.

'You're not so bad yourself, I suppose.' Lottie shocked herself with how effortlessly she spoke. *Where did that come from?*

He chuckled, the sound vibrating softly against her ear, then he abruptly swung her into a twirl that she somehow managed to step into gracefully, spinning out and then back into his arms. Her heart was racing, her feet moving naturally in time to the music.

'I hope I'll get the chance to show you how *not so bad* I can be,' he added, smiling. She found herself giggling as they continued dancing in their dreamy cloud.

Then the music stopped, plummeting Lottie back to reality. She blinked, then looked around to discover that everyone was staring at them – silent, except for the occasional muffled

197

whisper with eyes like pointed fingers in their direction. Anastacia's expression was cold, her eyebrows furrowed in what appeared to be annoyance, and then she turned to Jamie. Lottie had never seen him look as terrifying as he did then. He seemed to be radiating anger, and all her fears of him came flooding back like ice down her spine.

*I must have really screwed up this time*, she thought, feeling deflated.

She turned back to Edmund – and he was . . . smiling! He caught her eye, then took a flamboyant step back and bowed. Lottie put her hand over her chest and flushed at the gesture.

'It was an honour to dance with you, Princess.'

Lottie felt weird being addressed in that way but couldn't stop her cheeks and her whole face going hot as her fellow students continued to stare.

'M-much obliged,' she replied, trying not to let her nerves show.

*Thwack!*

The sharp crack of Lady Priscilla's cane tore through the silence in the hall with a deafening echo.

'That,' she shrieked, all eyes turning to her abruptly, 'was absolutely, outrageously, the most *wonderful* display I've seen in any of my classes for years.'

Lottie had to stop herself from gasping. Had Lady Priscilla just *complimented* her?

'Elegant, precise – a gentleman and a lady blending into their roles effortlessly.' Lottie found herself bristling at this statement. *What roles?* she thought in annoyance, but quickly quashed her feelings. 'It was everything a waltz should be. Marvellous.'

Then Lady Priscilla clapped her hands, applauding while the rest of the students stood awkward and confused. Her face had become almost comical, gushing so much that she looked as if she would burst into tears. Prince Ashwick winked at Lottie and she felt her whole body light up and looked away quickly to hide her blushes.

The class was breezy from then on. As long as Lottie was standing by the prince, Lady Priscilla was more than satisfied with her efforts, even though Lottie was painfully aware that she was doing everything exactly as she had before.

Lottie occasionally caught Jamie's eye. He no longer wore his disinterested blank-faced expression. Instead his jaw seemed permanently clenched, as if she were doing something very wrong, which didn't make any sense as Lady Priscilla was clearly overjoyed with her. When the class came to an end, Lottie was feeling a little smug. She'd gone from Lady Priscilla's most despised student to a 'shining example of how young girls can flourish when they step up to their responsibilities'.

Raphael had to cover his mouth to stop laughing, while Anastacia looked intensely annoyed for no particular reason. She nodded to Lottie briskly as they all left the hall. Saskia smiled sweetly at her and wiggled her fingers in a little wave.

'We have to leave. Now.' Jamie's voice came out low and cold behind Lottie, making her shiver.

Edmund narrowed his eyes at Jamie, then sighed dramatically.

'Well, it seems our time together is cut short, Princess Wolfson.' He stroked a lock of Lottie's hair, letting the silky blonde strand intertwine in his fingers. 'I will find a way to contact you.' He gently took Lottie's hand, before raising it to his lips and planting a soft kiss that sent sparks through her body. 'I eagerly anticipate our next encounter.' He winked at her before adding, 'I'm sure you understand why,' then he turned dramatically to the door as two terrifyingly large men materialized by his side to escort him out.

'Bye . . .' Lottie replied breathlessly after him.

Jamie began walking her back to the Ivy dorm. He was obviously angry, but Lottie was too elated from her encounter with Prince Edmund Ashwick to take in his sour mood.

'I could've danced all day and never got bored. Did you see how impressed Lady Priscilla was?'

Jamie's eyebrows furrowed, but Lottie simply danced around him as they walked through the grounds, skipping happily and giggling to herself in the waning rose-tinted light.

'I was brave and kind and I was totally unstoppable – aren't you pleased with me?'

'Yes, Lottie, I'm very pleased. Now listen . . .'

'Wasn't it magical? Lady Priscilla's face was priceless. It was like something out of a story, and Edmund –'

'Lottie, listen, you can't –'

'He's like no boy I've ever met before. He's the real deal; he's a real-life Prince Charming!'

'Lottie, you can't –'

'I'm so happy I could just –'

'LOTTIE, YOU ARE ABSOLUTELY, UNDER NO CIRCUMSTANCES TO SPEAK TO PRINCE ASHWICK AGAIN.'

Lottie froze and took in the furious resolution on Jamie's face. That had not been what she was expecting at all.

## 27

'EDMUND ASHWICK?'

Ellie's voice shrieked through their room loud enough to make Lottie's princess mug shake on the table. 'But he's a complete piece of –'

'You're forbidden from interacting with him, Lottie,' Jamie interrupted.

Ellie was pulling her fingers through her hair, filling the room with stress as she paced back and forth. Lottie sat firmly on her bed with her hands clasped in her lap, trying not to get annoyed that they were treating her like a stupid child.

'I think you're both failing to remember that he saved me in that class. Without him Lady Priscilla probably would have made me leave, blocking me from attending the Maravish Summer Ball.' Lottie tried to keep her voice as calm as possible after Ellie's erratic tone.

'He's gotta be a total sleazeball.'

'But Lady Priscilla –'

'Lady Priscilla is a backwards traditionalist bitch and if she likes you because of your association with Edmund then you definitely don't want anything to do with him.'

Ellie was furious. Lottie could practically see bolts of static electrifying the air around her.

As soon as the class had finished, Jamie had demanded an emergency meeting in their dorm room. Lottie had protested on the grounds that they might get caught, but she'd been overruled as Jamie could just dive off the balcony if he needed to – something Lottie actually kind of wanted to see.

'It's sick, *sick*, I tell you, that that . . . slimy toad Ashwick . . . I bet he thinks . . .' Ellie shivered then looked up at Lottie with a new conviction on her face. 'Lottie, I think we need to explain to you about my reputation.'

Lottie's brows furrowed. It was something she'd been curious about herself.

'Last year . . .' Ellie began, 'gossip was spread about me, saying I did all these things I didn't do. It said I was caught drinking with a guy at a rock concert and that's why I was being hidden away from the public. It spiralled out of control and people started saying I was going to be just like my uncle. It's all completely stupid.' Ellie looked away, her hands clenched in frustration.

Lottie's heart ached for Ellie – she understood her paranoia. *This is why she doesn't trust anyone.*

'Ellie, I think we need to start trusting people,' said Lottie gently. 'Maybe Edmund really wants to get to know the princess. Maybe there are people who want to know the real you . . . He was very kind and . . .'

Ellie's face softened as she saw the disappointment in Lottie's eyes.

'It's not just that, Lottie. If it did go sour with Edmund, think about all the gossip. It could further damage my reputation.' Ellie was trying to sound calmer but there was tension in her voice. Lottie didn't understand what Ellie meant. *What could go sour?*

'Well, shouldn't you know better than anyone what it feels like to have people make assumptions about you?'

*Maybe Edmund was the same. Maybe he was being misjudged.*

Ellie sighed as if Lottie was being a petulant child instead of a girl wanting to confess that she'd met the love of her life.

'You need to trust us, Lottie.' Ellie's voice was quieter now, but she still wore her fiery expression.

'Maybe you have to trust *me*!' Lottie exclaimed, standing up to face Ellie head-on. 'We can't judge a person based on rumours and hearsay. Surely you of all people can understand that.'

'Lottie, for once in your life would you stop being so painfully naive.'

Lottie jolted at the severity of Jamie's tone. She turned to see his face twisted into a furious scowl, and a cold feeling spread through her body. 'You're just a foolish little girl who's obsessed with fairy tales. You're being childish and you're going to put Ellie at risk.'

Lottie found herself lost for words. She stood frozen, tears pricking her eyes as she tried to compose herself. She was used to being called naive – she was even used to people thinking her interests were childish – but it was a whole different thing when she was being told her attitude could hurt someone else. She'd worked hard in that class and thought maybe she'd finally proved to Jamie she was capable. She'd failed: she'd failed to impress him and she'd apparently failed Ellie. It took all of her willpower not to burst out sobbing in front of them.

'I'm . . . so . . .' Lottie whimpered.

Ellie let out a massive frustrated groan. 'You,' she said, pointing at Jamie, 'shut up for a minute.' She turned back to Lottie and grabbed her by the shoulders, forcing her to look directly into her eyes. That storm was there, thundering in the background, yet Lottie felt calmed by it.

'Now listen to me, Lottie – *really* listen.' She took a deep breath. 'It's OK for you to daydream about boys –' the twitchiness in her voice suggested this was difficult for her to say – 'and I love that you try to see the good in everyone and, who knows, maybe Edmund really doesn't have an ulterior motive. I love you and all your wonderful quirks and I will never, *ever* call you naive.' She paused to scowl at Jamie. 'But –' she took another breath as she mentally prepared herself – 'I don't want you to be disappointed if things don't turn out the way you expect.'

'Ellie.' Lottie breathed her name softly, letting it clear her mind as it floated off her tongue. Guilt grew inside her as she looked at the pain on her friend's face. She didn't want them to worry about her; she needed to reassure them that she was capable of handling herself. She forced a smile, wondering what she'd actually do if Edmund contacted her.

'I promise you guys can count on me,' she said determinedly.

Ellie looked at her, her mouth breaking into her little side smile, though it didn't quite reach her eyes.

'Well, either way, Jamie's not allowed to shout at you any more. I'm forbidding it.' She paused before holding her index finger in the air. 'That's a royal order.'

Suddenly remembering he was in the room, Lottie turned to him, expecting to see him still furious and determined, ready to roll his eyes and lecture them both about the seriousness of their positions, but instead he looked . . . pained. He was looking away and one hand reached up and rubbed his forehead in a way that indicated stress. The guilty feeling in her stomach doubled. Once again she was overcome by the sad idea that Jamie had had to deal with far more responsibility than most other boys his age did. It was no wonder he reacted so harshly; Ellie and her reputation had to come first.

'Don't worry, Jamie.' She waited until he looked at her. 'I understand.'

They held their gaze for a moment and he nodded. She knew he understood what she meant, but now she had to prove it. *Ellie has to come first*, she repeated to herself.

'OK . . . are we all calm now?' Ellie quipped.

'I think so.' Lottie turned back to Jamie and put on her best happy expression. 'Now, Jamie, you've got to leave. Ellie has homework to finish and I think we could all do with some downtime.'

Jamie allowed a half smile to creep on to his lips as he turned to leave.

'Very well. I'll see you both tomorrow morning,' he said as he reached for the door handle. 'Oh, and, Lottie –' he caught her eye, the half smile still on his lips – 'try to get some sleep tonight.'

'Of course,' she said cheerfully, but a thick feeling of dread filled her stomach.

The door clicked shut and she pulled out the sleeping tablets Anastacia had given her. Something told her things were not going to get any less exhausting any time soon.

# 28

The end of the first term was fast approaching. Icicles lined the eaves of the school buildings and the pond outside the Ivy dorm had frozen over. Every day the sky threatened to snow, yet every day the air remained icy and still. It turned out it was easy not to speak to Edmund as there was no obvious way for them to stay in touch with the phone ban. Lottie had been working extra hard to be a 'perfect princess' since Jamie had lost his temper with her, partly because she didn't want anyone to see how tired she was but mostly because she realized how important it was to help fix Ellie's tarnished image.

*Be kind*, she reminded herself.

One Thursday evening was particularly quiet so the girls took the opportunity, before the rush of winter exams and the approaching fencing try-outs, to solve Binah's puzzle. Lottie reread the passage she thought contained the clue, hoping the answer would reveal itself.

> *And now within the master's office,*
> *Where he looks down on his house,*
> *His gaze on them with a gaze on him*
> *Of the Vixen and the Delicate Mouse.*

Ellie stared at Lottie as she recited the poem again. They stood at the foot of the stone stairs to the headmaster's office. The heart of the school.

'So "he" must be William Tufty,' Lottie deduced. 'And surely this must be "the master's office", right? I don't think it's talking about the one in Ivy Wood. So there has to be a painting of Tufty in the head's office,' she added. 'It's the only plausible interpretation.'

'I'll have to take your word for it.' Ellie raised her eyebrows. She was not the best at finding symbolism and hidden meaning in words, preferring numbers over letters.

'You really should brush up on riddles and clues,' Lottie cautioned. 'What if you need to solve one to get out of a sticky situation some day?' The scenario seemed unlikely but it was something she'd read in the Portman's diary. An old story of an eastern European royal's Partizan, who'd sent a coded message in a letter back to the kingdom by spelling the family dog's name wrong so they'd know she was being held captive. After reading this, Lottie had decided that you could never be too ready.

Ellie smirked, clearly not taking her riddle advice seriously.

'How did your first tutoring session with Saskia go?' she asked unexpectedly. Something about the way she said Saskia's name irritated Lottie.

'It was fine.' *I wish it was with you, though*, she added in her head.

'Just *fine*? I thought it was really cool of Saskia to offer to tutor you. I'd be thrilled.'

Lottie couldn't figure out why she was being so cagey about it. Saskia *was* a great teacher; she just felt weird when Ellie talked about her.

'It was great – she's great and I'm learning loads. Is that better?' Lottie realized she sounded an awful lot like Anastacia had back in the library and looked away embarrassed. 'Sorry, I think I'm just . . . tired, and I don't want you thinking her tutoring is better than yours.'

Ellie's face softened and she chuckled sympathetically. 'Well, of course she's not better than me,' she said, laughing. 'I just want to make sure she's good enough to tutor you.' Lottie couldn't help grinning at this. 'Now come on. We have some mysteries to solve.' Ellie grabbed her hand and they marched up the stone stairs together.

The plan was simple. They would knock on the door under the guise of wanting to ask about the history of the school for a class project. While they were inside, Lottie would examine the painting and look for any clues.

The large curved oak door to the headmaster's office had two twisted metal handles in the middle. The carved thorns and roses on them had been worn away over four hundred years of use, and were barely visible. Lottie took a deep breath as she knocked. The headmaster was a mystery to her. She was now so familiar with Dame Bolter, Ms Kuma and Professor Devine, but Headmaster Croak kept to himself, an invisible force quietly working away in the background.

She knocked twice and waited. There was no answer. Ellie looked at the door in annoyance then knocked even louder. Still no response.

'Hellooo! Anyone in? Excuse meee!' Ellie bellowed as she banged on the door with her fists.

Lottie nudged her. '*Ellie!*' she whispered harshly.

Ellie laughed, giving her the side smile that made it impossible to stay mad at her.

'Well, I guess he's not in,' she said, banging on the door again for good measure.

Lottie looked down in defeat. Their plan had seemed so simple and easy. She'd never considered the headmaster wouldn't be in.

She sighed. 'I guess we'll have to try again some other time.'

Ellie let out a single sarcastic laugh as she leaned on the entrance, completely disrespecting the authority of the door. 'Or we could just sneak in and take a look for ourselves. I'm sure that's what *the Vixen* would have wanted,' she said with a cocky grin.

'Ellie, we can't. That's too –'

But before she could finish, Ellie had turned the metal handle and pushed the heavy double door open like it was no big deal at all.

*I can't believe I'm doing this.*

This was definitely not 'perfect princess' behaviour, but she didn't stop herself following Ellie.

The headmaster's office was not what Lottie had expected. When she imagined this central point of the school – the room that held the most power and authority – large looming furniture and opulent ornamentation came to mind. Instead she found a quaint hexagonal room with a modest mahogany desk in the centre and piles of papers and books covering every inch of floor space. It almost seemed as if the room contained every document and book ever accumulated in the four hundred years that Rosewood Hall had existed. But there was one thing in the room that stood out: a gargantuan, gold-framed painting that peered down over the room with all-seeing eyes.

William Tufty.

'He's almost as messy as me,' Ellie said, giggling, sidestepping a pile of red books in an attempt to get closer to the painting. Lottie would have laughed, but she found herself completely mesmerized by Tufty's gaze. He sat within the painting, little half-moon glasses on the bridge of his nose, eyes staring down at her. There was a glimmer of thoughtfulness in his expression that the painter had perfectly captured in the soft way his lips turned up at the edges. His hands were clasped in his lap holding a small, circular mirror with a murky reflection of him. His delicate frame was a stark contrast to the vastness of the main hall in the background. Lottie narrowed her eyes at this depiction of William Tufty, at the way he looked out at them with a knowing smile.

*The Vixen and the Delicate Mouse.*

What did Binah want them to know? Lottie was about to articulate her feelings when a gruff male voice behind them said, 'He's quite fantastic, isn't he?'

Both girls almost jumped out of their skin. Headmaster Croak stood by the door, one hand planted firmly on a simple wooden cane.

'Headmaster Croak . . . we're so sorry . . . we . . .' Lottie trailed off, suddenly unable to speak. *You're going to get expelled*, a nasty voice inside her head whispered, a voice that for some reason sounded horribly like her stepmother. She looked at Ellie, who was also frozen. Lottie knew that getting in trouble would be far worse for her. She tried again. 'We were just waiting for you to –'

The headmaster laughed, a throaty guffaw. 'Oh hush! You think you're the first students to ever be wooed by the siren call of Sir William Tufty?' He let out a soft chuckle as he took a shaky step into the office. 'I had your friend Miss Binah Fae in here gazing up with that same look not more than a month into her first year at Rosewood.' Lottie felt a strange sense of comfort in this, that Binah had been caught too – and that thought quashed the voice of her stepmother.

'Sorry,' said the two girls in unison.

The headmaster smiled again. Then he turned to the painting, his face turning pensive as he gazed at the founder of the school. 'He was a very wise and extremely reserved man.'

Lottie regarded the patient face of William Tufty. There was something there, something she couldn't quite place.

'I've heard he was a kind man,' the headmaster said, turning to Ellie and Lottie and smiling. His face was wrinkled, covered in lines of experience and emotion. He tapped his cane thoughtfully before continuing. 'But his greatest attribute was his ability to be quiet.' Croak laughed to himself and Ellie cocked an eyebrow at Lottie, wondering if she'd heard him correctly. 'Sometimes the world can get very loud and people can get caught up trying to get their own voice heard and they end up silencing those that really need the space to speak. William understood this, and he used his position in the world to give others the chance to speak.' He turned his eyes to his weathered hands. 'I try my best to emulate that about him.'

Lottie wasn't sure why but this information resonated with her. She looked up at the painting again.

*Hide-and-seek.*

The frame around Tufty's image. She knew there was something there.

*Every day they'd play a game . . . she hid inside the painting frames.*

'And I hope I can be wise like he was, and give quiet to those that need it.'

*Wise and quiet.*

Lottie stared into the eyes of the man in the painting, then at Ellie, the girl living a dual life, secretly hiding in the guise of Ellie Wolf.

*The Vixen and the Delicate Mouse.* An explosive feeling erupted in her chest, a feeling like a distant memory crystallizing in her mind and she asked herself, *If William is the Delicate Mouse, then who is the Vixen?* Lottie looked up at the painting again and finally saw it.

'Thank you,' she said calmly.

The headmaster smiled at her, giving the signal that they were dismissed.

She gave Ellie a meaningful look, letting her know she'd figured out something important.

They walked down the stairs and out of the main building, pulling on their big coats and scarves. Ellie looked at Lottie but could see she was thinking very hard about something and, remembering the headmaster's words, gave her the silence she needed.

Once they were heading towards the Ivy dorm, Lottie paused – and Ellie paused too.

'I think . . .' Lottie lifted her fingers to her lips, not just in thought but as if conjuring a memory. 'I think William Tufty might not have been born who he became.' Ellie's face cocked to the side inquisitively. 'I mean,' Lottie continued, 'I think he was born a woman.'

'*What?*' Ellie asked in confusion. 'How do you know?'

'Do you know *The Arnolfini Portrait*?' asked Lottie.

Ellie shook her head.

'Well, in it, the artist hid himself in the background, in a mirror. Mirrors in art can symbolize many things, but they're most often associated with women, truth and, of course, reflection. I could tell there was something slightly off about Tufty's painting, and then I realized. The entire painting is reflected in the tiny mirror in Tufty's hand, all exactly the same, except one crucial detail. Tufty is painted as a fox.' Ellie's eyes widened. It was such an easy detail to miss if you weren't actively looking for it. You might just think it was a blurry image. 'The Vixen and the Delicate Mouse – they're both him; that's what the painting and the rhyme are saying.' She looked at Ellie in excitement. 'Whoever or whatever they were born as, they hid themselves as William Tufty, and that's who they were happiest being.'

'He's a little like me then,' Ellie breathed, her gaze distant.

Lottie nodded. 'I wonder who they were,' she wondered out loud.

'I don't know if it matters,' Ellie replied, a small melancholy smile on her lips. 'They were who they were and we should respect that.'

Lottie nodded again. If they were meant to find out Tufty's identity, she was sure they would one day.

Ellie's face went blank and then a look of comprehension crept into her eyes. Lottie suddenly knew what she was thinking.

*Binah knows.*

## 29

Lottie saw little of Jamie and Ellie over the next few days. She used all her time to study for their exams while Ellie focused on training for her fencing try-outs – both of which forced them to put Binah's puzzle and the revelation about Tufty out of their minds. For now there were more important things that they needed to think about.

The Rosewood Hall fencing team was one of the most highly regarded in the world, not simply because it had produced numerous Olympians but also because it was believed that joining the team would cast a spell on you. It was a centuries-old superstition that ordained you would be destined to be adored. Lottie had a feeling it was because the requirements of the team probably meant you were pretty cool already, but it was still a fun story.

One evening the tiered benches were packed with students of all three houses, yellow, red and purple, elegantly dotted among the stalls. Today they would be picking five Year Ten students who would be allowed to choose fencing as their option for the rest of their school years. Lottie envied anyone who'd picked an extracurricular class already. She'd only glanced at the list and found it horribly overwhelming.

215

*Antiques; archaeology; astronomy; badminton; canoeing; cheese appreciation; choir; classical studies; clay pigeon shooting; coding; debating; engineering; equestrian training; events planning; fencing; figure skating; film-making and theory; fine art (introduction to); fine dining; French; garden design; German; high fashion and design; horticulture; Japanese; jewellery making; kick-boxing; Latin (introduction to); law (introduction to); Mandarin; orchestra; Patisserie craft; philosophy; photography; poetry; sculpture; swimming (lane); swimming (synchronized); tea appreciation; tennis; theatre (drama); theatre (light and sound); theatre (set design); wrestling . . .*

The list seemed to go on forever and Lottie still had no idea what she should want to do. Lottie was feeling particularly rundown that evening. She'd got used to being permanently tired but today it seemed no matter how much coffee she drank she couldn't push the dizziness from her head. She was trying her best to hide this from her friends but found it difficult when they were all so close to her. Jamie and Raphael were sitting to her right, leaning close to each other, talking in their usual hushed tones. Saskia was sitting a few stalls above with some girls from her year, but she quickly came to say hi upon spotting Lottie.

'I was hoping to find Ellie before the try-outs and wish her good luck.' Saskia looked around as if hoping she might spot Ellie. *A perfect head of year*, Lottie thought begrudgingly, then quickly reminded herself that that wasn't a very 'kind' thought for someone who was taking time out of their week to tutor her.

'Thank you, Saskia. I'll let her know when I see her.'

Saskia smiled at her before running back to join the girls in her year, and Lottie turned to take a seat with the others.

Lola and Micky were scoffing a giant bag of pick-and-mix on her left; it was truly a wonder how they remained so small with the amount of sweets they consumed. The only person missing was –

'I wonder if they'll spar with a foil, épée or sabre?'

'Hello, Binah,' the group said in unison.

Lottie had become accustomed to her ability to appear out of nowhere, not even flinching when her voice miraculously chimed behind her. Lottie and Ellie both felt a little different around Binah now, not knowing how much she actually knew about the princess and the Portman situation, and knowing that they couldn't really ask her.

'Good evening, my fellow spectators!' Binah took a seat between Lottie and Lola. Her hair was up in two massive puffs on each side of her head, which somehow gave the impression of puppy ears. Lola wordlessly held out a yellow sweet that Binah popped in her mouth. She readjusted her glasses, causing the light to reflect off the lenses, obscuring her eyes. 'Lottie!'

*Please don't mention the princess thing, please don't mention the princess thing.*

Jamie squinted at Lottie and she held her breath, worrying that he could read her mind.

Binah simply smiled at her and pulled out a wispy-patterned green box from her bag. 'I got this for you; I thought you might need it.'

Lottie read the words on the top of the lid:

SLEEPY-TIME TEA: TO COMBAT STRESS

AND HELP YOU SLUMBER

217

Lottie blinked at the box for a moment. *Oh, come on! Does everyone in the school know I'm not sleeping?* On second thoughts Lottie realized that it was silly to think there was anything Binah didn't know.

'Thank you, Binah . . . I'll give it a go.' She smiled back at her with as much positivity as she could, desperately trying not to let on to how tired she really was. Binah gave her a soft look and gently rubbed her arm as if she could sense that Lottie was putting up a brave front.

'Sometimes the gifts people give us can help in more ways than we expect.' She winked and Lottie was sure she heard a little twinkle in the air as she did so.

How could sleepy-time tea possibly help her in other ways?

She began to rack her brain, knowing now that Binah's riddles were not to be taken lightly, but was quickly jolted back into the world when a horn blared out. It was time.

Dame Bolter stepped forward, effortlessly capturing the attention of the hall with her fierce authority. She was accompanied by a young man with fluffy brown ringlets, who stood a few steps back; Lottie instantly recognized him as the Year Thirteen fencing captain and head of Conch House, Jacob Zee. He was a big name at Rosewood to say the least and he was definitely 'adored'. Their vibes were comically different: Dame Bolter a scorching blaze and Jacob a soft, delicate brook. It was hard to believe they were from the same house.

'Good evening, students of Rosewood.' Dame Bolter's voice boomed through the gymnasium, effortlessly intimidating as usual. 'Tonight marks our three hundredth anniversary of the fencing trials. Today we will pick five students from Year

Ten who will be honoured with an invitation to join the Rosewood Hall fencing team next year.' She paused for a moment to take in the room and Lottie was sure her eyes lingered for an extra second on her. 'This is a grand turnout tonight and I expect the utmost respect from your spectatorship.' She turned to Jacob. 'Any words of encouragement for our young hopefuls?' He smiled brightly at her before bowing ever so slightly in respect, an act so subtle Lottie almost missed it. Lottie heard a few coos and titters as Jacob stepped forward, the same reaction she was used to hearing whenever Jamie entered a room.

'Today is not about winning your fights; it's about showing the most potential. There's some wonderful promise here tonight and I'm only sad that I won't get to lead you next year after I graduate. Good luck, everyone.' He directed his happy smile at the line of prospective fencing hopefuls.

It was impossible to tell which ones were Ellie and Anastacia. These was a line of twenty almost identical statues, their faces covered by mesh masks and bodies shielded by matching white uniforms. They were completely void of gender or personhood, transformed into a group of robotic dancers. One of them broke off from the group and flexed their muscles before turning to the others and shouting, 'BRING IT ON, LOSERS!'

*Yep, that's Ellie.*

Lottie turned to see Jamie cover his face with his palm and she had to stifle a giggle. A loud boom of laughter could be heard from the left side of the hall. It was Professor Devine, who leaned against the wall of the gymnasium, her presence somehow outshining the spectacular marble statues on either side of the giant door. Lottie gulped; she'd had no idea the professor would be attending and suddenly felt a thousand times more nervous for Ellie, even though Ellie didn't appear to be nervous at all.

The first match began. Two of the white-clad androids walked up to what Lottie had decided to call the 'stage' as the whole thing seemed so intensely theatrical. They bowed to each other before beginning and that was about all Lottie could keep up with. As soon as the match began, their swords were moving too fast for her to follow, a blur of white and silver elegantly parrying one another. It became clear that the person on the right was the one to watch; they moved with such lightning speed that their opponent could barely get a single strike against a barrage of unstoppable hits. She looked over to see Jamie and Raphael watching the match with squinted eyes, then back at Saskia, who winked.

Binah was grinning broadly. 'I wonder who that could be . . .'

The next match began, then the next, and Lottie found that she was being lulled by the movements, mesmerized by each feint and attack. She'd lost track again of which one was Ellie. The only one Lottie was aware of was the unbeatable person from the first match. She wished she understood more about the sport so she could know for certain who was doing the best, but she was worried that if she asked anyone they'd think it was odd for her not to know, so she kept her mouth shut and allowed herself to be hypnotized by the strange dance.

Dame Bolter called for the final match and the unbeatable person walked up to the stage to take on the other strongest competitor. The tension in the room seemed to triple as the two faced each other and the intensity emanating from the two duellers was palpable. This match felt different to the others. The two bowed and the atmosphere seemed to light up with prickly electricity. And then it began.

Their swords moved in furious flashes, the two fighters darting and lunging with such intricate precision that they seemed more like deadly ballet dancers than fifteen-year-old students. This time it was impossible to tell who was on top; when one forced the other to retreat, they effortlessly disengaged and brought the fight back to the centre until the other took over again. They twirled and twisted, bodies consistently taut, two relentless forces persistently attacking and feinting in a barrage of complex tricks. Lottie tried to keep focused, but her mind kept slipping. It felt as though with each clash of their swords a strange dark feeling filled Lottie's head, making her thoughts turn cloudy and confused.

And then it was over. In her haze, Lottie couldn't tell who had won.

The two duellers walked up to each other and began to remove their masks. The whole audience collectively held their breath. The unbeatable fighter pulled hers off and a cascade of luscious chestnut hair came loose. Lottie gasped at the sight of Anastacia, elegantly shaking out her hair. Standing there in her white gear, sword by her side, she looked ferocious and forthright enough to take on a whole army. Those in the audience wearing red began cheering wildly.

Slowly the other contestant pulled off her own mask and a thick mop of black sweat-drenched hair appeared.

A *prince!*

Lottie felt a sudden rush of heat enter her cheeks as she took in her room-mate. Ellie smirked at the audience as they cheered for her. Anastacia and Ellie held their hands out to each other and shook. As soon as their hands met, Lottie felt it – a swell of exhaustion hit her hard like a wave crashing over her and she swayed involuntarily.

*Focus, Lottie, this is Ellie's big moment.*

The hopefuls moved to stand in a line at the back of the stage, all masks off now. Dame Bolter cleared her throat as she approached the podium to speak.

'I will now read the names of the five students we have chosen to join the team.'

Lottie felt her breath catch in her throat; something was wrong. Her body felt as if it were suddenly moving in slow motion.

'Ellie Wolf.'

The audience cheered. Lottie tried to join in, but the dizzy sensation was overpowering her.

*I need to sleep*, she thought desperately, but there was something else, something clawing at the back of her mind.

'Marzia Hart.' The cheering began to get distant and Lottie helplessly bashed her hands against her ears, trying to will some clarity into her mind. What had Binah said about gifts again?

'Thomas Carter.' She looked up at the duellers, but their white armour seemed to be fading in front of her. Everything started turning black and she desperately tried to blink it away.

'Lottie, are you OK?' The voice was coming from Binah, but Lottie pushed her aside to get to the stairs.

'Riyadh Murphy.'

Lottie desperately began wading through cheering people. The world seemed to be spinning round like she was stuck on a nightmare carousel. She frantically racked her brain to figure out what her mind was trying to tell her.

'And, finally, the last person joining the Rosewood Hall fencing team will be . . .' The world was fading around her fast and her footsteps began to swerve as she reached the bottom of the steps.

'Anastacia Alcroft.'

The name smacked into her head, igniting a niggling thought until it burned so bright it blocked out all others . . .

*Anastacia's gift . . . The Princess and the Pea!*

She turned sharply in confusion just in time to catch a glimpse of Jamie's concerned face in front of her. 'There's something under my mattress,' she cried out over the noise of the crowd.

And then the world around her blacked out.

# 30

*I need to get off this carousel or I'm going to be sick!*

Something was spinning her round and round and she wanted it to stop.

'Lottie?'

*That's Jamie's voice.*

The distant voice called her name, but she couldn't quite get hold of it.

'Lottie, can you hear me?'

*Why is the room spinning so much?*

'Lottie, you need to wake up now. Lottie, hello?'

*Wait, it's not the room spinning. I'm spinning . . . I fainted . . . Where am I? Who did this?*

'Princess and the Pea!' Lottie jerked awake suddenly to see a crowd of people around her. Her eyes focused and she looked up into the face of a very worried Professor Devine.

'Sounds like you were having an interesting dream there, Lottie.' A concerned smile was on the professor's lips and Lottie instantly felt awful. She couldn't stand the thought of worrying anyone.

'Sorry, I . . . my bed.' Lottie fought to get the words out, desperately trying to form her thoughts into sentences through the haze in her head. 'I need to get to bed.'

She tried to sit up, pushing herself away from the professor's arms. Ellie and Jamie instantly appeared at her side to assist her, and the sinking feeling in her stomach returned as she took in Ellie in her pristine white fencing gear, hair slicked back.

*I ruined the tournament*, she thought despairingly.

'You've only been out for two minutes.'

Lottie perked up at Jamie's words, feeling a creepy sense that he'd just read her mind again.

'Now what was that about your bed?' Jamie looked at her very seriously, even for him. Ellie too seemed uncharacteristically severe.

'Yes . . . I have to get to bed. I seem to have remembered how to sleep.' She smiled at Jamie and held his gaze as she spoke, trying to convey that she wanted to tell him something – something important. He and Ellie exchanged a look, intimating that they understood the intention of Lottie's words.

'Absolutely not, Miss Charlotte,' blared out Dame Bolter's voice. 'You need to go straight to the infirmary to see Nurse Sani.'

Lottie didn't have time for this; she needed to know if her hunch was true. She turned to Professor Devine and gave her a pleading look. 'Please! I just need to get to bed!'

Her house mother raised an eyebrow and Lottie wondered if she might question her plea. But then the professor smiled at Dame Bolter and said reassuringly, 'Actually, Mercy, I think in this instance some good sleep is what's in order.'

Dame Bolter looked at Lottie suspiciously. 'Maybe so . . .' she said slowly.

The professor clapped her hands. 'Chop-chop, then. Jamie, would you kindly help Ellie take Lottie back to her room so we can finish this ceremony?'

'Yes, Professor,' they replied in unison.

The three walked out of the hall, both supporting Lottie, their arms round her waist. As they walked past Anastacia, Lottie thought she saw her clench her fists in a strange display of fury.

'Princess and the Pea,' Lottie said resolutely, her hands placed firmly on her hips.

'Yep, she's gone mad from no sleep. Told ya.'

Lottie scowled at Ellie, who was giggling at her own joke. Jamie and Ellie sat on Ellie's bed as if they were in a class and Lottie was their teacher. It always amused Lottie how perfectly the two of them blended into Ellie's dark, edgy side of the room.

'No, that's my clue,' Lottie said, rolling her eyes. 'Don't you remember the fairy tale?'

Ellie shrugged, but Jamie nodded.

'They place a pea under twenty mattresses and they know that the girl sleeping on them is a princess because she can feel the pea during the night and it stops her sleeping.'

'Ahh, yes,' Ellie said with a grin on her face. 'I can't sleep either when I need to pee.' Lottie snorted and quickly covered her mouth, and even Jamie allowed a taut smile to crawl on

226

to his face. 'But seriously,' Ellie continued, 'you think there's a pea under your bed?'

'Honestly I don't know . . . I just feel there's something . . .' Lottie turned to stare at the bed. It didn't look inviting any more; it felt as though something dark were nesting within it and she wanted it gone. The two nodded at Lottie in understanding and began wordlessly getting to work.

Lottie grabbed Mr Truffles and they proceeded to throw all the bedding and pillows on to Ellie's bed. Jamie walked over when they were done and effortlessly lifted the mattress as if it weighed no more than a feather. Lottie held her breath . . . and there it was.

In the centre of the mattress, taped down, was a piece of paper showing a wolf's head within a circle, crossed through with two thick red lines.

Ellie gasped and raised a hand to her mouth.

Jamie let out a furious curse. Lottie almost couldn't believe she'd heard him swear but this was not the time to protest.

'What is it?' she asked timidly. She almost didn't want to know; it had to be awful to get such a strong reaction from the two of them.

Jamie pulled the paper off the mattress and stormed over to the desk, slamming it down with such force it made Lottie jump. Ellie stared blank-faced at the desk, an eerie sense of calm exuding from her.

'That's the Wolfson House sigil,' Ellie said vacantly. 'And it's got a death mark through it.'

# 31

'We're telling your parents.'

'*BRIKTAH!*' Lottie cringed at the Maravish word as Ellie snapped out of her daze. 'No, we're not.'

Jamie was already flattening the paper, clearly with the intent of getting a copy back to Maradova as fast as possible. Ellie grabbed at him wildly, scratching and pushing to try to get it, but Jamie held her off easily. Lottie stood, stupefied and useless. Someone had put that paper there, probably someone she knew.

Another thought pinged into her mind and she felt sick. *It must have been the person who left the gift at the beginning of term. It's a curse and that's why I couldn't sleep – and somehow Anastacia had known about it.*

Ellie and Jamie continued to battle it out, the piece of paper with the death mark seeming to exude a negative energy. Lottie imagined tendrils of wispy dark smoke oozing off it and filling the room with a toxic tension.

It was here to scare the princess; it was here to scare her out of Rosewood.

'Jamie, you can't.' The words came out of Lottie's mouth before she even registered her own thoughts.

'But, Lottie, you might be in danger.' His voice was strained and it caught her off guard.

'So?' Lottie replied, feigning a calm demeanour. 'Isn't that the point of my job as Portman?' Jamie eased slightly and turned to meet her eyes. 'I deal with all the danger and problems so that Ellie doesn't have to,' Lottie continued. 'So that Ellie can *stay* at Rosewood.'

Lottie faced them, determined that whoever had done this would not jeopardize Ellie's time at Rosewood – she would not let them win. They would find out who was doing this no matter what.

Jamie released a long breath, then turned to Ellie and his expression seemed almost disappointed.

'Is this what you wanted?' Jamie hissed at Ellie in a low voice, barely audible to Lottie.

Ellie looked at the floor, a shadow hiding the unmistakable look of shame on her face. She refused to look at him, continuing to stare downwards.

'No, stop. You aren't listening to me,' Lottie said, surprising herself with her own determination. 'If Ellie gets taken away, then they win and the threat still remains. With me here we can lure them out. Whoever they are, they're getting bolder – we can catch them.'

Ellie flinched and Lottie realized what she'd just said. She was about to speak again but Jamie stopped her. His face was cold.

'Has something happened before?'

Lottie felt her breath catch in her throat. *Crap.*

Jamie slowly put the paper down and turned back to her, but she was unable to form any words. 'I asked you a question,

229

Lottie.' He gave her a look so forceful she could almost feel the blow.

'Yes,' she replied, unable to hold eye contact.

He turned to Ellie and she didn't look away this time.

'On the first day of school,' she said, straight-faced, 'Lottie got a library book with a message saying they knew she had a secret, so we sneaked out to find out which students had used the library that day.'

Jamie's lip twitched, but he managed to remain calm. 'And?' he asked, the chill in his voice more threatening than if he was shouting at them.

'And we found Anastacia, Raphael and Binah's names,' Ellie said. This time she did look away.

'And neither of you thought to tell me this?' His voice raised a little, making Lottie instinctively hold her breath. 'Even though I'm here to protect you, you hid this from me?'

Ellie shook her head violently. Lottie could see a storm brewing inside her.

'Maybe I don't want you to protect me!' she roared, baring her teeth like fangs. As soon as she said the words, she grimaced, a look of regret on her face. The silence that followed was painful. Lottie had absolutely no idea what Jamie was thinking and it scared her. Ellie's chest heaved up and down, her energy the total antithesis of Jamie's cool aura.

'I'll always be here, Ellie,' he said, his voice soft yet cold, 'whether you like it or not.' There was a weight to his words and Lottie knew something had just happened between the two of them that she would never understand.

*How did you become a Partizan?* The words popped into her head, leaving a burning curiosity.

230

Ellie slowly looked down. 'I didn't mean . . . I know . . .' she said, running her hands through her hair.

Jamie took another deep breath and turned back to Lottie, once again stoic and composed. 'Do you accept the danger of being bait, Lottie?' His dark eyes held hers, but she remained as poised as possible. She knew she had to remain calm and neutral if she were going to persuade Jamie that she wasn't affected by the messages.

*Who are you really?*

The words materialized in her mind as she looked at his expressionless face. She nodded once, not trusting her voice to keep up the facade.

He turned to Ellie once more and again they shared a look she couldn't quite understand. 'I want you both to be wary of Anastacia and Raphael,' he said coolly. Lottie could feel Ellie relax, yet she couldn't do the same. 'I don't trust them.'

*So that's why he's staying so close to Raphael.*

'You cannot let them know we suspect them. We need to keep a close eye on them.'

'Does this mean you're not going to report it?' Ellie asked, the eagerness in her voice pulling Lottie from her thoughts.

He frowned disapprovingly at his own decision and Ellie grinned in excitement. 'But if I feel for even one second that you're in imminent danger I won't hesitate to report back to your parents.'

Jamie was letting them keep it secret.

Ellie winked at Lottie. 'We'll catch whoever it is before it gets to that.'

Lottie found herself feigning a determined smile as a voice in her head whispered all the mysteries she needed to solve. *Who's leaving these messages? What do they want? Why is Ellie so uncomfortable with Jamie being her Partizan? How did Jamie become a Partizan?*

'Agreed,' Lottie said flatly. 'We'll uncover everything.'

She wasn't sure exactly which secret she was referring to.

## 32

A focused calm enveloped Rosewood Hall with the onset of the winter exams. The students gathered in the libraries and study halls, a collective hush as they concentrated on absorbing all that they'd learned that term.

Lottie was relieved that the years of hard work to get into Rosewood Hall had paid off. She found that revising and the exams themselves were not as daunting as she thought they'd be, especially with the support of her friends – and the endless supply of Tompkins sweets from Lola and Micky helped to keep their energy levels up too.

As soon as the exams were over, most students prepared to travel back home for Christmas. Lottie, Jamie and Ellie had temporarily halted their decoding of the message as they revised for the exams, but there was something else keeping Lottie's mind off the mystery. Ollie was upset with her.

*Dear Lottie,*

*I'm not going to lie: I'm really sad you're not coming home for Christmas, but I'm sure whatever this crazy thing you've got caught up in is very important.*

*If you do suddenly change your mind and want to spend Christmas at Casa de Moreno, there's always room for you at the table.*

*Don't forget about us in your new exciting school.*

*Merry Christmas.*

*Your first and most loyal friend,*
*Ollie*

It was far too late now to hop on a train back to Cornwall and see Ollie, but, worst of all, it had been her idea to stay over Christmas. She'd never been the type of person to be obsessed with her phone, but she wished more than anything that she could just call Ollie and hear his reassuring voice. To her dismay, you were only allowed to call immediate family from the school phones, so she still couldn't get in touch with Ollie.

Ellie had invited her to Maradova, but Lottie didn't know how she'd be able to cope with the strange setting. Ellie, however, was more than happy not to go home for Christmas as she was dreading seeing her grandmother, so here they were, spending the holidays at Rosewood Hall. But Lottie couldn't get in the Christmas mood.

She sighed deeply as she reread Ollie's letter, before folding it up and putting it in her pocket. She'd sent Ollie and his mum a hand-crafted Christmas card telling them that she wouldn't be coming home for the holidays, and, even though to most people Ollie's letter probably didn't seem too bad, she knew that he was upset.

'I thought Saskia said this was a small gathering!' Ellie scoffed as she prodded a large ice sculpture of an angel that had been placed on the food table. Saskia had invited some of the other students staying over the holidays to a small gathering in Conch House to exchange gifts, and the girls had arrived early to help set up.

Lottie was about to reply with her concerns about Ollie when the front door creaked open to reveal Anastacia and Raphael, who were effortlessly balancing trays of fancy foods on their arms like they were circus performers.

*Maybe those etiquette classes really are good for something!* thought Lottie.

She tensed as they placed their trays on the table. It had been easy to avoid Anastacia and Raphael since the winter exams started, but tonight would be Ellie and Lottie's first real test in pretending they didn't suspect them.

Anastacia dusted her hands off and, without looking up, she said, 'Ellie, stop eating the party food or I'll poison it.'

Ellie quite literally choked on the pig-in-a-blanket she was shoving into her mouth, making Lottie wince. That particular party snack was just too much for her animal-loving heart: a pig-in-a-blanket of its own flesh . . . The horror! Ellie gave Anastacia a little side smile before reaching for another one.

'Oh please, you don't need an excuse to poison anyone,' Ellie teased, making Raphael snort and instantly earning him a dangerous look from Anastacia. This poison talk was definitely not helping Anastacia's case.

Lottie was glad that Jamie was picking up a Christmas tree from the main hall as he was the only one strong enough to carry it on his own. If he were here to witness this, he'd be furious with them for 'fraternizing with the potential enemy'.

'No one is poisoning anything,' Lottie chided. 'We've put far too much effort into arranging every– . . . ELLIE, FOR THE LOVE OF GOD, STOP EATING ALL THE FOOD!'

Ellie paused with a chocolate roll halfway to her mouth, then slowly put it back down again.

'As you wish, Your Highness.' She gave her an over-the-top bow before heading to the door. 'I need to go and get my guitar anyway; Jamie and I are gonna sing you guys a little song.' She fluttered her eyelashes with a mocking, sickly-sweet smile on her face.

Lottie gasped in surprise. 'Jamie sings?'

The thought of Jamie pouring his heart out in a song seemed totally unnatural for someone so serious and once again Lottie found herself painfully aware of how little she actually knew about the two of them.

Ellie instantly turned back to her and gave her a sharp look that Lottie quickly realized meant, *'He's supposed to be your bodyguard; you should know he sings.'*

'You didn't know your own bodyguard sings?' The voice came from behind her and she quickly turned to see Saskia by the entrance to the kitchen, carrying a small table, and a posse of Conch House students behind her, all holding big bags of miscellaneous party items. 'Seems a bit harsh,' she added as she effortlessly set down the table.

Saskia truly flourished in the Conch House environment. It was clear she was the dominant presence in the room, and obvious why she was head of year.

'Well . . . no, I mean –' Lottie scrambled for the right words but somehow found it even harder to think in the presence of Saskia's questioning smile – 'I didn't know he sang in public . . . He's usually so shy about it.'

'Hmm.' Saskia began placing things on the table, giving Lottie a little sideways glance.

Lottie's eyes flicked to Ellie, but she was staring at Saskia strangely, not dissimilar to how she'd been looking at all the party food.

'What are you staring at?' Saskia asked coyly, flicking her hair out of her face as if she were a mermaid emerging from the water.

'Just admiring the view,' Ellie replied casually.

Saskia laughed a deep throaty laugh in response, a hand moving to her hip to smooth her dress over her thighs. Something inside Lottie bristled sharply at the exchange.

'Go and get your guitar and treat us to a song – then I might forgive you for pecking at my food, *pequeña pollo*.' Ellie smirked at the pet name and Lottie felt the prickly feeling intensify.

With Ellie gone, Lottie suddenly felt self-conscious, surrounded as she was by mostly Conch students who seemed to know each other quite well, so she resigned herself to meticulously arranging the food and decor in elaborate Christmassy displays. She might not be in a Christmassy mood, but she still liked decorating.

'You're surprisingly good at stuff like that.'

Lottie looked up to see Anastacia eyeing the snowflake patterns she'd made out of some paper doilies. It was hard not to take offence at 'surprisingly', but the fact she was getting any form of compliment from Anastacia made up for it. She wore a red dress and her chestnut hair was pristine as usual. She looked like something out of a Christmas advert and it made Lottie feel childish in the little reindeer headband she'd thought would be 'cute'.

'Thanks, actually I . . .'

'You're nothing like I expected you to be.'

Lottie blinked in surprise, not sure how to respond. *How exactly did Anastacia expect me to be? Does she think I'm a bad princess?*

Anastacia looked at Lottie seriously, her lips parted as if she were about to say something important, and Lottie was transported back to that time in the library when she'd felt the same determination radiating from her. 'Lottie, I know –'

'LET US ENTERTAIN YOU!' Ellie burst through the door dramatically, all eyes instantly turning to her as she raised a guitar in the air like a trophy. She was followed by a particularly irritated-looking Jamie. He too had a guitar in his hand but seemed less than thrilled about it. Ellie gave him a sharp kick in the shin and he reluctantly raised a party horn to his mouth and gave it a comically unenthusiastic blow.

*And he plays guitar? Does he also do ballet and sing soprano?* Lottie felt that wisp of curiosity about Jamie creep through her again.

*How did you become a Partizan?*

She turned back to Anastacia but she'd vanished, now suddenly at Saskia's side.

Lottie had to stifle a laugh as Ellie forced two Conch kids off the seats in the centre of the room like it was her own personal stage. They grumbled indignantly and looked to Saskia, but she simply laughed her delicious laugh and gestured for them to move.

'Sometimes I'm surprised you weren't put in my house; you're certainly resolute.'

Lottie instantly went cold at this. Ellie was in *her* house and no one could change that. Ellie winked at Saskia and gave her that trademark side smile, making Lottie's blood turn acidic. Why was this bothering her so much? She hated that she felt like this about Saskia, who was nothing but kind to her, yet every time she was around Lottie just wanted to get away.

Everyone gathered around Jamie and Ellie as they prepared to play. They didn't appear even a little bit nervous and Lottie envied how relaxed they were.

'Play something Christmassy!' called out one of the Conch girls, who was wearing a Santa hat.

Ellie made a disgusted face, completely dismissing her. 'No, we're playing something for Lottie,' she said bluntly as she twiddled with the strings.

'For me?' Lottie felt instantaneously nervous and happy. That unpleasant feeling in her belly diminished for a moment as she revelled in Ellie's attention.

Ellie passed a pick to Jamie and he stuck it in his mouth as he began adjusting his own guitar strings. There was something strangely alluring about the whole procedure, the shared concentration, the absolute assurance in what they were doing – two professionals engaging effortlessly with their craft.

'We're playing you a song from your country. Because you're not home this Christmas we thought we'd bring home to you.' Jamie spoke with that intense look he sometimes displayed and she knew it meant he wanted her to take this seriously.

'Thank you,' she replied hesitantly.

The rest of the room exchanged tentative looks with each other, as unsure as Lottie of what was about to come.

The room hushed as they got into position. They shared a private look and began. The first note pierced the air and the entire room seemed to shake. Lottie looked around but no one else appeared to have felt it. A collective chill ran through the listeners as Jamie and Ellie's voices rang out in a haunting harmony. The song was sweet and painful at the same time, filling Lottie's chest with a dull ache. Jamie's voice was hypnotizing and Lottie found herself swaying, bewitched by the spell of the music. Everyone was silent and wide-eyed, captured by the unexpected intensity of the performance. Each chord on Ellie's guitar plunged Lottie further and further into the enchantment. Her body began to prickle with pins and needles, the world around her fading as she shut her eyes, giving herself over to the song, letting it consume her completely.

And then she could see it.

The ancient Maravish lyrics came alive, thanks to the intensive princess lessons, and the story it told materialized in her mind.

Her name was Ester – she was both a Portman and a Partizan – and her princess was Liana. She was the most striking and devoted Portman the country had ever known, and she and her princess loved one another in more and deeper ways than just professional loyalty. Lottie could envisage them both, wispy ghosts of the past floating inside her head. They were a vision of red and black; they were fierce and forthright and adored by all who knew them. Princess Liana demanded that upon her emergence Ester would be declared her royal hand so that they might rule together. But upon the night of the princess's coronation and emergence, Ester was stolen from her bed in an act of war by a neighbouring country as a prop in negotiation. Instead of forcing her princess to choose between her people and herself, Ester took her own life. It was such a powerful act of loyalty that the gods took pity on her and allowed one last message to be delivered from her to her princess via a white dove. In a blinding rage and with the spirit of her fiery Portman inside her, the princess had the entire neighbouring kingdom destroyed. Lottie could see the flames bursting from the castle, burning her skin as they blazed around her. And then the song ended.

The ghosts blinked out of her mind and her eyes blinked open, plummeting her back into the real world to find herself reaching out, tears streaming down her face as she tried desperately to grasp at the vision and bring it back.

Everyone was staring at her.

# 33

Lottie coughed awkwardly a few times.

'That was . . . lovely,' she said casually as she wiped her eyes, pretending nothing was out of the ordinary and she hadn't just burst out crying over an imaginary ghost princess and her Portman. Everyone was staring at her as if she were some kind of freak in a circus show.

Her mind raced desperately trying to come up with anything to make the situation less awkward.

'I'm just . . . really homesick,' she said, wiping her eyes again dramatically and sniffing before excusing herself to the balcony so no one could see how shaken she was.

'Right. . .' Anastacia's voice echoed sarcastically behind her and mocking laughter followed.

Lottie grabbed the side of the balcony and gulped down as much of the fresh, frosty air as her lungs could take. She exhaled, the puffs of breath a mirror of her internal fog of confusion and panic. The light outside was pale blue, the dwindling sun hidden behind thick masses of curling clouds that mirrored the frost over Rosewood Hall. Everything around her was blue and white, as though they'd sunk into another world and were submerged in a strange muted version of her school. She looked down at her bleached knuckles, her hands gripping the balcony ledge.

*What was that? What just happened?*

The image of Liana and Ester burned in her mind as she squeezed her eyes shut. Suddenly 'homesick' wasn't so far from the truth. In that moment she wished more than anything she could be back in Cornwall, cuddled up reading about other people's exciting lives, far away from any of the madness herself. Maybe she wasn't cut out for this world.

'Lottie?'

Lottie quickly wiped her eyes again at the sound of Ellie's voice. She turned to see her and Jamie standing by the double doors to the balcony.

Slowly Ellie stepped over the ledge and Jamie moved to follow.

'I'm fine, guys. You don't have to come out –' Jamie wrapped a large red blanket from the Conch dorm round her shoulders without saying anything. 'Thank you.' Lottie pulled the blanket round her, not realizing until then how cold she really was.

'Can we have a moment alone?' Ellie said softly. It wasn't a question, and Jamie nodded before returning to the festivities and closing the glass doors. It was the first time Lottie had really seen Ellie take a tone of authority with him.

'Ellie, I really am fine –'

'What happened in there?' Ellie asked.

Lottie paused at the frankness of the question, then rubbed her forehead in thought. The truth was she didn't know what had happened and she didn't know how to explain it, but she knew it was important. Everything felt important since she'd started at Rosewood.

'Do you ever think . . .' Lottie shook her head and looked out over the school. 'Do you ever think that there's something weird about Rosewood?'

Ellie followed her gaze, a soft smile creeping on to her lips while her eyes remained distant. 'All the time. It's why I like it.'

Lottie watched Ellie's face for a moment before taking a step nearer and resting her head against her shoulder. They stood like that, intertwined, until Ellie huffed and turned to face her. 'Lottie, I'm really sorry.'

Lottie blinked in surprise. It was so rare that Ellie ever said that word and it was unclear what she was apologizing for.

'This is probably the worst Christmas you've ever had. Stuck at school away from home. It's not the same.' Ellie made a remorseful face and Lottie sniffled out a giggle at how silly it sounded.

'I don't really care about Christmas,' she said, 'and it was my idea to stay here.' Lottie pulled the blanket tighter round herself. 'I stopped really caring about Christmas after my mum went anyway.' Lottie hadn't known how true this was until she'd said it. It was why she was so scared to go to Maradova and see what Ellie's family Christmas was like. A Christmas with a full family. What if it wasn't like she'd imagined it?

Lottie was pulled out of her thoughts by Ellie making a growling sound.

'I'm supposed to be the one who doesn't care about stuff like that,' she griped, rubbing Lottie's head affectionately. 'You're supposed to love things like Christmas and carols and all the tacky stuff that goes with it.' Lottie laughed and Ellie gifted her that little side smile. 'Anyway, I was going to give this to you later, but . . .' Ellie pushed her hair back as she pulled something from her bag. 'I want you to have this now; it feels like a good time.'

She held out a poorly wrapped box with the word '*Lottie*' scrawled across it in black marker.

'Ellie, you shouldn't have. I really –'

'Just open it,' Ellie said quickly, looking away.

Lottie considered the gift for a second, then pulled the paper back thoughtfully. Inside was a large rose-gold velvet box with a dazzling embroidered sun on the lid. The little gems along the sides reflected the blue light in a milky moonlit glow.

'Ellie, this is beautiful.' Lottie's voice came out a soft whisper as she took in the box.

'It's for the tiara your mum gave you. I noticed how you just keep it in your bag or your bedside table so I thought you could keep it in here.' Ellie sounded shy as she said this, making Lottie smile even more.

'It's like us,' Lottie said, grinning at Ellie excitedly. Ellie looked confused. 'A crescent-moon tiara with a sunshine box. Total opposites that go together,' she explained.

As she said it, all Lottie's worries dissipated. She looked down at the box again, taking in the beautiful image on the lid. She wasn't worried about the message, or her exams, or the ball. With Ellie by her side she was sure she could do anything.

'Come on – let's go back to the party,' she said, grabbing Ellie's hand.

'Actually . . .' Ellie said, pulling her hand back. 'Why don't we just spend the rest of Christmas together in the Ivy dorm?'

Lottie beamed at her, not wanting to say out loud how much she didn't feel like spending Christmas in Conch House.

'I'll even steal some mince pies for us.' Ellie said, winking.

Lottie squeezed Ellie's hand. 'That sounds like the best Christmas ever.'

# 34

It was 9:30 p.m. on 31 December, and Lottie, Ellie and Jamie were making the most of the extended curfew for holiday-stay students by taking a late stroll around the rose garden by the main hall. It was freezing cold, the grass underneath them crunchy with its icy coat. Lottie pulled her heavy wool-lined Ivy cape tight round her shoulders.

'Look!' she cried, pointing up at a huge firework exploding in the distance over the walls of the school. It lit up the grounds in a gorgeous pink light and she couldn't help moving towards it.

'Lottie, wait.' Jamie reached out and grabbed her arm, pulling her back. 'Do you hear that?'

His voice came out in a cautionary whisper, instantly prompting Lottie and Ellie to mirror his silence. He held a finger up to signal them to stay silent and Ellie took a small step towards Lottie. Lottie stayed as quiet as possible, trying to hear what Jamie was hearing and wondering if they were in danger. A muted rustling came from a tree nearby and Lottie held her breath, her heartbeat increasing.

*This is it*, she thought. *Whoever left that message is coming for us.*

Slowly, crouching low, Jamie took five purposeful steps in the direction of the noise and before Lottie could register what was happening his arm reached out behind the tree and roughly grabbed their would-be attacker. Jamie kicked his leg out from under him and within seconds he had the figure on the ground with their hands pinned behind their back.

'PLEASE DON'T HURT ME! I'm sorry, I'm sorry!'

'Raphael?' Lottie said in confusion. Jamie didn't let up on his grip.

'Jesus Christ, Jamie! I was just coming to get you guys and then I thought it would be funny to scare you and –' Raphael yelped as Jamie pulled him up. Raphael rubbed his arm and chuckled to himself as he took in Jamie's serious face. 'I realize now that wasn't my smartest idea . . .'

Jamie considered him for a moment, then looked over at Lottie and Ellie. Lottie shrugged, trying not to laugh, partly because she'd been so terrified, and partly at how ridiculous the whole thing was.

'You never were one for thinking things through,' Jamie said sternly.

Raphael burst out laughing. There was something in his movements that seemed off, which Jamie picked up on.

'Are you feeling OK?' he asked, raising an eyebrow.

'I'm fine, I'm fine! We're doing something fun and I didn't want you guys to get left out.' He grinned at them, his charming smile slightly too bright.

'I guess you guys are having a pretty wild time then,' Ellie chuckled, taking a step towards Raphael. 'I've gotta see this. Lottie?' She turned to Lottie, grinning.

Another firework went off in the distance, this time it turned the ground red.

'Let me lead the way,' Raphael replied as the crimson air fizzled around them.

They walked to the outskirts of Conch House. Night had fully enveloped the school and the fiery lanterns by the doors were blazing enthusiastically like little dancing figures on each side of the entranceway. There was a commotion at the gate, accompanied by wild fits of laughter and muted conversation.

Ellie beamed excitedly. 'Sounds like a party.'

Saskia, Anastacia and a small group of other Conch students were standing against the wall of the dorm with bottles in their hands, looking giddy.

'What are you guys doing?' Jamie asked Raphael matter-of-factly as they approached.

'We're going to break into the Conch House pool,' he said, grinning wildly.

'But it's off limits!' Lottie immediately felt like an idiot for stating the obvious.

'Well, duh! That's what makes it fun!' This came from a petite Conch girl with a red bow in her hair.

Lottie looked to Saskia who was giggling. Why was she letting this happen?

Lottie thought about how incredibly uncool it would be for her to try to dissuade them. She wished Binah or Lola and Micky were there and she could just do fun safe things with them like drink hot chocolate and watch Disney films.

'Yes! A break-in!'

Lottie jumped as Ellie dived forward, wrapping an arm around Saskia's shoulder, saying, 'Y'know I always liked you, Saskia.'

They both burst out in senseless laughter and Lottie found herself feeling that familiar prickly sensation in her chest and scowled at them. She wanted to prise the two apart and tell Saskia to go away.

Ellie caught her eye and smirked at her as if she knew what she was thinking.

'We're not going,' Jamie's serious voice cut in, a stark contrast to the juvenile atmosphere.

Saskia squinted at him, her whole aura suddenly changing. 'It'll be fun –'

'Quiet!' Jamie gave her a sharp and furious look, and Saskia instantly fell silent, a cold expression on her face.

She shook her head and put her smile back on. 'Well, you know where to find us if you change your minds.'

Saskia made a signal and the group moved off down the path. Anastacia hesitated only for a moment, her eyes lingering on Lottie, before glancing at Ellie as she walked past. She didn't seem pleased and it was clear that Anastacia was the only non-giddy member of the group.

Ellie turned sharply to Jamie and shoved him, a totally futile move as he didn't budge.

He blinked slowly at her like she was a child having a tantrum. 'We are not going, Ellie,' he repeated.

She stared at him for a moment, then looked down the path at the others. When she turned back she had that determined look on her face that could only result in trouble.

'We have to,' Ellie replied. 'We can't let them think we're afraid.'

Jamie remained firm. 'No.'

'Well, *I'm* going. You guys can do whatever you want.' She stuck her tongue out at him and quickly pivoted out of Jamie's reach.

'Ellie, come back *now*!'

'You'll have to catch me!' she called, running to catch up with the others.

Jamie grunted in annoyance and took off in a sprint after her.

'Ellie, if you and Jamie go, then I have to . . . GUYS!'

It was too late. She would either have to stand there on her own or follow them. Begrudgingly she began walking after them.

*I'm definitely going to regret this*, Lottie thought.

## 35

Two plastic cups filled with clear liquid appeared in front of Lottie and Jamie.

'Here, have a drink, you two, and lighten up!' Ellie smiled down at them in an attempt to make them feel better.

Lottie and Jamie were stood by the side of the pool under the gazebo, wrapped in blankets and looking very much like they had accepted that the world was about to end. Lottie resented that she agreed with Jamie about how stupid this was, but drunk kids and a pool in December just seemed like a really terrible combination.

'I don't drink,' Jamie said firmly. 'I have a respons–'

'It's not alcohol; this is Anastacia's lemonade. We warmed it up,' Ellie said, rolling her eyes. 'I'm not a complete idiot.'

Jamie took one of the cups begrudgingly and allowed himself a tentative sip. 'Fine,' he said.

Lottie took the other cup, grateful for its warmth.

They sat under the gazebo in awkward silence, Jamie occasionally taking furious gulps of the hot lemonade, while Lottie warmed her hands round hers.

Ellie was dancing with Saskia on the other side of the pool, twirling and dipping her like she was some kind of Prince

Charming and Saskia was her princess. An involuntary pout crept on to Lottie's face and she told herself it was only because she resented being there and not because she was jealous of Saskia, because that would be completely and absolutely ridiculous.

'I bet you ten pounds someone falls in the pool,' Lottie said.

Jamie continued staring stony-faced across the water, gritting his teeth as hot air escaped from his nose into the cold. 'Twenty pounds says I push one of them.'

Lottie almost choked. Was that genuine humour? Her mind was abruptly thrust back to when they had first met, before she knew he was a Partizan, before she'd given her life over to being Ellie's Portman. It almost felt like there were two of him: the serious, mature mask he wore and the teenager that was hidden underneath him. Again that voice whispered in her ear. *Who are you, Jamie Volk?*

'Don't you ever wish you could just be an ordinary boy?'

Lottie blurted out the question before she'd even processed it in her own head. Jamie didn't reply at first and she instantly regretted asking such a rude question, wondering if she'd blown her chance of ever uncovering his mystery.

'I'll never be an ordinary boy.'

She tensed at his response. There was something undeniably vulnerable in his voice and she felt as if she were luring a deer towards her and had to be incredibly delicate in case she scared it away.

Jamie stood up slowly, knocking over the dregs of his drink as he shook off his blanket. She watched as he walked to the gazebo's edge, leaning on one of the stone pillars, and stared out almost wistfully into the water's sapphire surface.

Carefully, still with the deer in her mind, Lottie stood beside him.

The Conch House pool was hidden away behind thick rosehip bushes and crab apple trees, the red berries peeping out from the branches, contrasting to the dreamy blue atmosphere of the silky moonlit pool.

'But hypothetically,' Lottie asked gingerly, 'if you could be?'

He smirked and gave her a little sideways glance. 'I almost wonder if you're insulting my skills as a Partizan.'

Lottie was not expecting this response and Jamie laughed at her confused expression.

'What I mean is,' he went on, 'it's my job to try to blend in with the other students as much as possible. Do you not think I'm like other boys?' he asked, a glint of humour twinkling in his eyes.

Lottie pretended to think for a moment, tapping her finger on her chin as if trying to tap the thoughts out of her head. 'Hmm,' she began, 'I mean, for one you have about zero sense of humour, and you're so freakishly strong that you're basically a superhero. You're definitely not like other boys.'

A soft smile spread over Jamie's lips and he laughed low, the sound humming through Lottie's body. Then the twinkle vanished from his eyes and he was serious again. Lottie worried that she'd scared away the deer, but he turned back to the water and she could sense he was still with her.

'When you live your life for someone else, you find strength you didn't know you were capable of.' He spoke with a powerful sense of assurance – and Lottie found the words made her heart ache.

'That sounds awfully sad,' she said, involuntarily hugging herself as if trying to find comfort.

He looked at her earnestly, his head tilted slightly, his eyes glossy and intense. 'Really?' he asked. 'Are you not doing the same thing? Did you not sign your life over to the Maravish royal family?'

*But I had a choice*, Lottie thought, trying to stop the tears springing to her eyes.

And once again, as if he could read her mind, he leaned close to her and said gently, 'This is our choice, Lottie.'

His breath brushed her cheek, making her shudder. It had a strange sweet smell, like baby powder, which made her nose tingle. She looked up and realized how close their faces were.

Something wasn't right.

*Has someone spiked his drink?*

Jamie's eyes turned hazy and he leaned forward, causing Lottie to step back towards the wall that separated the gazebo from the pool, one hand resting on the stone for support.

'Jamie . . .'

The moonlight twinkled between them and the look on his face made her catch her breath. His manic grin reminded her of a wolf. His eyes were dark under his messy hair; it was a distinctly predatory look that made Lottie's heart race.

He sniggered as if reading her mind again.

'You're still afraid of me,' he said with a smirk.

Lottie felt a blush creep on to her cheeks, but not because she was embarrassed. His words had made her suddenly very angry. 'Afraid of you? Of course I'm afraid of you!'

This was obviously not the response he'd been expecting and his face showed it.

'Nothing I do will ever impress you,' she added.

He shook his head in confusion. 'You don't need to impress me –'

'But I *do*! I need to prove to you that I'm capable.'

'I don't think you're not capable.' His face twisted a bit as if he were struggling to summon the right words. 'I think you shouldn't *have* to be capable.'

'I . . . what?' Lottie blinked at him, perplexed.

'You're just a kid, Lottie.' He said this softly, whispering in her ear as he gently stroked a strand of her hair. Lottie felt the blush creep back, but this time she had no excuse for it.

'Well . . . so are you then.' She tried to sound confident, but her words were breathless and uneven.

Jamie looked distant for a moment, the haze completely consuming him. 'I never had that luxury –' he turned back to Lottie, a pained look taking hold of him – 'and I can't stand seeing it taken away from you.'

He leaned in so close Lottie could feel his heartbeat. She was leaning as far back as she could now without falling in the pool.

'Jamie, you're drunk or something – we need to . . .'

His expression instantly changed, all the softness being replaced by confusion.

'No, I don't drink. I'm . . .' Then realization dawned on his face, confusion shifting to anger. He grabbed his head in his hands, trying to will some kind of stability into his thoughts.

'Lottie, I'm going to pass out. Listen . . .' He scrunched his eyes shut, desperately forcing his mind and mouth to work together. 'You can't trust Anastacia . . .'

And then he fainted into her arms, plummeting them both over the wall and into the freezing-cold water.

# 36

Cold water flew up Lottie's nose, and her blood felt like ice in her veins. She opened her eyes under the water to see Jamie, still unconscious, a muddled blur sinking with her.

*I have to get him out.*

She wrapped her arms under his shoulders.

*Hold on, Jamie! Please don't drown! Please don't drown!*

She'd swum against wild currents in the sea in Cornwall, and she'd dived to retrieve coins at the bottom of the local swimming pool, but pulling another human from the water, fully clothed, felt like a gargantuan task.

*I will not let you drown.*

But no matter how much she tried to push for the surface they were just too heavy in their shoes and clothes. She was running out of time, every second felt crucial.

*I need more momentum.*

Slowly she allowed them to sink the two-metre depth, then firmly planted her legs on the bottom of the pool and pushed up with all her strength.

They broke the surface and Lottie desperately gulped in as much air as she could before struggling to the side. She could see people at the pool's edge calling out but she couldn't hear them. Hands came down and lifted her and Jamie out of the water.

They were hauled on to the grassy bank, and someone came to her side, saying her name but she pushed them aside; she had to get back to Jamie. She leaned over him. He was still out cold, his tan-brown skin coated by a porcelain sheen of frailty.

It felt wrong: Jamie was supposed to be strong, unwavering and unbreakable. She wanted him to wake up and shout at her, tell her it was a test, and chastise her for getting so worried – but, no matter how much she willed it, he remained still, not breathing.

*What do I do?* She felt tears pricking her eyes. *What do I do?*

Somewhere in her mind a soft voice replied: *Kiss the princess to wake them up.*

Her body moved on autopilot. She pushed down on his chest three times, covered his nose and gently placed her mouth over his, filling his lungs with her air. Then she did it again, and again and . . .

Jamie coughed underneath her abruptly, causing her to jolt back.

He drew in a shaky breath before mumbling, 'That's not how you do mouth-to-mouth.'

Lottie gasped at his voice, then he spluttered a few more times, his eyes trying to focus, before he reached up and stroked her cheek. His hand was freezing against her face. 'So warm,' he muttered, before passing out again.

Lottie sat beside him, still holding his hand against her cheek.

*He's OK. I did it. I saved him.*

Tears began to fall down her cheeks and she finally looked up. Everyone was standing around them, their faces glum. Ellie, in particular, looked horrified.

'It's OK, guys . . .' She hiccupped a little sob. 'He's OK.'

Slowly she looked up. There stood Professor Adina Devine, her winter cloak billowing in the wind like a whirlwind of furious power.

'All of you. To my office. NOW!' She stormed over to where Lottie was kneeling on the ground by Jamie. 'Raphael, Thomas, help me get Jamie to the infirmary.'

Lottie watched as they hauled him up, desperately wanting to go with them. Everyone began walking off but Lottie couldn't move.

A hand gently rested on her shoulder and she turned to see Ellie holding a blanket. 'I'm sorry, Lottie, I shouldn't have made you guys come out here . . . I'm . . .'

Lottie took the blanket from Ellie, still looking off into the distance.

'Someone did something to his drink . . .'

Ellie stared at her, dumbfounded. 'What? Who?'

'I don't know . . .'

*You can't trust Anastacia.*

It was the only logical conclusion. It had been her drink they'd been given; all signs were pointing to her. She looked at Anastacia as she walked off with the rest of the group, a blurry red figure slowly moving away. Lottie couldn't understand why she would do it. What could she have wanted to gain? It didn't make any sense.

'Lottie, you're shivering – we need to get you inside.'

Lottie let Ellie wrap the blanket round her and slowly they walked to the Ivy dorm. She wasn't even nervous about going to Professor Devine's office. Something weird was going on at Rosewood. It had nearly got Jamie hurt tonight, and she needed to figure out what was going on before it was too late.

# 37

As punishment for breaking into the pool, they were all given one month of leaf-sweeping and litter-collecting and had to write a five-page essay on the importance of respecting water. Saskia was grounded until term started again and Professor Devine stated, 'She should count herself lucky she isn't having her title revoked.'

Lottie had wanted to protest her punishment as she'd not wanted to go to the pool in the first place, but she remembered what the professor had said about how they needed to be responsible for each other, and held her tongue. The guilt was punishment enough for Ellie, judging from the sombre look on her face.

Jamie was released from the school infirmary after only an hour. They couldn't find any evidence of anything suspicious – no toxins, no poisons, absolutely nothing – but Lottie couldn't shake the memory of that strange sweet smell that she'd noted on his breath. Something wasn't right.

They sent him to his room to rest and he adamantly asserted that he was 'fine', even though he could barely remember a thing. He gave Lottie a particularly stern look as he told them to 'forget the whole thing ever happened'.

Meanwhile Ellie and Lottie had been left alone with Professor Devine.

She eyed them coolly, before gesturing to the cushioned seats by her desk. 'You may sit. I will keep this brief as I can see our young Miss Pumpkin is quite distressed.'

Lottie was still wrapped in blankets, enjoying the warmth of the fireplace in the corner.

The professor's gaze fell upon Ellie, and Lottie had to bite her cheek to keep from crying again, her eyes were salty and swollen enough already, as Professor Devine continued to speak.

'I can very well understand a desire to explore the many forbidden areas of the school –' even in Lottie's weary state her brain clung to the word 'many', holding on to the information for later – 'and, Lottie, it was quite tremendous indeed how you aided Jamie. It is not easy to think clearly in situations such as those and we will remember your bravery. But,' she said with a note of caution, 'what disappoints me is that two such promising Ivy girls failed to bring out the best in each other tonight.' She rubbed her forehead in thought for a moment and Lottie felt a soporific wave of warmth from the flames beside her. 'I shan't keep you here longer; I feel this is a lesson I cannot teach you in words. It's best now that you go back to your room and consider what has happened.' She gave them each a weighty look. 'You're dismissed.'

Lottie lay in her bed, staring vacantly at Mr Truffles as she chewed her lip. She didn't even register Ellie's warm body climbing in next to her.

'I really am sorry about tonight,' Ellie whispered, gently stroking Lottie's hair.

Lottie nodded, trying not to let any more tears escape.

'You really think someone did something to his drink?'

'It's the only explanation.'

Ellie hesitated. 'And you're sure you guys didn't just fall in the pool and he hit his head?'

There was scepticism in her voice, as if she were convinced Lottie wasn't telling her the whole story.

'No, Ellie, you didn't see him before we fell in the pool. He was . . . weird.' Lottie buried her face in Mr Truffles, feeling the blush creep on to her cheeks as she remembered just how odd he'd been. 'He said . . .' She paused. All evidence was pointing to Anastacia but Lottie still couldn't understand why she'd do it. 'He said again that we can't trust Anastacia.'

Ellie nodded soberly, then wrapped an arm round Lottie and nuzzled into her hair, making Lottie giggle as she felt her breath tickle her neck.

'At least I can trust you.' She exhaled the words slowly into Lottie's ear and Lottie's whole body lit up. Lottie turned so they were face-to-face, tears streaming down her cheeks and her nose running. Ellie held her against her chest until she stopped crying.

'I'm sorry,' Ellie repeated, though this time it was unclear what she was apologizing for.

They remained tangled together, sharing the warmth in their marshmallow cocoon, like two cubs in a den. Lottie's eyes and throat ached from crying, but gradually she began to relax in Ellie's arms, her friend's heartbeat pumping softly against her ear. Eventually Ellie climbed out of their den, switched off the lights and went back to her own bed.

That night, as Ellie slept soundlessly in her bed, Lottie awoke in a cold sweat from a terrible nightmare of Anastacia drowning Jamie.

She tried to get back to sleep, but her mind was too drained and frantic to rest again. A shiver ran through her body that she couldn't get rid of. She sat up and checked her clock. It was an hour into the new year. The chill ran through her again and she shuddered; it was too cold to try to sleep again.

She eased the door open as quietly as possible, not wanting to wake Ellie, and turned the corner to the storage room where she could get more blankets. On her way back she passed her post box and had to do a double take when she realized hers had something inside. It was a golden envelope with a delicate black pattern round the edges, winding up from the corners like smoke. She opened it carefully and found herself struck by the scent of peppermint. She pulled the card out slowly. It was black, with gold writing. It read simply:

*See you at the summer ball, Princess.*

*xx*

Lottie clutched the card to her chest, then quickly tiptoed back to her room and hid it in her bedside table under the box Ellie had given her. Jamie and Ellie would be furious if they knew.

*Edmund has finally sent me a message.*

Her heart was beating uncontrollably. She was sure this one little secret would be OK. What's the worst that could happen?

# PART THREE
*Presenting the Princess*

# 38

Spring term started on 9 January and with it came a soft sheet of snow over the school grounds. Everyone had switched to the thick, fluffy winter uniform, which made the whole school look as if it were filled with colourful sheep. The enthusiasm of a fresh start buzzed through the corridors, but for Lottie, Jamie and Ellie it was time to get serious about the mysterious threat to their lives.

They sat in the main hall waiting for the new term's opening speech to begin. It was far too cold to have the event on the field, but Lottie found that since the pool incident she felt a little claustrophobic in a crowd.

'I still think their plan must have gone wrong,' Jamie said. 'I think they intended to incapacitate both Lottie and me, but it's unclear why.'

'I don't think they intended for anyone to get badly hurt.' Lottie wasn't sure of this but whatever had been put in Jamie's drink had had no long-term side-effects and he'd pretty much recovered instantly. 'Otherwise they would have used something worse.' Lottie felt sick at that idea.

'Either way, we can't let Anastacia think we suspect her. We need to keep her close,' Ellie added, checking no one was listening.

Jamie chewed his lip in thought. 'I just wish we had a sample of whatever it was so that I could get it analysed.'

'What exactly did it make you do other than pass out?' Ellie asked curiously.

Jamie and Lottie froze. They both turned to look at each other and a stern expression appeared on Jamie's face. He had claimed a million times that he didn't remember anything and yet every time it came up he went rigid.

'I don't remember,' he said again.

'Well, Lottie must remember,' Ellie said helpfully. 'Was he manic or mellow or confused? It could help us figure out what it was.' Jamie gave her another sharp look and his words from that night pounded in her head.

*'I can't stand seeing it taken away from you.'*

Lottie gulped at the memory. 'He was straightforward,' she said at last.

'Straightforward?' Ellie's eyes narrowed, but before she could say more a cheery voice came from behind them.

'Good morning!' Binah, Lola and Micky took up the space next to Lottie, halting their conversation. Jamie let out a small breath as if he were actually relieved by their arrival.

'I heard about what happened over the holidays. Jamie, I hope you're all OK,' Binah said, real concern etched on her face.

'We're fine.' Jamie's eyes remained on Lottie as he spoke.

'I can't believe you dived in and rescued him, Lottie,' Lola said excitedly.

'You're like a superhero.' The twins spoke in unison.

Lottie wasn't sure how this rumour had started, but she could see it was making Jamie's lip twitch.

They all turned as Ms Kuma approached the podium, dressed in a fluffy yellow coat and matching hat that reminded Lottie of a daffodil. It seemed fitting with her bouncy and colourful presence that she would be doing the opening speech for spring term.

'Good morning, everyone, and welcome back to a fresh term at Rosewood. I am pleased to see such enthusiasm among you even with this dreadfully cold weather.' She shivered to accentuate her point. 'I hope you have all had a pleasant break and are ready to take on this term with even more passion and determination. Those of you in Year Ten and above will have the added pressure of preparing for next term's exams. It can be tempting to lose momentum in the spring term with no immediate examinations looming, but I have the utmost faith that all of you will rise to these challenges and face them head-on.' Then her cheerful smile turned rueful and she cleared her throat before continuing. 'On a less pleasant note, due to an incident over the holidays, the nine p.m. curfew will be upheld to the strictest order. If any student is not signed in to their dorm by this time, they will face an appropriate punishment; we would rather you didn't have to find out what that punishment is.' She looked over the students with pursed lips, making it clear that this was not something to be taken lightly. Lottie could sense something burning the back of her head and she turned to see Anastacia a few metres behind with Saskia and Raphael. Anastacia quickly looked away when Lottie caught her eye.

*You can't trust Anastacia.*

Lottie felt a shiver run up her spine. She couldn't get Jamie's ominous message out of her head.

She leaned over to Ellie. 'Anastacia is behind us. We should make sure to say hi to her later so she doesn't think we're avoiding her.'

Ellie nodded, resisting the temptation to turn round.

'Now before we let you get on with your day we have one final bit of news,' Ms Kuma continued. Lola and Micky let out a little squeal and she wondered what could be so exciting. 'This year the Tompkins Confectionery Company will be sponsoring our Valentine's Day celebrations so you can thank them for the extra-special displays. If any of you would like to get involved with the decorations, please do come and find me in my office this week.'

The twins turned to Lottie, Lola smiling giddily. Lottie attempted her best smile in return but the truth was she really didn't like Valentine's Day and she certainly didn't want to have to explain why to anyone.

*Another thing to worry about.*

The speech ended and everyone began making their way out of the main hall. Lottie could see Anastacia a little way in front of her and wondered if she should approach her. Ellie must have had a similar idea because as soon as they were outside, she ran past Lottie and grabbed Anastacia's arm to get her attention.

'Hey, Anastacia, we just –'

Anastacia turned abruptly, her bag falling off her shoulder, and the contents spilled over the floor. '*Mon dieu!*'

'Crap!' Ellie and Anastacia both cursed in unison.

Ellie and Lottie immediately kneeled down and began helping her pick up her stuff.

'Don't!' Anastacia cried, reaching to stop them.

'I'm really sorry, Anastacia – we just wanted to come and say hi. We didn't mean to –' Lottie's hand brushed over a photograph and she froze.

The photo was slightly fuzzy, but it was clearly Anastacia, grinning with a red bow in her hair. The Eiffel Tower was in the background and a huge ice-cream sundae was on the table in front of her. Next to her stood a girl with a large mop of tight blonde curls and caramel skin. It was Saskia. She was plaiting Anastacia's hair and the two were grinning. Lottie had never seen Anastacia look so happy.

'Don't touch that!' Anastacia snapped, pulling the photo out of Lottie's hand. 'You two do nothing but cause trouble.' She grabbed her bag and pulled it close to her, marching off furiously to catch up with the other Conch students.

'Wow!' Jamie chimed in sarcastically. 'That really could not have gone worse.'

Lottie barely even took in the words. She couldn't stop thinking about the photo and Anastacia's reaction. *You two do nothing but cause trouble.*

Anastacia was usually so composed. For her to react this aggressively definitely wasn't a good sign. Lottie looked at Ellie who gave her a shrug.

She couldn't help feeling like she was missing something important.

## 39

Lottie buried herself in her studies over the next few weeks, all the while feeling like there was something she was not understanding, until finally the worst day of the year came around: Valentine's Day. Or, as Lottie knew it, the anniversary of her mother's death.

Lottie awoke on the dreaded morning of 14 February and, as it was a Saturday, made her way to her early-morning princess lesson with Jamie and Ellie. She was grateful, at least, that she was able to sleep again, and that getting more sleep was helping her to keep calm, which she desperately needed to do, today of all days.

The whole school was thick with the oppressively strong smell of chocolate and red roses, while heart-patterned streamers forced their romantic agenda on everyone. Lottie was glad to have the lesson as a distraction. Jamie had picked the glasshouse in the rose garden by the main hall that morning, meaning they had a clear view of the Valentine's Day preparations. He had obviously picked it as a compromise to them missing out on the decorating, not realizing that Lottie wanted no part of it.

'Lottie?'

Jamie's voice jolted Lottie back to reality. 'Sorry! Could you repeat the question?'

Both Jamie and Ellie scrutinized her for a moment, Jamie's eyebrow lifting in muted concern.

'I asked you what your favourite story from Oscar's diary was, and how you've found it useful.' Jamie stood over her expectantly.

'Oh, that's easy,' Lottie replied. 'The story of Sun Dao and Shau Zu because – Have I said something wrong?' Lottie took in Jamie's face. His eyes had widened as if he'd heard something surprising.

'No, no. Not at all, it's just . . . That's my favourite too.' Lottie was overcome by a sudden inner warmth – it was so rare that he shared anything about himself and she felt like she'd just won a prize. He cleared his throat, bringing her out of her thoughts. 'Would you care to elaborate?'

Lottie nodded, happy to take her mind off Valentine's Day. She took a deep breath and prepared to plunge into the tale of Prince Shau Zu.

'It was 300 AD in China, a time when Portmans had become so accepted that you could assume most of the dynasty were not who you thought they were. Prince Shau Zu and his Portman Sun Dao were guests in the palace of Emperor Qin Shi Xiao, a powerful warlord and terrifying force. But their stay turned sour when it became clear that the emperor had invited them to his home to capture the prince. But Sun Dao was too smart for the emperor. Knowing that it was a great dishonour to harm a Portman once you knew their role, he double-bluffed and persuaded Qin Shi Xiao that *he* was the prince. The emperor unwittingly kept the real prince, Shau Zu, as a "special guest" within the palace, one who was not permitted to leave. Sun Dao, posing as the prince, endured eight whole days of deadly "games" – from crossing a tightrope over boiling oil to dodging arrows in the garden – until finally the prince's army arrived to rescue them. Once they'd escaped from the evil Qin Shi Xiao, the prince asked Sun Dao, "How do I reward such loyalty?" To which Sun replied, "Allow me do it all over again."'

Lottie had been looking at the roses as she told her story, doing her best to recall the details. When she turned her gaze to Jamie and Ellie, she was taken aback to find them both staring intently at her. Pride filled Lottie as she took in their enthralled expressions. It reminded her of how she used to look at her mother when she read her fairy tales and suddenly she felt a heavy ache in her chest.

Ellie blinked a few times before letting out a whistle. 'I need to read this diary!' she exclaimed.

Jamie's lips curved slightly and he gave Lottie a sideways glance. 'And why is this story useful?' he asked.

'Well . . .' Lottie looked down, feeling embarrassed by her answer. 'It shows that there's strength in loyalty. There's power in the duty of a Portman.'

Ellie snickered at the response, earning her a harsh glare from Jamie. Lottie felt herself getting annoyed: she was just too sore to find any humour in anything today.

'Hey, Lottie, you're not going to have to walk over boiling oil!' Ellie cracked up as she said it, and Lottie felt her brows furrowing.

Jamie glared at her. 'Ellie, that's –'

'You have no idea what we might end up having to do!' Lottie interrupted before Jamie could finish.

Ellie stopped laughing but a grin remained on her face, not realizing how distressed Lottie was getting.

'But that's *insane!* Don't get me wrong. I wish my life was that exciting but –'

'You *wish* your life was that exciting?'

Lottie couldn't believe Ellie had said something so ridiculous.

'Well, yeah! Being a princess for me has always meant I was just stuck inside all day and –'

'Ellie, you have no idea how exciting and amazing your life is. Most people will go their whole lives only dreaming of a world like the one you live in.' Lottie could feel her hands clenching in frustration. She couldn't seem to stop herself getting upset.

'Well, *most people* don't know how horrible it is. Lottie, what's wrong? You know how distressing my family can be –'

'At least you HAVE a family!' Lottie immediately covered her mouth as the words escaped but she couldn't stop the tears spilling from her eyes.

*Now you've done it*, she thought. *Now you're not going to be able to stop crying all day.*

'Lottie . . .' Ellie's voice came out strained.

Lottie knew she'd overreacted, but it was too difficult for her to get her thoughts straight. She rubbed her eyes aggressively and stood up. She didn't want to cause any more damage.

'I'll see you both later.' Her words came out in a little sob that she hated herself for and she ran to the garden's exit. She didn't look at Jamie as she ran past; she couldn't stand to see what he was thinking.

'Lottie, wait!' Ellie called after her, but she kept running.

She ran until her lungs were aching and she thought she might be sick until she finally reached Ivy Wood, but she didn't stop there. Her feet wouldn't let her.

And she ran straight into the Rose Wood.

# 40

Lottie's eyes and cheeks stung with the salt from her tears, and her nose was bright red, not just from crying but the biting cold. She stopped to catch her breath and found that she couldn't see the school buildings at all – she'd run deep into Rose Wood. She was covered in a sheen of sweat, but she realized too late that she'd left her coat back in the rose garden.

She walked on a little further until she found the biggest tree she'd ever seen. It was an ancient oak with a trunk large enough to build a home inside, its branches extending out in a huge circle. Lottie plopped herself down under the tree, letting her body absorb the cold to try to stave off some of the bad feelings. She felt embarrassed for being so melodramatic. Since her mother had passed away, she always got upset on this date, but usually she was alone in her room in Cornwall, able to deal with her sadness privately. Being at Rosewood somehow made her mother's passing seem even closer and more vivid than usual.

'Lottie.' She could hear her mother's gentle voice in her mind. The image of her in the hospital bed, skinny and weak but still smiling, pierced her thoughts. 'I'll be proud of you whatever you do in life, as long as you promise me –'

'I will be kind, I will be brave, I will be unstoppable.'

Her mother had laughed, the sound coming out in a pained wheeze. 'Yes, Lottie, I know you will be, but promise me you will also be happy. I want you to say it.'

Lottie had stared at her mother, knowing they didn't have much time left together. 'I promise I will get into Rosewood Hall and be happy.'

She couldn't do it. Lottie couldn't promise her mother she'd be happy because she wasn't sure she could be without her. But Lottie had been sure that getting into Rosewood would fix that. If she got into Rosewood, she'd be happy and fulfil her promise to her mother. So why wasn't she happy?

Another shiver ran through her body and she hugged her knees close. She didn't know how she'd find her way out of the woods or what she'd say when she saw Jamie and Ellie. She didn't want to think about anything; she just wanted to curl up under the tree and be alone.

'Lottie!'

Her head jerked up at her name, not sure how much time had passed. Her whole body was shivering and she could feel the chill in her bones.

The voice called louder. 'LOTTIE!'

She slowly got up, damp earth sticking to her clothes.

Someone was approaching on the other side of the tree, and she looked round the trunk to see Jamie standing there – with her coat and a blanket.

She rubbed her eyes, feeling the embarrassment creep back over her. *How did he find me?*

'I can follow tracks.'

Lottie blinked at him, her eyes sore and misty.

'Come on,' he said, holding his hand out. She took it and he tenderly wrapped the coat and blanket around her. His arms lingered on her shoulders and she was surprised by how comforting it felt to be close to him after the awkwardness following the pool incident.

'We're sorry. We should have remembered what today is for you. That was a significant oversight on my . . . I'm sorry.'

Lottie sniffed. 'I'm fine.'

A soft rumble of laughter escaped Jamie's throat. 'You always say that.'

There was a hint of regret in his voice that forced Lottie to look into his eyes. The tree cast a huge blue shadow over them, as if they were in their own milky world. His expression had a sweet ache to it and she knew she was witnessing something rare.

'I really miss her. But I don't want her to worry about me.' Somehow it didn't feel strange to be sharing this with Jamie.

Jamie nodded, his face solemn, and Lottie truly believed that he did understand. Yet there was something about his empathy that struck her. Did he have a sad secret from his past too? What happened? And there was that question again: *How did you become a Partizan?*

'Come on! It's time to go back now – Ellie's got something for you.'

Lottie let him lead her through the woods. He was so sure of where they were going, not troubled at all by the density of the trees.

She ran inside as soon as they reached Ivy Wood, eager to change out of her dirty clothes and wash her face. Clean at last, she paused by her bedside table and pulled out her tiara from the box Ellie had given her. She put it on her head and took a deep breath. *Be brave*.

'Do you want to go to the hall?' Jamie asked when she came back downstairs.

Lottie considered it for a moment: the other students in their pretty Valentine's Day outfits, everyone smiling and laughing. The promise she'd made to her mother echoed in her head, and a melancholy smile crept on to her lips. 'I want to see Ellie.'

Lottie followed Jamie to the main dining hall, where the Valentine's preparations were truly under way. Big bouquets of red and pink roses lined the tables against the walls, with strings of heart-shaped bunting across the sides and ceiling. Lottie couldn't even begin to imagine how they'd been strung up so high. In the centre of the hall, where there were usually large tables, was an enormous white chocolate fountain surrounded by an array of fruits and sweets, all emblazoned with TOMPKINS CONFECTIONERY.

As if on cue, Lola's voice squeaked from behind her. The twins stood beside each other, dressed smartly for the occasion in matching white and red. They both held wicker baskets filled with loveheart cupcakes.

'We've been looking for you!' Micky held out a pink cupcake topped with a loveheart that said PRINCESS LOTTIE.

'Everyone gets a cupcake. Except *Jamie*.' Lola said his name like it was poison. 'He's banned from having cupcakes because he said he doesn't like sweet food.'

'Which is sacrilege,' the twins said in unison.

Lottie blinked at them, taking in their serious expressions, then laughed. She'd been so sure that all she wanted to do that day was hide away from everyone, but here with the sugary-sweet twins she found it impossible to feel sad.

'Well, that's fine anyway,' Jamie said sarcastically, appearing at Lottie's side, 'because cupcakes are disgusting.'

Lola gasped as if she'd just received a blow and Lottie snorted.

'Blasphemy!' Micky replied. They both shielded their cupcakes as if protecting them from Jamie's harsh words.

'Thank you so much for mine,' Lottie said cheerily. 'It looks as sweet as you two.'

Lola instantly regained her composure and grinned at Lottie. 'You are most welcome.'

The two then skipped off happily to hand out the rest. Lottie turned back to Jamie, but her eye was caught by a sight in the doorway that made her heart skip a beat.

Ellie.

She spotted Lottie and came racing over, nearly knocking over a Stratus girl, who was carrying a plate of sugar cookies.

'Ellie, I'm sorry about earlier . . .' Lottie blushed as she said the words.

Ellie shook her head. 'No, Lottie, you have nothing to apologize for. *I'm* sorry.' She gave Lottie a tender look. 'I was so stupid. I know this is an important day for you . . .' Her voice trailed off and she ran a hand through her hair bashfully. 'I know this won't fix anything, but I got these for you.' From behind her back, she revealed a small bouquet of marguerite flowers, the flower Lottie's mother was named for. Lottie felt a wave of emotion hit her as she looked at them, and couldn't stop a tear escaping.

'That's . . .' She had to pause to take a breath. 'Thank you so much, Ellie, I love them.'

Jamie coughed, reminding them he was there. 'I'll catch up with you two later,' he said, and left them on their own.

Ellie and Lottie sat on the veranda outside, overlooking the rose garden, with their cupcakes. Lottie still felt raw. She realized she'd never opened up to anyone like that before, but Ellie and Jamie hadn't been mad at her or told her she needed to calm down. They'd both been so comforting. Thinking about it sent a warm feeling through her body.

'It's a blessing that Jamie doesn't like sweets really,' Ellie mumbled, her mouth filled with frosting. 'Because it means I always get to eat his dessert.'

Lottie giggled as she watched Ellie shove half the cupcake in her mouth at once, leaving a trail of frosting around her nose and lips.

'Let me get that for you!' Lottie leaned forward and gently wiped a bit of frosting off Ellie's cheek then licked it from her finger. Ellie grinned at her, shoving the rest into her mouth before starting on the next one. Lottie was about to take a bite of hers when she noticed something odd in the icing. There was a small dent in the decoration where a piece of paper had been poked into the frosting. She was about to tell Ellie when that feeling of dread that she'd become so familiar with lurched in her stomach, telling her to keep quiet. She pulled the paper out, making sure Ellie didn't notice, and carefully unfolded it, wondering if was from a secret admirer. It was not.

*Roses are red.*
*Violets are blue.*
*Watch your back, Princess.*
*I'm coming for you.*

She quickly shoved the paper into her skirt pocket, trying to hide away from the words. Her gaze went blank and she felt dizzy.

'Are you OK, Lottie?'

Ellie's voice startled her back to reality. Her friend's eyes were wide with worry, her concerned smile providing a small amount of comfort.

'It's nothing, I . . .' The message blinked in Lottie's mind and the writing blurred. She couldn't do it. She couldn't tell Ellie. She couldn't deal with another threat, not today. 'I'm just a bit emotionally rundown, but this cupcake will help.' She beamed her best reassuring smile.

She couldn't tell Ellie. If Jamie found out, and her family thought they were in danger, they might take Ellie away.

'Are you sure?' Ellie asked again, still looking concerned.

Lottie stared at her, face covered in frosting, strands of black hair falling around her comforting features. She couldn't lose her.

'Just peachy,' she lied.

# 41

Easter break was not much of a break at all. Lottie once again threw herself into studying for her end-of-year exams as an escape from thinking about the threatening message she'd received in the cupcake. There were no more scary messages and she was almost able to persuade herself there was no problem at all. As term wore on, everyone fell back into the routine of study sessions and revision groups. Rosewood Hall was not a place for students who weren't willing and ready to work hard.

Soon the trees around Rosewood were filled with colourful blossoms and the flowers and trellises bloomed, a flamboyant indicator of the approaching summer exams. Yet for all the colourful displays around the grounds, a lavender-scented calm enveloped the school, which accompanied a twitchy anticipation *something big* might happen. For most students this was the end-of-year exam results, but Lottie had another looming event: the summer ball.

Study leave began on the first day of May and Lottie's last exam was maths on the twentieth. They would get their marks on the final day of the month: 31 May. Once Ellie and Lottie had their results, they would fly back to Maradova and begin preparing for the ball – so long as they did well in their exams.

Lottie shot out of bed on results day, pulling herself out of a nightmare in which her grades had been so bad that she was not only banned from being a Portman and expelled but she had to become a court jester and perform circus tricks for the Maravish royal family. She clutched her hand to her chest, panting heavily, and looked up to witness the most shocking thing she'd seen all year. Ellie was awake before her.

'I'm nervous about the exam results,' Ellie said frankly as they left the Ivy dorm, chewing the cuticle on her thumb.

'Hypothetically, Ellie, if we had failed them . . . Couldn't your family just, I don't know, pay someone to change your grades?'

'Ha!' Ellie cackled. 'I wish. A wolf never cheats, Lottie.'

They met Jamie by the gate and Lottie noticed that his eyes were more sunken than usual, suggesting he hadn't slept well either.

Could he be nervous too? She couldn't imagine Jamie getting nervous about anything, but she felt too awkward to ask him about it. Ever since he had come to find her in the Rose Wood, she couldn't seem to look him in the eye, and she was sure he was avoiding her too.

They stood in the queue with all the other anxious students who'd woken up extra early to collect their results.

This was the make-or-break moment. If she'd failed, she'd not only have her bursary revoked but she'd no longer be allowed to continue her role as Portman.

Ellie was fidgeting, rubbing her fingers together as she chewed her lip, all the while gazing into the distance. This was equally terrifying for her. If she didn't get adequate grades, her parents would consider the Rosewood Hall experiment a failure and pull her from the school.

Lottie took a deep breath and held it. They were in the grand oak-walled reception hall, which she'd walked through on her first day of school and had thought so magnificent, but this time it felt overbearing and intimidating.

They took one final step forward in the line. Sitting in front of them was the Year Twelve Stratus head of year Angus Berkeley, the merlin symbol of his house visible on his yellow sash.

'Name – Oh! Lottie, we have your file here.'

*Princess perks!*

Angus reached to the side and pulled up a green hardback file with the three-rose symbol of the school on the front. 'Also your phone can be returned now,' he said as he handed everything to her.

'Thank you,' Lottie said, taking the file with shaking hands.


They stood together in the courtyard by the entrance next to the large archway. Binah had come to join them and her enthusiastic energy only made Lottie more nervous.

'I'm so excited!' Binah trilled, opening her file with no hesitation. Her expression turned into one of disappointment, though, as she glanced at the grade summary on the first page. 'Oh.'

Lottie's heart sank. If Binah had done badly, then how terribly had Lottie and Ellie done? But her worries quickly turned to groans when Binah added, 'Top marks in everything. How very boring.'

Ellie had to stop herself from snorting. 'You ready?' she asked Lottie, putting her fingers on the cover in readiness to open it.

Lottie puffed up her chest and nodded resolutely. 'Yep.'

They opened their files together, and Lottie saw Jamie twitch out of the corner of her eye. She shuddered at the thought of what his reaction would be if she'd failed. She felt sick. She felt like she was going to pass out. She finally looked down at the page before her.

She'd done it.

She'd passed everything with *seventy per cent or higher.*

She was in the top five in her year for English! Her heart skipped a beat as she took in her most difficult subjects. Maths, chemistry and physics were all in the top fifteen grades. She felt tears sting her eyes as she looked up at Jamie and nodded, then turned to Ellie who was still staring at her grade summary, her face blank.

'Ellie?' she asked apprehensively.

Ellie shook her head. 'I can't believe this,' she said slowly. 'I'm ranked seventeen in grades for the whole year. I made the top twenty.'

Lottie felt a huge wave of relief. She'd seen Ellie's exam results from previous years. 'Lacking effort' would have been an understatement.

'Of course you did!' Binah tutted, rolling her eyes. 'If any of you weren't in the top twenty per cent I would be furious.' She smiled at them. 'You're some of the smartest, most hard-working people I know.'

Ellie was still stunned at her grades. She looked at Jamie, who was struggling to suppress a smile.

'See what you can achieve when you actually apply yourself?' he said sternly, but then his expression softened and he nodded to both of them. 'I'm proud of you.'

Lottie grabbed a chunk of the huge celebratory cookie that was on the main table in the Ivy common room, with CONGRATULATIONS in big purple frosting. She sidestepped out of the way as two Year Thirteen Ivy girls came dancing into the room, singing and shouting with excitement at passing their exams.

'But I wanted top marks in everything – a B is not good enough!' Another Ivy girl was crying down the phone to her parents about her one 'bad' grade, and Lottie gave her a comforting smile.

Ellie and Lottie sat back in the purple chairs of the common room, watching and laughing at everyone celebrating. They were having their luggage flown back to Maradova the next day and would have a short stop in Paris to collect their dresses for the ball, so they were happy to spend the evening enjoying themselves before their next adventure.

While everyone packed and said their teary goodbyes for the summer, Lottie had one more thing she needed to fix before going to Maradova for the summer.

She excused herself, went to her room and turned on her phone for the first time since she had arrived at the school. It felt weird to have it in her hand again; she'd got so used to being disconnected from everything outside the Rosewood walls that it almost felt overwhelming to see it come to life in her hand.

Messages from Ollie appeared on the screen. The first was from the first day of school.

> I know you can't use your phone until the
> end of the year, but I wanted you to get this
> message when you finish your exams. I
> know I tease you a lot, but Mum and I are
> really proud of you and I'm sure you've
> done amazingly.

The second was from three weeks ago.

> I don't know what's going on with you but I
> hope you're OK . . .

Lottie shook her head and opened up Ollie's number. It rang six times before he answered.

'She lives!' came the humorous voice on the other end.

'Ollie!' She almost choked on his name as she uttered it. So much had happened since she had last seen him, and here he was, innocent Ollie, her best friend from a simpler time in her life, and she was going to have to let him down again.

'I assume you're calling to ask us to meet you at the station tomorrow? Which we'd obviously be happy to do.'

Lottie's heart sank. She hated having to keep things from him.

'Actually, Ollie, I need to tell you something.'

The other end of the phone went silent and she could feel the disappointment and anger radiating through the speaker.

'OK,' he said at last.

Lottie took a deep breath. 'I can't come home for the summer, or at all . . . I've written to Beady about it. I don't know when or if I can come back . . .' Her voice trailed off and she was met with silence again.

'Lottie, what aren't you telling me?'

Lottie almost gasped at how serious he sounded. It was so unlike him. He made everything into a joke. 'Are you in trouble?'

'No, Ollie, I'm fine. I can't tell you right now, but I promise I'm fine and I promise I'll come and see you as soon as I can.'

She heard a groan on the end of the phone. 'Fine!' He sounded hurt. 'If you're not going to explain to me what's going on, then . . .' His voice petered off and she heard him make an annoyed noise. 'Whatever. Just have a good life.'

The phone went silent in Lottie's hand and she looked down, tears trickling on to the screen. She'd done it. She just had to hope it was the right thing to do.

## 42

Lottie had grown up knowing the name Madame Marie's, dreaming that one day she might be lucky enough to see the white-pillared shopfront where the world's most glamorous gowns were sold. And yet Lottie found herself not just marvelling at the outside but actually *inside* the shop, trying on dresses as if she herself were someone special. It was a sunny Tuesday morning and the girls had been shuttled to Paris to collect their dresses for the ball. From the window in the consulting room, Lottie could see the Eiffel Tower glittering away – floating specks of dust caught in the sunlight, making it look like a statue within a snow globe.

'Welcome, Princess,' six sweet assistants trilled as they walked through the door, curtsying in their puffy powder-blue uniforms and white aprons. It was like stepping into a cloud kingdom; the white marble floor melted into the white walls, giving the impression that they were floating. They'd been shown to the bright consultation room by the notorious grandson of Madame Loulou Marie, Léon Marie. He had a pouf of white hair and a flamboyant grace that reminded Lottie of a peacock. He proceeded to bring out a bespoke selection of dresses, carefully chosen for the two of them. As planned, the staff of Madame Marie's believed that Ellie was Lottie's 'guest of honour' at the ball and required a dress of equal elegance.

'Princess Wolfson,' he'd declared with an elaborate bow, 'it has been my most aching desire to one day be privileged to dress you. I've heard such –' he lingered to raise his eyes at her theatrically – 'tantalizing stories about you.' He blinked and stood straight as if fully registering Lottie for the first time. 'Hmm,' he mused, a hand on his chin. He bent down low, his face coming awkwardly close to her own, and his icy-blue eyes in darkly lined sockets staring into hers.

'Yes?' Lottie asked tentatively.

Léon's eyes shifted over to Ellie, then back to Lottie. 'You're not quite what I was expecting, Your Highness.'

Lottie gulped nervously. What exactly were people expecting? She hoped it wasn't someone 'less ordinary'.

'I never like to be predictable,' she said with as much indifference as she could muster. This seemed to do the job as a glint appeared in his eyes.

'Day and night!' he called out abruptly, making both girls jump in surprise. 'Day and night . . . night and day. You two resonate opposition and unity, day and night. It's perfect.'

Lottie sat perplexed as Léon continued to bring out dress after dress. He glided around them with so much drama she felt as if she were watching an Olympic figure skating performance.

'Is this a freaking Cole Porter production?' Ellie hissed. She was less than thrilled about the whole excursion, finding little joy in luxury dress shopping. She'd been a bit off all day, worried about going back home, so Lottie was trying her best

292

to be as happy and positive as possible. The only thing that seemed to be softening Ellie's mood was seeing how much joy Lottie was getting out of it.

'Yes, and I love it!' Lottie squealed, beaming back at her, eyes sparkling.

Ellie rolled her eyes, but her smile gave her away. 'Let's just be quick, OK? We only have about forty-five minutes before Jamie comes bursting through the door all paranoid that we're in danger.'

Ellie spoke with a clear hint of exasperation, and Lottie had to admit there was a truth behind her words. Jamie had become both distant and almost oppressively protective since school had ended, and Lottie couldn't blame him. Which made her feel even guiltier for not telling either of them about the Valentine's Day message. She figured that because nothing had happened since, and as long as she was there to take Ellie's place, then it would be OK. All things considered, being allowed a little frivolity after all the messages and her argument with Ollie seemed fair.

Once Léon was completely satisfied with the dresses he'd chosen for them, he clapped his hands twice and two blue-clad girls appeared either side of him, holding gem-covered boxes.

'There's one final item to add to the equation,' he said. He picked up the box to his left and tossed the lid over his shoulder dramatically, revealing a pair of exquisite black heeled shoes with fierce yet delicate twinkling embroidery along the sides. 'These will be for our little goddess of night.' He thrust the box into the hands of the girl who stood in front of Ellie and grabbed the other box. 'And these,' he said, eyes widening like a mad scientist revealing his mysterious experiment, 'these are for our ray of sunshine.'

He lifted the lid slowly and Lottie gasped when she saw the treasure contained within. Lottie did not consider herself much of a shoe person, but inside the box were the most beautiful pumps she'd ever seen, white with veins of rosy gold that twisted and twirled amid hundreds of individual tiny glimmering crystals. The shoes quite literally glowed; the light seemed to emanate from the material itself. Lottie's mind instantly recognized this same sensation from the first time she saw her family's tiara, as if the two items were fashioned from the same magical substance.

'They're for me?' Lottie couldn't hide the wonderment in her voice, and yet even as she asked the question she felt as if the shoes were calling to her, like they were meant for her.

A broad smile appeared across Léon's face. 'They are *only* for you,' he replied. 'Custom-made to your measurements. They won't fit anyone else.'

Lottie took the box ceremoniously. She felt the moment – and the shoes – deserved a sense of ritual. She was sure she could hear the box twinkling as it moved.

'Thank you so much! I love them!' She beamed at him and he returned the look with a soft nod, before clapping his hands again as if turning off the spell.

'Right, my little birds, see to it that these delightful young ladies are taken care of.' And with that he turned dramatically to exit the room. The two 'little birds' immediately began undressing Lottie and Ellie with speedy efficiency. It lasted about ten seconds before Ellie nearly elbowed one of them in the face and promptly booted them from the room.

'We are perfectly capable of dressing ourselves!' Ellie shouted before slamming the door.

When she turned back she faced a displeased Lottie, arms firmly crossed over her chest disapprovingly. Something was definitely bothering Ellie, but Lottie had no way of figuring out what it was unless she opened up.

'Don't give me that look,' Ellie said, mirroring Lottie's stance. 'I'll play along with the dress-up game, but I'm not gonna be someone's doll.'

Lottie rolled her eyes and began flicking through the dresses on the 'day' hanger. They all had gorgeous heroic-sounding names like 'Celestial' and 'Solar'. One of them stood out from the others, seeming to glow in a similar way to her shoes. It had a small blue tag declaring the name of the dress to be 'Summer Calm'. She gently pulled it out from the rack and watched in awe as the fabric swished gently like liquid silk.

'Ellie, look at this dress – it's perfect!' She turned excitedly to Ellie but froze as she caught a glimpse of her friend's face. She was staring straight into the air between them, fingers lightly tracing the tip of her locket. There was no hint of sarcasm; her bravado had cracked and behind it was a very lost girl.

'Ellie . . . what's wrong?'

There was no point in asking if she was OK; Ellie would just lie. Lottie needed to be blunt or she'd risk losing her.

Upon hearing Lottie's voice, Ellie returned to the room. She hesitated for a moment and Lottie was sure she'd shrug it off.

'It's just . . .' she began slowly, clearly uncomfortable, 'Jamie and I had an argument before we left the hotel.' She relaxed her shoulders as she spoke, as though she were releasing the plug on her emotional bathtub. 'He wanted to escort us – he's so convinced something bad is going to happen – and I ended up losing my temper and saying something really stupid, and it came out all wrong. I'm just so sick of it, of him having to always . . .' It was rare for Ellie to trip over her words, an indicator of how upset she was. 'I said if he found me so difficult, why didn't he just leave?' She turned away abruptly. Lottie was about to respond with some comforting words when Ellie added dismissively, 'Whatever. You wouldn't understand.'

Lottie's heart sank. Not because she was offended but because she was right. For all the good it did having Ellie confide in her, Lottie couldn't really help because she didn't understand Ellie and Jamie's relationship. Her mind tumbled back to witnessing their spat after they'd found the message under her mattress. If she was going to be of use to her or Jamie, she needed to be part of the inner circle; she needed to know what they knew.

'Ellie,' she said firmly, 'you have to tell me how Jamie became your Partizan.'

# 43

Ellie cringed at the question, pushing her hair back as she turned to inspect the dresses laid out for her. She coughed, clearly trying to regain her composure.

'I don't know if we should get into this,' she said cagily, flicking through the dresses.

Lottie ignored her attempts to avoid the topic. 'It's just, well, you two get so – and he's so young!' She was tripping over her words, but she didn't know how to phrase it. Ellie and Jamie got so moody and serious around each other, and they were so close in age. She knew Partizans were trained from birth, but she didn't know where Jamie had come from. It just didn't make sense in her head and if she was going to understand Ellie and Jamie better, she had to know.

'Most Partizans are young,' Ellie said calmly, but Lottie detected a hint of regret in her tone. 'They need to be unassuming and blend in so it's preferable that they're the same age or similar to their master.' She paused and Lottie thought she might end the conversation there but she stopped flicking through the dresses and continued. 'They usually finish their base training at about thirteen and will be picked based on suitability; they get to know their family and master over their last three years and at sixteen they're fully registered. It's a very rigorous procedure. It's a bit mad really.'

Lottie took a deep breath, preparing to ask the obvious question, but Ellie's face became distant and sad and she couldn't locate her voice.

'Jamie . . .' Ellie's voice trailed off and she shook her head and turned to Lottie, a determined look replacing her previous melancholy. 'Jamie is different because he's been with us since he was born.'

Lottie had guessed as much from the pictures she'd seen of them as children in the palace.

'I've seen photos of her, his mum,' Ellie said. 'She was a Pakistani immigrant living in the city.' Ellie rubbed her eyes with one hand in thought before continuing. 'I don't actually know how, and I don't know why, but she got into the palace. She was heavily pregnant and sick and apparently she begged my parents to take her child and, well . . . they did.'

Although Ellie was not the most elegant storyteller, Lottie found herself enthralled: the fancy setting around them melting into images of a desperate woman determined to save her unborn child.

'What happened to her?' Lottie asked without thinking, but the answer was obvious and she braced herself for the terrible response.

'She died after giving birth,' Ellie replied bluntly.

'And his dad?'

'No one knows and no one cares; he's probably dead too.' There was a hint of irritation in her tone and Lottie couldn't place what it was aimed at.

*So that was it*, she thought. *Their response to an orphan baby was to turn him into a personal assassin?*

Something didn't fit right with that story.

'So . . . you made him a Partizan?'

Ellie turned to her, looking furious at the world, a storm raging around her that was ready to strike anything that moved. '*I didn't make him ANYTHING. My parents did!*'

The silence that followed was stifling, filling the air with a static energy. Lottie looked away, ashamed for asking something so stupid.

Slowly Ellie released a long breath and turned to the dresses once again.

'I hate them,' she said bitterly, a coldness in her voice that Lottie had never heard before. 'No one should have their life decided for them when they're born. Everyone should get to choose.' Her fists balled at her sides as she said the words. This was not just venting anger; this was an agenda. Lottie watched her and realized she was witnessing a private side of Ellie. This was a secret that she trusted Lottie with and yet Lottie was still hiding something big from her. She wasn't helping anyone by keeping secrets.

'Ellie . . .' she began, thinking about the Valentine's poem. 'I've been keeping something from you. I don't think it's fair to hide things from you. We need to trust each other.' Ellie looked up, her cold expression replaced with inquisitiveness. 'On Valentine's Day, in my cupcake of all things, there was another message.'

'What?' Ellie asked in alarm, her anger replaced with concern. 'What did it say?'

Reluctantly, Lottie recited the cruel rhyme to Ellie, shuddering at those final lines: *'Watch your back, Princess. I'm coming for you.'*

'Why didn't you tell us?' Ellie's voice rose slightly as she spoke and Lottie flinched.

'Because,' Lottie whispered, 'I don't want your family to take you away.'

The tension seemed to melt from Ellie, and a sad, achy smile appeared on her face.

'Lottie, I won't ever let anyone separate us. But I don't like the idea that you're in danger. I can't be responsible for that. I –'

'I'm not scared, Ellie, and you shouldn't be either,' Lottie lied. 'I would have told you guys if I was worried, but I'm not, that's why I don't want anyone to make a big deal out of it.' She forced out a determined smile, scaring herself with how good she'd become at lying. 'I'm fine, so we don't need to tell anyone.'

Ellie hesitated. 'You promise you're OK?' she asked, a pained look on her face.

'I promise.' Lottie felt the dread in her stomach flex as she said this, but she kept smiling.

The sound of singing cut off their moment, music chiming from Lottie's phone in her bag. She rushed to pull it out, wondering in the back of her mind if it might be Ollie. But, as if he knew he was being talked about, Jamie's name flashed up on Lottie's phone with a message reading:

You have ten minutes.

'Come on,' she said, grabbing both pairs of shoes from the table. 'Let's try on these clothes before we get *rescued*.'

Lottie happily pulled on her dress, then watched in confusion as Ellie kneeled down on the floor in front of her, reaching out to put Lottie's slipper on her foot.

'What are you doing?' Lottie asked, pulling her leg away instinctively.

'I'm being your Prince Charming!' she said, winking as she grabbed her ankle. Lottie felt her cheeks go hot as Ellie slid the shoes on before hurriedly pulling on the first dress she'd picked from the hanger. The two girls stood in front of the mirror side by side: storm and calm, night and day.

A feeling of rightness slowly began to return as Lottie took in the sight of them together. She had to admit they both looked silly – neither one done up properly to be in clothes of this sort – but somehow, standing next to Ellie, it didn't matter.

Ellie picked at a non-existent mark on the hip of her dress. 'I suppose this outfit will do, though I'd rather be wearing a suit. Are you happy with yours?'

Lottie turned to look at Ellie directly. 'Very happy,' she said, grinning. 'In fact, I'd quite like to never take them off.'

Ellie smiled back and wrapped an arm around her shoulders, their bodies and clothes merging in a pattern of black and white. They held each other until Lottie said what they'd both been thinking.

'I shouldn't have kept the poem from you and Jamie.'

Ellie was silent for a moment and Lottie could feel her hands fidgeting.

'I know,' she whispered, her gaze falling on Lottie's reflection in the mirror without meeting her eyes. 'There're a lot of things I shouldn't have done too.'

# 44

They arrived at the palace in the afternoon, the day before the ball. There was something painfully familiar about Lottie's flight to Maradova. Although the circumstances were different, she was once again avoiding Jamie and sitting next to Ellie on the other side of the plane. She just couldn't look at him in the same way since learning about his past. A terrible guilt filled her – she hated keeping secrets from him when she now knew so much about him. Her life now appeared to have become built around secrets and lies: the lie that she was a princess, the secret of Edmund's message, the lies to Ollie, and now this new lie that the poem meant nothing.

The air was possibly even colder than her first visit and the sky looked as if it were threatening to snow. She suddenly understood Ellie's mockery of the term 'summer ball'.

She expected to be met at the palace by girls who looked like they were in fancy dress, and to be deposited in an untouched and extravagant room and generally feeling out of place.

It was nothing like last time.

Lottie was greeted at the door by the queen, whose billowing embroidered gown danced around her as she came rushing down the corridor so fast she nearly knocked them over. Lottie was amazed that she managed not to yelp in surprise when Queen Matilde pulled her into a tight embrace, but instead she found the scent of lavender that surrounded the queen soothed her and she relaxed into her arms as if being greeted by her own mother.

'Our little pumpkin princess, we're delighted to have you back!' She held Lottie by her shoulders, taking in the full length of her.

'Thank you for having me,' said Lottie.

It was the only reply she could think of that would be appropriate, but she felt silly saying it. The queen smiled at her. They really could have been mother and daughter, her cascading golden locks and blue eyes matching Lottie's appearance far more than they did Ellie's. Anyone who didn't know better would easily mistake her for the real princess.

'I hope our Eleanor has been behaving herself.'

Ellie rolled her eyes and pulled Lottie out of her mother's grasp. 'Mum, would you please stop harassing my Portman?' she teased, dragging Lottie down the corridor as she stuck her tongue out petulantly.

Jamie took a step to follow them but was stopped by the queen. Lottie swiftly lost sight of him as Ellie took her on a long, winding journey through the sea of portraits of previous rulers to her room, a brisk reminder of how otherworldly the palace was.

Although Lottie had been in Ellie's room before, last time she'd been too overwhelmed to take it in. The lavish four-poster bed that seemed far too large for one teenage girl was on the left-hand side of the room as they entered. Ellie paid no mind to the Persian rug on the floor, happily traipsing over it in her shoes. There was an obvious disconnect between Ellie and the room – though it was decorated in dark colours to match her moody appearance, the room didn't have any of her personality.

'Why did you choose such different decoration for your dorm room?' Lottie asked, skirting around the fact the room was so bare.

Ellie snickered, understanding the unspoken message. 'This is just where I sleep; I'll show you my *real* room some other time.'

Ellie made her way over to two mahogany doors opposite the bed and flung them open to reveal the most extensive walk-in closet Lottie had ever seen. 'You'll probably appreciate this more than I ever did. Help yourself to anything in there.'

Lottie almost choked. The closet was filled with gorgeous dresses and accessories, all neatly stored and displayed, glittering jewels and expensive fabrics lining every shelf. In the centre, on two crystal mannequins, lit from underneath, were their dresses and shoes from Madame Marie's. Lottie was about to reach out to them when her phone vibrated in her cardigan pocket. She frantically grabbed it, hoping it might be Ollie.

It was not. A number she didn't recognize appeared and she turned round to see if Ellie was watching her before she opened it.

> I look forward to getting to know you
> properly tomorrow evening.
> Xx

Lottie instantly blushed.

*How did Edmund get my number?*

She involuntarily held her phone against her chest and covered her mouth. She felt silly for feeling so smitten over a message, but she couldn't contain herself.

'What are you looking so swoony about?'

Lottie almost jumped out of her skin at Ellie's voice behind her.

'N-nothing!' She rushed to put her phone away, only realizing too late that it made her look even more conspicuous.

Ellie cocked an eyebrow playfully. 'Who are you messaging that's got you so flustered?'

'No one. It's nothing. I love these rings by the way!' She could have punched herself for how painfully bad her attempt at swaying the conversation was.

Ellie squinted at her suspiciously and Lottie tried to pretend she hadn't noticed as she turned round to the closet. 'I need to pick some accessories for the – HEY!'

Ellie grabbed her arm, twisting her back round and pinning her to the closet doors, making them clatter.

'Ellie, what are you doing?' she spluttered.

Ellie loomed over her menacingly, her mouth in its little side smile and looking far more dangerous than usual.

'You are going to tell me your secret or I'll bite you,' Ellie growled teasingly.

Lottie felt her face going hot. *'Ellie!'* she exclaimed, laughing nervously.

Ellie responded by pulling her arm and giving it a little toothless nibble that tickled so much Lottie nearly kicked her.

'I can't!' Lottie blurted out through fits of laughter. 'You'll be mad at me.'

Ellie instantly stopped and Lottie was able to compose herself again. Ellie's face turned sweet and she slowly let go of her arm. 'Lottie, I thought we weren't doing secrets any more.'

Lottie looked away, hoping it might remedy some of the guilt. 'You promise not to be mad at me?'

Ellie let out a long sigh. 'If I promise, will you tell me?'

Lottie began biting her cheek in worry; she was so sick of keeping secrets and lying. It had to stop. It wasn't right. It was simply too un-princessy.

She looked into Ellie's eyes, her Ivy House room-mate. For some reason, their house motto sprung to mind: *Righteous!* An idea occurred to her suddenly. It was so simple.

'I'll only tell you if you'll let me tell Ollie about Portmans.'

Ellie hesitated, her face losing some of its excitement and she began chewing her lip as she weighed the pros and cons.

'OK,' she said at last. 'But . . . we have to tell Jamie about the poem.'

Lottie felt her heart skip a beat, but nodded slowly. Even though she was terrified of Ellie leaving Rosewood, she knew it was the right thing to do. Satisfied, Lottie squeezed her eyes shut, unable to look Ellie in the face as she confessed.

'Edmund Ashwick left a letter for me at Rosewood saying he'd see me at the ball and I really want to dance with him again tomorrow.' Lottie blurted the words out as fast as possible, afraid she might chicken out if she spoke at a normal pace. She opened her eyes, expecting to see an enraged Ellie but instead she just seemed shocked.

'And this has been going on how long?' she asked, her face still blank with shock.

'Since New Year's,' Lottie replied guiltily.

'And you managed to keep it from me *and* Jamie this whole time?'

'Umm . . . yes?'

Ellie's face unexpectedly lit up again. 'Well, I'm impressed!'

Lottie couldn't stop her jaw dropping; she'd expected Ellie to be as furious as when she'd spoken about the prince before. Impressed was definitely not the reaction she'd imagined.

'I mean, even I struggle to hide things from Jamie and I've been doing it since I was born. He has this way of just –'

'Knowing things,' Lottie offered in agreement.

Ellie nodded.

'Ahem.' Lottie and Ellie both jumped at the sound of the not-so-subtle cough coming from the other side of the room. They peeked out of the closet to see Jamie leaning against the door frame looking less than pleased.

'What sort of things do I just *know* exactly?'

They were well and truly busted.

# 45

'*Jamie!*' Ellie exclaimed furiously. 'Didn't anyone ever teach you to knock?'

He strolled casually into the room, ignoring her, and sat on the bed.

He looked up at them sternly in a way that told Lottie a serious conversation was about to be had.

'If you two are keeping something from me, you have to tell me. Now.'

The two girls exchanged a glance, trying to wordlessly decide what to do. Lottie gulped. She was sick of the secrets eating away at her and if she didn't come forward soon it might be too late. She turned back to Jamie, preparing to spill it all, but as she opened her mouth Ellie interrupted her.

'Jamie, you have to promise not to be mad.'

Lottie was overcome by a strong sense of déjà vu. It was an echo of the moment between her and Ellie just minutes ago. To her amazement Jamie's face softened in the exact same way Ellie's had; it was almost creepily similar.

'I can't promise not to be mad, but I'll hear you out.'

*That's more like Jamie*, Lottie thought to herself.

Ellie reached over and squeezed Lottie's hand before continuing. 'We found another . . . um . . . message.'

There was a brief silence in which Lottie could see Jamie's top lip twitching in a desperate attempt to stay composed. Ellie quickly filled him in on the details before he could ask any questions. She spun the story as if they'd found the message together. The entire time Jamie remained deadly calm.

'So we don't even know if it was really from the same person,' Ellie concluded. 'It could have been a terrible secret admirer for all we know.'

Lottie felt a shiver go up her spine at how good Ellie was at manipulating the truth. When she'd finally finished explaining, the room went cold – the only sound was their breathing. Lottie was sure Jamie was about to start shouting at them, telling them how irresponsible they were and how Lottie was putting Ellie at risk. But there was no shouting. There was an expression on his face that didn't seem quite right. He looked pained.

'You know what the queen just asked me?'

Both girls shook their heads at his question, racked with anxiety.

Jamie took a long breath before continuing. 'She asked me if I had anything worrying to report, and you know what I told her? I told her that everything was fine – *better* than fine. I told her you were both doing exceptionally well in school and there was absolutely nothing for them to be concerned about.'

Lottie could feel Ellie relaxing, but the information only made Lottie feel even worse.

Jamie looked directly at Lottie, forcing her to hold his gaze. 'I lied to my queen.' His face twisted in anguish. It was wrong to see him like this.

'No, you didn't. Everything *is* fine. You didn't lie,' Lottie said firmly.

Jamie's features regained some of their usual derision and she found she was actually relieved by it. 'I find it hard to see how death marks and ominous rhymes are *fine*.'

Lottie realized the answer he needed. The reason for his uncertainty was because he was stuck in a kind of purgatory. Torn between feeling that he was Ellie's sole protector and the knowledge that Lottie was there to take any, hopefully metaphorical, bullets for her.

'OK, listen. Both of you,' said Lottie decisively. She could feel a strong sense of resolve building up inside her. If she wanted Jamie to see her as helpful, she needed to stop doubting herself. 'I am Ellie's Portman, and I know you think I'm not cut out for it, but so far everyone believes I'm the real princess.' Something flashed across Jamie's face but she continued. 'You're clearly used to being her sole protector but you need to start trusting my judgement. I can handle whatever danger there is.'

Again the room filled with silence. Slowly a wry smile crept on to Jamie's face, Ellie watched it unfold and responded with a furious expression. Jamie had been acting, and they'd both fallen for it.

'You little –'

Jamie quickly cut Ellie off by standing up. 'Good job, Lottie,' he said calmly, all hints of his earlier anguish entirely untraceable. 'I knew things were fine so long as you were able to give me a response that eloquent.' Lottie stared at him dumbfounded as he sauntered over to them and patted her on the head condescendingly.

*The poem was a test.*

'I doubt we have anything to worry about from the sounds of your story.'

*A test from Jamie to see if I was serious.*

'But, just in case, I had to be sure you understood your role.'

*A test to see if I'd be willing to put myself in danger for Ellie.*

Lottie knew it was stupid after everything she'd just said, but she'd never considered that for Jamie to be happy with her as a Portman he'd have to also be OK with the idea that she might get hurt. That she might die. She suddenly felt like an absolute idiot. Ellie looked as if she were about to bark at him, but Lottie held up her hand to stop her.

'Of course,' Lottie said, feigning as much composure as she could. 'I'm glad you understand me.'

Jamie nodded at her. 'I'll see you both tomorrow then.'

And with that he walked out of the door, leaving them alone again.

Jamie walked calmly to his quarters. He walked past Hanna and smiled warmly at her. He walked past one of the cooks on a break and nodded in recognition, all the while being absolutely sure to give nothing away. After all, it's what he'd been trained to do from birth. He finally reached his room and pushed the door open, entering just as he would normally. He waited until the door was firmly shut behind him before he allowed himself to be consumed by his dread, and he broke down.

# 46

Lottie's hands fidgeted nervously in her lap as her mother's tiara was carefully lowered and clipped on to her head. She had requested permission to wear it with her gown and no one had protested. She was convinced it was the only way she'd get through her nerves.

Any moment now she would be joining the ball; she could hear the guests on the other side of the white doors. Ellie had failed to inform her that as this was the first time the princess was attending a royal function, she would be getting a grand entrance and official announcement. Lottie thought back to when she'd been in the Ivy dorm all that time ago with Ellie and Jamie, before any death marks had appeared in her room, before the pool, before all the secrets. She'd been so excited to attend a real ball with real royalty, and she was determined to find that part of herself again. She couldn't let the dreadful feeling in her stomach win.

Lottie looked over to her left and saw Ellie, wringing her hands, equally nervous, wearing a dress she resented, to please people she didn't like. She reached over and grabbed her hand like Ellie had done for her all that time ago during their trial.

'It's going to be fun,' Lottie said, offering her best reassuring smile.

Ellie turned to her with a fleeting look of surprise that melted into a genuine smile. 'I'm so glad you're here,' she replied, furrowing her brows comically.

The two girls paused as the hall beyond the doors went quiet.

It was time.

'Good luck.'

Lottie was genuinely startled at Jamie's voice behind her, not just because he was so committed to rules and logic that she didn't imagine 'luck' was in his vocabulary but because there was no hint of irony at all. She turned to him and gave him a little wink, like she'd seen Ellie do a million times.

'I don't need luck,' she teased, before turning in preparation for her grand entrance.

A short fanfare played out, and then the words she'd been waiting for. The words that weren't really meant for her.

*'We are delighted to introduce Her Royal Highness, the princess of Maradova.'*

Then the doors to the ballroom opened and light flooded over her, illuminating her dress and shoes like glowing liquid over her body. She stepped out gracefully and stood at the top of the marble stairs, looking out over the assembly below her. Lavish golden streamers hung from the ceiling, dangling elegantly between cherubic paintings. It was as if the heavenly scenes were extending out into reality.

The congregation below her was like something out of a fairy tale, a display of opulent and over-the-top gowns and suits. Dresses flared out in colourful puffs across the shimmering white floor. Many heads were topped with different types of ornamentation. It was a room filled with royalty. The wonderful array of magnificent flowers bowed and curtsied as Lottie began her descent. The crowd parted for her as she made her way over to her 'parents' and once she was safely at their side the announcer gave the order for the festivities to continue, and Lottie became fair game for conversation.

Ellie's mother happily embraced the role of pretending Lottie was her daughter, whereas the king continued to keep himself apart from her, which to most people probably just looked like a stern father–daughter relationship.

'A wonderful entrance,' the queen praised, tenderly brushing Lottie's cheek with her hand. 'Don't you agree, Alexander?'

The king nodded briskly. 'Yes,' he said, giving Lottie a sideways glance, 'quite the natural it would seem.' It didn't feel like the words were intended as a compliment.

The queen leaned over to Lottie and whispered in her ear softly. 'Go and find Ellie and Jamie and they will take you on the rounds.' She finished by giving Lottie a gentle push into the crowd.

Lottie had taken no more than three steps before the person she'd been hoping for appeared before her.

'Edmund,' she breathed.

The prince was wearing white again, but this time he wore an elegant but subtle crown as well as his pristine regal outfit. He bowed low in response, but before he straightened up a hand grabbed Lottie from the side and yanked her away, leaving Edmund looking around in confusion.

'Let go of –'

Lottie looked up to see Jamie's face looming over her. They stood close together as if they were about to dance. He looked incredible. In the short time she'd been in the hall he'd changed into his black suit, the shoulder pads and ruffles making him look like a valiant knight.

'Wow!' The word came out a whisper.

Music began to swell and she looked around to see various couples pairing up to dance.

'You are *not* dancing with Edmund,' Jamie said sternly.

Lottie pouted indignantly. 'Well, who can I dance with then?' she asked, fully aware that she sounded like a petulant child. She wanted to have a perfect night and that included at least one royal dance. •

'I don't know. Ellie will be here soon; you can dance with her.'

Lottie had every intention of doing that, but it seemed that was not a choice right now. The dance floor filled up and Lottie found herself and Jamie in the middle of them. She looked at his grumbling face and it became blindingly obvious what needed to be done.

'As your princess, I order you to dance with me.'

Jamie gazed down at her, completely bewildered. He had no choice. Couples around them began to get into position. He couldn't leave now without causing a scene. Lottie smirked at him and to her amazement his expression turned to begrudging acceptance and he effortlessly moved her into position just as the music started.

'As you wish,' he muttered, as he placed his hand on the small of her back.

315

He was far too rigid to be a good dancer, yet there was something comforting in the way they moved and stepped together. It probably looked very awkward to anyone watching, and it definitely was, but somehow Lottie didn't mind. She was happy he was allowing her to be close to him again and figured this might be the first opportunity to talk with him candidly since the pool.

*No more secrets.*

'Ellie told me how you came to be her Partizan,' she said gently into his chest. If it was possible, he went more rigid. 'I know you have a complicated relationship with Ellie and her family, and I know you think I'm just some naive girl, but –' the music swelled again and she had to tiptoe to reach his ear – 'I want to help you, if you'll let me.'

Jamie abruptly spun her out and pulled her back in under his arm so she was facing forward with his arm wrapped round her waist. He leaned his head down over her shoulder and murmured in her ear. 'I don't think there's anything that can help me since you showed up.'

Before she could react, he spun her again and when he twirled her back he dipped her, leaning in again and Lottie found herself blushing at how close they were. 'But thank you,' he added, before returning to a standing position.

*Not such a bad dancer after all.*

They came to a stop as the music faded, the two of them slightly breathless and still holding one another.

'Jamie . . .' She said his name delicately, as if she worried it might break in her mouth if she spoke too loud.

*'Ladies and gentlemen, if you would please gather with a partner in the middle for the royal waltz.'*

Lottie looked up at Jamie hopefully, but his gaze was behind her. He leaned down to her again. 'Our princess is here.'

Lottie turned abruptly, all at once forgetting Jamie as she turned to see Ellie. Jamie slunk away while he had the chance, leaving the two of them alone.

They stood opposite each other: Ellie in her deep black gown twinkling with crystals, making her seem as if she were wearing the night sky itself, and Lottie, a vision in white and peach, the gold lining of the fabric shining like a gilded dawn. With her dress flowing behind her Ellie took a confident step towards Lottie so they were face-to-face, their breath in sync.

'May I have this dance?' she asked with only a hint of irony in her voice.

'It would be my pleasure.'

## 47

Ellie took Lottie's hand and kissed the back of it dramatically, causing a particularly sharp version of that familiar static to shoot up her arm. She spun her into an embrace, making Lottie giggle as she landed comfortably in her arms.

'Hi,' she said, their faces mere inches from one another.

'Hi,' Ellie breathed in response, the air from their words mingling together.

When the music started the two girls began moving together so fluidly it was as if they were a single being effortlessly floating across the hall. As they spun around the marble floor, the liquid fabric of their dresses melted into each other, the black and white forming a yin and yang effect as they twirled gracefully. Ellie led naturally, a strength and determination in each step that seamlessly matched Lottie's subtle and delicate movements. Lottie gradually leaned into Ellie, resting her head against her shoulder as they slowed down.

'I forgot to tell you how amazing you look in that gown,' Ellie said gently.

Lottie smiled, a warm feeling spreading through her body. 'Thank you . . . I'm sorry you had to wear one too, though you look lovely in it . . . if that helps.'

Ellie chuckled, its low rumble vibrating against Lottie's cheek. Lottie let herself completely relax into her as they swayed together. As they turned, she was abruptly taken aback by three familiar faces. Anastacia, Raphael and Saskia were standing by the wall near a massive spread of fruit on a gilded table.

Anastacia was dressed in a deep-red dress that puffed out at the sides like one of the flowers from the overhanging bouquets, her chestnut brown hair partly up, the rest cascading down her shoulders. Lottie felt as though she were looking at a character from an old French film. Raphael was dressed in a deep burgundy suit, matching Anastacia, though it was unlikely she'd agreed to that. Lottie was surprised Saskia had chosen a dark suit instead of a dress and yet it was so comfortable and natural on her that she could have been born in it.

But it wasn't their effortless beauty that caught her eye. Anastacia seemed on edge, fidgeting in a way that was out of character. Saskia slowly looked up and her gaze fell instantly on Ellie and her. She smiled and Lottie returned the gesture, relieved she was there to calm Anastacia.

'I can distract Jamie if you *really* want to dance with Edmund, but *just* a dance, OK?'

Lottie looked at Ellie in surprise. She had entirely forgotten about him while dancing with Ellie and she was reminded that the main thing she was supposed to be looking forward to was seeing him. She tensed up suddenly.

'Lottie?' Ellie asked questioningly. 'Are you OK?'

Lottie buried her face back in Ellie's chest. 'I'm nervous.' The words came out muted against Ellie's skin. 'What if he kisses me?'

Ellie laughed outright and Lottie immediately felt embarrassed.

'Bite him,' Ellie said frankly.

'Ellie, I'm serious. I've never kissed anyone before!' Lottie looked at her pleadingly.

'Good.' She chuckled again and Lottie grumbled at her lack of sympathy.

'Haven't you ever been with a boy?' Lottie asked.

Ellie raised an eyebrow. 'Lottie, the only thing I've ever been *with a boy* is annoyed.'

Lottie almost laughed, but she was too nervous. She sighed wistfully. 'I just want it to be perfect.'

Ellie looked at her seriously, slowing them down so she could be as clear as possible. 'Listen, Lottie –' she lowered her hand to pull her even closer, so their foreheads gently touched – 'if anything isn't exactly how you want or expect it to be, then I will be there for you to break his pompous nose.'

'Ellie!' Lottie tried to groan, but it came out more as a giggle. 'Thank you.'

The music came to an end and Ellie quickly spun Lottie. 'I do not condone this, but –' she gave Lottie a gentle push, not dissimilar to her mother's actions earlier – 'go dance with the prince.'

Lottie felt a strange physical loss as she moved away from Ellie, but she didn't have time to think about it as she practically fell into Edmund's arms. He caught her as she tripped forward ungracefully to where he had been standing patiently at the edge of the dancers.

'I was starting to think I'd never get my turn,' he said with a cunning smile.

Lottie felt her heart skip a beat as he escorted her back to the dance floor. They assumed the same positions they had at the etiquette class and Lottie smiled up at his icy-blue eyes. Now that he was there in front of her she instantly remembered how he made her feel.

'I thought it would be good to make you wait,' she said, amazing herself with how casual she was being.

He purred a low laugh as the next waltz began. It wasn't the same thrill as it had been with Ellie and their movements were far more predictable than when she'd danced with Jamie. Instead they were the poster children for a classic waltz, just as someone would expect of a prince and princess.

'I'll be honest, I was hoping a girl like you would have found a way to contact me,' he said, spinning her out and bringing her back in, closer than before. Lottie found her cheeks going hot at the feel of his heartbeat through his clothes, failing to understand the undertone to his words.

'Too many watchful eyes,' she replied honestly, missing the thrilled look in the prince's gaze.

He tutted. 'Ah, I understand that very well.' The smile on his face turned wry, and he gave a sharp look in the direction of where Lottie assumed his parents were. When he glanced back he gave Lottie a knowing look, which she didn't quite understand.

'But . . .' Lottie said as they glided through another step, 'I'm sure I can make it up to you.' *By you giving me my first kiss,* she added in her head.

He looked down at her again, the smile on his face replaced by a considering look. The waltz wasn't even halfway through when he leaned closer and whispered gently in her ear, 'Let's go somewhere quieter, away from all these *watching eyes*. I have something I want to share with you.'

Lottie's breath caught in her throat. *This is it!* she thought. *I'm going to have my first kiss . . . at a ball . . . with a prince . . . and I'm not dreaming!*

She beamed at him, forgetting she'd promised Ellie that she'd only *dance* with the prince. 'I know just the place!'

He smiled back, mirroring her excitement. 'Of course you do,' he purred softly, and grinned at her.

Lottie took his white gloved hand and guided him through the pairs of dancing figures, the two of them gliding across the floor almost unnoticed as they pivoted among the other guests. She led him out of the ballroom, deeper into the palace, already knowing exactly in which room she wanted their first kiss to take place. It would be in the creamy, floral room with the huge arched window overlooking the fountain, the ideal mix of innocent and lavish, which Ellie had shown her on the tour of the palace earlier.

He laughed as they approached, giving her a sideways glance as they came to a stop. 'Such a hurry,' he panted, leaning against the wall to catch his breath.

'Sorry,' she replied breathlessly. 'I'm just excited.'

She felt her familiar blush creeping on to her cheeks and didn't mind that it wasn't just from the running and dancing. She opened the door, anticipation building in her stomach as a million butterflies danced around inside her.

'Follow me.'

Edmund complied, stepping behind her, a grin splitting his face. He gently closed the door, a sharp click echoing through the room as it shut. Then he turned to her, the strange manic smile on his lips seeming out of character.

A chill ran through her and a voice in her head whispered: *Lottie, you're a fool.*

## 48

'Finally we're away from all those boring pests,' said Edmund. A malicious tone crept into his voice, making Lottie feel uncomfortable.

Then, before she could register what was happening, he grabbed her head with both hands and crushed his lips against hers. Her eyes widened in shock; things were happening too fast and forcefully for her to comprehend. He pulled away, leaving an odd dryness on her lips. She froze. She didn't feel wonderment, as she would have expected after her first kiss, but underwhelmed and confused at how unpleasant the experience had been.

*This isn't right.* The kiss lingered on her lips with a sickly alcoholic taste that she wanted to wipe away. He didn't even look at her as he proceeded to walk over to a side table and pull a flask from his waistcoat, before pouring a stream of dark pungent liquid into two glasses.

*I have something I want to share with you.*

Lottie gulped. Confused by what she was seeing and feeling, she sat down hard on the chaise longue in the centre of the room, her fingers still hovering over her lips, her mind telling her that something was wrong. This was not the kind of behaviour she'd expected of Edmund. This is not how she'd wanted this to go.

'What do you mean?' she asked, a realization dawning that she may have completely misunderstood him horribly.

'You *know* what I mean.'

He shrugged off his jacket and unbuttoned the top three notches of his shirt before running his hands through his hair. When he took his hand away from his face Lottie almost gasped at how different he looked. The transformation was terrifying. He'd entered the room as a bright and elegant Prince Charming and was now a messy, feral animal.

It was all backwards: she'd kissed the prince and he'd turned into a frog.

'All these tedious airs and graces,' he continued, taking a large gulp of his drink. 'Everyone so pathetically easy to fool.'

Lottie felt her hands start to tremble and quickly stood up, moving to the other side of the room, away from this stranger. They'd both got each other completely wrong.

*Does he* really *believe I'm like him? How on earth am I going to explain this misunderstanding?*

'I think –'

He cut her off before she could explain. 'I can't tell you how thrilling it was when I saw you at Lady Priscilla's.' A sarcastic snigger escaped before he carried on. 'I'd heard so much about you and then to see you were just like me, pretending to be a good little royal.' He smirked as if laughing at his own joke. 'Unfortunately your reputation precedes you, but we can remedy that if you do what I say. I've been tricking people for years. I'm an expert.' His eyes narrowed in a menacing look of plotting.

Then there was that inner voice again: *Lottie, you are a fool!*

She'd fallen for Edmund's charming persona and conjured up naive ideas about her first kiss, her fantasies running away with her. Ellie and Jamie had warned her and she hadn't listened and now she was trapped in a room with a boy who thought she was someone completely different. And the worst part was he didn't even think he'd tricked her. She had been so stupid that even he didn't expect her to have fallen for it. He thought she was like him. Lottie's mind raced, trying to figure out how she could get out of this situation without causing any more trouble.

'On second thoughts,' she said carefully, 'I think I should get back to the party. I have royal duties to attend to and I can't have people getting suspicious.' Her heart was racing and she became hyper aware of the door. She slowly edged towards her escape.

'You can cut the act now,' he said. 'Though I have to say, even I'm impressed by your commitment to this role.' He casually sat down on the chaise longue, swirling the drink in his hand steadily. 'We all know what you're really like, Princess Wolfson.' The name came out like a purr and he gave her a look as if he expected her to do something.

Lottie froze, her mind going completely blank. 'I think maybe there's been a misunderstanding.' She could hardly get the words out with her shaky voice.

He leaned his head back and gave a brutal bellowing laugh that made her flinch.

*This is not Edmund. This has got to be an evil twin.*

Her brain was trying to come up with a million other explanations other than just *'You're an idiot'*.

He stopped laughing and gave her a terrifying sharp look, like an animal about to attack. 'OK, I'm getting bored of this now.' He stood and downed his drink in one chug and threw the glass against the wood-lined wall, grinning at her as it smashed. He grabbed the other glass and held it out to her. 'Show me that notorious girl I've heard so much about.'

She slowly stepped backwards as he edged towards her, feeling for the door handle behind her.

*How could I have been so stupid?* she thought desperately. Flashing through her mind were images of Jamie and Ellie telling her how careful she had to be because of Ellie's fake reputation.

'I'm such a fool!' she breathed.

'What was that?' He took a step forward. 'I can't hear you.' He was grinning maniacally, his expression making Lottie simultaneously feel sick and want to slap him for thinking that Ellie would ever waste her time with a slug like him.

'I said, *you're boring me.*'

She turned to the door, forcing herself to act as calmly and dismissively as possible. She placed her hand on the door handle.

Edmund slammed his arm against the door, banging it shut and trapping her. She jumped at his sudden forcefulness and turned to find him looking confused.

'Let me go,' she said assertively, glaring furiously at him.

He faltered for a moment, caught by the intensity of her expression. In her anger she could now see all the cracks in his persona. He wasn't a Prince Charming of any sort; he was just a spoiled little rich boy.

'What did I do wrong?' he said playfully, the strong odour of alcohol making her even more annoyed.

'I said,' she repeated firmly, 'let me GO.'

She thrust her palms into his chest as hard as she could and he toppled backwards a little in surprise before catching his balance.

She held her breath expecting him to be angry, but he laughed again.

'Now *that's* more like the girl I heard about.' He held the drink out for her again and she grunted in exasperation. There was just no getting through to this idiot.

She lifted her hand and smacked the glass hard out of Edmund's grasp. It smashed against the floor, spilling the dark liquid across the embroidered carpet. Taking advantage of Edmund's surprise, Lottie rushed to the door. But before she could reach the handle she felt a hand grab her dress.

A harsh tearing sound ripped through the air and Edmund succeeded in pulling her away from the door. Her tiara flew off her head and clattered on to the floor.

'My dress!' she cried as she landed roughly on the chaise longue. In a mirror on the wall she could see that there was a huge rip up the back that caused one of the sleeves to fall down. Uncontrollable tears pricked her eyes and she wailed, 'No, no, no! You ruined my dress, that was a gift from –' She quickly covered her mouth with her hands, but it was too late – she'd given herself away.

Edmund stood very still in front of her, looking blank. Slowly, like blood seeping from a wound, a dark smile wormed its way on to his face.

'You . . .' he began, taking a step forward so he towered over her again. 'It wasn't an act, was it? You really thought I was –' He laughed again, a nasty mocking cackle, and he grabbed his stomach as if his sides would burst. 'You fell for my charming routine, didn't you?'

Lottie cast her eyes to the floor and hiccupped back a sob.

'Stop that, I'm the real victim,' he chided unsympathetically. 'Here I was thinking I'd finally found a wild royal girl, someone just like me who –'

'I'm nothing like you,' she said fiercely, outraged that he would ever think he and Ellie had anything in common.

'Apparently so,' he said vacantly, as he leaned down, propping her chin up with his hand. 'You're just as boring as everyone else.'

His words rekindled every insecurity Lottie had about her place in the world of royals. She felt the tears building again when the door burst open with a crash.

'YOU SON OF A –'

Everything suddenly moved very fast yet very slowly, all at once. Ellie and Jamie surged through the door furiously. Edmund turned in surprise to see Jamie trying to hold Ellie back, but she evaded him and came storming towards them. Lottie didn't have time to explain the situation; it was too late. Ellie balled one hand into a fist and with the other grabbed Edmund by his collar.

And then Princess Eleanor Wolfson punched Prince Edmund Ashwick, hard, in the face.

# 49

Edmund fell back against the wall, clutching his nose as a bright stream of blood gushed out between his fingers, running down his lips and neck, and leaving a crimson crescent mark on his shirt. It was a violent display – Lottie had to cover her mouth to stop from screaming – but the fact that Edmund was still conscious, and cursing loudly, indicated that he wasn't *that* badly injured.

Lottie hiccupped back another sob as Ellie rushed to her side and squeezed her. 'I'm so stupid. I'm sorry. This is all a stupid misunderst–'

Lottie was cut off by a furious growl from Edmund. He looked down at his blood-covered hands and cringed. 'You filthy little commoner!'

*Oh no*, thought Lottie.

'How dare you interfere –' He stopped as Ellie turned and gave him what could only be described as a death glare, her eyes like daggers. It was as if there were tendrils of electric air surrounding her, threatening to awaken a storm. Edmund hesitated for only a moment before continuing. 'You broke my nose . . . you . . . you *animal*!'

'I'll break more than just your nose if you don't keep your dirty mouth shut,' she barked, her face contorting into a furious snarl.

*What is it with these people calling each other 'dirty' and 'filthy'?* Lottie couldn't help but think.

'That's enough.' Jamie's voice came out clear and sensible, his pragmatic manner welcome under the circumstances. 'Ellie, see if you can fix Lottie's dress, and, Prince Edmund –' he turned sharply to the bloody mess that was the prince, his eyes and voice becoming icy – 'I will fix your nose.'

Edmund froze as Jamie approached him, his whole body going rigid as the dark shadow of an uncompromising Partizan stepped closer, hands outstretched.

'Don't touch me!' Edmund cried dramatically, covering his face with his other arm.

Jamie let out a terse growl and pushed the prince's arm out of the way, holding it firmly so Edmund couldn't move. 'Don't be melodramatic; I just need to look at it.'

Edmund remained cowering, backed against the wall like a scared little mouse, while Jamie turned to Lottie and Ellie, still holding Edmund's arm to stop him from making a run for it.

Ellie looked at Lottie, who gently reached out her hand and gripped it tightly. Choking back another sob, she took a deep breath and spoke as clearly as she could. 'He's not going to hurt you, Edmund.'

Edmund stared at the two girls, eyes wide as if seeing them properly for the first time, then slowly he relaxed. He'd managed to leave a bloody handprint on the soft floral wall behind him. Carefully Jamie let go of his arm and silently began working his fingers over his nose. Edmund watched as Ellie, who was simply the dark-haired girl to him, assisted the princess in trying to salvage the dress. His vision blurred, the two fading from human figures to a white-and-black glittering haze that danced around each other and an unpleasant feeling in his stomach began to build, as if his own blood were telling him to be ashamed of himself.

'Keep your eyes forward.'

Edmund jumped as Jamie's voice yanked him back to reality, pulling his eyes to his so he was face-to-face with the burning hazel of Jamie's irises.

'She was . . . I didn't . . . I mean . . . I thought she was like me!' Edmund spewed out the words quietly, tripping over his tongue as he said them. Jamie remained silent as he continued to delicately feel the bridge of Edmund's nose. 'The dress was an accident.'

Jamie's fingers carried on with their methodical work, the lack of response making Edmund tense.

'I know,' Jamie said finally, his face remaining blank.

Edmund regained a semblance of his previous posture, mistaking the reply for Jamie being on his side. 'Good, because I'm really completely innocent. I was just –' Edmund yelped as Jamie pushed his nose back into place.

Jamie leaned forward slowly, so his lips were in line with Edmund's ear. His words came out cold and ominous, leaving no room for misinterpretation. 'If I thought for even one second that you'd intentionally hurt her, you'd be leaving this room with more than just a broken nose.'

Edmund gulped. He managed to muster an indignant pout, but his silence made it clear he'd got the message.

Lottie watched Jamie as he expertly dealt with Edmund; somehow he'd managed to keep him keep silent for a while. She turned her attention back to Ellie as she attempted to pull the back of the dress up with no luck; it was well and truly broken and yet . . . Lottie found she didn't care any more. She was still upset, mostly with herself, but she'd realized something when Ellie and Jamie had gallantly appeared. She'd been wrong. She'd spent all this time dreaming of her wonderful Prince Charming who would sweep her off her feet, but the truth was she didn't need a valiant prince: she already had two. She'd had them all along. Their names were Jamie Volk and Ellie Wolf and they were more courageous than any prince from any fairy tale she'd ever read. But she couldn't always rely on them; she needed to be strong herself. She needed to show she could be tough in her own princess way.

'It's OK, Ellie. The dress is a lost cause.' Lottie carefully sat up and rescued her tiara from the floor. She slowly lowered it on to her head, feeling it rejuvenate her.

*Kind, brave, unstoppable.*

*Righteous, resolute, resourceful.*

'As long as my shoes are OK!' She allowed herself a little laugh at that. 'I think what we all need now is to –'

'What on earth is going on in here?'

Lottie faltered as an unexpected voice came from the door and the group looked over in surprise to see a mop of thick blonde curly hair. Saskia.

Even Jamie appeared caught off guard. Lottie assumed he had been too preoccupied with Edmund's nose to be aware of his surroundings.

'Lottie, your *dress*!' Saskia gasped. 'Are you OK?'

Lottie was amazed it was her dress and not Edmund's bloody nose that caught her attention.

'Saskia, what are you doing here?' Lottie asked. The last thing she needed right now was another person getting involved in this mess.

'I saw you come up here and then I heard some commotion and, well, here I am.' She smiled at her and Lottie found that even Saskia's brazen personality felt comforting under the circumstances.

Ellie sat up, taking in the situation. 'It's fine – we're fine. Lottie's just upset because she ripped her dress.'

'Oh! I can help,' Saskia chirped. 'I brought loads of spare dresses. We'll get you cleaned up no problem.' She winked at Lottie, who had to admit the idea of getting out of that unpleasant room was very welcome. The three looked at each other in silent deliberation.

Jamie gave Saskia a once-over before reluctantly nodding his head. 'We'll meet you downstairs in the hall by the ballroom in twenty minutes,' he announced, leaving no room for discussion.

'Perfect,' Saskia replied with a reassuring smile. 'I've helped other girls in situations like this a million times.' She held the door open for Lottie, a practical look on her face. It made sense that Anastacia would be drawn to someone so straightforward.

Lottie paused, decidedly ignoring Edmund. She gave her best *I'm OK, really* smile to Jamie and Ellie before leaving with Saskia.

Saskia escorted Lottie quickly to a room at the end of the wing they were in, which overlooked the back of the manor through a large white-panelled sash window that was cracked open slightly. Lottie thought it a little strange to have the window open on such a cold day but found the coolness in the room soothing.

Saskia poured Lottie a cup of hot tea from an ornate flask on a side table before going to the wardrobe. 'Anastacia's father requested they could keep some extra outfits in here. I'm sure she'd be more than happy to lend you a dress.' Somehow Lottie doubted that and the grin on Saskia's face suggested she knew very well how Anastacia would really feel about it.

A thought crossed Lottie's mind. *Maybe this is a good time to ask Saskia about Anastacia.* She couldn't pass up any opportunity to get more information.

Lottie took a small sip of tea, letting the warmth calm her. 'That's really kind of you, both of you. I'll take anything that fits really. I'm not fussy. Actually . . . I wanted to ask you about Anastacia,' Lottie said, smiling awkwardly at her. Saskia didn't respond. 'If that's OK . . .' she added, feeling a chill creep up her spine.

Saskia returned the smile, but there was something not quite right about it. The chill worked its way through Lottie's body and she suddenly found her vision blurring. She coughed a few times but found she was struggling to catch her breath. The cold chill gripped Lottie's stomach; a thought crystallized in her mind.

*I've been poisoned.*

She gasped, trying to muster the breath to scream. Saskia kept smiling, a nasty tranquillity resting on her features, and then it hit Lottie.

'It was you . . . the note . . .'

Her thoughts became hazy and she lost control of her senses. She dropped the teacup and could barely register it smashing on the wood floor.

'You could ask me about Anastacia, I suppose –' Saskia's tone changed dramatically, her voice dripping with an icy humour – 'but she's not the one you should have been watching.'

The room began to spin around Lottie and she desperately tried to make sense of the words as Saskia stepped towards her. She frantically reached a hand out to the bed as her knees gave way.

'Five, four, three . . .' said Saskia.

Lottie gripped the bedding, trying to pull herself towards the door, but her limbs weren't cooperating. *I have to do something.* In a moment of clarity, she kicked her left shoe off and shoved it under the bed.

'Two . . . one . . .'

Saskia's voice slowly faded away and everything turned to black.

# 50

Only nine minutes had passed since Lottie had left with Saskia to find another dress, and Jamie was already getting agitated. He put a last bit of tape gently over the bridge of the prince's nose. He saw no point in causing more commotion by hurting him unnecessarily, the broken nose Ellie had gifted him was harm enough.

*Ten minutes.*

'Finished,' Jamie said matter-of-factly, pocketing his emergency mini first-aid kit.

The prince let out an exasperated groan, which was very clearly a desperate attempt to regain some composure. 'Finally. I need to get away from this –' he turned to scowl at Ellie – 'unsavoury company.'

*Eleven minutes.*

Jamie rolled his eyes discreetly. He knew he could easily put this spoiled boy in his place, but felt no need to lower himself to his level. Ellie let out a cackle and ground her knuckles into a fist. This was exactly the behaviour that worried Jamie the most. Ellie was tough, and the truth was she could probably handle most situations on her own, but she was undisciplined and irrational, and he worried that one day she might take on someone and be out of her depth. And that's exactly why he needed to be by her side.

*Twelve minutes.*

'I thought you liked *wild* girls, Ashwick?' she said mockingly, cracking her knuckles again in a particularly menacing display.

The prince glared at her, his face twisting into a snarl. 'Only pure breeds like myself,' he spat furiously, 'not some common rabid mutt like you who's somehow wormed her way into our society.'

Jamie couldn't stop a chuckle escaping his lips at the irony.

A look of total bewilderment planted itself on Ellie's face before she let out a sardonic howl. 'This is too much!'

She laughed, clutching her stomach. Jamie gave her a sharp look and she held up her hands to reassure him she wouldn't say anything stupid.

Edmund stared at them in irate confusion, frustrated at being the butt of a joke he didn't understand.

*Thirteen minutes.*

'This is ridiculous,' he declared. 'It's your princess's own fault that she created something sentimental between us.'

Ellie instantly stopped laughing and Jamie tensed, prepping himself in case he should have to intervene.

*Fourteen minutes.*

They needed to get out of there and back to the ballroom before people started getting suspicious.

'Sentimental?' Ellie questioned, a furious calm in her voice. 'How can you expect her *not* to be sentimental when you sneak love letters into her dorm?' It took Jamie all of three seconds to realize what this meant. Ellie and Lottie had been keeping *another* thing from him.

*Fifteen minutes.*

'Love letters?' Edmund almost spat the words as if they left a bad taste in his mouth. 'What on earth are you talking about?'

Jamie turned to face Ellie, his hands crossed over his chest in a questioning stance.

She glanced at him with obvious guilt before quickly turning back to the prince. 'You know,' she demanded, though he continued to stare at her as if the very idea were outrageous. 'The one you had left in her letter box at New Year's?'

*Sixteen minutes.*

Edmund's face turned from disgusted to genuinely perplexed, and acid began to creep through Jamie's body.

'I've never sent a love letter in my life.' Edmund's confusion was turning into mockery. 'Why would I waste the energy on such an easy conquest?'

They both ignored the childish jab, but Jamie could feel the acid in his veins bubbling away as his mind began to clear.

*Seventeen minutes.*

'I mean, it wasn't a love letter,' Ellie began. 'It was more like a *see-you-soon* kind of thing.' She was rambling, so Jamie knew she was getting nervous. 'The one in the golden envelope? That said you'd see her at the ball?' She continued staring at him as if this would jog his memory, a hint of desperation creeping on to her features.

Jamie turned to Edmund, his face serious as he looked him in the eyes.

*Eighteen minutes.*

The prince exhaled sharply through his nose and raised his hands. 'Listen, I know you both despise me,' he said slowly, 'but I've never sent a card like that.'

'Well, then who –' Ellie blinked, but Jamie had already arrived at the terrible truth.

*Nineteen minutes.*

Whoever had left the death mark had also left the 'love letter'. Ellie's eyes were electrified as she locked her gaze with Jamie's.

'Lottie's in trouble!'

# 51

Biting cold nipped at Lottie's nose. She imagined droplets of ice surrounding her in a quiet floating pool.

*Where am I?*

She was awake, but her eyelids were leaden, too heavy to open. Her fingers felt stiff and numb as the cold wriggled over her skin.

*You have to open your eyes*, said a distant voice inside her head.

*Who is that?* A metallic thumping noise made its way through the fog in her mind. *I'm in trouble.*

*Unstoppable. Resourceful.*

Lottie willed her eyes to open and made out the shape of a van, and it was getting closer. Tiny dust like snow was falling around her.

*I'm tired.* Her eyes became heavy again.

The voice chimed in: *The prince and princess need to be able to find you.*

*What prince?* Her body was numb, but she could feel herself being picked up and tumbled into the van.

*Ellie . . . Jamie.* Tendrils of the memories of the night flittered in her mind but she struggled to grasp them.

She blinked and looked about groggily. The van door was open.

*Resourceful.*

One foot felt lighter than the other. She remembered – her shoe had come off; she'd hidden it. She frantically kicked off the other one before sinking back into sleep.

*'She's not here.'*

They had run back to the ballroom as fast as they possibly could, leaving Edmund alone and confused.

They'd checked the buffet, the stage and every inch of the marble floor.

'She's not here,' Jamie repeated. His face was inscrutable, but Ellie knew he was worried. She'd never seen him this concerned about anyone except . . . well, except her. Lottie should have been there ten minutes ago, according to their arrangement, but she was nowhere in sight.

'I can't believe you two kept something so important from me. I can't believe you would do something so stupid.'

Ellie looked away in shame, her fingers curled into fists at her sides, nails biting into the skin of her palms so hard she thought they might draw blood. It took all her self-control not to start trashing the buffet. She so badly wanted to break something; she had half a mind to storm back upstairs and pick a fight with Edmund, but she knew it was nobody's fault except her own. Jamie was right, how could she be so stupid? STUPID! STUPID! STUPID!

She inhaled sharply and squeezed her eyes shut, preparing to say the most difficult thing she'd ever had to say. They would have to tell her parents that Lottie was missing.

She opened her eyes and turned to Jamie. 'Jamie, we have to –'

'Is something the matter?'

Ellie shut her mouth suddenly at the sound of the cool voice from behind them.

The two turned to find Anastacia, poised elegantly in her lavish red dress, her calm demeanour the total antithesis of their frantic energy. 'You both seem awfully disturbed.'

Jamie tensed noticeably and Ellie took this as a sign not to say anything.

'Everything's fine,' she lied, her teeth gritted.

Anastacia seemed unaffected by Ellie's taut mood. 'Are you sure there's nothing at all that I can help with?' She spoke so steadily that Ellie didn't catch the edge in her voice.

Jamie instantly picked up on what Ellie missed, his eyes narrowing before he discreetly, but very firmly, took Anastacia by the arm and moved to the edge of the room. Ellie flinched – not at the sudden movement but at the deadly look on Jamie's face, one she recognized well.

'What do you know?' he whispered sharply.

Anastacia laughed, patting Jamie condescendingly on his chest with her free hand.

'A true Partizan,' she said, the humour not quite reaching her eyes. 'Nothing gets by you, does it?'

'Don't play coy, Anastacia,' Jamie growled. 'If you know so much about Partizans, you should know that they'll do anything to protect their masters.'

Anastacia held her ground, not allowing herself to be intimidated, and Ellie was impressed. Then Anastacia said something neither of them could have prepared for.

'If you need to protect your master, surely you should be focusing on Ellie and not . . . whoever the hell Lottie is.' They looked at her, confused for a moment, and she gave an exasperated sigh. 'I know she's your Portman, Eleanor Wolfson.'

Ellie's mind whirred, then realization dawned that Anastacia knew *everything*. But how? Had she told anyone? And more importantly – where was Lottie?!

Before Ellie could speak, Jamie broke the tense silence. 'What on earth are you talking about?'

Anastacia let out a humourless laugh. '*Quels imbéciles!*' she hissed. 'Ellie Wolf, Eleanor Wolfson, the rebel princess from Maradova . . . How anyone who knows anything could have mistaken such a ludicrous attempt at a cover-up! I mean, Pumpkin alone is a completely ridiculous –'

'Enough!' Ellie commanded. 'How long have you known?'

A subtle blush had crept up Anastacia's neck, her brow had furrowed slightly, a light sheen of moisture upon it. Ellie realized this was the most perturbed she'd ever seen Anastacia. Ellie so badly wanted to tell her they'd have to kill her now, but not even her dark humour could distract her.

'Since breakfast . . . the first time I saw you. Lottie introduced you as her room-mate and I just knew.'

'But how? There's no way –'

'You can't escape who you are, Ellie. It's in our blood. We'll never be like them and they'll never be like us. It's etched into us the second we're born.'

Ellie stared at her. In what way was she anything like Anastacia?

'What could you possibly –'

344

'Privilege,' Jamie interrupted, slowly releasing Anastacia's arm. 'She's talking about privilege. But we don't have time for character growth right now; Lottie might be in danger.'

'Danger?'

Ellie felt annoyed at what seemed to be genuine concern on Anastacia's face.

'Yes, she's missing, and the last person she was with was your good friend –'

'Saskia!' Anastacia spat the word out, cutting Jamie off and surprising both of them with the hurt reflected in her face as she spoke. 'She's been obsessed with the Wolfson princess ever since she found out she was attending Rosewood. She wanted to know everything about her. She demanded I introduce her and get close to her. It was . . . not like her at all.'

Jamie and Ellie glanced at each other, both coming to the same conclusion.

'Anastacia, do you know if she left anything under Lottie's bed?' Jamie asked hurriedly.

Anastacia looked down in a sheepish manner that was uncharacteristic of her. 'No . . . All the messages . . . that was me . . .'

'*What?*'

'You don't understand. I was doing it to protect her . . . I –'

'By putting a *death threat* under her bed!' Ellie exclaimed.

'No. Shut up! Listen!' Anastacia took a deep breath. 'I was trying to scare her away – both of you . . . Saskia, she's not just a friend. She's my –'

Jamie grabbed her by both shoulders. 'Anastacia, spit it out – we might be running out of time.'

She bit her lip and turned to Ellie, such intensity in her gaze as though she were trying to communicate something to her that only Ellie could understand.

*She's not just a friend. She's my . . .*

'She's your Partizan.'

It wasn't a question; Ellie knew it was true.

Anastacia nodded and Jamie slowly released his grip. It felt as though light had exploded over the situation and Ellie all at once understood what had happened and why Anastacia had done what she'd done. For some reason Saskia had been obsessed in a dangerous way with the princess, who she believed was Lottie. Anastacia couldn't turn her in. Ellie tried to imagine turning Jamie in. It just wouldn't be possible; she could never do it. So Anastacia had done the next best thing, and tried to get her and Lottie as far away from Rosewood as possible.

'I understand,' Ellie said gently. She'd never imagined she'd feel any kind of connection with Anastacia, but in that moment she felt she understood her better than anyone else.

'OK,' Jamie said, trying to remain calm, though his teeth were clearly gritted in frustration. 'We have to overlook this for the moment because it's now been well over thirty minutes and Lottie is still missing and presumably abducted by a rogue Partizan, which –'

He stopped, horrified as he took in the severity of the situation. Then he shook his head, a determined and furious look resting on his features, before he said decisively, 'We have to find her – *now*.'

Ellie pushed her hands through her hair. It would take literally days to search the grounds. 'Where do we even begin?' Her voice came out strangled and desperate, and she resented not being able to keep steady like Jamie.

Anastacia's voice pulled her out of her despair. 'Have you tried calling her?'

They both blinked at her for a moment.

No, they had not.


'Yes, I have the princess. No, she's unharmed. I think she's waking up. OK. We'll be there. *Svobadash!*'

Lottie tried to make sense of what she was hearing. She felt a gradual tightness round her wrists, the squeezing sensation snaking her back into full consciousness.

'You're awake.'

She opened her eyes to see Saskia kneeling in front of her, meticulously binding her wrists. This time there was no murky feeling; the world and her thoughts were fully lucid.

She'd been kidnapped.

She pulled her knees together, willing the nausea not to win as she sat up straight. Feigning as much murky confusion as possible, she looked around the van, discreetly taking in everything she could.

Saskia had tricked them all. Saskia had been planning to kidnap her since the moment she had met her. Lottie couldn't feel movement from the van, so that meant that they might still be within the palace grounds. She was missing her shoes.

But the main mystery was . . .

'Why are you doing this?'

Lottie was relieved by how groggy and choked her voice was, hoping it would lower Saskia's guard.

Saskia turned to her. There was an eerie soft smile on her lips that made Lottie shiver. Yet Saskia didn't betray any hint of instability. If she was unstable, Lottie was sure she could distract her, but she was too alert, too primed. It made her think of . . . Jamie.

'Well . . . the short answer is –' she made a sign with her fingers, rubbing them together – 'money.'

Lottie jumped on this, saying the first thing that popped into her head.

'OK then, why don't you take me back? I'll tell my parents you rescued me and we'll give you a big reward.'

Saskia laughed, reminding Lottie of all their time together over the past year. 'Nice try, princess, but there's a bounty on your head bigger than you could imagine. You're top of the list.'

Lottie shook her head; the words didn't make sense.

'Whose list . . .? Who were you talking to on the phone?'

Saskia's 'friendly' smile melted away and she looked off into the distance. '*Them.*'

She spoke with a reverence as if she were talking about a god, and a chill ran up Lottie's spine. 'They're called Leviathan and they're here to change things. And you're my ticket to being fully initiated. I have no idea why, but they want the Maravish princess – you, more than anyone.' Saskia pulled a package from her suit jacket and began fiddling with it. Lottie noticed it contained two small knives and gulped, wondering how many other weapons Saskia was concealing.

'These Leviathan,' Lottie began, trying to continue her groggy and confused tone, 'do they have bounties on lots of people?'

'Not just any people, the children of royalty and important, wealthy families. They want to –' Before Saskia could finish, a pleasant melody floated out from under Lottie, accompanied by a harsh vibrating noise.

Her phone.

Saskia knelt down by Lottie and gently tilted her to retrieve the phone from her evening bag, still on its delicate silver chain over her shoulder. The action could have been mistaken for an embrace.

'Answer it.' She shoved the phone in front of her face. 'Convince them you're safe or I won't be so nice.'

Lottie looked at the phone, watching it vibrate in Saskia's hand. Ellie's name flashed on the screen and Lottie's heart began to race frantically. This could be her chance. She racked her brain for every book she'd ever read, every ridiculous espionage and trick and code she'd absorbed.

'Well, hurry up, Princess,' threatened Saskia.

*Princess* . . .

Lottie knew exactly what to do.

'Hello.'

'Lottie, oh my God, are you OK?' It was Ellie's voice.

'Yes, I'm fine. Sorry I missed our meeting time. I'm just a little frazzled. I think I'm gonna crash.'

'Are you sure? We could come and see you?'

Jamie. She was on loudspeaker. They must be away from the ballroom.

'No, no, it's really fine. I just wanted to get out of that stupid uncomfortable dress – and shoes too . . .'

There was a brief silence on the other end and Lottie felt as though she were about to burst.

'OK.' Ellie's voice came out so steady that Lottie worried she may have missed the hint. 'Is there anything we can do for you at all?'

'Actually –' at that, Saskia gave her a sharp look and gestured to hurry up – 'you could save me one of those apple tarts I saw in the buffet?'

'Of course. I'll make sure they know to save you one.'

'Thank you.' Lottie squeezed her eyes shut and on instinct she added. 'I love you guys.'

She opened her eyes to see Saskia's finger on the hang-up button, her lips twisted into a satisfied grin.

Now Lottie just had to pray they'd figure out her message.

## 52

Jamie watched as the phone went dead.

*'I love you guys.'*

His heart was pounding; he knew something was not right but he had to remain calm and rational.

'So she's fine?' Anastacia said hopefully.

'No,' Ellie replied bluntly. 'She's left us a secret code.'

Anastacia's face melted into despair. 'Oh, Saskia,' she sighed. 'What have you done?'

Jamie pointedly ignored her. Anastacia's worries about her dishonourable Partizan were not their top priority.

'What are our clues?' he asked, already preparing to make a move.

'Well,' said Ellie, 'she's allergic to apples – that's how we know she can't say she's in trouble, and then the shoes . . .' Ellie rubbed her forehead in thought, looking desperate. 'I know she's trying to tell me something by mentioning they were uncomfortable. They were tailor-made for her; she loves them. I just –'

'It's Cinderella, you idiot!' Anastacia barked. Tears were pouring down her cheeks now and she sniffed loudly and wiped her nose, but continued talking as if she weren't crying at all. 'She's probably put her shoes somewhere as a way to find her.'

Jamie nodded. 'We can't alert the guard yet. If the palace goes under lockdown, she'll have a separate escape plan and Lottie will be in more danger.'

'How do you know?' Ellie asked, not sure of his reasoning.

'Because that's what I would do,' he said simply. 'So, we have to find the shoes.'

It took them all of ten minutes to find the first shoe. Jamie rationalized that it had to be on the west side, as that's where Saskia had found them, and it had to be in one of the rooms with a gate-facing window for quick escape.

Ellie was drawn to the broken teacup and from there she spotted the missing shoe and called out to them. There it was, shoved under the bed, almost completely hidden but with the light glittering off it, just enough to catch her eye.

'She went out of the window?' Ellie asked in disbelief.

'Yes,' Jamie said. Saskia's plan was obvious to him now, and she had clearly underestimated both Lottie and the situation. It was a classic polite parting, a cute name for a procedure they were taught as Partizans in case an event arose in which they needed to escape a high-profile event unnoticed.

He'd never considered someone might use the same technique to kidnap someone.

'This means they'll probably be leaving any moment.'

'So why don't we just tell the guard not to let anyone leave the grounds?' Anastacia suggested. She'd calmed down and was determined to help, evidently feeling somewhat responsible.

'Because then she might start killing people,' he said frankly.

Anastacia scoffed. 'Saskia would never –'

'I'm sure you thought she'd never kidnap anyone either.'

Anastacia instantly bit her tongue. It was insensitive, he knew it was, but the stress of the situation was getting to him. Lottie was being held by another Partizan, she was in imminent danger, and he needed to save her without prioritizing her safety over Ellie's.

'Guys,' Ellie called over. 'I think I've found them.'

Jamie dived over the bed in a rush to join Ellie at the window. He followed her gaze but it was hard to see anything in the frosty dark. He was about to tell her she was imagining things when he saw it.

A van, not more than a hundred metres from the building, seemed to be glowing from underneath. It was subtle enough that you might assume your mind was playing tricks on you. The three teenagers ran downstairs to the veranda by the entrance, the cold wind slapping them in the face as they crept outside.

Anastacia kept her hand on the door to stop it from shutting. 'Are you sure that's the one?' There was a pained look in her eye, knowing that she was about to condemn her Partizan forever.

'Positive,' Ellie replied. She didn't bother trying to reassure her; there was nothing to be said.

Anastacia bowed her head, flinching from her feelings. 'I'll alert the guard. You guys keep watch.' She turned to run back the way they'd come, but paused and grabbed Jamie's sleeve. 'Don't hurt her,' she whispered.

He wondered if he should spare her feelings, but realized there was no point in lying.

'I might not have a choice.'

# 53

'Anastacia has informed the guard. We'll wait here until they arrive.'

Jamie was trying to persuade a shivering Ellie to go back indoors, but she was refusing. Instead she stubbornly rubbed her arms to stay warm. They hid in the shadows of the veranda, keeping out of sight of the van but peering out occasionally to check it wasn't moving. She'd acquired a golf club from somewhere and propped it by her side, apparently hoping to use it as a weapon.

'But what if it's too late by then?' she cried.

Jamie shook his head, knowing what she was thinking but trying to stay as logical as possible.

There was no way he could put Lottie's safety before Ellie's. He wasn't allowed to do so, even though it was killing him to leave her. He had to protect Ellie, no matter what.

'I have to keep you safe, Ellie,' he said sternly, even though every fibre of his being was telling him to run to the van. Then, just as he finished talking, he heard the soft low rumble of an engine starting up.

There was a sound of tearing and Jamie turned to see Ellie ripping her dress.

'I'm sorry, Jamie, but I'm not risking it,' she said. And then she grabbed the golf club.

Jamie reached out to stop her, but it was too late: Ellie had flung her shoes away and dived over the veranda's edge, racing towards the van.

She was running to do what Jamie wished he had the freedom to do. Running to save Lottie.

Lottie had been moved to the front seat of the van, wrapped in a shawl so her tied wrists were covered. She was shivering; she didn't know if it was from the cold or fear. The instructions were simple: she had to act upset, so upset that she wanted to temporarily leave the palace, and that Saskia, a registered Partizan, had kindly offered to drive her around. If Lottie failed to convince them, Saskia would start hurting people.

Saskia had assured her that if anyone looked at the CCTV footage, it appeared as though Saskia was simply helping the drunken princess. An easy-to-believe story considering Ellie's reputation and her run-in with Edmund. It was smart and it matched the story she'd given Jamie and Ellie that she didn't want to return to the ball.

*Please – I hope they've figured out my code.*

Saskia looked down at her watch, waited a few more moments, then put the key in the ignition.

'OK, Princess, are you ready for your performance?'

Lottie could have laughed if she wasn't so terrified. *I've been performing the whole time.*

Instead Lottie nodded mutely; it wasn't going to be hard to pretend to be upset. Then the van rumbled underneath them and they were moving.

*I guess this is it then*, Lottie thought to herself hopelessly.

Saskia pulled them out of the spot and pushed her foot down on the accelerator, taking them on to the path to the gate.

They had moved no more than a few metres when everything went completely mad.

A figure dived in front of the van, arms outstretched, a feral shriek roaring out of its mouth.

'What the –' Saskia cried out as she rammed her foot on the brake.

The van halted suddenly and Lottie jerked forward. The figure shone in the headlights, a wild mass of black hair flying around her head, teeth bared in a furious snarl.

*Ellie!*

Her dress was torn and she was standing barefoot and furious in the snow with a golf club that she swung violently, smashing one of the headlights as she screamed a vicious war cry into the air.

She was terrifying.

'WHAT DID YOU DO?' Saskia screeched.

Lottie jumped as Saskia grabbed her. She faltered, unable to answer.

*What the hell is Ellie doing?*

'I didn't –'

Her words were cut off as the driver's-side window was smashed, shards of glass falling around them. She shrieked at the impact, and the biting whirlwind of cold that accompanied it.

'Saskia, get out of the car *NOW!*' Ellie barked, the words a ferocious growl as she prepped her club to swing again.

Saskia's face turned cold in front of Lottie and a chill that had nothing to do with the wind ran up Lottie's spine. Saskia grabbed Lottie by her hair and threw her into the back of the van. Lottie screamed as she landed. Unable to cushion her fall with her hands tied, she smacked her head on the floor, her tiara flying off. She heard the driver's-side door open and called out for Ellie to run as she tried to pull herself up.

The van doors opened. Saskia stood there restraining Ellie, from whom she'd wrestled the club. Ellie threw her head back and spat on her. Saskia let go of her abruptly, and smacked her hard across the face before shoving her in the van next to Lottie.

Ellie looked up at Saskia and grinned. 'You're so screwed,' she cackled, her freshly bleeding lip making her look as if she'd just feasted on a live animal.

Saskia raised an eyebrow, then Lottie saw what Ellie meant.

Jamie was hurtling down the snowy track so fast he was almost a blur in the frost. Alarm registered on Saskia's face, and Lottie watched as she spun gracefully, pulling something from the inside of her jacket and aiming it at the figure thundering towards her.

'JAMIE, LOOK OUT!'

Lottie screamed the words hopelessly into the air but they were needless. Before Lottie could comprehend what was happening, Jamie was in front of them, ducking out of shot then surging upward.

He swung his left hand, pushing away the barrel of the gun, followed by his right hand, which struck Saskia's wrist hard. He deftly manipulated her hand so that the gun was now pointed at her. It happened so fast that Lottie could barely process what she was witnessing. Saskia reacted by stepping on Jamie's foot and twisting round, causing both of them to drop the gun. She kicked it out of reach. If she couldn't hold the gun, it was better to have it out of reach than risk it being turned on her.

Jamie grabbed Saskia and flung her as far away from the two girls as possible before storming towards her.

And then the dance began.

They moved in a fluid mix of elegant and punchy steps, a sophistication and precision in every movement that made for a deadly but beautiful display.

Lottie watched in horror as they laid into each other, amazed by the intricate accuracy of their dance.

*This was a Partizan fight, and it was deadly.*

They seemed to be a perfectly even match until Jamie thrust his elbow to block her arm and was able to land a blow to her stomach. Saskia doubled over and he used the chance to knee her in the nose. Lottie covered her face at the impact, disturbed by how effortlessly violent Jamie could be. Then, before Saskia could right herself, Jamie dived into the air as though he were weightless. Lifting his knee up, he easily spun his body to deliver a bludgeoning kick to Saskia's head before landing and pulling a gun out of his jacket.

It was clear that the move could have been lethal if Saskia hadn't managed to hold her arm up in a last-ditch attempt at defence.

She fell to her knees and slowly raised her head to see the barrel of the gun, all her previous composure beaten out of her. She looked at him, manic and bloody. She laughed, but it came out more as a wail. The sound made Lottie flinch.

'You are such a perfect little pet of a Partizan, aren't you?' Blood spilled out of her mouth as she spoke, and she spat on to the floor as though she were a snake shooting venom.

'You've lost, Saskia,' he said coldly, his face calm as the frosty wind howled around them.

She laughed again, the sound becoming a wheezing cough. Lottie recoiled, but Jamie remained unchanged, pointing his weapon at her with no hesitation.

'I haven't lost anything,' she cackled. 'I found myself years ago. You're the one who's lost.'

Jamie didn't say anything, and there was no sign of the biting cold having any effect on him.

'You could be free of them,' Saskia went on. 'You could use your training to fight for a righteous cause instead of being wasted on these fatuous fools.' In the clouded moonlight Lottie was sure she could see tears forming in Saskia's eyes. 'They don't care about us. We're just tools to them; everyone is a tool to them. They'll never let us live how we want.' She reached a hand out desperately. 'Join us.'

Lottie held her breath, the wind billowing between them as she sat helpless in the van, not knowing what Jamie was thinking. Her heart lurched as he opened his mouth to speak and she thought she saw his hand quiver for just a second.

Before he could respond a voice blared out. 'Put your hands in the air where we can see them.'

Lights flared around them so brightly that they almost blinded her as twenty or so figures in black swarmed them. They grabbed Saskia and instantly cuffed her, pushing her up against the side of the van. Jamie carefully deposited his weapon on the ground and sat in the van beside Lottie, completely unaffected by the sudden siege, as if he knew they were coming all along.

They were all escorted to the palace entrance and Lottie saw one of the masked figures pull off his headgear to reveal a weathered face with a severe scar. He nodded at Jamie, who responded with a salute, and the man bowed in return.

Someone untied Lottie's hands and wrapped a silver blanket around her. Everything melted into a warm and confusing blur of questions and anxious voices. Jamie and Ellie both shrugged off their questioners and bolted to Lottie.

'Are you OK? Are you hurt at all? Either of you – Ellie, your lip!' Jamie frantically fussed around them in a way that seemed very unlike him.

Ellie shook her head, not really paying attention, and pushed past to grab Lottie and pull her into a tight embrace.

'Lottie! Oh, Jesus Christ, I'm so sorry. I'm so, so sorry.' Ellie kept repeating the words as she held her, but Lottie was distracted by what she could see over her shoulder.

By the door to the palace, standing tall and unflinching, was Anastacia. She didn't look at Lottie, Ellie or Jamie. Her eyes were on Saskia, a trail of moisture on her cheek, obscured by her chestnut hair, and her dress flapped around her in a blaze of deep red. Saskia was escorted to where Anastacia stood. Her guards paused by Anastacia and one of the figures bowed.

'We'll be taking her in for questioning, ma'am. Your father will also be informed.'

Anastacia didn't respond; she simply stared at Saskia, a fire burning in her eyes.

The Partizan's face turned from anger to something akin to determination. They began pulling her away again and Saskia cried out, 'Ani, I was going to come back for you. *Ani!*'

But Anastacia didn't even turn round as her Partizan was dragged away. She clenched her fists so hard her knuckles turned white. Tears spilled in an uncontrollable wave of woe. These were not the tears of a shocked young girl; this was something more.

Lottie's mind conjured up the photograph of them in Paris. And suddenly it hit her, and she couldn't believe she'd missed it before.

They were in love.

## 54

Lottie, Jamie and Ellie once again found themselves standing outside the main hall in a perfect line, waiting to be allowed into their trial. Fewer than twenty-four hours had passed since the ball. The festivities had ended early and the guests had been asked to vacate the premises. What had followed was a sleepless night of blurry questions and emotion, and Lottie was desperate to throw on some pyjamas and sleep for a hundred years. Her world had altered, and she knew that things were going to be drastically different now.

They had all agreed to stick with the story that they hadn't had any clue that the attack was being planned and that Anastacia knew nothing about it. Except, it wasn't a story. It was the truth.

Ellie and Lottie had both sustained mild injuries: Ellie had cut her lip, but not badly enough to leave a scar, and Lottie had a bruise on her cheek and a sore bump from where she'd hit her head. Jamie remained unscathed, outwardly at least.

Lottie held her breath as the doors slowly opened. The light hit her again in that same flooding bright stream, but this time she did not flinch from it. Instead she marched forward confidently to embrace her fate.

362

In the hall sat the king on his throne, his wife and his mother by his side, with Simien Smirnov, the glass-eyed man, standing behind him. To Lottie's surprise a fifth person was present, the gruff man who Jamie had saluted the previous night, who sat with a permanent scowl on his face.

'It is clear, after the events last night, that there is a serious and present danger among us.' The king spoke intensely, leaving no room for questions.

Lottie stood firm, eyes straight and emotionless as she'd seen Jamie do so often. She understood now the importance of presenting yourself as unflappable. It was like a suit of armour, not just to protect yourself but to protect those who might worry about you. Lottie could not have Ellie worrying about her if she was going to remain her Portman: she needed Ellie and her family to think the traumatic events at the ball were easy for her to brush off and that she'd readily put herself at risk again for Ellie's sake.

It wasn't true. Lottie had never been so terrified in her life, but that was exactly why she needed to be there, to make sure it never happened to Ellie.

'Sir Olav –' the king gestured his hand to the scarred man – 'we understand that we have the rogue Partizan in confinement but she will not speak.'

Lottie thought of Saskia, a girl she'd been jealous of and trusted as a mentor, and her heart lurched. She couldn't imagine what Anastacia must be feeling right now.

Sir Olav rubbed his hands together in thought and Lottie could see a strange dagger-shaped tattoo just above his wrist.

'So far the only information we have is from your Portman.'

Lottie mentally stored the fact that he knew she was a Portman; it was important to know who was high-ranking and trustworthy.

'The Alcroft parents knew nothing,' continued Sir Olav. 'Their daughter, Anastacia, claims her Partizan had an unusual but not worrying interest in the princess.'

Lottie knew that was a lie. Jamie and Ellie had filled her in on how most of the notes had been left by Anastacia as a way to scare them out of the school.

The king turned to Lottie and gave her a sharp look. 'I see, and what exactly have you learned, Miss Pumpkin?'

Lottie took a deep breath, trying to remember the information without slipping back into the memories of the van, of Saskia's bloody face, of Anastacia weeping. She shook her head, shaking the thoughts away. 'We know they're called Leviathan, Your Majesty,' she began. 'We know they're targeting the children of important families, particularly royalty and –' she prepared herself before she said the next words, worrying about the reaction they might provoke – 'we know there's special interest in the capture of the Maravish princess, but we don't know why.'

The king simply nodded his head. 'Good work.'

It took everything in Lottie's power not to start squealing in excitement. *Did I just get praise from the king?*

She had to quickly remind herself of the circumstances, but it didn't stop her feeling a little elated. The queen smiled at her, as if she could read her thoughts, and Lottie returned the look with one of the respectful nods she'd so often seen Jamie and the king exchange.

'Well then.'

All Lottie's good feelings evaporated at the raspy voice of the king's mother.

She tapped her fingers on her cane irritably as she looked at them with a scathing gaze. Her hair was down this time, a flowing wave of silver cascading over her waist, which made her look as if she could at any moment cast an evil spell on whoever crossed her. 'Let us move on to the more pressing matter.'

The three teenagers held their breath, knowing what was coming.

'Why on earth was the real princess, our Eleanor, allowed to be put in harm's way for this girl?'

Lottie felt her body go hot and her hands twitched nervously at her side. She was amazed at Jamie's ability to stay completely calm.

'It is unacceptable that the princess should put herself in danger for her *Portman*.' She said it like it was a dirty word. 'The idea is simply atrocious.' She looked at each of them, as she tapped her cane. 'Well, do you have anything to say for yourself?'

Lottie gulped, feeling all at once furious and ashamed. She'd believed there was nothing she could have done to stop Ellie running out to the van, but that was not the truth. She could have prevented it by truly pretending everything was fine when they'd called – but she hadn't even considered that. She had to remember that she was expendable. 'I'm sorry, Your Majesty, I –'

'Not you!' the king's mother screeched. 'Her Partizan!' She gave Jamie a fierce look before turning back to Lottie. '*You* behaved exactly as a Portman should in that situation.

Portmans are very difficult to come by; it would be most inconvenient if we lost ours.'

*Inconvenient.*

Lottie's mind went blank. They didn't know. They didn't know that she hadn't even remembered she was a Portman in the van. She hadn't been thinking about how *inconvenient* it would be if they lost her. She hadn't thought about surviving for her princess. She'd only been thinking about herself. She wasn't what they thought she was, and part of her resented them for it, but a larger part resented herself for it. She didn't want to react like a regular kid would in that situation. She wanted to be strong; she wanted to have a place in this extraordinary world no matter how dangerous it became.

She turned to Jamie. He continued to stand tall, accepting the scolding words without flinching.

'Quite,' the king said, though his posture and tone suggested he disliked having to agree. 'Sir Olav, would you please prepare an appropriate punishment for your student?'

Lottie felt a sense of injustice building in her. *Jamie had saved them. He'd done everything he could to . . .*

Jamie gave her a look of warning. She bit her cheek hard to stop herself from saying anything. Before he could give the same look to Ellie, she stepped forward to speak. To Lottie's amazement, she didn't protest. She didn't even raise her voice.

'May we leave now?' Her fists were clenched as she spoke, but that was the only indication of how she felt.

The king rubbed his forehead as if he had a terrible headache, and then sighed. 'You may leave.'

They all slowly turned to the door, and as they did the king spoke again.

'I'm glad you are all safe and I'm impressed with how you handled yourselves – but these are our rules.'

Ellie paused at the door without looking back, then they made their way out, leaving an uncomfortable silence behind them.

# 55

Before the three of them headed back to Ellie's room, Ellie asked Jamie to give her a moment alone with Lottie. He nodded somewhat reluctantly and went on by himself.

'Come with me,' she said softly, grabbing Lottie's wrist. Her words were slightly muffled through her swollen lip.

She walked Lottie through the corridor, up a winding staircase to a tower room with a huge balcony overlooking the back of the grounds, an endless garden covered in thick snow. Ellie leaned against the stone balcony, her face inscrutable, looking more like Jamie than herself. Lottie followed her gaze out over the garden, wondering what it would be like once the snow cleared.

'Lottie,' she began, not looking at her, 'I have something important I need to ask you, but I need you to promise me something first.' She turned to her then, holding eye contact in a way that Lottie couldn't pull away from.

'Of course,' she replied, ignoring the hesitation in her gut.

Ellie shook her head. 'No, Lottie – that's the point,' she said with a sigh, the lack of sleep suddenly showing on her face. 'I want you to promise that before you answer my question you're not going to think about me. You're only going to think about yourself and how you feel.'

Lottie froze, thinking of her mother and the promises she'd asked of Lottie on her deathbed. There was that strange and awful crawling on her skin, the knowledge that this was not a promise she could possibly keep. She couldn't explain it to Ellie; it was something only Jamie would understand. She couldn't answer only for herself, because this was her life now, being there for Ellie. But she didn't vocalize this; instead she held her breath and nodded.

'I promise,' she said reluctantly, knowing it wasn't quite true.

'OK.' Ellie looked shaky, her hand fidgeting. 'And I want you to really think about this before you answer.' Lottie nodded again. Ellie let out a short breath before continuing, looking as if it hurt her deeply to ask. 'Would you be happier if you'd never become my Portman?'

'No,' Lottie replied, almost before Ellie had even finished the question.

She didn't need to think about it, and it had nothing to do with devoting herself to Ellie. She knew deep down that it was true. She didn't care how scary things became, or what she had to sacrifice, the last year she'd spent with Ellie had been the happiest she'd been since losing her mother. This was the closest she'd ever been to fulfilling her promise to be happy. She felt like she'd found a part of herself that she didn't even know was missing.

'This is where I belong,' she said earnestly, grabbing Ellie's hand and squeezing it. Tears trickled down her cheeks, but she didn't care. 'Being with you is the happiest I've ever been; you make me a better person.'

Ellie's face scrunched up in a desperate attempt to hold her emotions in and she sniffed loudly to try to maintain her composure. She pulled Lottie into a tight embrace, squeezing her so hard she almost couldn't breathe.

'Me too,' Ellie whispered in her ear.

## 56

The three teenagers sat in silence on Ellie's black satin bed.

Jamie had propped himself on the edge, head in his hands, looking remarkably like Rodin's *The Thinker*. Ellie lay sprawled in the middle, staring up at the patterned wood ceiling, her head resting on Lottie's lap while Lottie absent-mindedly stroked her hair.

'This is my fault!' she exclaimed.

Lottie paused between strokes, but she didn't know what to say.

'We all know it's my fault,' Ellie continued. 'They know it's my fault – and they're doing this as a punishment for me.'

Jamie made a strange noise that sounded a little like a laugh. They'd been discussing the fact that Jamie was getting punished and Ellie had regained some of her usual fire.

'Sir Olav will just make me take some extra training classes –' he pushed his hair back so he could look at them properly – 'and I like training, so it's not really a punishment.'

Ellie grumbled. 'But it's the *principle* of it!' she said, punching the air as she pouted with her swollen lip.

Lottie smiled to herself, remembering how fierce Ellie could be. 'I think it was worth it, though,' Lottie said with a giggle.

371

Ellie stopped punching the air and Jamie turned round questioningly.

'Not just the punishment,' said Lottie. 'The whole kidnapping ordeal – it was definitely worth it.'

Ellie shot upright suddenly, causing Lottie to move back to stop their heads colliding. Jamie and Ellie both stared at her in confusion, sharing a look as if she'd gone mad.

'In what way is any of this worth it?' Ellie asked, raising an eyebrow.

'It was worth it because –' she sat up straighter as if she were about to tell a story – 'I got to see that wild show of you smashing up a van, Ellie, barefoot in the snow like some kind of feral, murderous animal.' Lottie burst out laughing as she spoke. The more she'd thought about it, the more she'd decided it was funny. If she had to choose between traumatic and hilarious, she'd go with hilarious. 'When the headlights first shone on you I thought you were –' she had to pause to catch her breath through her hysteria – 'I thought you were an angel.' She wiped a tear from her eye as she continued to laugh.

A wry smile appeared on Jamie's face, and Lottie knew he understood that her way of combatting the situation was to keep positive. He understood because his method was to stay cold.

'An angel?' he said mockingly. 'More like a demon. I mean, really, who goes after a Partizan with a golf club?'

Lottie burst into a fresh set of giggles, falling back on the bed.

'Hey!' Ellie exclaimed, trying to look angry. 'I was going for full-on banshee, thank you very much.'

'That explains all the irate screaming,' Lottie teased.

Ellie gave her a look of mock indignation before jumping on her. 'We'll see who's irately screaming,' she said menacingly as she held her hands up preparing to attack.

'No, no, no, I surrender!' Lottie pleaded playfully, holding her arms up. 'You make a wonderful banshee.' She snorted the words out, fully prepared for the repercussions.

'That's it!' Ellie howled, an evil grin on her face. 'You're gonna regret that!'

The three of them spent the whole day in Ellie's room, watching films and playing video games. Lottie was determined that they should have some fun and forget about the previous night before they had to go back to reality and face their problems.

At some point in the early hours Ellie passed out in the blanket fort they'd made. Lottie wanted to join her, but she knew that sleep wasn't an option for her right now; her mind was too chaotic.

'Lottie.' Jamie's voice sounded uncharacteristically vulnerable and it brought back memories of the pool. 'Lottie, I have to know something.' His face was serious but there was a soft edge to it.

'Go on,' she replied apprehensively.

'You didn't think about Ellie when you were in danger – your only thoughts were on how to survive the situation. Correct?'

Lottie stared into his eyes for a moment, not giving in to the sick feeling of shame.

'Yes.' She forced herself to say it even though it hurt. It was true – she hadn't thought once about her responsibility to

Ellie while in the van, only about escape. Before the ball Jamie had tested her to see if she placed her safety lower than Ellie's, but when it had counted she forgot completely and Jamie had anticipated it. Even if Ellie's family hadn't realized, part of her already knew that Jamie had.

'Good,' he said briskly.

'What?' Lottie almost choked. 'I failed. I'm every bit as disappointing as you expected me to be.'

Jamie shook his head, a sweet smile appearing on his lips. 'Lottie.' He grabbed her shoulders and held her gaze, squeezing her slightly to hold her attention. 'The only thing I could ever be truly disappointed in is myself if I lost you.' The intensity in his eyes was enough to leave most people breathless. 'I don't mean you losing your life. I mean I'd be disappointed if I lost *you* – your character, your unwavering positivity. You must never let anything in this world take that away from you.'

There was genuine concern on his face and Lottie felt a happy warmth at the knowledge that he wasn't OK with her getting hurt in Ellie's place, but that was instantly quashed by anger. She'd spent this whole time trying to impress him so he'd trust her to be a Portman and *now* he's telling her he's worried about her! There was only one solution to all this.

'Well,' she said, the irritation in her voice catching him off guard, 'if you're so worried about losing me, teach me to fight.'

'I – what?' This was not the reply he'd been expecting and he faltered, tripping over his words.

Lottie quite liked seeing him flustered. 'You heard me. I want you to teach me to fight, so I can protect myself and Ellie and you. I was so terrified in that van. I had no idea what was coming. I never, ever want Ellie to be in that position. Also, my life choices aren't allowed to be your source of weakness, is that clear?'

His face went blank for a moment as if he were questioning his entire life, and then he laughed. He laughed genuinely and openly, the sound of it warming her as Lottie realized it was the first time she'd seen him do that. He finally composed himself and smiled at her.

'You are the most unpredictable person I've ever met, and I've lived with Ellie for fifteen years,' he said affectionately.

'Is that a yes? Will you teach me?'

He rolled his eyes, but the smile remained. 'Yes, I'll teach you.'

# A Note from Connie

I would like to say a big thank-you to you for picking up my book. Whether you're a fan of mine or totally new to my world, I hope you have had a thrilling experience and that it has left you excited for what is to come.

As you may have picked up, there are whispers of enchantment within the walls of Rosewood and surrounding Lottie herself. It is not the magic of fantasy books and wizards – it's the magic you feel when you find a person or place with which you feel an unexplainable affinity. There is an ancient and enigmatic force guiding our heroines, with a story behind it that spans hundreds of years and that connects our characters in ways you may not expect.

There are still many mysteries, new and old, to be solved in the world of the Rosewood Chronicles and a lot of danger is brewing around our three heroes. When you come back to Rosewood in the second book for their next year of studies you will get a chance to learn more about the other students and their own battles – with some unexpected allies joining our royal trio.

You may have many questions you're itching to have answered. *What will become of Saskia? What is Leviathan and what do they want? Who is William Tufty and what does Binah know?*

And to all these questions I can only say . . . you will have to wait and see!

Until then, be kind, be brave and be unstoppable.

Connie x